Grounds for Tenure

Grounds for Tenure

Barbara Lalla

THE UNIVERSITY OF THE WEST INDIES PRESS
Jamaica • Barbados • Trinidad and Tobago

The University of the West Indies Press
7A Gibraltar Hall Road, Mona
Kingston 7, Jamaica
www.uwipress.com

A catalogue record of this book is available from
the National Library of Jamaica.

ISBN: 978-976-640-621-9 (print)
978-976-640-622-6 (Kindle)
978-976-640-623-3 (ePub)

Cover design by The Invisible Creative, theinvisibleisland.com
Book design by Robert Harris
Set in Dante 11/14.5 x 27
Printed in the United States of America

The two lines from "Riddle", by Nicholas Laughlin, *The Strange Years of My Life* (2015),
are used with the author's permission and with the consent of Peepal Tree Press.

All quotations from Chaucer, used in the epigraphs, are taken from *The Riverside
Chaucer*, 3rd ed., edited by Larry D. Benson (Oxford: Oxford University Press, 1987).

"and here is a whole book to help you say,
Here is one more chance just in case."
　　—"Riddle", *The Strange Years of My Life*, Nicholas Laughlin

"Of sondry folk, by aventure yfalle
In felaweshipe."
　　—"The General Prologue", *The Canterbury Tales*, Geoffrey Chaucer

Contents

Prologue to a Tale

And turnen substaunce into accident

Watch me. It have no such thing as solid ground. The earth is riddled with oil and guano and dead bones, enriched through rot and scoured away by wind or water. This book, though, *this* book rests on bedrock. At the mercy of the subcommittee as I am, I admit what follows is a story and not a treatise, but it came first hand from those concerned. I too was connected indirectly though crucially – even though the thought of using first person sets off all sorts of bells jangling in my head.

That said, I adopt as objective a stance as I can. To say these matters came to concern me closely is not to say I was there at all the critical moments. I pass on what I heard, and errors that slip through are not, strictly speaking, my own. Also, as an academic (apart from a teller of tales), I can't let slip the chance for critical comment, so at this point, readers uninterested in scholarly observation should skip to chapter 1.

But I'll be brief. What concerns me most is plot, but since some people of letters nowadays look down on suspense, I'm prepared to tell you from the outset: It ended, according to a more prominent scholar than I, in catastrophe. Nothing melodramatic about that to my mind, however snootily modern critics wave plot aside. True, accident plays a part in plot, but accidents happen every day, some set in motion millennia before, and others we stubbornly bring on ourselves – now and then along the dimensions of a visitation (which suggests there are no accidents but only mortal error).

Accident, curiously enough, is what accomplished storytellers centuries ago might have called the sort of cataclysm that lies ahead – *accident*, as distinct from *substance*. Substance was not what you felt firm to the touch; it was an intangible reality beyond our faulty senses. And the material world? Only a trick of physical sensation that made the slippery ooze seem solid: *accident* – the stuff of fabliau or of farce. The fact that we divine substance only through accident is what prompts the "moral" tale I feel called on to relate.

Chapter 1

Headhunter

To been avysed greet wysdom it were,
Er that he dide a man dishonour.

Morgan Shade was lying in wait for her in the car park, when she left her evening class at the Learning Resource Centre. She could not possibly have known what he was, with his brisk all-inclusive grin, except that the flash of teeth remained fixed a few seconds longer than need be and did not light the deep-set eyes in his somewhat hollow face. In dark no-name jeans with a black T-shirt and worn shoulder bag, he bore no reassuring mark that might encourage her to talk to him – unless it was supposed to be the carefully preserved accent of a man educated in Britain decades before. But a few warmed-over diphthongs were not enough to win around Candace.

Having materialized from behind a traveller's palm and edged up to her car under the low trees that dripped rain water and fine sodden yellow flowers, he slid his card across the worn bonnet of her foreign-used Toyota with the stern gesture of one serving a subpoena while, somewhat irrelevantly, baring another swift cold grin. "I've been authorized to seek out appropriate persons," he said, "and to invite them to apply for truly attractive positions in tertiary learning that are about to open up."

Dr Candace Clarke was bone-weary after chasing back and forth across the St Augustine campus in the most waterlogged month of Trinidad and Tobago's rainy season so as to deliver a course in academic writing to a thankless generation. Outside of the few students with any interest in language, all too many cared nothing for distinctions between valid and invalid logic, let alone the proposition that such distinctions might reside in adverbs. Candace gloomily suspected most students of eyeing adverbs with contempt and repulsion, if, indeed, they ever eyed them at all.

The University of the West Indies had increased student intake in recent years, though not along lines that raised the proportion of fluent writers. On other campuses the relatively new Accelerated Foundation Programme had drawn off large numbers from the traditional courses, but the AFP had caught on less at St Augustine and throughput was still slow. Even at seven-thirty p.m. in late November, when class attendance was falling, parking on campus was tight enough for Candace to wonder where this character – Shade, he called himself – had found a place for his car, and whether he would find his wheels clamped when he returned to it. Despite her parking permit, she had come on campus half an hour early so as to circle mon-otonously until a space came free. So she could hardly suppress the feeling that a clamped car wheel would serve him right for taking space better deserved by those with work to do. A twinge of guilt for the ungracious reflection prompted her to accept his card, but she took it mainly to be rid of him. When shaking Shade off proved complicated, she mendaciously arranged to telephone him by Friday.

Naturally, she did no such thing.

She was amazed on Saturday morning, when Cassidy announced him at her modest town house in Curepe, first by the two brief, low-toned, business-like barks reserved for strangers who paused outside the gate, a voice for conveying straightforward and unbiased information. The dog was so clearly located inside the house that Shade did not hesitate long about entering the front yard. At the creak of the wrought iron gate, though, Cassidy, an impetuous ridgeback, leapt up with a deeper bass volley of expletives. These cut off abruptly at a nod from Candace. Brief enquiries about Shade had confirmed that he might get on her nerves but would do no physical damage. Still, she washed and cleaned on Saturdays and had no time for him. When Candace unlocked the door, her voice coldly polite, Cassidy relaxed momentarily, but then, at Shade's nervy glance about the room, she tensed again, muscles tightening to a quivering knot of suspicion.

"A minute or two, then," Candace said, "to leave whatever information you must." She drew the door back grudgingly, a mere slot through which his narrow frame slid smoothly as if immune to physical resistance, as if he could have oozed in under the door had she not opened it at all. But, once in, he seemed to take over and fill up the small sitting room, unpacking and spreading brochures, tokens and glossy flyers liberally on couch and side tables. When Candace's icy response cracked to betray annoyance, Cassidy's expression (misleadingly mournful, normally) tightened at the jaw, narrowed at the eye and wrinkled around the muzzle to one of loathing.

"It ent going to bite, right? It looking kinda miserable." Candace could not repress the chuckle that escaped her, as Shade flipped endearingly from British English to Trinidad Creole. He positioned himself to ensure an armchair between him and the dog, betraying his limited understanding of the more athletic breeds. "Is a pothound, ent? Not so? To me, all dem skinny brown dawg is pothoun. Big, though. Is bad?" He peered more closely. "What wrong with it back? What it have down the back there?"

"*She* wasn't exactly expecting visitors," Candace replied, with such good-humoured emphasis on her friend's personhood that Shade, riding the crest of his own smooth apologies for the intrusion, missed the rebuke entirely. Before she could gather herself to dismiss him, he fanned out more handbooks, and invitations in bold black font to apply for the position of Lecturer at the Institute of Tropical Studies in Portmore, Jamaica.

He began to reel out figures surprisingly higher than UWI salary scales. "Yes, tenure track." She could apply for tenure by her second year at the Institute of Tropical Studies, instead of waiting through two three-year contracts as she would at the University of the West Indies – if she ever did land a full-time, tenure-track post on a UWI campus.

Sharing out complimentary ITS pens and flash drives, Shade assured her he had studied tertiary institutions in the region and taken advice from Professor Dexter Danraj, who would obviously be clued in on that kind of thing and on Caribbean institutions in particular. As one of the luminaries in the Caribbean world of letters (besides being everybody's pardner and having their good at heart), Professor Danraj had lectured far and wide and knew the people who counted. Based on Dexter Danraj's assessment, Shade said UWI's days of being top dog in Caribbean tertiary education were numbered.

Who should know but Dex? Shade rolled his eyes at the obvious. The whole bureaucracy for admissions, examinations, appointments and promotions – and tenure, most of all for tenure – stifled creativity at every level. As he grew more expansive, Shade lamented that this tenure thing turned the oldtime universities into a niche for has-beens, and when some of these senior people stopped producing, it was hell to dislodge them. At the Institute of Tropical Studies, one progressed on merit and that was that. If Candace joined up, she would see for herself.

She watched, rapt, as Shade concluded with a final flourish of knobbly fingers and another grin that was little more than a revelation of teeth. Droll and creepy at the same time, he gathered his hoard of oddments with the promise that they would meet again to sew things up, and he slid back out the door. Candace regarded him in silence as he inched past Cassidy towards the gate, but Cassidy turned her back and squatted to send a stream of urine surging down the drive. Suppressing an inclination to snigger, Candace reached for the hose she kept on standby. Still, she was as much annoyed at herself as at the man who had invaded her weekend. The irony was that her own search activity had called this vulture down.

In her midnight siftings through university websites for vacancies, she had hunted out job search engines – all the while swatting away pop-ups advertising a range of trash. In the process, Candace had left behind a virtual trail for university recruiters, and some had sent advertisements or solicitous enquiries. But she had visualized such recruiters as snappy, well-heeled experts in educational data systems, the type that sought and screened job seekers, analysed résumés, tracked training grant customers and liaised with fulfilment teams in wealthy institutions.

Candace doubted whether this Institute of Tropical Studies in Portmore, Jamaica – the very Portmore where she had passed her earliest years – was laying out even the US$50,000 per year on one recruiter for academic staff, however rich the parent of the offshore campus might be. Besides, surely no institution would invest in anything as unprofessional in appearance as Morgan Shade. Yet she could not suppress some sneaking gratification at being sought out at all. She had, after all, been waiting to be discovered for seven years – well, five to be more realistic (but there *were* people who landed posts before completing their doctorates). Since the award of her PhD in 2004, each year had been an eternity. So. How unimpressive could this place be, anyway?

As she strode back to the house, Cassidy plunged alongside her, a droopy ear lifted, apparently in doubt. "But suppose it's on the level, and I ignore it," Candace insisted. Cassidy swerved in front of her, then heaved a sigh and slumped across the doorway, making it clear Candace was on her own as far as that decision was concerned. Candace stepped across without grumbling, because the dog was trying to shield rather than trip her. "You must want to go back to JA," Candace insisted, with a mischievous poke of her toe at a satin flank. "More work for you too."

Precisely. Cassidy closed her eyes. There was work to be had outside of academia. Some people refused to consider the options.

Candace could not help it. She was born into an academic family – or rather, her father was academic to the bone. Earl Rider had graduated in 1972 with honours in literature and history along with a few courses in economics, then headed straight on to an MPhil, his 1975 thesis on something to do with the migrant male in the emergence of a Caribbean world of letters. From there it was inevitable that he contemplate a doctorate, and he began toying with the title "Money, Machismo and the Written Caribbean". His supervisor cast a look askance at such frivolity, for it would be a while before titles like that stopped attracting disparaging glances from traditional scholars.

From what her mother said, alongside his initial reading Earl had practised unstintingly on his own machismo until a Tobago girl with a wide, playful grin confided that she loved Jamaica rhythm but that her favourite song was still Louisa Marks's "Caught You in a Lie", and what did he think of that? He said what she was missing was a firm grounding in rocksteady and that he was the tutor to take her education to new heights. Or perhaps they could begin with a quiet evening beside his new record player? Was she ready for a little Burning Spear?

Sheena Candace had not come along until 1979, a couple years into their marriage, which was already straining under the pressure of Earl's focus on the doctorate. Her mother, Patrice Rider, yearned to join the flood of migrants putting as many miles as possible (and preferably the whole Atlantic) between themselves and the Manley experiment with democratic socialism. "You want to stay here while Michael turn Jamaica into another Cuba?" she demanded.

"Not if you have a tenure-track position at Oxford for a black Portmore boy," Earl replied irritably.

It was an exchange Patrice quoted and re-quoted later when he complained of getting nowhere at UWI. Still, his 1980 PhD came just in time for an appointment as Assistant Lecturer at the University of the West Indies, on the Mona campus, fixing his domestic life firmly on the back burner.

Often enough as a child, Candace had thought of striking off on her own. "They sailed away for a year and a day," she intoned, and perhaps she could as well. She fantasized about directing affairs, especially in the evening at around five-thirty when it was cooler but still light. There she sat on the rocks, a leggy seven-year-old with her underlip caught anxiously by upper teeth that were still a bit large for her face and a determined set of her jaw, looking out to sea and imagining herself an admiral overseeing the defeat of the French, for someone had given her a book called *A First Story of Jamaica*, and she had recast herself as Admiral Rodney. Or she huddled behind a tree, a maroon lurking in wait for the enemy, scrutinizing the shadows on the stony faces of the hillside for Taino ghosts she would marshal to a massive uprising that would turn history around. Outside she had been in charge of the battle. Inside her parents' two-bedroom house, the bickering overwhelmed her. Sometimes when it got too late to wander outside, she sat just beyond the door, mentally relocating to the inside of a favourite tale, preferably in verse: *The moon was a ghostly galleon tossed upon cloudy seas.*

She had begun what she could remember of that life in Portmore only a limestone hole or two away from where this new campus had grown up. Candace thought back to the landscape of the Hellshire coast that had provoked her wildest imaginings. Perhaps if her parents had left the old house for her she could have scrambled down over some rocks to the grounds of the Institute of Tropical Studies. Perhaps not. The decades had muddled whatever sense of local geography she had gleaned before leaving Jamaica as a child. Despite the intervening years, she had never grown to feel at home in Trinidad.

Perhaps that was unfair, for she felt at home once she retreated into her head, usually by way of a book. Her earliest bookshelves had been in her bedroom under windows that the helper, Eudine, called *jealousies*, first a simple white case that she decorated with pressed ferns, for it was hers alone and little taller than herself – *The Three Billy Goats Gruff* Robert Louis Stevenson*The King's Stilts* . . . The next stood so tall she needed a chair to reach the upper shelves. Mr Toad Scrooge *Escape to Last Man Peak The King Nobody Wanted*. Then, there was the story of the cat that walked by himself.

And all places were alike to her. Well, not true either. It had been different outside, beyond the sad confines of the Portmore house. It came back to her, the pale grey structure on level rocks that reached to the back of the Riders' land, curved down towards the sea and then crumpled into jagged stone interspersed by tufts of whiplike vegetation. Behind that, the hard ground fell away to the sea that churned and sprayed up at her on Saturday mornings, when she lay on her belly to peer over the edge for small pinky-orange crabs scuttling in and out the crevices below. Some ventured unwittingly within reach of the homemade net she slapped down to pull them up and flick into her bucket. Washed with salt and lime, seasoned and fried, they had no meat to offer, only the flavour of shellfish teasing the tongue, while she drew on the meagre claws and then spat the shell back out. It was a sort of self-inflicted torment, this sucking at the merest taste that left the mouth empty and intensified the craving. "Make no sense, Sheena," her mother muttered, before shrugging and searching the fridge again for limes.

In Tobago, the crabs were dark grey blue and heftier, and she did not catch those. During Candace's visits each July from the mid-1980s to 1990s, Silver, her grandmother, would bring the crabs in from a man who sold them with their claws laced tight with coconut fronds. After a long scraping of hairy legs and scouring with lime and salt, they were curried with big flat dumplings that soaked up the flavour, so you ate and ate until you could barely crawl onto the cot under the window and collapse there, dazed by the fullness of your belly and confused by the lingering flavour of curry and shadon beni, the sting of salt, pepper and sea wind, and of Silver's wit, swift and penetrating beneath her hard deep laughter that drummed down like rain on galvanize.

Through Silver's house lay a path beaten by relatives or neighbours stopping for portugal juice or sweet drink, dropping a bag of eddoes or picking up a helping of warm pone. Among them were those who thought a young girl should be learning the household, busy with pot spoon or needle and thread; but as far as Silver was concerned, Sheena Candace could climb a mango tree and read herself to sleep in it. Not that Silver didn't loathe idleness of every sort; only nothing could bring her to believe that reading was idleness. Certainly not the reading of thick books of verse or novels from every age, not that avid sort of reading in which the child submerged so deep that she came back out with her eyes wide and dark, the pupils dilated like those of someone summoned from an unfathomable place.

Candace's father being from Portmore, at that time a small forerunner of what was to become a flourishing dormitory town of Kingston, it had been natural enough for him to settle his family there, as the area developed. Earl Rider was only a temporary part-time lecturer at UWI Mona before the award of his doctorate in 1980, when what he described as a lucky death in the faculty opened up the rare vacancy into which he fitted himself seamlessly.

Right away, he published feverishly from his thesis or on related topics he worked up along the way; then he began to branch out more daringly – at times in areas well off his usual path. So, as a child, she would hear him holding forth on the phone to a colleague regarding some snide remark – one that had filtered back from a subcommittee meeting on assessment and promotions – about whether he actually had an area of specialization. A comment like that was born not just of ignorance regarding the disciplines involved, her father would say. These people had no concept of interdisciplinarity. And what was so dangerous, he continued, was this blindness lay at the heart of his own faculty, so there was scant hope of understanding when the case went further up in the system to committees and boards populated by those philistines in science and technology.

Candace had taken down her *Pocket Oxford English Dictionary* (third shelf from top, extreme right) and found the word *interdisciplinary*, but through the intervention of her grandmother, she had already met the Philistines in her Bible. How they now came to be working at UWI was unclear, but she realized they were what Eudine would have termed *iignorant* people, reinforcing that with a prolonged suckteet. It was a category in which

Eudine fitted all employers, especially Dr Rider, who objected to her playing dub music while she ironed. "Plodding and unoriginal" was what he called dub, when Patrice protested that the woman was not playing it loud enough to disturb him at his desk. He would have thought, he said, that his wife could see the need to balance a certain aura of refinement against the (unavoidable) celebration of indigenous culture. Candace looked up *indigenous* and decided that was what she was.

Meanwhile, her father concluded he was getting nowhere because of academic jealousy and spite, so when a full-time post opened up in Trinidad on the St Augustine campus in 1988, he pounced on it. Patrice gave herself up to the euphoria of contemplating life in easier reach of her mother, because even if Tobago was a different island, at least it was still the same country – which meant, Patrice said, having the sort of support she had craved for years. Most of all, Candace's mother basked in the promise of domestic bliss. For appreciation was what Earl had needed, Patrice explained to the neighbour who came to help pack up. Earl had been utterly undervalued by his colleagues at Mona, and now, here it was: he would be happy at work and come home to them, well, content.

At first Candace did not want to leave Jamaica, but it was different when her mother pointed out how much more time Earl would spend with them.

"We'll be happy, Sheena," her mother said in that wheedling voice.

"Why can't you call me Candace like everyone else?" She pulled away, but looking back she recalled anticipating long talks, questions her father would no longer brush aside but pause over, conversation.

Candace had always liked questions more than answers, and most of all, she liked questions that had no answers. She collected them the way other children collected stickers, gossip about film stars or pictures of rock singers with shiny hair. She uncovered questions like those wherever they cropped up in her mind and dusted them free of whatever rubbish adhered, to take them to her father and hold them up – not so much for him to answer as to consider. Except, she would discover, he found all this provoking to the nth degree.

One particular question that sidled up during her early years and followed her through her teens had to do with words – which seemed adhesive and manoeuvrable (for how else could they connect and rearrange) as well as wildly variable in texture. The question, which she could not for a long time articulate, clung and nudged at her, and rubbed itself along her mind almost like the words that she turned over in her thoughts and played with, marvelling at the hard, clear transparent ones that scattered light in dim places, and others that sliced sharp, cut deep or echoed hauntingly. Then there were those that felt silky, like the stray kitten she had cried and cried to be allowed to keep, but the tiny mewing in the box came to her fainter and fainter, as the gardener bore it off obediently to the pitch oil tin full of water, and a neighbour distracted her with his puppy, all smooth damp nose and velvet ears, like words of incredible softness and tenderness that smoothed the jagged ones.

She grew more and more susceptible to words and to the formations in which they came together, in which they could be brought together to stir and govern how people felt, thought and behaved. Or wanted others to behave. Or seem to behave. How was it possible to control the insides of people with words? Candace wanted to know.

She locked herself up with them the way a few of the older brothers or sisters of children she knew locked themselves up to smoke or even locked themselves up with each other to find out . . . whatever it was – she had not known or cared. At first most of the words that attracted her came in writing from other places. Pulling the curtains as wide as she could, so the light could come in, and she could see the kiskidee alight weightlessly and then soar off again, she shut herself in her room with snatches of language that darted near, and she surrendered to them. Rendered light-headed by the lilt of "Meg Merrilies" and the interlocking narratives of *The Hobbit*, she dipped into books for older people, and she found herself breathless with the ripple of meanings that spread and intersected in some lines from what seemed a longer poem, called *A Midsummer Night's Dream*. It was the sort of thing she intended taking a few bits of to her father, when they finally got to Trinidad and he was . . . content.

Only, once they were there, he said, "Yeh. Great. Run along now." Only, he immersed himself deeper in his publications and graduate students so as to cross the merit bar and nail tenure fast.

And more and more Candace retreated from her parents' unrelenting discord, reeling herself up into a space in her head that vibrated with words and the sounds of words and the rhythm of sentences. There she occupied herself contentedly, hung up on verse, rocking on anapaests, lulled by unravelling iambic pentameter. There she declaimed *The Ancient Mariner* loudly to herself in the one solitary place that was hers, where she could shout without anyone hearing, only herself listening for the twang or thud or swish or chime of consonants, the echo of vowels. There she hovered, strung out on the way phrases clung together or broke loose suddenly, hurling her aloft; or she might just let go and float, soar, plunge – there was a sort of free fall one experienced in some sequences. Words, sentences – she unwrapped them greedily, sense after sense. It was her own, secret, space.

In a few years, she tried to throw herself into the bustle of Trincity Mall, to complain about extra lessons in maths, to share the flap over a male teacher as old as her father and equally uninterested in her, to yearn admission to hot spots and all-inclusive fetes. At home she looked longingly at the hills barely visible from her window, leaning out dangerously, remaining motionless so long that a swallowtail wafted up drunkenly and settled on her arm. When it fluttered off again, she drew back inside and surveyed herself in the mirror without satisfaction, feeling herself too tall, wondering whether her breasts would ever fill out, doubting whether she cared. She loved clothes of cool colours in light fabric, but not transparent or clinging. She loathed the constriction of a bra but put up with it for Silver's sake. Her eyes were dark, bright, wide as if taken by surprise. Her hair curled disobediently in every direction, whatever she did with it. But what really occupied her thoughts was how it was possible to word the wind howling Heathcliff's anguish, and whether the letters *Man-man* inscribed on Miguel Street were a sign of his madness or some part of the cause.

Silver seemed unfazed when Candace's interests swerved off the beaten track, but at school it had been weird sometimes, being bright. Twinges of guilt or self-consciousness cramped the thrill of catching on more quickly than the rest in subjects that came easily to her; then, when she floundered in some area that was not her own, an irrational shame pinched her, as if she had found herself out and was small and commonplace after all.

By the time she outgrew that, there was the pretending – to the other girls, her parents, even sometimes herself – tapping her foot to music turned up to the level of gross noise so she couldn't make out the lyrics, let alone carry a separate line of thought in her head. Tapping her foot, bobbing her head, as if she were into it. Talking about a boy who played football for Hillview, when neither he nor football interested her one jot, and shutting up about things that did but were boring to normal young people, like her conviction that Hamlet was no madder than most people she knew.

"I always want to go to the party," she admitted to Silver. "I think, *It's going to be different this time*. But it never is. And it's me: I don't know how to . . . be fun."

"You *are* fun." Silver's face tightened to grim loyalty. "Who can't see that, is because they stupid." She stopped and stroked a cheek. "And it have nobody worthwhile could help looking at you."

Silver had something to say about everything, and when she pursed up her lips and clenched her mouth in silence, it was because the subject was too fraught for the caustic remarks it warranted. Her son-in-law, Earl, inevitably prompted this voluble silence. But nothing else was safe from her tongue, not the slack lyrics that accosted them from the radio, nor the skimpy dress Candace's mother had bought her for Christmas, nor the rude glance of the porter at Crown Point Airport. Silver never hedged, never said, "We'll see." There was enough *we'll see* at large already, Silver pronounced, and it spawned wutless men and miserable women, subjects on which she let fly unstintingly. "That is one good-looking boy," Silver said once, following Candace's eye, as they sat under the almond tree watching passersby on the beach. "Soft-spoken and nice. He fool up two young girl already and leave them with they baby to mind by themself. Like he now looking for another fool. Make him come round here, let me put him out of business for good."

Some women never managed to take charge of themselves, Silver reflected. For that was what she had done, when her husband had persisted in his own wayward life, flitting from woman to woman in Port of Spain and drinking out every penny he made, while she struggled to bring up the little girl-child. She had left him right there, gone back to her mother's tiny house in Tobago and taken care of the old lady as well as the child. Not everyone had the belly for that.

Husbands, Candace concluded, were pure crosses, and since husbands went along with routine plans for a home with children, she turned her dreams instead to a life immersed in books. Meanwhile, from mid-July into

August, year after year, Silver made her a home with real food every day and church on Sundays. Sometimes the rain set in, and they read and played rummy. Otherwise – sky, sea, sand – everything that was the make-believe of travel magazines was the one real place of her childhood, when she and Silver read to each other under the almond tree until their voices croaked. So, in yearly instalments, Silver grew her up, strait-laced and private.

At fifteen, Candace might sit still, poker-faced in the midst of heated conversations, while her brain cavorted around, nipping at fallacies, tearing into weaknesses of content and mauling preconceived positions and stereotypes in the verbiage that flowed by. Occasionally she let go of herself and closed ferociously on whatever had provoked her.

She was studying for CXC, when it became apparent to her father that UWI ought have promoted him to Senior Lecturer, and he glimpsed the post he deserved, in Canada – by which time verbal cruelty and whining were years deep in the Curepe house. (Sometimes Candace could lock it out. Works of Jane Austen *Wide Sargasso Sea Collected Poems* Emily Dickinson *In a Green Night Crick Crack, Monkey.*) When the University of Toronto turned down Earl Rider's application, he moved to a more comfortable house in Valsayn, coming back and forth only for food and laundry, so it was possible almost to ignore him. Yet still Patrice and Earl tormented each other, one suffocating and the other slashing away.

Till Candace met Randall, there was no one but Silver with whom to discuss books, dogs, parents, the nature of debate itself or the efficacy of words. Hers were not views most people would engage with, so she hugged them to herself. Her temper did not, like his, take ages to ignite nor burn on even when there was nothing left to consume. But teased, she snapped hard. Randall discovered that procrastination particularly agitated her and meandering argument brought on some intellectual equivalent of motion sickness. She was incapable of polite circumlocution. But how, Silver demanded, would any child who didn't sit down to regular Sunday lunch with her parents learn how to talk to people in a civilized way? As usual Silver had seized on the meat of the matter and then boiled it down dry. It was true, though, that having established her father had no interest in any debate with her, and her mother no spirit for it, Candace kept her more exciting thoughts to herself unless forced out of silence. Only, when that happened, she found herself unable to back off; instead she plunged on, worrying the argument, diving after its most elusive detail like a mongoose at a snake.

Silver's moral framework being the only one available, Candace grew up viewing her father's more obvious flaws through the eyes of her grandmother. Earl Rider, amoral and coldly self-absorbed, proved ruinous in his effect on women, especially the wife who idolized him until he wearied of her, and who clung on obsessively. After the Riders moved from Jamaica to Trinidad, Candace's recollections of her early life concentrated over years like the Salt Pond at Portmore, and eventually she wondered whether her memories had reshaped, even distorted under the intense conditions of her childhood, so as to enable her to survive. It had been a relief, however Candace resented it, when her father left and set up an independent establishment. But Candace's mother, long teetering on the verge of collapse, fell apart. And ever afterwards, even after she recovered, he belittled her for weak-mindedness.

Ever fair-minded, Silver pronounced that Patrice's story was the tragedy of a woman unable to command respect. Patrice was her daughter, and she, Sylvia Veronica Clarke, should know her own child. Not that that was any excuse for the Mr Earl, she added.

Candace stayed on with her mother and gave not a thought to Earl Rider's polished house in Valsayn. During Candace's last year in secondary school, she encouraged her mother to take a job in the registry on campus and employ a Guyanese illegal to clean once a week. Earl Rider's full-time position allowed his daughter to enrol in 1997 free of tuition costs. Patrice's salary covered the books and entitled her to hold forth on Candace's choice of programme. "Linguistics? What is that? And English? But you not serious, Candace." By that time, her mother had given in and was calling her Candace. "You have the grades to do law. Bad enough you refuse to choose the sciences in school. You could have got into med school easy, easy. But no – you cling to these arts subjects, and now, with a string of As, you refuse to do the law. And where you will get to with an arts degree? Into some paltry teaching job. I can't believe you have so little ambition."

By the time Candace was nineteen and one year into her bachelor's, all she wanted or could remember wanting was for either or both of her parents to go away.

Then they did.

Chapter 2

Spent on Books and Learning

gladly wolde [s]he lerne and gladly teche

When Earl Rider stopped by on the way to the airport, to announce his departure for Canada and leave his forwarding address, her mother did not hesitate.

"You're almost ready to graduate, your courses are paid for, and I'm leaving you the house," Patrice said to her daughter the next day, as she rifled frantically through a cupboard for warm clothes to take with her. "What it is you want me to do?"

Candace proclaimed their departure a good riddance. Her father's blatant infidelities disgruntled her, and her mother ricocheted between agony and denial, incapable of dumping him. Candace could block it out – in softly lit corridors, book-lined. She wrote an essay on Shakespeare's Gertrude as a criminally inept mother, and the first marker declared it fanciful, while the second argued that Gertrude came through in the end. But for scrupulous research and intrepid argument, it drew an A–. Candace chuckled and bled. She pressed on the wound, immersing herself in morphology and semantics that slowed and then staunched a flow invisible to everyone else. She threw up a sturdy schedule for her existence – a time for everything under the sun.

She immersed herself in her courses but otherwise clung to the margins of campus life, a fascinated observer. She registered the smell of hot oil, pepper and garlic, the rustle of grease-proof paper, the crunch of fried channa. She picked up the rhythm of the Soc Sci student who hoisted a thick Econ text in one hand while dipping French fries in ketchup with the other. All the while, his right leg jiggled so furiously that the bench shook, and a girl sitting farther along it slung on her backpack and then swigged a Gatorade and took off, two free fingers curled around a brown bag of doubles.

Candace wandered back into the library. She kept off from fetes, cricket, protests. She would have gone on hikes, if it had not meant throwing in her lot with strangers. She would have driven up into the Northern Range, if she had a car. She received an occasional call from her mother and tried to listen. But nobody interfered with her or quarrelled over her head. Safe place. Immovable mountains presided over meticulously labelled trees and bush that outlasted dry season to spring and bloom again. Between lectures she sat on a bench under the shade of a samaan with her laptop and a bag of crumbs to scatter occasionally at her feet. Candace nailed her routine in place and felt quiet descend.

There were students who pursued a UWI degree only for the security of a certificate, and now and then, someone grumbled about the odd staff member for whom UWI amounted to a shelter, a sure salary and pension plan, juggled against another life in business, politics or industry. Perhaps priorities wavered and reformed in situations where rules existed but were not rigorously enforced, but the staff Candace encountered proved a decent lot – not that one knew or speculated on their personal lives – and she found her lecturers accessible, knowledgeable, mostly caring. If there were others, she never encountered them. The campus seemed as good a place to be as any other, and her father's discontent with it inexplicable.

Although August of 1998 saw Dr Earl Rider relocate with the stated intention of taking up a good position in a Canadian university, Candace's mother quickly found herself domiciled in Toronto on her own. Earl had simultaneously negotiated two contracts and had moved to Texas, where he selflessly accommodated their divorce. Patrice had a comfortable home, provided she remained where she was, unless she preferred to return to Trinidad. Patrice hung on in Toronto and hoped.

Candace stayed put in the Curepe town house and went through the official procedure for whittling away Rider associations by assuming her mother's maiden name, Clarke. Years before, Candace had adopted the hyphenated existence summed up in Clarke-Rider, which appeared on Patrice's official documents, and she had glowered when her father jeered about whether, when Mr Right materialized, she would become Clarke-Rider-Right. She had recovered swiftly enough to promise she would drop the Rider. As for Mr Right – she had laughed. Fantasy was not her preferred genre.

Randall Jefferies, though – Candace's first and, for a long time, only friend – had proved unrealistic. Untethered to this world – that was how she described him to Silver. It was as if it fascinated but had no hold on him. Yes, he had devoured Silver's pelau with gusto and engrossed her in lively conversation about everything from the Tobago population of leatherback turtles to the ethics of Dan Brown's novels. After spending seemingly unending patience on the float in the toilet tank, he surprised them with a rare but incendiary fit of temper and hurled abuse at it. Still, he applied his compulsion to fix things liberally in Silver's kitchen – tightened a doorknob, cleaned out a toaster, replaced a light bulb broken from its base in the socket. But as for sparing good shoes from salt water or even positioning himself for employment in the long run, such considerations occupied Randall's mind not at all. He cared even less about securing comfortable and reliable transportation. He strode along everywhere at top speed and with a bounce in his step, lean as Candace, despite eating twice as much, radiating health and exuberant good spirits – if her observations were to be trusted. Even after years apart, she had to admit she could draw up his long narrow face in her mind, that humorous curl of full lips, sharp-cut smile lines under high cheekbones and intent eyes that, she insisted, danced with mischief.

She had first caught his voice emanating from a huddle of students to whom he was recounting a tale made interesting only by its delivery. When the others sat forward, the teller came into view, and she thought him attractive enough, but it was not that – it was the abandonment with which he threw himself into it.

"Who's the raconteur?"

The chap beside Candace said, "Jefferies. Good sort. Not usually so excitable – well, only when he gets into a story."

Riveting eyes, she thought, even four years later, bright under thick black brows and the stiff wild tangle of his hair. "Like a pile of twigs," she grumbled. "What?" he asked, preoccupied with an overheated radiator under a dented bonnet.

"Your hair. Twigs." Randall's grey polo shirt and worn sandals prompted her to add, "Except for lack of a tonsure, you look like a friar. Do you know that?"

"Oh well." He had grinned in response to her critical gaze. "Lots of 'em were okay."

There. That unquenchably bright outlook could scarcely be viable.

"A decent young man," Silver had protested, groggy from multisymptom tablets she took for flu, her breathing laboured. They couldn't know then that pneumonia had set in and would carry her off. "You never meet up with the other sort, or what?"

Sylvia Veronica Clarke, Candace's grandmother, had been her earliest connection with Trinidad and Tobago, and she had not minded her grandmother calling her Sheena Candace, even when her mother gave up and stuck to the second name – the only one her father used, when he used one at all. At first Candace and her parents had visited Silver together, then Candace and her mother alone, before the pattern set in of leaving Candace in Tobago over July and August, when Earl would go off on study leave, Patrice tagging doggedly along. Eventually Candace confessed that she would not have wanted to be anywhere else but in Tobago with Silver; yet over the years, her resentment pierced deep, particularly when adult experience of campus life revealed that UWI travel grants for staff included an allowance for children. The university had more idea of parenthood than Earl or Patrice, Candace complained to Randall.

Randall himself had no parents to complain of, his father having decamped so early that no one had any idea who he was – except, presumably, Randall's mother. But she had taken this information with her when she died in childbirth. His mother's brother was a kind fellow with no family to think about but Randall. He had run a bar, though, and, eighteen years later, intervened when bandits held up his cashier one busy Saturday night in August of '97. So Uncs took a bullet and reached the Port of Spain Hospital dead on arrival. By then, however, he had paid for Randall's first year at UWI, and a scholarship was to take care of the rest. That was how Randall found himself entirely on his own, with no hang-ups about anything except government inability to address crime.

Candace had hang-ups, and they went way back.

What little she relayed about those days amounted to memories of childhood that she could connect only with holidays in Tobago, sporadically lighting up against the dim background of the Rider household. Rooms, garden or even events she tried to conjure up from the Portmore days remained out of focus, their specifics dulled by routine disappointment. Something in that shadow, a sort of settled sadness underlying humour, or a wistfulness that hedged wit, aroused Randall's curiosity when he first saw Candace, painfully out of place at a student lime.

"On the contrary," she objected, when he recalled it months afterwards, "I was the life and soul of the party." *That* was when he recognized the role of flippancy in her fabrication, the ongoing pretence that she was not unbearably shy. When she said it – "I'm shy" – that too was part of the disguise, thrown out to avoid sitting on stage, and everyone accepted it as frivolity. "She likes to have her little joke." They exchanged knowing glances. "Don' mind she looking serious the whole time." No one took her carefully artless claims to shyness at face value.

But Randall's uncompromising curiosity cheerfully stripped layers of skilful wrapping from fictional characters, or from narrative embedded in other narrative, and he approached Candace with the same wild mix of glee, rigour and sensitivity that he brought to critical inquiry. Besides, like her, he could listen in silence for a long time. Somehow she would find herself recounting incidents to him, startled at how unselfconsciously she bared sensations she had tamped down over years.

In the late 1990s, as she pursued her double major in linguistics and literature, once her parents had taken flight, Candace discovered the well-being of a peaceful house. More and more, she found herself in the same tutorial groups as Randall; she wondered idly whether he had engineered it and, then, whether she minded. It was impossible to be bored by a man from whom the ending of a novel could draw a gasp of satisfaction or explosion of fury. To romantic involvement, she gave no thought whatever.

"Frigid" was how a would-be suitor summed her up in Randall's hearing.

Randall eyed him dangerously. "A word that has nothing to do with the referent's temperature and everything to do with the speaker's pique."

The connection between them fell into place, comfortably, undemandingly. Wide green spaces of the campus dappled her moodiness with light and transformed the emotional sparseness in her parents' wake to lush receptiveness. Anything, it seemed, could flourish.

The campus now bustled with an enrolment of more than eighteen thousand, and buildings were springing up in pursuit of a runaway growth in student intake. The land on which the campus had taken root boasted its own rich past. At the end of the nineteenth century, a thriving sugar estate had gone bankrupt and been transformed to green land for grazing animals, before the whole physical property went up for sale at last. The agricultural college planted there grew into the Imperial College of Tropical Agriculture and eventually one of the three campuses of the University of the West Indies. The fourth, the Open Campus, would not be launched until 2008.

Long before that, in 2000, Candace had completed her degree with first-class honours. She wrote her last examination barely in time to catch a flight to Toronto, where her mother had been hospitalized following on dizziness and fainting. Candace arrived at the Princess Margaret Cancer Centre, only to find that after innumerable tests, Patrice had been diagnosed with stage 4 cancer.

Patrice tried to speak. Her lips soundlessly formed the name *Sheena*. In the end, she could not even call Candace by the name Candace preferred. But after that jab of disappointment, Candace's reflections mellowed around the thought that her mother had used the name *she* loved best.

Dr Rider flew up from Texas for the funeral, accepted condolences from colleagues and acquaintances, and made a touching tribute. To Candace, the gathering after the service and the conversation that ensued seemed to exhume and re-inter her father's Caribbean past. Amid a hallucinogenic mix of odours – greasy finger-foods and lilies – the room tipped and spun around her. During the queasy two days afterwards, and to her surprise, her father dropped by and made solicitous enquiries. And on the day she was packing up, he invited her to visit him at his home. As he had covered her mother's final expenses and Candace's airfare, it seemed churlish to refuse, so she arranged to go in a couple weeks – but briefly, because she and Randall planned to travel together to Kingston so as to begin a graduate programme at UWI Mona. That, however, she kept to herself.

Tucked up against the plane window, she wrapped herself in *A Suitable Boy*, which she had wanted to read for months, but she had been too distracted with examinations to indulge in hefty novels off her syllabus. She was startled when the attendant came down the aisle to collect trash in advance of the landing, extending a hesitantly hopeful hand and receiving disposable cups and napkins with a shy dip of her head along with a prolonged *thank youuuu* and a gratified – no, obsequious – smile, as if being granted what she had long hoped for but knew she did not deserve. Just the sort of thing for Randall, Sharon thought, when he got started on that novel. She made a note for him.

En route from the George Bush Intercontinental Airport, she berated herself for expecting her father to collect her. Instead, here was the back of a turbaned taxi driver, who spared but a surly word or two regarding her destination. Under the rear-view mirror, an air freshener in the form of a cardboard pine tree dangled from a glow-in-the-dark shark that bobbed about, until she felt slightly sick, in the way she had, over the years, reacted to her father's disregard.

After a forty-minute drive, the Texas College of Arts and Culture lit up on the left. A few swift turns brought her through a residential area to a well-illuminated house behind a car-lined curb, with strains of soca music and laughter to be heard. Earl Rider raised his voice above David Rudder's "Calypso Music" to greet her in his offhand way and wave her towards a table with drinks. She wanted coffee but knew better than to ask for a cup from his cache of Blue Mountain, so she took wine. After that, the evening went forward as if she were not there. Having been starved by an uncivilized airline, she picked at nuts and over-salty fragments of chips shaken from the bottom of some bag, while the Merlot soured her stomach.

A few days later, the old Earl did take her along to a faculty get-together and, once, when he had to entertain a visiting colleague, to a steakhouse. The waiters said, "Abslutely", when she gave her order, "'preciate it", when

Professor Rider paid the bill, and "Have a good one", when Candace and her father were leaving the restaurant. Otherwise, as the rest of the ten-day visit unfolded, he suggested she grill a couple chops, and he passed on a shirt or two for ironing.

He pointed out the advantages of her doing her graduate work right there at TCAC, where she could stay with him at no cost, but when she asked point-blank whether he would help finance her graduate programme at UWI, he refused. He was only prepared to support her at TCAC. Candace issued a resounding suckteet and informed him he could stuff his money or just invest it in a maid, because she was going to a proper university and not some little half-arsed college.

He said, "Suit yourself."

⸻

Their Firsts having secured scholarships, Candace and Randall flew into Kingston on the same plane, moved into their respective rooms and plunged into their MPhil programmes on the Mona campus. She had wanted to go back to Jamaica, and Randall encouraged her, saying, "I feel I going too. Ent you don't mind?" Their landladies and classmates assumed he was her boyfriend, for they ate and studied together and analysed everything under the sun. In a group, he stayed on the outskirts of arguments, as she did; but where she tuned out non-issues, he stayed entranced, eyes darting from one combatant to the other in lively interest. He was even less likely to engage than she was but hung on the edge of his seat, caught up in the drama.

His one-to-one encounters seemed to absorb him less, though. The girls he went out with had nothing of interest to say, he complained to Candace. She used to call them his adverbs. "Only, if they're meaningless or, at best, non-essential, what are they for?"

"For marking time," he replied inscrutably.

They were driving along a residential road in the suburbs one day, when he drew suddenly to a halt, opened his door and shot out a surprisingly brawny arm to scoop a puppy from the gutter – only it turned out to be a rabbit. So he drove along with it on his lap, until he found a game of cricket in the street and slowed again. A small boy was crying on the outskirts of the game by the roadside, and Randall called him and handed over the rabbit.

"Just in time," he muttered, putting his foot on the gas before a parent could turn up and object.

"Hardly. It's peed on your pants."

"Could have been worse."

He was part of her by the time that first semester drew to its close. They had actually just returned from the supermarket in Liguanea Plaza, when he remarked that he should have looked around in the shops. Then he sheepishly explained that he was shifting programmes. There was another application he had sent out almost as a joke and eventually warmed to. When the letter of acceptance found its way to him late, he decided he wanted to take it up, and they were willing to admit him in January. They were almost back to her flat, just off campus, when he told her he would need to buy warm stuff somewhere.

"Warm stuff?"

"Well, for London."

That was when he confessed to the ridiculous research topic that had led him out of Caribbean letters altogether and on the path of traditional British canonical verse. He had not entrusted Candace with the idea before, he admitted. He had postponed talking about it, because he knew she would carry on, when, really, he hadn't even been serious about the medieval at first. "And it was not to say that you wanted us . . . wanted . . ."

"No. Well, by all means, continue to keep your thoughts to yourself, and I'll do the same," she responded, wrenching the car door open before he had quite drawn to a halt in front of the gate where Cassidy was watching eagerly, then slamming the door savagely behind her.

What did he know of what she wanted? What did she know, for that matter – except that she had valued the openness between them. Anyway, she was bad at surprises. He moved to crank down the glass to call her back, but that was the window with the missing handle.

All she flung over her shoulder was, "Don't waste another word on me."

The deluge of work kept her from sinking as low as she might. Her supervisor, Leslie Crichlow, returned timely feedback on the design she had beaten out, so she plunged into the reading that bore her up through ten months of blocking Randall out. When the silence hardened to pain that distracted her, she sent off a brusque e-mail enquiry as to whether he was all right. Then they started writing back and forth.

Meanwhile, like any number of other graduate students, she began teaching a few hours a week in the Foundation courses.

By virtue of being compulsory, most of these courses were unpopular with the student body across the region. In particular, innumerable students moaned about the first-year writing courses, cursing and often ignoring them to the point of failing and having to repeat them years later, alongside finals and beyond.

"We should put that to work for us," Candace once said, in chatting with Marcus Walters, a tall, strikingly handsome Barbadian who was in the same research methods course. "Offer them the chance to take all those courses before they even start – for a price."

"Like a shot against seasickness before embarking." Marcus laughed. He really had the most engaging smile, she realized. "Only, what would they do with the space for those courses, when they do come in?" His eyes were lively with interest.

"Don't know." She reflected. "Nothing. Finish a semester early. Or if they did extra faculty courses, maybe the university could calculate the level of the degree on the best of a larger number of courses. Students who couldn't afford the package could fulfil the requirements in the old way. But what about equal advantages? It would need tweaking."

"You should patent that," Marcus responded.

They chuckled over a few more details, and then he waved cheerily and strode off to his car. Nice car too. His father was a businessman who had relocated to Jamaica recently and seemed to be doing well.

A week later, Marcus put a proposal to the Head of Department, who bore it off to the Dean, and they rushed it through Faculty Board, Academic Board and the Board of Undergraduate Studies, before the news percolated down to insignificant part-timers like Candace. In its essentials, it remained the same idea. Students could choose to take the package if they knew (as the blurb said) that they had better things to do with their university years and wanted to avoid dragging closer and closer to graduation failed courses they would continue to repeat after satisfying their other degree requirements. No reference to the fact that most students could pass simply by applying themselves to the courses, Candace noted. *Take the tears out of Final Year*, coaxed a notice on the university's website.

The Head of Department congratulated Marcus Walters on his initiative and massaged some empty and about-to-be-frozen post to get him appointed as a full-time instructor in time for the next semester. If the thing took off, the Head and Dean might even be able to negotiate an upgrade of the same Instructor post to Lecturer. The Dean undertook to push this, offstage, on the strength of all the university would save if the fee-paying package replaced the traditional route for a sizeable number of registrants. "Hundreds of students," the Head predicted.

By the time Candace and Marcus spoke again, he was Programme Manager for what promised to be a thriving enterprise. "And in a way, you inspired me," he said, in a tone of heartfelt appreciation that set every nerve jangling. "Why don't you change your registration to part-time, so you can teach a few more groups with us?"

Her future was so unstable that she found little to say except, "Who knows?"

By February of 2002, Candace was in a position to defend an upgrade from the master's to the doctoral programme. Just before signing his support, her supervisor asked her the question most supervisors never ask: Did she know what she was doing? She gazed at him blankly. Everyone knew an upgrade meant registering for a doctorate rather than the MPhil. Deeper research, longer thesis. It was daunting, the stipulation that your work must add to existing knowledge and push the limits of a discipline beyond what experts in that field had marked out; but she had already discovered in herself the weird mix of arrogance and humility that seemed called for. For a second her heart stopped. Dr Crichlow could not be wondering at this stage whether she had the brains.

"No." He read her face. "You meet the requirements, or I wouldn't support the upgrade. The question is about what you're doing to your life, changing track. How you intend to make a living."

She saw his lips moving, heard superfluous words. She was not changing track, only trying to clamber onto the only track there was.

The upgrade approved, she argued for an extension to her scholarship and probed deeper into how writers represented Creole in direct speech.

As she grappled with issues of getting Jamaican on the page, it flashed in her mind that a few creative writers were also linguists, and she began juggling correspondence with her applications for funding. She was sorting and storing data gleaned from local writers, when she landed a grant to examine postcolonial discourse in the University of Toronto's Robarts Library. She began requesting interviews with authors and critics in the Toronto area and made arrangements for Cassidy. Then she flew over and settled into temporary student quarters. In the unearthing of sweaters and jackets, memories of her mother's departure, then Randall's, had flooded back. But the thought that it was now her turn had lifted her beyond such griefs as habitually shadowed her.

However warm Canadians asserted themselves to be at any one time, Candace was always aware of a chill wind lurking around each towering block of concrete and glass. But she liked her six weeks in Toronto, especially St George Street, with its students rolling by on bicycles, preoccupied staff, and even the young man on the shady deck of a house – one that looked, otherwise, abandoned – who sat on a stool playing with a snake twelve to fourteen feet long, gleaming gold medallions on black, coiling round and over and under his body in a ceaseless sinuous flow. Another day that house was utterly empty. Leaves drifted across the wooden deck as if no one had walked there for years. A different world, yet . . . legible. She unwound, reading it.

Leaves turning. Her interviews done, she moved between libraries in the deep contentment that settled among bookcases radiating to present shelf upon shelf of spines, titles, authors. Lights flared as she advanced along the corridor of books and faded behind. The weeks drifted by.

~)\~

Back in Kingston, from Monday to Friday her mobile launched her from bed at four a.m. to hammer on the computer for three hours before bolting out of her back room in Mona Heights. It was as well that her landlady had taken to Cassidy, who followed her to the gate and would be there to escort her in at night. Each morning Candace hovered at the edge of Hope Road, watching for the minibus named Good Shepherd that raced past the main gate to the campus. Somehow in all of this, she picked up temporary tutoring in linguistics or in literature.

"You don't know how lucky you are to land those," Marcus said, his Bajan accent thickened by longing. "The writing courses just eat up time. Marking, marking."

She took note of the glottal consonants in his pronunciation, which had once seemed cute to her, and wished he would choke on them.

It had been during those years of graduate research that the Institute of Tropical Studies sprouted up, but she paid little attention to begin with. Years before, a public announcement had been buried some pages into the *Gleaner*:

> ### Green Light for Portmore Institute
> The Global Knowledge Institute of the Americas in association with the International Consortium for Borderless Education, having negotiated with the Jamaican government over the past three and a half years, has eventually been granted a charter by an act of Parliament to establish an offshore campus in Jamaica, more specifically in the Portmore area of St Catherine.
>
> The location of a campus in this thriving locale is expected to generate thousands of jobs locally as well as widening opportunities for higher education for Caribbean and, especially, Jamaican youths. Because the campus will also welcome students from the United States and others in our global village, it promises to bring in much-needed foreign exchange.

Candace vaguely remembered that even before she had registered for her bachelor's at St Augustine, an acquaintance in Jamaica had sent her mother that *Gleaner* clip to show how *bright* Portmore was getting. But it wasn't until she was fashioning those first chapters of her thesis at Mona that the opening of ITS sprawled itself flamboyantly across the papers.

> At a gala dinner yesterday evening, the Head of the International Office of the Global Knowledge Institute of the Americas announced that "the breathtakingly beautiful campus, with its sweeping vista of the Caribbean Sea and background of the Hellshire Hills, will offer the ideal environment for adults embarking on lifelong learning."
>
> The Principal of the Mona Campus, UWI, when asked for his opinion,

stated that he wished the founders of the new offshore campus and its Institute of Tropical Studies every success. Asked whether he foresaw significant competition with UWI, he smiled and said he had nothing to add to his earlier comment.

Apart from public discussion of the terrain, after construction began, nothing much about ITS or UWI responses to it had impinged on Candace, until the conference that eventually lured her back to Trinidad.

In lacing together chapters of her dissertation, she had sensed her student life moving towards its close. The future blanked and then over-shadowed and pressed in, so she began wondering about prospects at St Augustine. Waking one morning to a foretaste of despair, she propelled herself from bed to desk and drew up an application form for funding to attend a conference.

Details of her first publication accounted for her previous grant, so now she attached the abstract for the new presentation and a list of appointments she had made with sociolinguists and literary critics at St Augustine. She sent a copy of her request to an invited speaker from the University of Miami, for an appointment to discuss direct speech in autobiography. She even referred wistfully to a rumour that Walcott might visit the campus during the conference and implied she might land an interview. In her dreams – but never mind. Unless a full-time position evolved from nowhere, she would be lucky to have hourly paid teaching once the dissertation went in, and no hope of funded travel once she was neither registered student nor permanent staff. The conference offered a chance to arouse interest on another campus. So she laid it on thick.

Then rumour of a vacancy opening in linguistics at Mona set her rein-forcing her vitae, while she refined the conference paper and kept plowing away at the dissertation draft. At the same time, the logistics of conference attendance sent her into her old phone contacts: Driver, TnT, Solomon.

Solomon, who had helped get her mother to and from sessions with a psychologist, agreed to meet Candace in Trinidad at Piarco Airport and to drive her during the conference and then to visit an aging aunt in Toco. But she barely recognized him at the arrival door.

"Miss Sheena," he hailed her.

"You lost so much weight," Candace exclaimed, stepping from the morgue-like temperature out into a blast of heat.

"You nearly didn't find me here at all." Solomon pushed her hand luggage into the back of his Sentra. "Is weeks I there in hospital."

"What happened?"

"*If* I tell you, I hardly know myself what taking place. I just wake up and see I in hospital. And tests? You say, test?"

"So what it was?"

"I fine now, as you see me here. Sometimes I does be a little forgetful, like I catch myself and don't know what just happen. But on the whole, I good. Them doctors don't know nothing, I tell you. They saying was sugar, but it wasn't no sugar."

"But the doctors must . . ."

"Here nah. I is not no diabetic. You think I taking a set of tablet costing *money*, when I feeling good good? I know myself. I must know my body. I can tell you I ent no diabetic, because – watch me – I eating everything right through. Dem doctors doesn't know nothing."

Perceiving she was in the hands of a noncompliant diabetic who was subject to blackouts, she converted a hysterical laugh to a hiccup, and when they pulled up at the guesthouse, she jumped out of his taxi thankfully. There, she apologized for some unavoidable rescheduling. (And a day swerving through the mountains to Toco? No way.)

"I'll be back in TnT soon." Her enthusiasm must have been infectious, because he smiled back. "Meanwhile," she said, "give those doctors another chance."

"Nah! You see, they does only like to *pretend* they know."

By midmorning she had relocated to a guesthouse on the conference shuttle route and was headed for the library. Then she was upstairs, feeling again the falling-away of the outside world and the salute of books, row upon row, a gentle crowding round of titles, authors' names, publishers' logos. The reassurance of typeface on book covers – Baskerville, Times, Helvetica, Book Antiqua. The inhalation of a new page and salve of unfolding concepts. When she forced herself outside, the square in front of the library and even the walkways overhung by flowering creepers teemed with students. Across at the Learning Resource Centre, where the conference would kick off with an informal get-together, she recognized enough people to greet but no one she knew well enough for conversation. That was okay; as a child, she had not played easily with others but had refined the art of pretending to play.

The next morning, she mounted the steps of the LRC half an hour before the first session, but soon enough the crowd expanded beyond organizers and junior participants to local staff, and the next shuttle swung in to set down miscellaneous international players: men in shorts or jeans, wearing caps and sandals; women in sleeveless or strappy floral cottons and floppy hats. There was a babble of voices, a few raised in complaint about the bitterly cold registration room, and an exodus of bright colours back into the sunlight. Then the region's senior luminaries rolled in, some dropped off by colleagues they were staying with near campus in the cool foothills of the Northern Range. Several of the St Augustine crowd remembered Candace from their undergraduate courses.

A huddle of senior academics on the steps ignored the organizers signalling the opening session, as Dexter Danraj asked the crowd whether they really hadn't heard about this place that had opened up at Portmore. For those new to the Caribbean, he added that Portmore was a coastal development in Jamaica that was growing steadily on the overflow from Kingston.

"Why should they have heard?" Under slightly raised eyebrows above his somewhat hooked nose, one of the poets she had recently interviewed cast his eyes in a characteristic faraway glance. He continued innocently. "But I suppose you mean the Portmore Institute of Tropical Studies?"

"What? The PITS?" A noisy retiree emitted a yelp of delight, and other voices piped up with increasingly wild acronyms.

"But let's not be vulgar," a genial voice intervened from somewhere behind her, over her shoulder. "Just University of Portmore should cover it."

A couple historians broke away into an argument about what Portmore would have been like when Lady Nugent, the Governor's wife, used to hurry from Spanish Town to Port Henderson for stylish morning gatherings at the beginning of the nineteenth century. The original group tightened and flagged away an undergraduate conference assistant sent to call them in to join the scanty group in the auditorium. As the student slunk off, cowed, they turned back on Dexter Danraj to pump him for some confession regarding his involvement in ITS.

"You seem very well informed," one of them teased.

She couldn't see, but the second vowel in *informed* summoned another well-known face to mind. The campus enfolded her again and began to fit.

"Dexter, invite us to your installation as Chancellor." A husky laugh shifted her attention from Danraj to one of her favourite lecturers, Roger Gayle, who enveloped her in a bear hug.

Yes, she'd come back, she thought, if they'd have her.

"Me? You mad or what?" Danraj gestured ITS away with a flourish of the wrist. "You feel I ent have nothing better to do? If they pay me as a consultant, I would give advice, yes."

Dexter Danraj was a tall, sturdy figure with an imposing profile and wealth of black hair. Lines were chiselled deep into his face and a sag had begun under the chin that open-neck wear of the tropics framed so ruthlessly, but he came across as confident of his ageless appeal. More important, he was a formidable critic, habitually surrounded by aspiring scholars, and not for the first time, Candace wondered if she should have asked Professor Danraj whether she might list him as a referee in her job applications. But she knew him only through his visits to UWI and the odd conference, though he had complimented her on a presentation once or twice. He might not even remember her. Besides, her mind flicked back over times she had heard his nickname, Dextrous, supported by whispered anecdotes.

⁓∕⁓

Back in Jamaica after the conference, she resumed her routine, investing more than time and energy in the campus itself, coming, unthinkingly, to trust it. Students so utterly unlike her, and bewildering in their variety, proliferated the challenges in preparing for tutorials to reach all or even most of them. In the unending tug of their scripts and the grating of excuses – dull, fanciful, or heart-stopping in a ring of truth – they took her over. Department politics flared or simmered around her, and she was aware but outside of it, so it remained a curiosity, safely barricaded off in that other life she hoped to have one day.

In the library, she dropped her guard, plunging into books, journals and occasional papers to the obliteration of everything beyond the fluid swirl of concepts. Without glancing at her watch, she would find herself packing up, and by the time she wandered out, the alarm was sounding and night had fallen. The basic routines of the campus entered her unseen as she battled with the next draft of the thesis. Now, chapters written months apart had strayed wilfully from her original design, and she was in the process of wrestling them back in line when her father forwarded a notice of a vacant post in the Texas College of Arts and Culture.

Resentment churned in her: it was a little late for paternal interest. He wanted someone to keep house for him, to be trapped by contract and eventually tenure at his insipid college. Her finger hovered above the delete button, then jerked back before making contact. Against the clock she felt ticking inside (she prayed it was only a clock), other forces competed – a skewering regret, a weight of nameless grief, sensations that impaled or crushed her from so far within that it was impossible (perhaps unwise) to locate them. She scrambled back into the thesis, turning the second draft inside out into a third, tugging the words tight around her line of reasoning, plugging gaps, hacking redundancies.

"I'm tying up too," Randall told her, "and I suspect the hardest part of the exercise will be parting with it."

Over the past year, they had sent each other almost monthly updates on their work, on the humorous or crazy sides of staff and students around them and on the freedoms and deprivations of student housing. Her resentment at his decamping three years before had evaporated, leaving only the unacknowledged speculation of where they might have been if he had stayed – like an occasional plaintive echo of a cry she denied ever uttering even to herself. Overwhelmed by work as she was, it was enough that they were together undergoing an entirely new form of separation trauma.

Indeed, submitting the thesis proved an excruciating release of what seemed to have become a vital organ and left her more hollow than relieved. To plug the gap, she approached Marcus about working for the Accelerated Foundation Programme.

"Submitted?" Marcus demanded. He looked appalled. "I never knew you were so close. You kept that real quiet." His supervisor, he confided, was trying to push him into all sorts of unnecessary fieldwork. "Well. All the best, then."

He gave her shoulders a congratulatory squeeze, though Candace felt he would rather have had his hands on her throat.

Unkind, she reflected, not to mention paranoid. She glanced back apologetically to thank him, only to intercept a gleam of keen hatred, as if his mind were slicing *PhD* across her face. So. Perhaps it was just as well there was no vacancy in AFP at this time.

The two months before she could expect results flashed past in preparation for tutorials, in writing papers and job applications. But then the third month passed, and a fourth. She awoke one morning to the certainty of something gone horribly wrong, and the calm she had fashioned began to come undone in a frenzied sifting of possible causes for the delay. The examiners hated her work. It could only be that. She would not even get the opportunity to resubmit. She was out of it, out of the life that meant everything to her.

Meanwhile, the Mona campus, secure on its own firm base of shale and metamorphic rock that undergirded the Liguanea Plain, had imperceptibly worked its way not only beneath and around her as a support but into her system. Now it was the point from which she measured anywhere else she might go. When she turned in through the gate, green lawns spread away to the stone chapel and the ancient aqueduct arching against a riot of bougainvillea, while, ahead, beyond the bright mosaic wall, rose trees with flowers tumbling from the sky, or so it seemed. Beyond the library and other buildings – beyond it all, Long Mountain spread its arms in an all-encompassing embrace. One day, when she woke up and prepared to go to campus in the spirit of one not leaving home but going back to it, she realized she had allowed the campus to become the place where she belonged.

In the warnings that set off, the urgency of her applications seized her. Somewhere good, Lord, to widen experience and adorn the vitae. Her mind played with Goldsmiths, Warwick, Nottingham. Her heart urged London. Randall forwarded every notice he could find.

A letter arrived, stating that referees for one of her applications had been contacted, and now she must send the results of her doctoral work. She invested in a phone call to the United Kingdom, relieved at the concerned tone of the HR officer who enquired about the date by which her university could provide the transcript. But when she explained her lack of further information, the voice chilled, and she could hear the very possibility of the job slipping away.

Now, alongside a growing sense of calamity regarding her thesis, and the threat of rejection on the job market, it dawned on her that she had no hold on UWI. The thesis that was to open the way to the profession she wanted had closed the door on the way of life that had been hers and had left her in limbo. She dangled in a state of impending loss – waiting, waiting – as the dull ache of unease intensified to anguish and deepened to gloom. She envisaged acerbic remarks by the examiners, the massive dissertation gone astray, an examiner dead and replaced, causing the process to begin again. Or some deep-rooted problem in the thesis: a crucial study of which she was ignorant and that had wiped out the originality of her work.

No. Everyone she asked said that the examiners were just late in responding. Just. *Just?* But what to do? Sue? Write the newspapers? What about the rest of her life? The Caribbean was where she wanted to be, what she wanted to research, and turning on UWI would be mauling herself.

Then suppose everything speeded up, and the oral rushed down. She got hung up on the thought, then impaled: They could ask anything. Did she fully remember this work she had packed off months ago? And what of more recent findings? She reread frantically, tripping over missed references and turns of expression she hated now, conceiving questions she could not answer. Then, oh Lord – she had taken her mind off the post she had applied for. She called Admin about the status of her application.

"Oh no!" exclaimed the helpful young man on the other end. "You didn't know? That ad was withdrawn."

"Why?" A little wail slipped out before she could stop it.

"The post's been frozen."

The only vacancy left was in literature, and in an area not even remotely applicable to her.

So that was that, doctorate or not. No responses to her applications abroad, and at Mona the department expected its full contingent of staff in the coming academic year – no sabbaticals or other leave. The financial crunch meant the part-time allocation was cut and posts for tutors reserved for registered students. Registration for the PhD had helped her to teaching hours; finishing it had wiped out her claim on the institution.

She rushed in a formal application to the Accelerated Foundation Programme and asked her supervisor to put in a word to the Head. Through the AFP, the department had set up what amounted to a shortcut past the old system of delivering Foundation courses alongside degree programmes. Their mostly online delivery rendered AFP placeless, so students could access the courses from any territory and complete those requirements before leaving home. If unsuccessful, they re-registered online or signed up for these face-to-face and took them parallel to their other courses in the old way. But with improved throughput, AFP had mushroomed.

From her supervisor's office, Candace observed Marcus bustling by with two would-be instructors in tow.

"Onto a good thing," she remarked.

Dr Crichlow followed her glance. "The accelerated programme? Definitely. Brainchild of a brilliant young man. Smartest student I ever had, and I've been teaching over twenty-five years." Candace maintained a wooden silence. "Still," Crichlow continued, "he needs to keep a balance. Hasn't presented a seminar this year, even though I hear he's hustling now to get the dissertation in. Teaching with him?"

"Hopefully. Nothing available in linguistics, so it's AFP or nothing." She thanked him for his reference.

Meanwhile her dissertation had lurched through the examination process, and arrangements for the oral defence now tangled around an external examiner's schedule. Candace's applications abroad for jobs and post-doc fellowships choked on her unchanging status, *PhD under examination*, and she tortured herself over whether she looked foolish or dishonest. But the oral bore down. She surged forward to meet it, delivered an unflinching defence, embraced some suggestions for improvement and parried others, thanking the examiners for questions she wished in hell.

She accepted the congratulations of the panel in dazed disbelief that it was over. Someone shook her hand and called her "Dr Clarke". The letter with feedback on the thesis came anticlimactically, sharing examiners' recommendations that demanded only minor refinements. *Superb argument*, one said. *Timely*, remarked another.

But what next? Every vestige of employment for which she was fitted had dried up, and no post-doc had materialized. She was not, like Randall, susceptible to subtle gleams of hope. Edging around the victory lunch and cloying sweetness under Riccadonna bubbles lurked a sense of deflation, of a plan gone flaccid, a future being erased.

Weeding old messages, she encountered one from earlstroserider@ tcac.edu, which so nearly tempted her now, years late, that she took the precaution of deleting the message at last. Then she sent off applications to the St Augustine campus in Trinidad and Tobago for full-time or part-time teaching. For anything.

Dangling there on the job market with no prospect but that of clutching at one temporary position after another for years, she felt the old adversary closing on her. A heaviness smoked down, concentrated just beyond the border of her conscious undertaking to think positively – a shadow seeping in unbidden through any unpoliced crevice. That natural slant of her mind tipped more steeply towards despair as if the distribution of weight shifted throughout her body under the thickening fog that weighed down her limbs, dimmed the morning and dulled the taste of food.

A toehold in UWI, somehow, please God. "What's Marcus Walters doing now – apart from AFP?" she asked Dr Crichlow.

"Dissertation going in, but no papers out yet," he responded.

"I thought he'd do it in his sleep," she remarked sulkily. "Didn't you say he had the best mind you ever encountered?"

"No. I couldn't have. Probably said the smartest. That's different. It takes more than intelligence to make a good mind."

Whatever. The curtain of gloom crept closer.

Then, a response from St Augustine: Part-time teaching would be available for Semester 2, beginning early in 2005.

There could never be a prompt reversal of mood, only a slow, almost imperceptible lightening. Withdrawing her application to AFP, with a note of thanks to Marcus and the head, Candace set about obtaining a pet import permit to move Cassidy and packing up for her return to Trinidad.

And there she was, still. Not Mona, nor anywhere in easy run to hills or shore imbued with the smell of roasting breadfruit or jerk pork. But if she was not Trini to the bone, as the locals expressed it, nor was she exclusively Jamaican any more. She was UWI in the marrow.

So now the St Augustine campus began its work on her. Not good either, for she was no nearer a secure post. St Augustine too had lush green grounds and stunning trees, canopies of pink samaan and poinciana in gold and flame against a background of mountains, but she was as part-time and temporary as ever. Three years had seemed a lifetime, then five. Some part-timers dangled for fifteen years before landing anything . . . or dropping out of sight. Remembering the mid-1990s when the Learning Resource Centre was being built and, later, staff grumbling about how student numbers had exploded, Candace realized she had returned to St Augustine under the delusion that the expansion on campus meant increased job opportunity. Nada.

By this time, the students engaged her as they had not when she was one. She saw them in another light now – as youngsters reaching for success, some by legitimate means and some by short cut, a few through outright fraudulence, but all with some claim on her. Beyond their requests for explanation, pleas for time, fabrication of lame excuses and, sometimes, tentative upholding of an original idea, she caught a strain of something like ownership, as if a dimension of herself rightfully belonged to them.

This proprietorship – did it originate with them, or had she somehow conferred it? – extended well beyond matters pertaining to her classes. A student whose husband resented a wife's effort to better herself asked Candace how to ensure no one from UWI called her landline; and another whose mother was dying of cancer brought the oncologist's report for advice on getting leave of absence. A gentle-faced young woman whose hijab cast soft shadows here and there over her forehead and cheeks asked about arrangements in the graduation ceremony for students who must not touch hands with the Vice Chancellor.

They bustled in from every corner of the country, every condition – well-to-do offspring of successful store owners (fabric, furniture, jewellery), managers in the oil and gas industry, surgeons and attorneys with huge practices, dealers in real estate. Others had family who had scraped and saved by wrestling with the land over generations. Their grandparents, descended from slaves or indentured workers, had laboured on the estates, walked alongside the bull-cart urging the hog-cattle with a stick, or thrown a banana leaf over a left shoulder to keep off the drip from the cocoa bags, or plodded through rows of cane, swinging machetes. The parents had torn a desperate living from whatever land they had managed to buy or just occupy, and had, mostly, never in their wildest dreams foreseen their children penetrating beyond primary school. Those who had dreamt such crazy dreams had whipped and coaxed and done without, and now hired a car to bring this child from the trace to the university, against its background of mountains with its wide green lawns and spreading samaan trees and low-trimmed hedges of bright ixora.

And there were parents in a different kind of shock, those who had for decades put aside money to educate their children anywhere, in any field, who were prepared to pay for Oxford or MIT or Princeton – anywhere the child wanted and performed splendidly enough to be admitted – and who found themselves with children who could shine anywhere but were adamant that they were not leaving the Caribbean – that it was UWI or nowhere. And when you told them to write the SAT, they said, "For what?" And if you talked about the opportunities that would open up if they went to the United States or Canada, they said, "To ketch me tail in the cold? You mad or what? Nah!" Or if they were more polite, more sensitive to acknowledge all you had given up to put aside this fortune for their education, they thanked you, patted you reassuringly and said, "Maybe later. If I run mad and go on to postgrad."

Between her students' concerns and class preparation, Candace stuffed the days and nights with her own research. Sometimes she was still fixed at the computer when the smell of parching geera rose at the window, announcing that old Madame Indira next door who woke before dawn was beginning to prepare the roti she supplied to a nearby parlour.

In her rudimentary bedroom, Candace regarded herself in a mirror spotted with grey-brown patches and struggled to don Randall's outlook for at least a moment. She had good bones and a fine-shaped face with direct fearless eyes. "And at least I've controlled my weight this time," she reflected, meaning she had successfully battled bouts of inability to swallow anything. "I can keep charge of my mind, once I have work." But however frantically she clung to her temporary post, she knew how widely misunderstood this work was. Living among the philistines, as Randall described it (there they were again), meant recognizing how many of one's colleagues viewed English language teaching as trivial and linguistics as nebulous. Besides, hers was not a job but a string of short-term appointments.

Yet once more her mind cried out: How could it be possible for UWI to have no need of her? This was an institution spread over more than a million square miles of sea strung with countries that included fifteen contributing territories. She was qualified, unattached, free to go anywhere. And apart from the unlimited target of its Open Campus with its virtual access and nearly fifty actual sites fanned out across the islands, the three physical campuses were expanding so rapidly that Mona had spawned a western campus in Jamaica, and there was talk of a south campus in Trinidad for St Augustine. Little more than sixty years since its inception, UWI had a thousand times more on-campus students than it had started with, and students wanted Candace. They manoeuvred to get into her classes.

At St Augustine, the students absorbed her in the diversity of their needs. Well-to-do kids from posh homes in Diego Martin or Cascade seemed to her, at first, to have few problems besides labouring back and forth through the Port of Spain traffic and finding parking spaces for the Honda Accords their parents had supplied. Later she realized they suffered through their own traumas, from a father's bankruptcy to a mother's battery by the same ruined father, or from the frustration of parents pressuring bright children to do law rather than literature and scoffing at a son bent on music instead of medicine.

Others students travelled the Eastern Main Road or Churchill Roosevelt in route taxis or maxis from more straitened circumstances, boxlike concrete houses clinging to a rocky overhang in Morvant or tightly clustered dwellings rank on rank uphill in Laventille. They set out over the gouged and tightly fenced roads, out from behind walls, mildewed, cracked or fallen, or stubbornly scrubbed and painted – set out hopefully despite the black-clothed police pointing their guns at overturned trash bins and leaning poles with drooping electric wires, and at human debris snoring on the narrow sidewalk. Bulky policemen glowered at anything that moved, suspicious (from hard experience, they would say) even of a small neat girl in a lavender top and hair ribbon tied in a bright bow, filling her plastic container with water from a burst pipe for which she could not be responsible, since it had gushed so long that the concrete was shiny dark green. And she was so neat and self-contained and certain of herself, because her brother had set off for UWI, and she would go one day too. She could see herself, tall, slender and graceful, like the only really beautiful thing in their yard, the palm tree that soared up above the galvanize walls and over the forgotten roadworks, and despite the sullen, disappointed, disbelieving face of her father and exhaustion of her mother. She too would effect the miracle of one day, one day breaking out and making her way along the highway to UWI and studying harder than anyone else, and coming out a lawyer. But now her brother might miss a test, because he had to stay home to take care of her, when their father disappeared, and their mother went off to look for him, because there was no leaving the child alone at home after the shooting on the road the night before. So Candace might set the brother a make-up test.

And there was the woman in her late twenties, older and wider than the average undergraduate, who turned to Candace a broad face with its close-cut, almost-shaved hairstyle, her tight mouth and direct gaze. Her skirt stopped well short of the thick knees, and her legs were heavy but firm and smooth right down to the constricting black pumps that clamped down her toes and made her feet swell up painfully around the leather or whatever material the shoes pretended to be. This lady needed to be in an evening tutorial on Friday, because she commuted from Tobago. Otherwise, how was she to get this course UWI said was compulsory? It was not a big class, though, Candace protested, never more than three tutorials groups. Oh well. Perhaps.

Only, there was that other woman who could only come in the day, while her children were in school and didn't need her to drive them back and forth to extra lessons or make them do homework in the evenings. She was a short square white woman in her mid-forties, festively attired in bright shorts and floral sleeveless top, muddled by re-immersion in class and study, still distracted by her recent divorce but trying to put behind her the betrayal at which her husband had merely shrugged with a derisive comment about her abilities in bed. She had to qualify herself while getting past his desertion – not to mention his clearing off with everything in their joint account – and the inevitable hauling and pulling of house, cars, time-shares, even the blasted dog. Her wide eyes vaguely travelled over the youngsters in the room, who were so certain of what they were doing, or not about to do, and so comfortable with their laptops or tablets, or so superior to whatever might be going on as they focused on their smartphones, incapable of grasping the hopelessness of what she was trying to do, getting into a classroom at this stage when she was barely computer literate enough to check e-mail, certainly not to download e-books, and she had no money (don't mind she white), no money to buy books, not even the text, not if she was going to buy school books for her son (as if he was likely to open them). But this girl who was teaching the course seemed a good sort, this Ms Clarke – doctor, they said, only she looked so young – and was it possible, just possible Dr Clarke might lend material if one explained a fraction of the whole exquisite mess.

And Dr Clarke found herself with no choice but to hand over her own copy of the text and say, "Just remember to return this, okay? It belongs to the department." Because Dr Clarke was not permanent staff with a book grant.

But the students wouldn't know the difference. They inhabited a different dimension of the UWI world. The gorgeous full-bodied girl with black silk skin and almond eyes, her intricately braided head crowning the regal bearing that was not affected or even assumed but entirely unconscious and totally compatible with regular attendance and prompt, well-worded essays – she knew nothing and cared less about the university's necessarily unequal provision for different types of staff. She was about her own business, as she should be, hugging her tablet and looking forward to her Upper Second.

On the other hand, Candace feared for a fragile, almost gaunt brown girl, her too-thin arms and jutting clavicle perhaps testifying to some eating problem, hair teased into a mass of curls to supplement her own personal lack of bulk, walking a little awkwardly because her back was to the wall or more or less sliding along it, her hip bones a little too prominent, her bony legs delivering a stilted, disjointed gait.

Candace felt far more comfortable about the young man with the long drop earring, because even if he was not about to do any work for her class (and he might well be, but he was still keeping that to himself), he was clearly about something that mattered to him. He would probably segue into creative and festival arts, because he had recently sprouted innumerable plaits that in her experience were a sort of vague indicator, and his bright sharp eyes were hard with resolution and purpose rather than hostility – in fact, rather kind, just not to be messed with – quick eyes that watched everything and might even be a little amused but definitely *not* to be messed with, and hands often raised at chest level looking ready for anything, to catch or ward off something, or to beat pan with Exodus if they would have him. All night.

So the students broke down her barricades, broke her up, broke her heart, put it back together.

Which was all very well, but she had to eat too. And how long would the succession of part-time contracts continue? She looked around, and the sitting room was dismal – so drab she had not had the heart to put up the few paintings and the odd ceramic she had bought. Everything around her screamed *temporary*. Against this disquiet persisted an uncertainty about how to proceed with her own writing. All around the cry was for collaborative research, when she worked best on her own and when scholars in the arts valued the single-authored book. The pressure of science and social science values filled discussions of staff assessment with prattle about criteria less applicable to the arts, and the idea that linguistics was a science meant little to either artists or scientists.

Then the call for interdisciplinarity issued from scholars collaborating across disciplines, even while some of them secretly viewed each other's work with suspicion. So die-hard linguists poured contempt for fuzziness and mush on literary interpretation, while the more stubborn critics seethed with impatience over technical detail and blindness to the expressive and aesthetic. Only the extremists, as usual, but these were so vocal, it meant that even within the humanities, close colleagues fell out over different perceptions of meaning. Unsurprising, Candace reflected, that outside the humanities (but for a few shining exceptions), complete cluelessness seemed to reign on issues of language and discourse. She clung to a deep-set belief in her work, once she could hold onto it, but over the past months, a sense of hopelessness had glided in and begun its insidious coiling under her diaphragm.

For, after years at St Augustine, she had no foothold. Whether she would ever be first choice or even proxy on a shortlist was a moot point. In a faculty chronically strapped for funds, no substantive post had materialized for her, and here she was, in 2009, beginning her third decade, still clinging to hourly paid teaching in the Foundation courses. The work was unrelenting, and the workers rendered largely invisible by the low status of the courses. For decades, English language teaching in secondary schools had been palmed off on any teacher with a few free hours in the timetable, regardless of qualifications. Those in a position to affect employment might shrug off graduates in Linguistics as remedial teachers. The Ministry of Education had eventually revised its requirements to insist on language training for qualified English teachers, but general perceptions had altered little.

A post in Language and Culture at the Institute of Tropical Studies would take Candace back to Jamaica at a good salary, as well as offering permanent employment, and it would bring her closer to teaching in her area of research. A suspicion nagged her that – considering her circumstances – turning her nose up at a full-time post at this institute amounted to foolish pride. She had applied for jobs abroad and once got through the initial phase, and referees had been contacted. But she had never passed the shortlists. Anywhere.

So why now? Shade having invoked Dexter Danraj in the sales pitch, she wondered whether her recruitment fitted some subterranean agenda of the wily professor. But his interests were entirely literary. His most recent book focused on the poetry of exile in the Guyanese diaspora. She had neither studied nor worked with him. Nor in his area. Why would he think of her? Unless it were God, she reasoned, at last opening an avenue – or at least a fissure – for her in Portmore. But *Portmore*, Lord?

Candace shrugged aside the burden of memory to hoist the heavy pot of dog food onto the kitchen counter, because it was 6:45, and that was what happened at 6:45. She scraped heaping spoonfuls into the bowl while Cassidy sprang forward then back and forth across the kitchen in her expect-ant, bouncing gallop, with a little feint to the side just beyond Candace's restraining hand and a hearty swipe of her tail across the girl's thighs.

Girl? With age forty lurking at the end of the decade, Candace saw little choice but to accept a job that offered a steady salary and pension plan.

She felt a jab of regret regarding some of the students, but there would be students enough to occupy her wherever she went.

On Candace's kitchen table lay a half-marked essay from the composition course she taught as an itinerant part-timer. A heavy pencilled circle marked the sentence where the environmentally conscious student proclaimed that "hunters should be fined for pregnant animals". And that was a mild example. Candace's personal favourite was more extreme, a line from a student of biology who had claimed, "The theory of evolution state that man has descend from ape and shall return to ape." You laughed and mourned over that sort of thing, but to grapple it indefinitely as a way of life – Jesus wept. She expected to cope with blunders of style in essays on language variation, pragmatics or discourse analysis, not to make actual composition her life's work. Yes, it was valid and valuable work, but for her, martyrdom.

Time to move on. With something of a skip in her step, she bore the outsize bowl out to the landing, where Cassidy, a sloppy eater at best, could sling her jowls around without restraint. Watching the hail of rice grains as the dog swung her head to grin briefly before resuming, Candace felt the tension between her shoulder blades unknot and the grey mood circling her thoughts lighten.

Refreshed after cavorting around while Candace heaved the pot off the stove, and gratified by warm rice redolent with beef mince, instead of day-old food that had been refrigerated or (shudder) frozen and thawed, Cassidy entered uninhibitedly into a spirit of jollification that Candace might capture but never quite maintain.

Candace displayed, according to Randall, the reverse of ridgeback personality. Hers was a cheerful expression underlain with deep mournfulness. Which was just keeping one's chin up, Candace protested, there being no one to share out treats to her. This Randall had denied, in that first carefree semester at Mona, with enough prancing exuberance for her to compare him to Cassidy, then a pup of three months old – a rebuke he joyfully accepted. He had offered to lick her face for it, but she declined with dampening dignity, her eyes sparked with suppressed laughter. And Randall had bent again to the task of getting Faint back onto the road. This was the pathetic vehicle he had acquired in Jamaica on arrival, "at a good price", and managed to keep going, while he put off visits to the mechanic – a collection of groaning metal that he fondly named Faint Yet Pursuing.

Now that she was actively considering ITS, Candace Skyped Randall for his thoughts. She had more faith in his assessment of academic institutions than of cars, she said. She mentioned her refusal to apply to TCAC years before, and since then, so many part-time contracts had elapsed, she had begun to wonder whether she had been foolish. Here was this new place taking root in Portmore, on home soil, as she said, and it would obligate her to no one.

Randall's questions about the respectability of ITS echoed hers, but then his own weird career choice occurred to her. Who was he to advise, really?

"You see, Cassidy," she said after ending her call with Randall, rubbing a silky ear between her fingers, "it's like this. As things stand, I go on as I am forever, in a panic every few months about employment, or I become a drudge for my father or Mr Right. Best I ditch this forlorn hope of a UWI position and strike out for any institution that will have me."

"So here I am," she announced to Randall the following night. "Redy to wenden on my pilgrimage." Scary – but one thing in favour of ITS as an unknown quantum, she told him, was the number of solid scholars it had attracted.

In particular, the UWI grapevine buzzed with the name of a prominent professor who had served not only on UWI boards but on national and international bodies. He had attracted awards for seminal work on drainage systems to reduce breeding grounds of vectors associated with dengue and similar fevers. Anyone with leverage over Aedes aegypti in the region could draw a spotlight, and the word on the corridors had been that Professor Clyde Seuraj stood a good fighting chance of being appointed Vice Chancellor one day, and meanwhile as Campus Principal, when the next of these posts came vacant.

The result of that next set of deliberations over a campus principal had upset all expectations, the distinguished professor suffering bitter disappointment as the pro vice chancellorship went to another candidate. ITS wooed Seuraj in the first heat of his resentment, offering a massive pay hike and a promise that he would succeed the first provost at the end of his term. Professor Clyde Seuraj had actually been planning his departure from the UWI for a hefty government post, when Morgan Shade got at him. As pictures of the glittering farewell for the first provost had occupied some of the material Shade had later shared out to Candace, everything pointed to Professor Seuraj coming into his own almost immediately. It must mean something, Candace reasoned, a man like that running the place.

Anyway, Candace had no intention of settling into ITS indefinitely if she took the job, and she would cling to one frail link with UWI – a group or two in the Accelerated Foundation Programme. The AFP population was so now huge, she felt almost certain of acceptance. Indeed, she had decided to invest in a town house in Kingston rather than Portmore. Over the causeway and left onto the Parkway, then the turnoff on Portfront Avenue. How long could it take? Twenty minutes, thirty tops – from what Shade had said. The Institute of Tropical Studies looked increasingly attractive to an unrecognized scholar. Candace could not picture a campus on landfill overlooked by limestone rock and cactus, but the mountains that presided over the Mona and St Augustine campuses offered no niche for her either.

And it would be Jamaica.

Jamaicans who say *Jah mek ya* fall into two groups: those who attest the claim seriously, as a matter of fact, and those who pretend they are not serious. Most Jamaicans, as Randall early divined, remain infuriatingly patriotic in the face of every flaw that outsiders perceive, because Jamaicans too perceive the flaws and shrug them off with a sigh – of regret, not of denial – while they remain focused on those essentials that, in their view, establish Jamaica as utterly superior to every other place on earth. Give thanks for Jamdown, they say. Me baan ya.

It *would* be Jamaica.

So she got the documents together. Morgan Shade hustled in her application while invoking his pardner, Professor Dexter Danraj, who was now something called a Fellow of ITS. A letter of acceptance came back under the signature of the acting provost, an unfamiliar name she could not decipher.

The move to Jamaica was relatively straightforward as far as her own person was concerned. But the ferocious quarantine laws of Jamaica, which was free of rabies and intent on remaining so, meant tedious procedures for relocating Cassidy. They involved prolonged incarceration of a dog by nature unsuited to confinement. The conflicting logistics of moving between countries and visiting Cassidy in quarantine meant hurling a nine-year-old dog down again and again from ecstatic reunion to apparent abandonment. In the protracted upheaval, events outside of the actual relocation slipped by unnoticed.

So she was officially on staff and unpacking in her compact New Kingston town house, before she spun the pages of the glossy *ITS Newstime*, the issues for June, July and August 2010. In the background wail of classic reggae against the clatter of the police helicopter overhead and the relentless heat and humidity of a Jamaican August, a bold dark headline wavered before her eyes, and she passed her hand across them and then stared in disbelief. The June issue of *ITS Newstime* was proud to announce the appointment of its new Provost, Earl St Rose Rider. From a spectrum of international scholars considered for the position, the article quipped, behold a dark horse – named Rider. In a tone evolving from revoltingly playful to high-minded, the writer continued: a local Portmore boy had been selected to establish the Institute of Tropical Studies as the prime tertiary institution in Jamaica. *Selected.* The absence of any named human agent left room for the reader to assume divine intent behind the appointment.

Then the diverting effect of eccentric syntax evaporated in the realization that she would be working for her father. It came together in the pit of Candace's stomach like vapour condensing to a puddle and then congealing to ice.

"What happened?" Skype produced an unusually clear connection, and Randall's brow furrowed with concern.

"Nothing to be done at this stage." But she told him anyway, reaching for the Tia Maria she kept for emergencies and measuring out half a liqueur glass meticulously, as if there would never be another bottle.

Desperate to comfort her but at a loss, he slid into his supply of Uncs quotes. "Nothing happens without a reason," he said, goading her reply before he could think better of it and retract.

"But not necessarily designed in my favour," she snapped. The sensation of an abrupt tilt over a chasm seized her brutally, and something pinched hard inside her, as if Morgan Shade's bony hand had clenched her gut.

Chapter 3

The Road In

I trowe his habitacioun be there.

Once when Candace reflected that she had no heart left to speak of, Randall had responded that she had belly. The ground had unsettled beneath her, but, hell, she had come this far, and her new Suzuki had negotiated the Kingston traffic, edging around an enraged higgler and a quick-fingered youth exchanging obscenities in the middle of Hagley Park Road. Candace made her way along, past Kingston Port onto the toll road.

Rough grass and coarse bush slid past, light poles with solar plates, huge shipping containers and weirdly shaped equipment, but at last the sea spread like unpolished steel, and the smell of the lagoon rose from behind bordering bush. She crossed the causeway over the harbour and drove slowly past the Salt Pond, until Greater Portmore unfurled before her, an utterly unknown terrain.

She knew there was old Portmore – itself distinct from ancient Portmore – and there was new Portmore. Bigger and better, as Morgan Shade had pointed out. How was it possible to get so much more on a small strip of land squashed between hills and sea? By filling in the sea; of course, she remembered the hype. Landfill and drainage supported this new Portmore, as it expanded to accommodate housing, businesses, schools, a community college – and now, at last, a sizeable university campus. *Attractive grounds with an excellent prospect*, bragged the shiny brochures Shade had spread along her couch.

Hellshire Hills – originally Healthshire Hills (before the inevitable whittling of consonants) – looked out over the Portland Bight. The protected area included hills, caves and scrubland with cactus, as well as beaches of such white sand as gladdened the hearts of tourists and locals alike. Mangroves rich in lobsters, whistling ducks, hawksbill and green turtles edged the coast of the Portland Bight. Beyond that coast stretched seagrass beds and, still farther out, teeming coral reefs. Long ago Columbus had admired the manatees, but of those there was word no longer.

On land, nearer to Portmore, acres of dry limestone forest extended over the Hellshire Hills that lay in the rain shadow of the Blue Mountains. Between clusters of thorn bush, wiry vines with dry tan-coloured flowers crept around the edges of sinkholes – for the ground was hard yet not invariably solid. Here in the rain shadow, the dry land yearned for moisture, and when it fell, the water, innocent on its own, picked up the carbon dioxide in the atmosphere, becoming weakly acidic, so as to gnaw the calcium carbonate, lingeringly, the rain pitting the surface of the rocks over millions of years.

On unconsolidated ground extending way beyond any original foundation of rock, the campus of ITS rose up suspended, it seemed, over the sea to offer Candace her foothold in the academic life to which she had been clinging by her fingernails for years. Having driven past the entrance, she circled back. Only for a fraction of a second as she slowed on the Portfront Road approaching the turnoff did she pause to ponder again the connection between her father's post of Provost and her own recruitment by Shade to the more lowly one of Lecturer – but that was a no-brainer.

From the exit leading to ITS, the campus seemed particularly dry, even with August giving way to September and a few years of landscaping having already kicked in. Once salt manufacturing by Europeans and then the production of indigo and lime in ancient Portmore had given way to farming, and especially grazing, the forest had been stripped away. The landscape had continued to transform radically, and now from its efficiently contrived shoreline, the campus could boast an outlook on the sea that would have gratified even Admiral Rodney in the old days.

Hosts of students, reassuringly labelled the institution's most important stakeholders, swerved in and out of the turn-off to the institute. Others climbed out of the unofficial taxis that were everywhere, some driven by policemen, Candace had heard. So no one would challenge them. It was not a residential campus, and students had to get there somehow.

The Institute of Tropical Studies, as she coasted up, presented itself as a cluster of white buildings with slate grey roofs, connected by covered walkways with a fountain of silver-grey aloes at each upright. The hills behind it marked the skyline with bonaire cactus, and the sea glittered in front. Maximizing the island's wide variety of cactus achieved an effect of greenery along the white-hot shore.

Glimpses of deep green prickly pear cactus camouflaged whatever lay to the back. At the front, a rock garden included mamillaria, green globes veiled by a network of fine thorns, and dramatic stripes of carroto shot out at the base. Along the central walkway to what must be the main administration building, rose-shaped echeveria filled and overflowed urns.

Randall's voice inserted itself unbidden in Candace's thoughts. In response to her belated fretting about an offshore campus's lack of academic clout, he had said, "You're accepted, you've moved, you'll have to raise the standard yourself. And, hey – they may have parking." He persuaded her that Portmore was not the backwater it had been in her childhood and might now support a more distinguished institution than she expected.

As for her father's appointment, Candace thought, they would hardly meet at work, and she would not be living nearby. She could, if nothing materialized at UWI or once she had tenure at ITS. Good, affordable residential areas neighboured the campus just fourteen miles from the city. In fact, she had learned, her father had invested in a posh place in the hills nearby. He would. But then – who wouldn't, given half a chance?

The last vestiges of misgiving slowed her as she approached the barrier at the main gate before a metal arch that declared a welcome to the campus. The sun glared between the cut-out letters in little fiery jabs of light that made her cringe with last-minute hopelessness bordering on an inclination to swerve into a U-turn and speed away. But she had parted with the St Augustine campus and shipped everything over to the New Kingston town house she had bought with the sale of the Curepe place. Cassidy had survived quarantine, Silver was long dead, and Randall was far away. So Candace pressed on the gas and passed in on the broad black asphalt drive that shimmered with the heat.

To her delight and wonder, there seemed, in the distance, to be abundant parking, and she began to reassess Randall's ability to discern a ray of sunlight at midnight.

At first this difference between them had escaped notice. Then one midnight in 1999, after nailing a particularly stubborn exercise in sociolinguistics, she whispered, "I wonder if I should say this? Here's the thing: I sometimes . . . slide into this state of mind . . . No. Go on home. Just leave me to work."

But he had dumped his bag beside the table and sat down in silence over his books, all night, without comment or question. At six a.m., he put up two fingers to touch his forehead and said, "I could say, 'Good morning'? Permission please?"

And she laughed and called him an ass but added with a catch in her voice, "Short for astounding," because, before Randall, she had never encountered friendship outside the pages of a book. Many an evening, even as recently as the night before, an e-mail had come in from his London flat, beginning: *Still working at your table . . .*

Yet that all-nighter in 1999 had been just two nights before the thing with the TV. A newscast revealed that the government had declared zero tolerance for crime, and Randall had reared up and grabbed the set.

"What are you doing?" she shrieked.

And he put it down gently. "You know I nearly pelt the thing through the window?"

She walked over in shock, as he sank onto the hassock and ran his hands over his face. "They actually acknowledge that they tolerate every outrage for years. This man who owed me *nothing* and brought me up, bleeding to death in my arms. And they now deciding not to tolerate . . ." He stared at the figures bantering on the screen. "I could take a blowtorch to them, yes."

She grieved for him, but she had not held him or asked anything more.

Now she tried tempering the flood of longing (which was out of all proportion to their situation) by casting her mind over routine annoyances – apart from his foolish choice of research area. The inexplicable love of a man for an old car, she reflected, the childish frittering away of attention lavished on the scratched bonnet he caressed with chamois. The toleration of car windows that did not close fully, so that fixing the AC was postponed, while the wind tore her hair to pieces. "But you look great," he would insist, raising his shoulders in bewilderment and waiting patiently for her to stop glaring at him and get out, because the door on the driver's side did not open from inside, so he had to slide across her seat. He had bought Faint as soon as they arrived in Jamaica, and he was inordinately proud of his first car. "I don't know why you batter around on the minibus, when you're welcome to use this anytime."

"But how could you possibly want to drive something beat-up and unreliable?" She glowered at it. "Not to mention ugly."

"I don't know what you have against her." He regarded Candace with his head cocked to one side. "And look how nice I am to Cassidy."

It was true he romped with the puppy as if spawned in the same litter, but that did not mean his friendship with Candace could have grown into anything else.

Candace made a left at the next sign and stared in disbelief. Unlimited parking. On her way into the main building with almost a bounce in her stride, she nodded jubilantly to a janitor negotiating the steps with an oversize bin.

The first person she met of standing was Harindra Baldeosingh, the Registrar, who seemed distracted by more pressing duties but shook hands pleasantly enough and directed her to Dudley Sandiford, the aging Master of Studies. Dudley Sandiford had been there from the beginning and helped set up the place. He was not an academic in the area of culture but could tell her about the Centre for Caribbean Cultural Studies, because he had heard it all from Professor Danraj. Mostly, though, Dudley Sandiford's information was about the institute as a whole.

"It would be impossible to deny that we haven't intransigent problems still unsolved." He peered up at her over thick glasses, his drawn face lowered between hunched shoulders, behind which his short thick frame had rounded by osteoporosis to the steep curve of a tortoise. "But no one can say – not, at least, without a certain degree of duplicity – that the essential framework has not been hammered out to accommodate the development of quality programmes and that whatever remains in the system that could tend not to facilitate accreditation hasn't been – if not rooted out – at least discouraged." He ran on through a spreading maze of subordinate clauses that hedged each other's verbs, and negatives that interacted as if they could indeed cancel each other out, and passives that postponed responsibility indefinitely – leaving her bewildered but fascinated and watchful. Yet he was harmless, she decided, just tired and habitually defensive. "I don't have long before retirement," he concluded. "But I shouldn't expect anyone to be able to say we've made an unimpressive start."

He nodded rapidly and proffered a limp handshake before turning Candace over to his administrative assistant, a thin woman of indeterminate age and downturned face, clad in white. With a gesture of austere disapproval, Ms Mackhail pointed in the direction of staff offices for Cultural Studies.

The organizational structure had crystallized, as Candace moved beyond Morgan Shade's glossy brochures to handbooks and intranet. The three main arms of ITS governed physical resource management, general administration, and academic programming and delivery. This last was overseen by the Master, Dudley Sandiford, from whose somewhat grubby office she headed towards the Centre for Caribbean Cultural Studies. This, he had explained affably, was generally called CuSt.

CuSt was one of three academic units, the others being the Centre for Small States Governance and Development Studies, and the Centre for Tropical Sciences. In addition to their teaching programmes, these other centres boasted research projects in areas like tropical disaster preparedness and marine environment conservation. Such projects attracted substantial funding, though none as generous as the Dengue Eradication Grant. Candace had heard colleagues on the UWI campuses scoff at the quality of research likely to emerge from what they called "the PITS", but she clung to the thought that serious scholars managing a sizeable grant could make a mark from anywhere.

ITS boasted a number of distinguished academics. The institute shored up its scholarly base by the simple procedure of angling for staff, usually but not always retirees, from established institutions. They drew from UWI through generous offers of remuneration. So there was some truth to accusations that ITS built credibility through what suspicious UWI staff termed intellectual phishing, and that was a short step, by way of the pun, to what alarmists decried as a sort of institutional identity theft.

At the same time, though, ITS also attracted less distinguished academics by dangling senior lectureships or professorships. Critics at UWI argued that this type of recruiting would accumulate grumblers and non-achievers – or, at any rate, those who (for whatever reason) had not attracted the recognition they felt themselves to deserve from their previous employers. Very early on, a senior lecturer in UWI's Faculty of Social Sciences had pronounced that the ITS system of attracting staff would produce hotbeds of dissatisfaction in each academic unit simply by drawing in dissidents, even as it fostered mediocrity by rewarding the undeserving. "But let them phish the swamp by all means," said this Dr Mendes. "Good riddance to whatever they catch."

That, however, reflected a callously inexact assessment of UWI's temporary staff. It took no account of the overflow of qualified academics – some able and thoroughly deserving scholars – swarming at the margins of the university for want of space within. New UWI posts were few or non-existent. The lingering throughput of doctoral candidates well outpaced staff turnover.

Deciding, after some quick accounting, that she was more fortunate than many of her colleagues, Candace ran her eyes over the names along the corridor. Her appointment with Professor Danraj, who as Fellow chaired the Centre for Caribbean Cultural Studies, had shifted from eleven a.m. to two-thirty p.m. That evening, as Dudley Sandiford had also reminded her, was the Provost's reception for welcoming new staff and, incidentally, for formally introducing himself, although almost everyone had met him over the past couple months.

Meanwhile, Candace settled into an office as yet bare of books, with her collection of papers on programmes and timetabling. She had also acquired a cup of tea with condensed milk, which was used in Trinidad and Tobago but not enough to be sure of in a coffee room.

"Or cocoa?" an older woman seemed to enquire but turned out to be pointing out an option. "Cocoa's one of the wonder foods, isn't it?"

Candace hated cocoa but recognized an overture and smiled. "And is this bought water, or can we drink from the tap?"

"Of course, the water's potable," answered a colleague – Francine, her name was. "The amount of money and research invested in polishing –" She broke off. "Don't polishing is what they call it?"

"Polishing the sewage?" jibed a good-looking man with what Silver would have described as a slack mouth.

"Oh stupidness, Courtney." Francine put down her glass, and a graduate student someone had called Anthea said, "Gross."

"The water's good, gyul," Professor Danraj raised his glass to her in salute and drank it down. "See you this afternoon." He collected his papers and was gone.

"Those are just courtesy calls." Francine's tone was low, confidential. "If you need to genuinely talk, call any of us. My office is down the corridor."

"Unless you want real information, in which case you have to brave the Mackhail," put in slackmouth. (Unfair. Really not bad looking. Courtney, they'd called him.) Then he added, "Dudley's harpy, the one in white."

"You mean she always wears white?"

There was a hoot of laughter at her awed tone, and a number of voices chorused, "Always!"

"Mackhail is *called* Administrative Assistant, but she is ultimately the one in control," said Francine. "She does as she sees fit, and no one dares intervene. She keeps Dudley's records and releases them to no one – sometimes not even to Dudley. Mackhail's is the last word on what is confidential."

"Old witch," added Courtney. "The only thing that frightens Dudley more than Mackhail is the thought of doing without her. Even Dexter gives her a wide berth."

"Disagreeable?" Candace asked.

"A terror," confirmed Francine.

Back in her office, in between sips of her second cup, Candace's brief survey of the room revealed that the stack of new material added nothing to what she already knew from the intranet. So she added to the pile for dumping, alongside what the earlier inhabitant of the office had abandoned. Her door safely closed, she settled back to take stock.

There seemed surprisingly little to learn about ITS. She already knew that the Institute of Tropical Studies had been established essentially by fiat as an offshore college of an American institution. Basic policies and procedures had been imported or worked out along the way. Some of these had found their way into brochures to attract funding and clientele, but nothing more had as yet accreted in formal ordinances or regulations. There were no institutional memories, marks or symbols.

Distinguished names were being collected, like that of Professor Dexter Danraj, Fellow in the Centre for Caribbean Cultural Studies, and presumably the other Fellows were equally prominent figures. It had to be so, she thought. Professor Clyde Seuraj, having been passed over as Provost in favour of Earl Rider, was not even listed as Fellow in the Centre for Tropical Sciences. So that had to be some other high-flyer.

These posts of Master and Fellow were strange to her. They had a familiar old-world ring, an echo of ancient British college tradition. No resonance from North American university circles of which she had any knowledge. In the UWI system, there had once been Research Fellows, but these did not appear to correlate with the ITS posts. It seemed the offshore campus was allowed a different system of governance to its US parent, or at least one in which familiar posts were renamed for effect. But what effect? Some sort of modish antiquity?

She was not clear how the place ran. Candace knew nothing of the president of the organization, except that he was a CEO rather than an academic.

"And even as far as being CEO is concerned," Professor Danraj said that afternoon, with that smile that was a little spiteful yet somehow winning, "that's a titular rather than a dramatic function." President Simon Bosworth's background was the bauxite industry, with particularly impressive connections in South Africa, and as Dexter Danraj pointed out, Bosworth's doctorate was just honorary. With his usual camaraderie, Dexter waved a finger at the picture of the Provost on the department wall and then brought the same finger back to tap his own chest. "Is we a run tings."

She looked up with that familiar pang somewhere between anxiety and unassuaged hunger at the heavy frame hanging above them. The portrait was faithful to Earl St Rose Rider, elegantly greying at the temples above the dark smooth good looks of the kind that cultivated the more European features of his particular mix – close-cut hair, tightened lips, nostrils drawn in as if forever testing the air. No. That was mean. Her father really was a handsome man. In the picture, as in reality, her father was broad-shouldered in a suit that was unfailingly custom-made and always seemed new, revealing an impeccably ironed shirt and matching tie. His eyes looked straight back at her, bright and knowing – not the mocking eyes of Danraj, but that keen appraising glance that fixed their object and recorded details.

She need have very little to do with him here, she reminded herself. Whether or not he had contrived her appointment, she had been unaware of his impending connection with ITS when she signed the contract. In any case, it was Danraj she would encounter almost daily, the Guyanese-born East Indian professor who had joined ITS on retirement. She had heard him, as a visitor to St Augustine, holding forth after his presentation in the Distinguished Lecture Series.

"I say, leh me see what I could do for the poor bastards," he told a past colleague, who had reminded him how he had earlier scoffed at the idea of serious people taking jobs in places like ITS. "If I find they really beyond help, I done with that." Danraj busied himself covering tracks he had not yet made.

"We putting together a good team, girl," he assured Candace during their meeting, "and in a large measure – thanks to UWI. UWI is way behind progressive American colleges that have dispensed with a mandatory retirement age. These idiots at Mona and the rest throw away their best people by the time they become internationally recognized as distinguished scholars. All we have to do is sit back and wait for them to enjoy a well-publicized send-off with a nice little thing in the press, and then we get Morgan Shade to catch them – after a couple months when the holiday spirit has worn off and post-retirement panic set in." In response to her stiff smile, he added, "But we need bright young people too. You will do well here, man. Tenure in a year or two. Well, of course, we taking those years of part-time teaching into account. Oh Gawd, gyul! What you tink we is? UWI?"

After leaving his office, she walked out to look at the sea and try to locate the campus in relation to what she remembered of Portmore and what she had read of that sort of terrain. She knew that under rugged honeycomb limestone, way beneath this surface made jagged over countless centuries of corrosive rain, deep deep down underground, there might yawn submerged caves and flooded chambers eaten away by groundwater over tens of thousands, hundreds of thousands of years. It was the sort of action that compromised the integrity of stone, wearing it thinner and thinner in the roofs of limestone caverns, unsuspected by those who walked in the world above.

Her eyes wandered along the coastline and then up to the hills, pausing over small houses perched here and there, for the human inhabitants of the area and its surroundings were relatively recent, however loud their claim to the space they measured and carved up. She wished she could get up into the hills with someone who knew them, and sit stock-still, until the wilderness forgot her, relaxed and came alive around her. In Hellshire, the dry forest had for far longer provided a home for countless elusive creatures, some of which vanished for years, even decades, then were glimpsed again, only to disappear once more, leaving their survival a matter of speculation. Here lived the endangered and the simply shy – the iguana, the tree frog and the thunder snake; the coney, the fish-eating bat and (one or two would say) the wild hog, some of the last long-tailed skink that remained on the island and, possibly, the few blue-tailed galliwasps left on earth.

These last, if they still existed, were born alive and incredibly vulnerable, and they stayed alive by hiding. Threatened not only by natural predators but by the loathing and fear with which lizards were generally regarded in Jamaica, the galliwasp especially – a half-mythical, secretive coil of coldblooded yet harmless existence – had remained the subject of irrational horror. Believed to be venomous, it would be merely one timid inhabitant of a pile of dry palm fronds. She supposed that disturbing the debris might produce, at most, a passing impression of a glossy streak and hint of a skitter of tiny legs, before it was gone again into a hole in the rock. Misunderstood.

Candace turned back to the buildings that spread inward from the sea, deciding to give herself a walking tour of the campus, and she returned to the main entrance from the Portfront Road, which ran under the intimidating metal archway to meet Circuit Road. To the left lay the parking lot by the sea, and to the right a lavish Physical Resource Management building that overshadowed the modest office of the Master of Studies. The walkway led to the administrative centre, the Paul Bogle Building, which turned out to be a nostalgic attempt at recapturing the charm of a 1920s bungalow. Latticework bordered wide porches cooled by huge fans. The Office of the Provost to the left seemed mysteriously familiar, until she recognized it was a smart copy of the fine old house that served St Augustine campus as the Principal's office.

Unusual, Candace thought, for a North American–based institution to adopt this old tropical style, surely inadequate for office space. But then, perhaps she had expected the administrative complexity of UWI and extensive face-to-face interaction. Instead the charming bungalow helped cultivate, out of nothing, an impression of historical continuity. She felt around in herself for a frisson of simplicity, of bureaucracy denied, but found only mild perplexity.

Beyond these buildings, everything changed. First Street connected the jazzy Tropicourt Restaurant overlooking the sea to the other arm of Circuit Road, where a white tent arched vast as a Romanesque church. Here gradu-ation exercises were conducted, or other solemn ceremonies, according to a solitary security guard who looked touchingly thankful for a chat. Farther on, behind a cluster of offices and lecture rooms, lay what a student termed the "entertainment region", resulting in Second Street being fondly termed The Bourbon. This only meant that the Marley Student Centre, with its crowded café, gym, table tennis and benches on which dominoes clattered, spread to the right of the squash courts and cricket pitch. To the left, the vegetarian Ital Café overlooked the boardwalk along the seawall, and it resounded with student chatter and dancehall music. Between these stu-dent facilities and a Learning Complex lay a construction site that chimed with the voices of imported Chinese labourers.

On Third Street, she stepped from brick pavement onto black pitch that softened in the hot afternoon and sucked at the heels of her shoes, leaving sticky gobs on the low cream wedges. Too late she noticed that classrooms beyond the walkway could also be accessed across scrubby patches of grass, where the young people tramped along not just in Nikes and Crocs but in vulnerable Bridget Sandals and less pricey Azizas. A cleaner hurrying through the door watched sympathetically, as Candace twisted her ankles around and examined her shoe heels. "In future, Miss, please to walk pon the grass. Don't stick to the walkway." She gave a wide grin and whisked her broom across the landing.

Three old buildings towards the back of the campus must have been standing long before landfill set in. Tropical Sciences loomed in ancient red brick, bearing barely legible signs that announced the Dengue Project and some sort of library, the latter being a one-room affair at best. *Dengue Town*, read fading graffiti on its front wall.

Beside the red-brick lecture rooms for the Centre for Small States Gender and Development, the Cultural Studies classrooms occupied an unpainted concrete block, and Candace recalled Dexter grumbling about CuSt scrunting for teaching space and being at the mercy of the technocrats and social scientists. Farther inland lay only a dusty track of shattered stone with a faded signpost that said Fourth Street. But it was only rubble and scraggy hillside. She was glad to head back to the more finished buildings and attractive frontage.

—)\~

"Good Lord! What were you doing on Workhouse Lane?" The imposing woman she had met earlier in the coffee room took her by the elbow as soon as she got back to the offices on Main Street. "We met, remember? Francine Forbes-Garcia? Right. You're Candace. I saw you conducting your own tour, and I said, 'Leave her in peace to find her way.'"

"Workhouse Lane?"

"At the back. That awful brick building was a workhouse once, they say. Never mind. All to be torn down, as well as our own eyesore. The construction is working, road by road, back to the hill. So, what do you think of us?"

"Well, I don't believe I got right around. I never found the library, for one thing."

"Oh, that's forthcoming." Francine fluttered vague fingers towards the construction site. Temporary quarters for now, behind the CTS Lab. Squatting in Dengue Town, you know." She dropped her voice confidentially. "Now that everything's online, no one misses any library – least of all the students." Then she added hurriedly, "But, of course, it has to come – I mean, how would it look? And it'll have all the high-tech stuff the young people like, so I suppose we'll get them into it somehow."

Candace stared at the students through the window of Francine's office, bemused at the transformation in expectations among the denizens of Portmore. Long before the signing of any agreement regarding the environment, residents of Salt Pond District (as the area had then been called) had lived and worked in scattered settlements, fishing or labouring on plantations, and later, in growing communities. By the time Candace was growing up, there were houses of all sizes, buildings for shops, schools and medical care; postal service and police presence. The traffic jams and crime came later. More land was reclaimed from swamp, as the city spread out on landfill extending from the alluvial plain near the Rio Grande and holding its own through a meticulous canal system for efficient drainage. Even as a flourishing residential community, though, Portmore continued to attract passers-through who came to frolic on the beaches, stuff themselves on fried fish or poke around in caves.

"It's hard to relate all I actually see before me to what Portmore was when I was a child," Candace remarked lightly.

But she knew the development of Portmore had taken off from the 1960s, when WIHCON spawned identical houses for the huge overflow from Kingston, and its inhabitants toiled back and forth along the road through Bernard Lodge. By the mid-1970s, when Candace's parents were hunting for a place in which to start life together, the causeway arched across the harbour to connect Kingston to its dormitory town. Setting its back against the Port Henderson Hill, with its hidden meshwork of Arawak burial caves, Portmore had swelled over thirty years to an independent urban community.

"Well worth the battle with the environmentalists," Francine said. "In fact there was still a hullabaloo over building ITS."

The parent institutions had commissioned an environmental hazard assessment, and Candace did recall this EHA being publicly debated. Then concerned groups in the country had clamoured for an environmental impact awareness study. Committees and subcommittees shifted into high gear, arguing more and more shrilly about air quality, noise and effluent discharge standards, traffic implications, and ecological and socio-economic impact.

There had been placards and marches regarding the future of vegetation and wildlife in the area, while scholars held forth passionately on surface and groundwater. Then a handful of small farmers in the area got stirred up about soil fertility. But construction companies salivating at the prospect of contracts pointed out that a campus would in the end have less effect on ambient noise and air quality than, say, an industrial plant. An engineer pointed out that Portmore had big building development lang time, and no autoclapse to date. Short-term noise from excavation, drilling, concrete mixing and the lumbering along of heavy equipment was inevitable – unless the area was to be left a wilderness for all time. (Duh, said the students in environmental science; but who paid them any mind?)

Francine surveyed the bustling campus with satisfaction. "Isn't the transformation marvellous?" she asked.

"Unbelievable," answered Candace.

⌁⁄ı∖⌁

That evening at the Provost's reception, she steered clear of her father, joining a group in which Dexter Danraj held forth on the progress they were making.

"That ass, Sandiford, eternally bragging about how he defined operations and set up systems and worked out modalities – Dudley Sandiford is our biggest obstacle to progress." They hadn't been looking for any scholar, when they chose Dudley, he explained; they brought him for his administrative experience, primarily in the business sector, and (when he retired from that) in the international office of a South African university. That was how he had met the President, over some negotiation for bauxite money to fund equipment wherever he worked in those days. After Dudley left South Africa, he spent one year – *one year* – as Registrar in some outpost in northern Scotland before leaving that for "medical reasons". Which meant (here, Dexter dropped his voice politely) they were freezing his balls. So Dudley leapt at ITS's promise of a relatively stress-free position in a warm climate.

What the fools never grasped, Dexter pointed out, was that a college administrator needed academic experience. Dexter cast his eye across the reception area outside the Provost's office, a sweep of mosaic tiling, and waved cheerily at the Master of Studies. "Now the old Dudley watching the current three-year contract shrivelling to an end, and he see he going have to give up sunshine for drizzle, so he whining about how he longing for home, but he love the Caribbean, and it have work here – he *ought* to finish. I say why he don't retire (for the fourth time) to Irish Town or Beverly Hills or wherever he means to make his senility official." Dexter spread his hands palm down and patted the air with a conciliating smile. "I mean – don't mind he is my good friend – when is time to go, is time to go."

Candace turned a somewhat bemused face to the colleague at her elbow, as Dexter sauntered off to the group that included the Provost and Registrar. Francine shook her head but sounded a note of commiseration. "If the post of Master is to come free, I suppose the sooner the better as far as Dextrous is concerned." She threw an appraising eye over their surroundings. "I think our Provost could have asked us to The Habitat. His grand new house, you know. I'm dying to see what all the flak was about."

"There was flak?" Candace knew she was temporizing. High time to reveal her connection with the Provost before Francine said anything embarrassing, but Candace's mouth seemed unable to frame the words. "Environmentalists, I suppose?"

"Not so much that. The hoo-ha was about some archaeological site no one had ever heard of. Underground. Some nearby cave no one had even seen. You know."

As if they were easy to find. It was not a matter of tripping over caves yawning by the main road. Candace remembered hearing of one in the area, unknown to anyone except the more foolhardy children, perhaps a few steps beyond ITS. She vaguely recalled making out from the road a curve in the jagged rock face, as if the stone wall were concave just above water level, but she had heard tell of a substantial cave there, its mouth submerged beyond view. She had known from childhood, by hearsay, of other caves – some shielded by bush or overhanging vines, and yet others with narrow entrances facing away from the road. She had seen nothing of what lay beyond their entrances.

"But what would the Provost's house have to do with caves?" Candace asked.

"Exactly. Not to say he erected a mansion on bones and shards and that sort of thing. I mean it was prime residential land, and the man bought it. Wait." Francine paused. "Dudley?" She raised an arm to get the Master's eye and flagged him over, strolling forward to meet him partway. He struggled minimally to straighten up, but diminishing bone density had bowed his spine irreversibly, and he contented himself with cocking his head sideways to meet her eyes.

Francine tucked an arm through his. "My dear, why are you eating pastry?"

"Only cocktail patties," he protested. "See the size? Little more than food for the soul." He wandered off into tortured aphorisms. "Man shall not live by work alone . . ."

"But they add up," she scolded. "And then your acid reflux will keep you up all night, *if* you plan on going to bed at all. I hope you've stopped taking work home. What? *Board minutes?* My friend, listen to me. You want to fall down and give Morgan Shade a wo'k looking replacement for you?" As he leaned attentively to her, his trousers bagged in front to a degree that drew a pointed finger and snigger from a man Courtney had been chatting with. Francine regarded them severely and turned back to the Master. "Dudley, how long again you have?"

They were wandering away, arm in arm, when a cool hand on Candace's shoulder startled her, and she spilt the chardonnay slightly before righting her glass.

"Dr Clarke, I assume?"

Earl Rider's disarming smile flashed at will under hazel eyes that were jewel bright and cold, with always the same effect on her – that stir of hope that should have been long dead, and then the plummeting of her spirits, as common sense kicked in.

A sliver from her father's disavowals had long worn its way into her, deep and visceral, and it shafted her every time she encountered him; but she donned her expression of composure and released the one bland word that came to mouth. "Indeed."

"You've met our Provost?" Francine had released Dudley and materialized at hand again to make introductions. Her head tilted with interest in the looks exchanged – one triumphant, the other evasive. "Our centre's newest adornment, Provost – Dr Candace Clarke. Candace has done this really remarkable study in the course of her doctorate that is just going to feed right into the unit's expertise in Caribbean language and cultural history."

Candace recognized her duty and rose to it unhesitatingly in the relief at having something to say. "Well, but your articles on race, class and gender in the Caribbean postmodern were indispensable."

"Ah, yes." He gripped Candace's hand warmly and held it. It was too open to provoke suspicion. "And, of course, I know of the doctoral thesis. What was your title again? You'd have told me years ago, but the exact wording . . .?"

She forced herself to let his claim to communication between them pass unparried. "'The Operation of Person in Direct Speech'."

"An application to Caribbean poetics, I think?"

"In a way. But the focus remained on operations of discourse rather than on literary interpretation." An attentive silence prompted her to continue, but already the chill had set in to shut her down. Swiftly as her thoughts took form in words, her father's indifference erased them before they could leave her lips. It was not intimidation but the proven pointlessness of talking to him. Her dissertation topic was the sort of thing her father would already know if he cared and needed to be told – and he didn't, so he needn't. Sensing the blood ebbing from her face, she bent over a passing tray of plantain chips and avocado dip.

"You know, of course." The Provost flashed his brilliant smile at Francine and a warmer one back at Candace. "We have let too much time pass."

"Know what, Provost?"

He turned to Francine with an expression of incredulity. "That Candace is my daughter. I married very young and, well, sometimes these things don't quite work out." A moment of sad reflection, then he brightened. "Candace constitutes the very best of us both, and I hope to know her better, now we've found ourselves in the same place at last."

"I read of your appointment here after I arrived. I could hardly believe my eyes," Candace threw in, instantly appalled at the hackneyed phrase that rendered her unconvincing even to her own ears.

Francine's expression announced how heartening it was to have a touching story shared so forthrightly, but she included a knowing curl of her mouth. Still, this was a fleeting impression, deflected by the clasp of the Provost's hand that (cool and dry as it was) left Candace's clammy. She barely refrained from wiping her fingers on her skirt, as she had more than twenty years before, when the same firm palm on hers had pressed her to be silent lest she make her mother sad – not because of anything he had done to Candace nor even because of all he had left undone, but because of betrayals he had not cared to conceal.

"But where are these waiters?" The Provost flicked an imperious glance over the gathering. "They're starving my guests. Better if we had gathered on Hellshire Beach for fish and festival."

"Don't let's keep you," Candace said. "Perhaps we should let Francine finish my tour." Candace's eyes skimmed the semi-barren landscape for escape.

"We have time," he agreed, "at last."

He turned away – no doubt in search of someone useful, Candace reflected, someone yet to be hypnotized by his startling professional profile. This emanated from more than charm and dynamism. His résumé, honed to meet the challenge of the most punishing traditional standards, seized attention through titles that flashed on bold forays into controversial areas. Earl Rider not only engaged with hot topics but took up disobedient yet unassailable positions on the cutting edge of troublesome issues. His list of publications was shot through with the glint of titles like "Cultural Identity Theft and the Mindside of Trafficking", "Alternative Sexuality and the Fracturing of Caribbean Masculinity/ies", and "Race for the Environment: Eurocentric Gardening in the Re-Mapping of African Diasporic Spaces".

Registering a familiar sense of time-up, Candace turned away, even as the Provost moved off, and she glanced around at the other guests. "Who's that?" She forestalled any questions from Francine by pointing out a woman she had glimpsed at the centre earlier that day.

"Come and meet Sonja," Francine agreed, beaming delight in being the person who knew everyone worthwhile. Sonja Palmer was a visiting professor whose publications in eighteenth- to nineteenth-century roots of Caribbean culture were impressive, although, in a situation that placed value mainly on contemporary experience, she was particularly valuable for her connections. "You see, she's got to be thick with Stuart and Cornel and the rest," Francine explained, "which is going to be incredibly helpful when we get the conference I'm proposing off the ground. Meanwhile, she's so able she can teach useful courses, like the one I'm designing right now, on the Caribbean Unhomely in Diaspora Studies." She sang out, "Sonja. Sonja, this is Candace. Candace, Professor Palmer. She's our distinguished visitor – Swanton Professor of World Literature, Emeritus. Emerita, I should say."

"English not having restructured to ape Latin grammatical gender, I'd have said not," Sonja remarked, smoothing the edge of the remark with a smile. "But that's what we've come to." Then she glanced sharply at Candace. "We met before?"

"I'd remember," Candace said. Sonja's was a memorable face, smooth-sheened black with high cheekbones and pointed chin, wide-browed above lustrous dark chocolate eyes. Tall and flat-chested with generous hips, she carried herself with an easy upright bearing and somewhat inquisitive incline of her head with its profusion of dreadlocks.

Seemingly unaware of her stature, she glided smoothly in a crush of strangers whose murmurs rippled in her wake. "Palmer, is it?" The recognition rendered her familiar yet distinguished, like the references to her work strewn profusely through texts and journals – what colleagues in other disciplines termed the impact factor. ITS had wooed her with as tempting an offer as it could muster and would have been unsuccessful a couple years before. Now she had come for a few years in the Caribbean after retirement – as a distinguished visitor, when her reputation as the Swanton Professor was too sound for an obscure appointment to damage.

If one were just starting out, though, Candace thought – the frying then drizzly September day replaying in her mind as a sort of panicky blur, with her father shaking hands urbanely two steps away – things might not be so clear-cut. She found herself wondering how mad Randall had been, after all, signing up for courses in Anglo-Saxon, Medieval Latin and paleography. Even Old French, for God's sake. The reflection jostled her own choice of discipline, let alone her leap into the unknown as far as employment was concerned. Here she was, in an academic area that was widely misunderstood and under-valued – as Randall liked to quip, "sentenced to the study of language". And ITS may well have drawn her beyond hope of respectable employment.

She thought back to those anxieties that had been loudly aired before the institute opened, but she could not recall hearing or reading one demand for reassurance about academic standing. Her connection to the physical Jamaica and her own background in Portmore had made her naturally curious about headlines relating to the physical setting. Online, Candace had picked up the outcry about effects from disposal of construction rubbish and other waste. The site was reclaimed land, in any case, the builders replied to the environmentalists – who were not comforted. Landfill. In the long run, it was all waste anyway, quipped the construction firm.

As it turned out, the debate over environmental impact made less news than the hue and cry that resumed and intensified regarding environmental hazard. The safety of our youth, intoned by a series of portly middle-aged social commentators and one or two fiery scientists from UWI, depended on land stability that the area could not claim. The south coast was all too familiar with the visitation of hurricanes, and it was vulnerable to storm surge and to water damage from inland as well – what with the Rio Cobre and the area's history of urban flooding. It was true that much of this had been addressed from the 1960s by building dykes, but there were still narrow and blocked drains and possibilities for backflow from sewage systems. These needed just a breezeblow and rivercomedown to set them off. As if all that were not enough, another group had begun playing on the natural Jamaican paranoia regarding earthquakes by announcing that the proposed campus location fell squarely on a seismic hazard zone.

The residential area nearby was equally vulnerable, some argued, with population growth concentrated in the area – already fifty-one per cent of the population in St Catherine and growing faster than anywhere else. So there were calls for the government to intervene in any development that could compromise safety. Even those who thought a tertiary institution the very thing for Portmore added their strictures. At the very least, the campus would need an evacuation plan, and well-wishers began to flourish templates for the sort of thing that was necessary and to refer to approaches set out by NOAA.

With the faith one has in that apparently solid land on which one walked with confidence as a child, Candace had dismissed much of the debate that raged through the Jamaican media or found its way to her through Facebook and YouTube. The Portmore landscape was far more home to her than the concrete structure in which she had lived with her parents. The years since then had helped to flog the old Portmore days back to their corner in the unmemorable past. The old house from her early childhood was gone, and she would no longer recognize the primary school she had attended. She had been a doctoral student and part-time instructor on the Mona campus when Portmore graduated as a city with its own council and mayor, and this morning, almost another decade later, the toll road that led to ITS had been entirely new to her.

The changes she had found had been disorienting, even as they brought back to mind snippets of news she had heard along the way. All around was rampant progress. Land developers had gouged and shattered, and she recalled the images from YouTube of real estate people emitting suckteet in response to threats from coal-burners who had made their own living – destructive, yes, but in a small way – for as long as their grandparents could remember. Building projects had sliced up acres into development blocks, some (if the protesters were to be believed) inattentive to the 1992 Biodiversity Convention. Conservationists were still loud in their objections, which were largely ignored by politicians, who had more votes to gain through urban sprawl than through upholding the welfare of the galliwasp.

But as she searched her mind for any outcry about academic or intellectual standing, nothing came in focus.

Yet, surely it couldn't be that bad. Could it? Trying to get her head around the job she had gambled on, she encountered from every angle the same yawning gap that sent her scurrying to the computer as soon as she got back to her desk, her laptop, with the door key still between her teeth and her handbag slung over her shoulder. They got a good Skype connection almost at once.

". . . but no library, Randall." She saw his eyes widen as the shock reverberated, and she leaned forward to rest her forehead on the image of his face, but the screen was cold and unyielding.

"Plan B?" he urged.

"Circus act. One foot on the ITS job and one on AFP teaching." The UWI link was more urgent than ever.

By the following week, Candace had landed two groups especially for repeaters in the year-one writing course, each in a two-hour slot, one after the other on Wednesday evenings. Marcus had welcomed her home on behalf of the faculty, his delight apparently genuine, when she explained she had full-time employment elsewhere. As she met other instructors she learned more. Brilliant, winning, energetic, Marcus managed not only course material, timetabling and examination records but course instructors and students – and managed everything with endearing smoothness.

The AFP flung its net across fifteen countries, and registration had doubled, then tripled over the past five years, but there was still face-to face teaching.

Marcus took upon himself, rather than passing on up to Heads and Deans, the tedium of steering something vast, unwieldy and unpopular; so he became the darling of administrators. "How are things, Marcus?" they would ask, hoping not to be told, and the answer came back, "Cool runnings, Prof." To the beleaguered officer in a heavily bureaucratic institution, he was a dream come true, untangling timetable clashes, fielding student discontents, advising which of innumerable job applications seemed most promising. And prospective students gravitated to the package, so as to leave their *real* university years free for chemistry, economics, anatomy or dance. The fees poured in. It would even have been worth funding such a programme – a programme that delivered sixty-seven per cent faster throughput than the traditional Foundation courses. But it wasn't necessary, because it was self-supportive.

So UWI had concluded that there could be no question of expending the sum that used to be required for delivery, if another approach could work better. The drain began: funding for the Foundation courses that students took on campus alongside their degree programmes could be reallocated. From the outset, some of these savings had gone into a new tenure-track post for management of the accelerated programme. Marcus was worth it. Naturally enough, because the university was now supporting his post, its associated duties would include administration (on his home campus) of all Foundation courses, however delivered. With all this, Marcus Walters was now consulted on Foundation matters across the region, his advice sought and his attendance required for campus and intercampus meetings. Lecturers in charge of each of the Foundation writing courses, including those outside the AFP, were selected on the basis of his advice. All of which Marcus found highly gratifying.

"Problem is, he's published nothing since submission of the doctorate." Professor Critchlow shook his head, when Candace dropped in to hug her old supervisor on the award of his Chair, and they got talking about her teaching in AFP and then about the organizational flair of the AFP manager. "And his publishing particularly matters now that the post is tenure track. Hence the riddle: What do you need most but have least, the more you get of everything else?"

She thought of Marcus controlling more and more, wielding the AFP like the One Ring. "Time," she said. What with the effect of all that on his research output, he must be hypersensitive about more prolific writers on the job market in fields related to his own.

Then she thought about how all she wanted was to survive, and she told herself: Stay invisible.

Chapter 4

─╼╱╲╾─

Hazard

Hasard is verray moodor of lesynges,
And of deceite, and cursed forswerynges.

Randall liked to say, "Time longer than rope," but Candace had little patience with most things and even less with Time. She was here at ITS because she couldn't wait any longer for something or nothing to *evolve* at UWI. "And I have to make some mark on academia soon or give it up," she harangued herself. But give it up for what?

She decided to feel out Sonja Palmer for advice, and began one wet November day with an innocuous remark or two on ITS, before Francine came in to put down her mug.

"A grisly mix of students," Sonja admitted. It was the usual 10:50 of Candace's trip to the coffee room. Candace had asked how Sonja adjusted to teaching undergraduates after what must have been years out of the fray. "I've always liked first-years, though," Sonja continued, twirling her spectacles dangerously. "So unspoilt. I can do without them when they become blasé. Still, these are a varied bunch as far as attitude is concerned, and not altogether prepared for tertiary level."

Varied was one word for it. Candace cast her mind over the students. Among the cynical, troubled, credulous, humble, terminally lazy, jittery, earnestly plodding or mortally uninterested, others threaded their way, unalarmed at the prospect of reading a book, unoffended at the suggestion of work, not maddened by abrupt release from parental supervision or by sudden availability of unlimited sexual opportunity. Here and there gleamed the curious, the committed and, in occasional breathtaking encounters, the gifted.

In the little silence that rippled from Sonja Palmer's gently delivered but massive understatement, Candace picked up glances of interest from those around – except for a somewhat gormless young man whom someone had introduced to Candace apologetically as Percy Stone and who, having once nodded at her, maintained an unblinking stare at nothing in particular.

"I'm afraid we do bend the rules regarding admission just a teensy-weensy bit." Dropping her voice to the murmur of the confessional, Francine held up two fingers barely apart and shuddered. "I've whispered that to our administrators, but no one listens. And, you know, they're right about one thing. We've got to be accessible." She pulled herself together. "The days of elitism in education are long gone, and we'll get nowhere by following extremists like Harvey Barham." By now Candace knew Barham's marking was so savage that students called him The Butcher. "There are some wonderful young people among them, you know," Francine added. "We have to be prepared to go that extra mile, that's what."

"Aah." Sonja was noncommittal.

"What about the conference, Sonja?" Francine charged on. "You travelling at the same time as the rest of us?" The rest except for Candace, too recently arrived to have made it into the group application for funding. Even to attend an attractive conference in London, Candace was not about to submit a personal request to the Provost. But she had made a mental note to be ready next year. *Make* at least *two presentations a year and turn them into articles. Submit an essay or chapter. Keep a thread and weave it to a project. Carve a niche.* Years ago she had heard her father mentoring a glamorous Assistant Lecturer and seized on this advice as a template, more recently adding an addendum: *Gather data non-stop, and document everything.*

"But of course you must be there, Sonja?"

Without looking around, Candace recognized Marion Bailey-Brown, a retiree from the University of Guyana whom Morgan Shade had harvested for ITS. Marion somehow imbued every sentence with a rising intonation, so it was never clear whether she was asking a question or making a statement on which she invited debate. That upward pitch projected a sense of self-depreciating distinguished scholar, intellectual strength in a somewhat fragile frame. Colleagues said Marion's publications crowded against deadlines, until she let go of one to get on with the rest. They backed up, each paper with its solid core, one overtaken by the next, eventually to be polished by some beleaguered editor. The profile was entirely compatible with that characteristic interrogative, giving off around Marion an aura of slightly addled brilliance.

Candace could release nothing before it was perfect, which it could never be, and in the living room that doubled as her study, a comfortingly book-lined room lit by wall and ceiling fixtures, as well as standing and table lamps, the written articles piled up – on Bajan shifts for signalling class superiority, on Trinidadian linguistic choices for communicating solidarity in electoral campaigns, on Jamaican *im* as a class and age marker in literary characterization. Edited and proofed, the papers lingered excruciatingly for one last read. Inability to let go held her back, like a trap she could escape only by gnawing off a limb. Everything depended on output, but all that she laboriously gathered from informants and noted from articles by other experts – this whole mass of data – called for ongoing strenuous effort. It was not only a matter of accessing and verifying the information and of recording it in some appropriate linguistic format. There was the problem of keeping the contribution of others distinct from thoughts exclusively her own, through scrupulous documentation. She was eager for the perceptions of others, part perhaps of that deep-seated craving to belong to a community of scholars. But obsessively validating and managing facts and sources swallowed up time.

In between, Candace would distance herself from the material, and when she returned to it, she would notice that some strands had begun to mesh. Meanwhile, details that had dangled, meaningless at first, had begun to loop around others across the months, even years. Because hers was a long process, she kept several projects going at one time so as to publish regularly – separate undertakings maturing each at its own pace. And now and then, the projects seemed to talk to each other. She was beginning to suspect some would eventually merge into a book.

In the interim, frequently enough to keep her afloat, material came together for an article. Came together? Another stupid expression to imbue the inanimate paper with agency. It never happened by itself. And she wasn't one of those who churned out papers, pulling together a presentation in flight to some conference. She lived in horror of being stood up by her own mind, of letting herself down in front of her peers. Randall slaved over every presentation, compulsive like herself, but in the end, he enjoyed delivering them. He was a performer, she said. Her own upcoming oral presentations would churn in her belly, and the possibility of a *written* paper coming out rife with embarrassing flaws nagged her into multiple rereadings.

Candace was the sort who studied fine print on responses from publishers. Satisfied with the online journal that had accepted her last paper, she cast an eye over its Consent to Publish form one last time. Its precision appealed to her. A firm that stipulated *non-exclusive rights to publish by any number of systems including Internet and intranet delivery and all other forms of electronic publication not known or hereinafter invented* at least had thorough forethought on its side.

Could she have worked up the urge to outshine her peers, that would have delivered the kick she needed to release her hoard of almost perfect papers at once, dramatically expanding her vitae. But she knew herself to be terminally uncompetitive. Once past third form, she had never by thought or inclination moved to outdo anyone except versions of herself. Thank God colleagues in a small institution like ITS must be scattered over such widely different interests as to be unlikely to find themselves vying for turf.

"And while you're there, you can help us arrange for a keynote address, for our own conference next year." Francine's voice brought Candace back to the discussion that had prompted her mind to stray in the first place.

"Help you where?" Sonja's bewilderment was patent.

"You mean you're not going to the 2011 conference in London, Sonja?" Francine seemed scandalized. "We *need* people of your calibre. And you know the organizers will accept *your* abstract even at this stage."

"You want me to apply to a grants committee chaired by our Provost – or does *he* constitute the grants committee? Whatever. I must ask Earl Rider for funding to attend something called 'Taking Another Swing: Her Breasts at History 2'? Or is it 'at History Too'?"

Sonja had a faraway smile. One could not always say whether she was seriously engrossed in the conversation or had drifted elsewhere.

"Well, that's just the quote," Francine exclaimed, "picking up on the last one that adopted the NourbeSe Philip phrase – *swinging her breasts at history.* I wouldn't have missed the 2001 conference at Goldsmiths for the world, and now the people at this other place are taking another swing, as it were, from their own angle. Come on, Sonja. You can't be offended at that."

"Offended? No. Just excluded."

A curious group had clustered round. A force-ripe graduate student, Anthea O'Connor, took it upon herself to update the newcomers. Sonja gestured the conference away with a dismissive lift of one shoulder.

"Leaving aside the fact that I am woefully unequipped (personally) to engage with the conference theme – it feeds the stereotype." Francine stared at her blankly, so Sonja resumed gently. "I mean, it implies that we're all supposed to have breasts of swinging proportions. No, no. Great metaphor – but quite overlooks my build of woman. Oh well." She shrugged, falling back on a turn of phrase more familiar to the eighteenth-century scholar. "At least I can be said to have bottom." A consequent bray of laughter halted her, and she looked askance at the gathering, as if for the first time seeing how many were there, and how uninformed about the idiom of earlier writers. Sonja hung poised, an anachronism among the guffaws and appreciative slapping of hands on thighs, seemingly suspended in time itself. Then, with the slightest toss of her head, she appeared to consign a host of well-worn metaphors in gender and postcolonial theory to some intellectual trash heap. "Make Danraj send off an abstract," she threw out.

Yeh, right. As if an international player like Dexter Danraj would pay his way to conferences, even with institutional funding. Danraj attended gatherings by invitation, to make keynote addresses on Carter or Dabydeen or the Caribbean diaspora, and to launch books hither and yon, enhancing an occasion by passing through. If you brought out a book, you might send him a complimentary copy, but not because you expected a review. For that you pestered a solid scholar a rung or two below Danraj (if you found one with extraordinary ideals of professional responsibility). You sent Danraj your book on the chance of his mentioning it in an address or in conversation with someone who mattered. Dex send an abstract?

Too bad, as far as Sonja was concerned.

Anthea O'Connor was still fuming a week later, as she waited in a lecture room that CuSt had borrowed from the Centre for Small States Governance and Development Studies after painful negotiation.

"I don't care how famous Sonja Palmer is."

The group of ten or twelve had gathered for an address by a visiting Distinguished Lecturer on sexual faultlines in Caribbean folk tales.

"You could be bright and backward same time." Anthea was a particularly noxious graduate student from the Eastern Caribbean, who had taken it on herself to set Sonja straight regarding conference attendance as a scholarly obligation, and who had declared herself alarmed and insulted by the discovery that Sonja was entirely unaware that she, Anthea, even existed. "I mean, if she's too big to notice what's going on in the centre or to participate in international exchange, what she good for?"

The few other students present were so busy tightening sweaters and shawls round themselves and snuffling wretchedly in the frigid air conditioning that no one managed more than half-hearted acknowledgement.They had come in the frail hope of picking up some application of queer theory to gild whatever seminar they had in the pipeline. Under Anthea's baleful eye, Monique, the secretary who scheduled such events, maintained her politely ironic smile, unreadable as ever. Monique had inherited from her Chinese mother the flat back and front with slightly bowed legs that gave the impression of her being firmly planted, so that there was no point in trying to push her anywhere. A slight cast to one eye, which made her seem to look this way and that at the same time, had provided Francine with an excuse to say Monique invited the stereotypical label of inscrutable Asian. In fact, Francine grumbled, Monique not only bought into the cliché but exploited it. "Coldly calculating, that one," Francine had pronounced darkly. But about what? Francine's comments sometimes left Candace uneasy in ways difficult to define.

For Candace, the very existence of graduate students at ITS was mystery enough, when proposals for master's and doctoral programmes were only just under design. The forethought involved in accepting and registering students while hammering out details of their programme made Candace's head spin but did not seem to unnerve the students themselves, or their supervisors. Francine said, "Once the formalities are in place by the time they're to graduate, who cares?"

Today Monique regarded Anthea O'Connor dispassionately and enquired about the morning traffic over the causeway from Kingston to Portmore. Before she closed the deal on an apartment in Kingston or sold her little place in Portmore, Monique explained, there was the traffic to consider – not to mention the $150 on the toll road. She understood, though, that Kingstonians like Anthea were getting in to Portmore much earlier. Anthea muttered about the traffic always being deadly, and then she dried up.

How, Candace asked later, had Monique silenced The Anthea? Monique replied that some students were such committed researchers, they spent nights on the premises. She refused to say more, only warning Candace there would be hell to pay if the remark got back to Anthea's supervisor, Dr Forbes-Garcia.

Why Francine should be overly concerned about such a thing dropped swiftly from Candace's mind. Francine was actually more easygoing on students than Candace. Indeed, an anonymous student had singled Candace out by spray-painting her office door with the warning: *Slave driver: Bewear.* Still, whatever Monique thought Anthea might be up to, that was just the sort of trivia that churned below the surface of CuSt and, to Candace's mind, deflected attention from matters of consequence. At ITS, students and staff seemed oddly aware of each other's personal lives in a way Candace had never been, even during her doctoral programme. As a student, she had rarely thought of staff as existing off-campus. Here, snide remarks on the marital problems of lecturers passed through student Facebook walls and took wing on Twitter. At the same time, abrupt reversals in staff relations around her made Candace wary of forming connections with colleagues.

Yet she came upon stability where least expected. Convinced that Administrative Assistant Mackhail held her in dislike, Candace rarely sought her out; but when she asked about regulations for recording coursework marks, the AA said, "None, Dr Clarke, but I've found a format from elsewhere you might like to try." As pleasantly as you like. Sonja confirmed that Ms Mackhail could be quite forthcoming, subject to her own stringent assessment of who deserved attention. Her views on the faculty at large proved caustic, though, especially in relation to those she categorized as having yoked themselves to Baal.

As Candace acclimatized, she caught up with the profile of other units, and especially of the Centre for Small States Governance and Development Studies.

CSSGDS boasted a colourful collection of older, relaxed scholars (other than the ferocious Mr Barham) and younger appointees fervently fighting their way forward. Ravindar Sumra, turbaned and heavily bearded, kept strictly to himself, taught his classes scrupulously and then withdrew from sight to bolster the curriculum vitae that would get him out of ITS to a safe appointment in the United States. His responses to any remarks were polite but guarded, before he wrapped himself up again in his work, the fabric of his days and nights tugged tight and symmetrical around him. Percy Stone, on the other hand, delivered his courses fitfully and kept chaotic records. His was not the disorganization of the overworked but of the inattentive; a befuddled lethargy appeared to beset every area of his life and displayed itself in slurred speech and dilapidated clothing. Insolvent and moth-eaten, Percy drifted openly between unwholesome bars in shady company. Useless asking his opinion or requesting information. "Attention spam," sighed Francine. It was immediately obvious that Percy's was a brain divorced from its surroundings by alcohol or cocaine. Or both.

Another of the younger set, Denise Quintin, had grabbed the ITS offer as a respite in which to seek greener pastures. The fiery Grenadian gender specialist was beautiful to a degree and intensity that Francine said undermined that savagely feminist stance. "You don't find even Courtney tiptoes round her?" Marion was heard to ask. Denise projected this posture through pungent comments on men at large and a stubbornly high failure rate that inspired the students to spray-paint on her door *bad bitch* – unless that was a reference to her sideline for supplementing her income: a thriving business of breeding Rottweilers for nervous Jamaican property-owners.

Less readable than staff members was the overarching administration. Policies, procedures and general infrastructure mystified Candace, until she realized that these were, mostly, absent. "I guess I'm blinded by the little I've glimpsed of UWI's red tape," she confided in Sonja. "But then, I have no experience of other institutions." Having discovered they lived ten minutes away from each other in New Kingston, the two women had met at Scotchies, analysing ITS over jerk pork and festival. "You're the one with international experience. What do you say?" In the wax paper Candace pushed across the table, the outer surface of cornmeal was still hot and crisp and the inside of the festival warm and fluffy.

"No systems in place to speak of," Sonja said, "except for what Mackhail has beaten out and enforces without regard for Dudley or, for that matter, the Provost. Courtney tried to wheedle his way into some record he needed the other day and met with stony contempt. Mackhail said he had no right to it and ignored him, even when Dudley signed the release. Then Courtney inveigled Marion into approaching Mackhail and protesting that Courtney was only trying to help out a colleague. But all Marion got out of Mackhail was a stricture on the regard that ought to be accorded to "Cain and his offering". Sonja broke the last festival in two and reached for another piece of fiery meat.

Gesticulating with half of the festival, she said, "Even the Registrar can't get anything Mackhail is intent on locking up. So, you see, decisions are left up to the individual. Of course, the old British system is extreme, and sensible places nowadays try to simplify their operations – but there must be some infrastructure. What's odd is how far ITS seems prepared to go in putting up an appearance of the old ways, while preaching contempt for them. Like the function this evening, deep into the semester, when such a ceremony is designed to usher in new people as they begin."

The matriculation ceremony was the Provost's innovation on the offshore campus of an institution that had little truck with traditional formalities, even those as common as graduation exercises. At its central location, the Global Knowledge Institute sent out circulars, and students dropped in to collect their diplomas. At ITS, the first-years were now already preparing for examinations – but it was never too late, Professor Rider insisted, to ensure a proper introduction. He rode over the half-hearted protests of the Fellows and Registrar. People who had little education themselves, he said, delighted in seeing their children cross the stage and shake hands with the man in the black and emerald gown with the gold trimming. Then don't forget there was the press to keep interested and donors to be wooed, and for that sort of thing, there must be ceremony.

This was the Caribbean, Rider declaimed in his speech at matriculation, where the *best* of the old ways of British education were still revered,
however savagely critiqued by the politically correct. No need to throw out
the baby with the bath water. He added, "The fact that UWI has retained
such ceremonies doesn't make them pointless."

Once the obedient snicker died down, the Provost's address pounded the
right notes on institutional standards and the establishment of ITS as the
prime tertiary institution in the country, if not the Caribbean. In his words
on student well-being, however, he became incantatory. He pulled off a
miraculous representation of students as customers who were somehow
transformed to raw material and then to product. As Sonja remarked in the
general post-mortem next day, the same students were eventually (with a
flourish) transubstantiated into consumers.

"We are very serious about student friendliness here, Professor Palmer,"
Anthea remarked coldly.

"So we commercialize our dealings with them? Of course, we must run
the place in a businesslike way, but I would think we're here as scholars, not
shopkeepers. Well, never mind – I'm devoted to metaphor myself. Probably
why I hate seeing it mangled." She turned to Francine. "It's good to see
young staff so loyal to their institution." She offered Anthea an approving
smile guaranteed to infuriate her.

"I'm not staff, Professor Palmer," Anthea said icily. "I'm a graduate
student."

"Visiting, like myself, then." A statement rather than a question.
"Graduate programmes here are still in the pipeline, I believe." And Sonja
drifted away.

Candace turned the topic adroitly. "And do we really have all those
student associations he spoke of?" She put it to the gathering at large, and
Francine pounced.

"Oh yes. As well as professional societies for both students and staff.
I have to say it's been a struggle getting our own society, for cultural
ownership and sensitization, to convene regularly, but we're doing better
than hitherto. And CSSGDS has a strong group – the Conservation and
Wild Life Survival Society, CWiLS they call themselves, and they go on
field trips and put out a newsletter."

"The Students for Jesus Association is active too," added a young woman called Nadine. "At least, they have regular services on Wednesdays and process every Holy Thursday." Candace remembered hearing singing and clapping, when she was leaving the campus for her UWI class.

Francine resumed without acknowledging the interpolation. "Some have been the province of staff only, societies with mainly supportive functions, like the OED – no Candace, not the dictionary." Francine flashed a tolerant smile. "The OED programme aims at assisting orphans, elderly and disabled. Fund-raising mostly: barbecues, cake sales, that sort of thing."

"Are you involved in any?" Candace sensed Francine holding back the best for last and felt obliged to ask.

"Actually, I chair one. I do feel that so many of our staff have spouses and partners who for one reason or another are at a loose end. You know, temporarily unemployed, waiting on visas, shut in with children and so on. So we have a support group, the Association of Significant Others." She smiled modestly. "I try to do my little bit."

"Ha," Randall wrote that evening in response to an update from Candace. "The very thing for you – a significant other." Her sense of contentment at having spent the afternoon at the National Library, and coming home to put up the first real painting she had ever bought, prevented her from hitting the button before he could continue. "Only, if you had a practising significant other, he would not be at a loose end," he mused. "He would be writing papers, even if he were out of a job, in between offering up a dish of cold stewed guavas with coconut cream he had prepared with his own tender and able hands."

This was exactly the direction in which they had tacitly agreed not to go, but a reluctant smile broke away from the corner of the thundercloud edging over her mind, because Randall really had made stewed guavas once. The coconut cream was more recent wishful thinking. But then, it was all wishful thinking, now that he was an ocean away. She had better fit into ITS, because teaching and research comprised her life.

So she changed the subject. "I bought a landscape today, done by a new artist – for what else could I afford?"

"And another lamp?"

"Of course. Desktop, with a Tiffany shade."

Yet what sort of teaching comprised this life, when ITS stretched its requirements to squeeze in unready students? Barham had raged about administrators who caved under political pressure, and Candace had demanded where political pressure came from in an offshore campus of a foreign institution. But Barham's wry smile from between his stubble of moustache and beard was tinged with pity. Did she really think any locally sited organization could be immune to political pressure?

"The thing is, if we admit them and take their money, we are saying they are ready." Candace got back to her core problem. "After that, how many is it reasonable to fail?"

"Well, in the first place, we don't fail them," he returned. "They fail themselves, and are welcome to, so far as I'm concerned."

"Student friendliness," Anthea began, but he swung a fierce eye at her, and she shut up, delivering a sullen mutter only after he had left the room. "That man is such hog."

A grouch perhaps, Candace thought. Possibly a bully – she was not sure. But not a hog.

The last thing she expected was to find herself accused of bullying, but shortly afterwards, in her eleven a.m. class, she paused by a desk inscribed in a kaleidoscope of inks that coloured in gouges of varying depths and widths. "If only you took notes in lectures," Candace said to the student with the penknife, "instead of defacing the institute's property. That might be a more constructive approach to learning."

"Miss, why you picking on me?" The young man regarded her with the expression of one cruelly maligned. "Dr Sumra does not speak to me like that, you know, Miss."

"He may or may not speak to you at all. However, I'm advising you with a view to saving the institution the cost of a replacement desk *and* preventing you from failing the course."

"Miss, you know how depressing that is – for your lecturer to talk to you about failing?" He bundled together his folder, soft drink bottle and greasy brown paper bag, and he slouched out.

"But what was he doing in my class anyway?" Candace grumbled to Sonja. "He's CSSGDS, and they have optional courses he should take in preference to mine."

"Those guidelines are never enforced," Sonja said. "Mackhail ensures such regs are relaxed for the girls, and the guys have to get the same consideration, or they'll scream gender discrimination." In answer to Candace's look of surprise, Sonja continued. "Mackhail advises the young women signing up for Sat's courses to register for another (almost any other), so as to save themselves from this wicked generation." Yes, Candace had heard rumours about Satnarine Nagassar, a lecturer in CSSGDS. "Precisely," Sonja said, watching Candace's face. "In this way, the faint-of-heart beat their paths to our doors. But you're right. The fellows have fewer problems."

Whatever the demands of undergraduate teaching, however, it was straightforward in contrast to staff relations. As the weeks unfolded, Candace increasingly discerned frail links that formed among colleagues or between academic and non-academic staff, trembled there briefly, and as easily broke and re-formed elsewhere. These fragile connections set up ranks that overlapped or confronted each other. So in drifting inattentively along between classes and meetings, discussing a field exercise with a technician or consoling a student, it was possible to find oneself in an embattled camp before perceiving that anyone was at war. Indeed, it was scarcely possible to find a lecturer, secretary or janitor not somehow aligned in a shifting mesh of loyalties and hostilities. Apart from Sonja.

Sonja sailed smoothly among them, leaving in her wake (however briefly) an altered dispensation. Locating herself beyond the level of staff discord, she remained impervious to venom. She was caught up in juggling the pros and cons of a research methods course preceding or following one on theory – regardless of the order for which Anthea and company had already signed up. Sonja enquired into how soon entering students might be sent on field study and speculated on ways in which they might be monitored. She grumbled about Young's thoughts on hybridity being uncritically applied to Guyana, Haiti and Barbados alike, as if the Caribbean was a smooth purée from one end to the other. She injected actual matter that neutralized the type of poison that operated in a vacuum of real issues.

Not that ITS lacked controversy. Ideas, carelessly aired, sprang up and spread riotously – often, it seemed to Candace (raised in a sterner system), without firm root in real enquiry, so they withered overnight and gave place to others. Sometimes it was a student matter that prompted dissent.

A brief flurry of scandalized outcry arose over an exchange student from the Global Knowledge Institute who had found herself in the Fort Augusta prison for women. A cadre of supportive students and junior staff upheld the detainee's contention that this was entirely a matter of gender discrimination, having little or nothing to do with the charge against her as a cocaine mule. Then she was forgotten, and some other colourful concept seized attention, flourished over the lunch hour or for the space of a presentation and faded.

In one graduate seminar, a student proposed "To Articulate the Modality for Eliciting Cyberliterature from Socially Marginalized Groups", but the young woman did not care to identify any particular methodology – as yet. "But will this be a literary, interpretive study in a postmodern framework?" Sonja probed. "Or are you considering critical discourse analysis? Could it be a sociological study – perhaps the business of CSSGDS?"

"It will be eclectic," the student retorted. As even the less inhibited of her peers exchanged glances at her outburst, she went on to explain patiently, as to an imbecile, that she was arguing, ultimately, for the decriminalization of cyber-smut. But then, as Sonja insisted on hearing how the research was to be conducted, Candace found herself wondering *why*. And beneath her irritation, she became aware of a sort of resentment: whatever she did could never offer that tingle of naughtiness, that glitz of the rebellious. Was this some form of academic jealousy? she questioned herself ruthlessly. No. But how could she ever distinguish herself against an underlying aridity that drained away energy even from what she saw as serious subjects? And did this enervation matter, when issues that engaged her were not of obvious social urgency? Let alone racy. The thought took hold that as a scholar she would never seem progressive, that, as a result, her work might never *take*.

Certainly Anthea ignored anything that smacked of the traditional, especially if it came from Sonja, whom she regarded with studied contempt. Anthea O'Connor threw herself on the controversial side of any argument. Regarding toxic gender relationships in the fiction of Jean Rhys, Anthea subscribed loudly to the view that Antoinette's suicide was sublimely triumphal. Francine egged her on, countering Nadine's protests with the reminder that the whole world of Caribbean letters was built on intellectual disobedience and that she would not have a student of hers stifled for expressing forthrightly an opinion that was offensive to the right-wing ear.

"Wings have ears now?" Sonja moaned, almost inaudibly.

"But there's a difference between articulating an independent thought and making spectacular but baseless statements," Candace broke in. Having held back at first, she had spoken more loudly than she intended. A silence fell, in which she could hear perceptions of her alignment shift and slide.

"Too bad," she said afterwards to Sonja, when they had found their way to Jolly's, having been assured that was the place for seafood on Tuesdays. Sonja had enquired tentatively about the fish, in view of all she had heard regarding pollution in the vicinity, but Francine had waved her fears aside.

"The fish is fine. It comes in from way, way out, because the harbour itself is pretty dead."

"So that's all right, then," Sonja mused. "I could have sworn I once saw a shark drift by under the jetty at that beach along the Palisadoes. But tell me, whatever happened to Rodney's Arms?" It had been one of Candace's favourite places too, with wooden tables for eating fried fish or grilled lobster in the open air overlooking the sea. The rest from that row of historic buildings were falling to pieces but for a few darkening grey brick walls weathering around murky pools, as the very bedding on which they rested dipped treacherously. "We must find out," Sonja said. "Meanwhile, come for breakfast one Saturday. Bring the dog."

Candace's mind had hung up on the cyber-smut seminar. "People fabricate these immoderate pseudo-academic claims, just to prop up some pet philosophy," she complained.

"Not even that," Sonja objected. "I don't think people like that little girl – or Francine, for that matter – believe what they're saying or make statements that emanate from a *philosophy*. They feel impelled to say something original, and they confuse that with saying something startling."

"That's dangerous." Candace reflected on a presentation the day before, a seminar that had examined themes of commerce in the writing of Austin Clarke and identified prostitution as empowerment in *The Polished Hoe*. "But don't you see" – Francine's voice had trembled with passion – "the presenter is arguing that it enables Woman to set her own value on her own Body." Anthea leapt on it at once, so the discussion took its usual course, Anthea pursuing her foregone conclusion through heady non sequiturs, until she arrived at a state of intellectual intoxication in which she could voice any immoderate claim.

"But dangerous to whom?" Sonja asked, breaking into Candace's recollections. "I mean – *who's listening?*"

It startled Candace that they were talking not about debate but about talk as a prop for staging intellectual exchange. It forced on her a glimpse of herself in an academically moribund society, with the real world of letters out there and herself on the margin. Again. She had been on the margin at UWI, because there was no way in. Here, she was in. But in what?

"Yes. You shall have breakfast with me Saturday," Sonja was saying. "It's the only time I cook. Bring Cassidy. That's his name, ent?"

"Hers." With an effort, Candace drew herself together. At least ITS provided a new situation, she decided, and pliable, because a mesh of regulations and tradition had not yet worked its way into a stranglehold on institutional procedures.

But it was hard to feel one's way.

The following day, finding no guidelines regarding the treatment of plagiarism, Candace followed an old principle instilled by Silver and asked an elder for advice. She knew Harvey Barham was a despotic assessor of student presentations but had a sharp analytic mind and had known ITS from its inception.

"Policy? Rider runs this place like a plantation," Barham grumbled, scraping his fingers savagely through his short, wiry beard. "He responds according to his own agenda and on a case-by-case basis. Procedures? You think this is an institution of higher learning, or what?"

Yet the need for constraints of all sorts grew daily more apparent. Another student assignment fluctuated between inept sentence mechanics and elegant academic prose, and by tossing a phrase or two on Google, Candace had reeled in chunks of the essay's better passages about speech acts, carved from online journals on pragmatics or websites on context and utterance meaning. Plagiarism was a problem worldwide, but she had some guidelines for her UWI scripts. From what Marion said, ITS committees bickered over the problem, every draft gumming up in a web of legal and ethical issues. Back it would go to the Committee of Fellows, the tight group that headed the three centres. Each Fellow held forth on procedures that had pertained at the school he came from, but they could never resolve their differences among British, North American and West African approaches into consistent guidelines for ITS.

The Fellows attempted to rope in Professor Clyde Seuraj, who had for years chaired boards and committees on professional ethics. This produced a situation.

Professor Seuraj had come to ITS after UWI passed him over for Campus Principal, only to find himself passed over as ITS Provost, but he could hardly ignore the call to help strengthen professional ethics at the institution in which he now worked. Although ITS had gone on to issue the crowning insult, appointing a lesser man Fellow over his head, he determined to sit down with this Professor McGregor – a decent chap, Seuraj knew from UWI, though not in his league at all – and see what he could do to clean things up. He now had further assurance, directly from the Global Knowledge Institute of the Americas rather than through Morgan Shade, that the GKIA would make good their promise to appoint him Provost, when Earl Rider was taken up into the clouds after his brief ministry in Jamaica. But even without that, Seuraj would have done what he considered to be the proper thing. So he had already been arguing passionately for regulations on collusion as well as cheating, when a comment by Dexter Danraj got back to him. Dextrous had suggested that when the Fellows had the matter sorted out, they could all take Seuraj out for a Passover meal.

Clyde Seuraj cut communication with the Committee of Fellows and, still determined to contribute, sent a detailed proposal of his own directly to the Provost. These were suggested regulations he had drawn up, based on his experience of several serious institutions. It may have been the word, *serious*. The Provost was not amused. Not only had he never invited a submission from Professor Seuraj, but this document represented exactly what he was trying to avoid for ITS. "We will *not* be tying ourselves up in the sort of cumbersome regulations that hamstring UWI," the Provost ruled.

Candace suspected it was not regulations that hamstrung institutions so much as inconsistent or tardy enforcement, but there was no opportunity to say so. Professor Rider did most of the speaking at those meetings he attended, though he often appointed someone else to chair; or he might attend to issue a welcome with some guiding comments on particular items of the agenda, before leaving for his next event. The Provost of ITS featured prominently on well-publicized panel discussions and television interviews, like those on intergenerational programmes for lifelong learning. He was sought-after for public addresses on repression of the strong male role model in Caribbean family structure. A television host invited him to speak at prime time on why the government should fund an ITS student learning hub devoted to senior self-sustainability. As far as routine ITS meetings were concerned, he contented himself with Dudley's summary of salient points and recommendations, and then he took his own course.

At a meeting of the Academic Committee, when the failure of the last Proposal for Addressing Plagiarism was discussed, Dudley reflected, "The result cannot be said to have been unexpected."

But in the corridor afterwards, Dexter Danraj remarked that matters of urgency like that needed strong action, and nothing would ever get anywhere as long as the faculty remained in the hands of that hunchbacked old fart.

"Well, he really isn't pulling it off," Francine conceded, but she referred to the Master, with greater propriety, as *poor Dudley*, with that inflection of pity that betrayed she had come unwillingly to the conclusion that Master Sandiford really had worn himself out. She was concerned for *him*, she began, only to be drowned out by Satnarine Nagassar guffawing over some pun his friend Courtney Straker had brought off regarding Dudley's inability to control a hump. Like so many other discussions in which the two men took part, the talk veered away in bantering exchange.

Candace determined to introduce her questions in a more formal context. And now that she perceived among the faculty undercurrents as duplicitous as a Jamaican river, she made the time, in advance of a meeting scheduled for the next day, for preparing to word her concerns delicately. It was a graduate programme planning meeting, and she wisely skirted the issue of graduate students being already engaged in programmes that did not yet exist. Instead she enquired tentatively, recognizing that every question was presumed loaded, whether a full graduate programme (including a taught master's) should be brought on board at all before glitches that plagued the undergraduate programme, like failures in examination security, were worked out.

The room bristled instantly with hostility, and Candace stopped stirring in the condensed milk. She put down her teacup. She glanced around.

"What did I say?"

"No, wait." Francine relaxed, her eyes roving over her colleagues anxiously, and she set her placating smile to defuse the situation. "Candace is still *new*. Don't misunderstand her. There are things she just isn't aware of yet." She turned respectfully to the Chair, Professor Danraj. "Dex? Would you grant me a minute or two, Mr Chairman?" With his permission, she explained to Candace that funding did not come easily to undergraduate courses in cultural studies. One obtained funding for research projects and for the graduate work aligned with it.

"And do we have a project?" Candace asked, meekly as she could, recognizing the voice of a self-appointed mentor.

"You see? You are going at once to the heart of the matter. Indeed we do have a project, and I'm getting to that, but – just to put it in context – you need to know that the other centres, Small States Governance and Development Studies, as well as Tropical Sciences, have well-established projects laced to graduate programmes already on stream. So it's essential that we don't fizzle away into second-class citizenship here."

It seemed to Candace that inadequate exam security would undermine the entire institute if not dealt with before building on a graduate level, but all she said was, "I hear you."

"And interdisciplinarity is the thing," Francine went on, her listeners nodding sagely. "That's how the CSSGDS's project on disaster preparedness attracted all that money: Apart from the social and economic stuff, teamwork with CTS covered environmental and engineering issues. We build the graduate level and tie in the research. Then the undergraduate programmes fall into place." She smiled at Candace sympathetically. "It's all right – I mean, you couldn't have known the politics of the thing, and certainly not about our own Cultural Studies project." The atmosphere was friendly and nurturing again. "Chair. Chair, a moment to tell Candace about our project?"

Francine explained that the Cultural Studies project was entitled "Unstable Skins: Towards a Caribbean Posthuman", and was jointly conceived with CSSGDS to promote a focus on race and gender.

"Different," Candace pronounced, feeling her way carefully. "I can see multiple possibilities for studies in any number of disciplines. You know" – she warmed to her theme – "a graduate student could do some really interesting work on books by Hopkinson and Chariandy. And, oh Lord, James . . ."

"Right." Francine laughed. "But we won't take over the whole meeting. So, thank you, Chair. On with your agenda."

"I'd love to see details of the project, Francine," Candace said afterwards. "Can I contribute?"

"I knew you'd see the value right away, and as soon as we reach that point, we'll just rope you in."

The central movers in the project besides Francine were two men from CSSGDS, Courtney Straker and Satnarine Nagassar, with support from graduate students like Anthea. The combination made Candace uneasy, but she was determined to keep the peace.

"Interdisciplinary and collaborative. That's the way things are moving now. And there'll be space for everyone as it grows," Francine explained. "The funding will just open it up. Right now the three of us are putting everything we have into it, and we need to keep it very tight and get it off the ground. Mind you, Anthea isn't asking for any money. So committed. I tell you, that girl is amazing. But we can't expand or add to the existing concepts before we deepen what we have."

Afterwards Francine suggested that a good way for Candace to get into the culture of the place itself was to join a club or two. What about their own centre's association?

When she had bustled away, Candace tried it out on Sonja. "The Society for – is it Ownership and Sensitization of Culture? Or Cultural Ownership and Sensitization? What?"

"Not me." Sonja shook her head vehemently and then gathered her locks neatly behind her back again. "Not signing up for something that isn't even grammatical. No sir. Nope."

As the Chair disengaged from the brief aftermath of the meeting and turned through the door, Candace headed him off. "Advice, Prof. What does the Society for Ownership of Culture (or whatever) do?"

"Do?"

"Well, own what, sensitize whom, and what about and how?"

Dexter put down his file and assumed what Candace now recognized as his encouragement-of-junior-staff expression. "You must get into that and help them build it up," he said. "They need energetic young thinkers. Last meeting was joint with the Caving Club, I think."

"That's a history or archaeology group?" she asked tentatively.

"Oh, but how deadly." Francine had circled back. "Our associations aren't flat disciplinary assemblies – no set of doddering old men talking to each other. No. Here we are trying to get something together that is *applied*." At Candace's bewildered expression, Francine added, "Hands on. You know, giving something back to the community."

"I'm trying to get a sense of the Culture group you mentioned," Candace said. "Or even CWiLS – isn't that what they call the environment one?"

"Let's go on one of their field trips," Francine replied, as if that would decide it once and for all. "You're not afraid of caves, right? Nothing risky. These guys" – she waved to Courtney and Satnarine as they wandered past – "they're always going on field trips, and they'll take care of us."

"Nothing on heaven or earth could get me into a cave," Candace responded apologetically. She did not add, *particularly along with Courtney and Sat.*

Chapter 5

The Fellowship

Herkneth, felawes, we thre been al ones;
Lat ech of us holde up his hand til oother,
And ech of us bicomen otheres brother.

*C*ourtney Straker and Satnarine Nagassar had started off as rivals rather than friends, from what Dexter Danraj had let drop, and Francine said she was the one who had brought them together through the project. Others, like Denise Quintin, recalled early exchange of mutual hostilities between the fellows, until they saw that no one else cared which of the two was in the right. All that mattered to most colleagues was that the barrage of corrosive mail, copied to all and sundry, should stop blocking up the limited space allocated to staff inboxes. Denise's and Dexter's versions agreed on one thing: it came to both men that the rest were a weak-spirited lot from whom no support was to be expected, so they turned to each other and joined forces. By the time Candace joined ITS, Drs Straker and Nagassar were so inseparable that they were referred to as a unit, Courtney'n'Sat.

Whatever their differences with other staff in CSSGDS, Francine said, that had nothing to do with her. She had proposed the interdisciplinary topic that benefited from Sat's expertise in transnational alliances as well as from his technical ability. Francine said the project equally depended on Courtney's span of interests and expertise. Yes, Courtney's official area was the economics of small states, but the man was multitalented. People had to understand this. The problem was, his colleagues were limited to their own little intellectual cubbyholes and had no concept of the *range* of a mind like his. And that was one of the challenges of ITS, she pointed out to Candace: the quality of some of the staff. "The material is, well, uneven," she pronounced delicately.

By now sworn colleagues, Francine, Courtney and Sat had determined to raise the tone of the institution, to stave off (as Francine put it) the academic extinction everyone was so ready to prophesy yet do nothing about. A viable research project offered an obvious way forward, and the international conference they planned to mount that year promised another. But dazzling the scholars of the region, let alone the globe, required substantial funding. So it would be necessary to win over the Old Man.

Dudley Sandiford would have to push the thing in a management meeting if they were to strike gold. "And once the money's set, you'll help us with the conference, won't you, Candace?" Francine was wooing all the part-time, temporary full-time and new permanent staff. "All hands on deck. It'll be a labour of love," she promised. Then she leaned closer and murmured in Candace's ear, "The problem is that so many of the older ones are such stick-in-the-muds. No, their thought processes are blocked up with obsolete crap. Excuse me, but I can find no other way to express the . . . just, *turgid* reasoning." She thought about it some more, eyes raised heavenward.

Even a recent arrival like Candace knew to expect limited input from CSSGDS staff, including their genial Fellow, Olatunde – whose other name no one could pronounce and, therefore, few knew. None of them would rally behind Courtney'n'Sat. This was particularly true of Harvey Barham, who, at sixty-seven, had been at ITS longer than anyone else besides Olatunde and was disenchanted with the younger set. Barham had been recruited as an excellent teacher who read voraciously and thought profoundly but did not publish and could not, therefore, get tenure at UWI. In fact, the renewal of yet another temporary contract in Barbados on UWI's Cave Hill campus had been in question when Morgan Shade went to work on him. As a Senior Lecturer, Barham could have thrown weight behind the application for conference funding, but he was unbending in his gruff contempt for all considerations besides the intellectual, and he dismissed the idea of the conference being for academic exchange. "It's for show," he summed it up, his stark, spare view unaccommodating to the benefits of an institution displaying its assets.

The conference organizers cared not a whit about Harvey Barham. Backed by Courtney'n'Sat, Francine was contriving a gathering with four simultaneous panels running over three days. She was lobbying for a flashy reception on the first evening, at Vale Royal, not only hosted by the Prime Minister but rounding up an array of prominent figures from the Minister of Education to the US Ambassador and the Indian High Commissioner. If the British High Commissioner came through with funding to bring Stuart Hall or if the Global Knowledge Institute of the Americas that had spawned ITS in the first place unbuckled so as to cover a Homi Bhabha or Cornel West, the conference was made.

But surely Sonja knew at least one of them? Francine enquired tenderly.

"I did meet Professor Hall at his 2004 lecture at Mona," Sonja responded. "Never before or since. What about the people right here in the Caribbean?"

Yes, yes, she would call on the Caribbean luminaries across the region, Francine said – but their business was to come anyway, out of professional interest, not put her to the trouble of finding foreign currency for them.

The finale was to be an equally glittering affair. Francine would never lay her hands on enough money to bring Machel Montano from Trinidad or whatever part of the world he might currently be touring. She might not even pin down a Jamaican singer like Lady Saw, for whom she hoped no airfare need be found, but she had spoken to Mutabaruka and believed he *might* give in and do a poem or two. He had to do "Dis Poem" – because that was the one everyone knew – whether he liked it or not. She speculated on a range of possibilities for the readings, like "It Was the Singing" or "Yellow". Yes, *that* was the level of artistic involvement they needed.

Courtney had tried getting her to settle for some little backward singing group, Francine said, for, of course, he didn't care about poetry – he was just one of these big handsome philistines whom one forgave everything. Candace registered once again the prevalence of Philistines in higher education and entertained a frivolous thought or two about whether they didn't create even more havoc in the Caribbean than in the ancient world.

When she came to, Francine had hurtled on. Sat was harder to deal with than Courtney in some ways, Francine murmured to her, and, she *had* to say, he had certainly noticed Candace. He had been asking about her and whether she had *someone*. So since they all had to work together on this thing, it would be better, don't you know, if Candace spoke to him a little more nicely so as not to rock the boat, because there was no time for that. It wasn't a matter of having to take him on, but Candace just mustn't alienate him right now, because he was *not* good at rejection.

Candace was more concerned right then with improving her curriculum vitae – or résumé, as they liked to call it at ITS – with a view to consideration for tenure. When she settled in front of her computer, Sat was the furthest thing from her mind. She jumped on a message just in from editors of a new journal. They declared themselves impressed by an article she had published the year before, and they invited Dr Clarke to follow up with one for their publication. "Your paper seemed to our Board of Governors to set the discussion of the issues raised on an entirely different level, and we would be pleased to include your work in our next issue."

After the first wave of euphoria, though, she wondered about the reference to a Board of Governors. She searched the letter for the composition of the publication's editorial committee, but without success. She Googled the title and, outside of the journal's own web page, found mention of it only through a website called publishit@acadamentor.com. With an involuntary grin, she reflected that serious people would have put in an underscore, but she saved the address anyway and turned back to the vitae that she wanted to discuss with the Cultural Studies Fellow.

~)|~

"Okay. What you have?" Dexter shuffled his papers in a businesslike fashion.

"Eight articles in peer-reviewed journals. Three book chapters, one of which is forthcoming in a book for which I'm an editor. Six conference presentations."

"Good start, good start."

"Start? Three of the items have appeared over the last year, and a fourth is in press. I happen to know it's more than some Senior Lecturers here have to show in total." Even a likkle house lizard like Percy Stone seemed to feel safe enough with his one four-page article on handicraft in garrison communities. But she managed not to say that.

"Okay, nah. Don't vex. Wait. We vex or what? I say is a good start, because I feel you well on your way. You not like a set of them getting nervous about this Landau thing."

The news of Fred Landau had shaken people who were coasting contentedly in ITS. Everybody knew Fred, because he had worked in a range of institutions across the region before getting a UWI contract. After thirteen years on the Mona campus, however, Landau had been refused renewal of contract and would have to go. As a tutor and eventually a part-time instructor who taught well and cared for his students, he had eventually been offered a full-time post, but despite the tenure-track contract, he had published nothing at the end of three years. Still, his Head of Department argued that he had good material in the pipeline and was a valuable staff member, so somehow they gave him another whirl. The second three-year contract was running out, and the Head was trying for a two-year, which would make the point to Landau, he argued, but the Principal said no. Chaps had to publish. Not two years, not one.

Nada, Dexter reported. So as far as UWI was concerned, Landau was history.

It occurred to Candace that Marcus Walters must be climbing the walls. However indispensable he had made himself to date, he must be ready to tear out the throat of anyone with a vitae going into bloom. The Landau story was everywhere. And suddenly everyone knew someone that had happened to, people terminated on a UWI campus or at some other university that someone at ITS had recently visited, and, as they compared notes, it was as if academics were getting the axe across the region on different campuses, and, beyond that, all over the world, university staff were being terminated for being unproductive.

And now Dexter explained his uncertainty about Candace's readiness for tenure by insider knowledge of how the Provost planned to tighten up on performance right here at ITS, because they had to plan for accreditation. There was nothing Candace could do but contain her fury with what grace she could muster.

Francine felt that a heavy-handed approach would be a retrograde step and could only be cosmetic, but she concluded that the change in atmosphere made it all the more important to bring off the conference and get the papers published with as much press coverage as possible. The image of ITS had to be polished up, and that meant roping in the press.

By now Candace had heard rumours about Francine's recruitment to ITS. Unless the promises had been empty, there should be a Chair in the offing, and Francine was bolstering her CV but expected the institution's full support in order to make good its promise. She spoke as if accepting a Chair would be a selfless thing she would do for the honour of the institute. The Provost could hardly fail to live up to her expectations.

Candace, however, would not be depending on advancement through the Provost's nurturing care. She set about hewing her own path, and it was neither broad nor straight. Nor was it firm. She watched for advertisements UWI might put out, and she enquired in the faculty and department offices before they closed for the evening.

It took less than no time to confirm that not a post was to be had in linguistics, nor was anyone retiring in the near future from a subfield in literature for which she might claim to be qualified. The number of students signing up for Foundation courses in the old way, alongside their degree programmes, was shrinking, but there was talk of new full-time Instructor posts in the AFP. She thought of approaching the Head of Department directly, but the other instructors warned that the AFP manager would advise the Head in any case. It was better to win him to one's cause from the outset. So the following Wednesday, she went in early to see Marcus Walters.

Delicately she explored the possibilities of full-time appointment, watching him intently – the winning smile becoming fixed, his eyes narrowing.

"Why would you give up a tenure-track position as Lecturer for a temporary one of Instructor?" Then, the warmth came flooding back. "Candy, Candy. No one who had your good at heart could encourage that." As he saw her out of his office, he said, "Don't let them get you down, girl. You hang on to that job."

Candy my foot. As she drove home after class, chance remarks came back to her and clicked in place. The elaborate trust built on Marcus Walters was taking its toll. Severely overloaded, he had done a couple columns in a newspaper, spoken at a high school prize-giving, and made a conference presentation. But his scholarly output had ground almost to a halt. Concern had overflowed for a most valuable staff member. An administrative assistant had whispered that the Principal's solicitous enquiries about the progress of young Walter's research (such a promising chap) had reached his Head of Department and made him blanch at the thought of any threat to the well-being of the person who stood between him and the potential for chaos in AFP. Meanwhile, two articles Marcus had listed as *in press* slid back to *in progress* on his vitae, and the idea must have formed that experienced instructors in the programme with more time to publish might not only complete their doctorates too but push out papers so as to seem more qualified than himself. As that fear took hold, he began throwing up obstacles to staff research time, to block anyone else who might edge ahead.

Even as cancerous growth in the AFP strangled the regular Foundation courses, cutting off money required for their delivery, Marcus had begun to squeeze the instructors harder. He had no wish to stand in the way of colleagues he had known from his own undergraduate days, he told his Head. But if they failed to deliver quality work or made themselves difficult to other colleagues – not himself; he was willing to put up with almost anything, because who knew what troubles people faced at home – then (for the sake of the institution) one would have to look at other applicants whose requests poured in constantly.

So the tension tightened within the section. Murmuring muted except among those who had relatively firm footholds, those, for example, who had regular tutorials in the linguistics or literature programmes. But instructors who depended entirely on the AFP began to feel the wisdom of looking satisfied; the eye that had been cast over the shoulder instead fixed itself expressionlessly ahead. Everyone knew himself, or herself, to be replaceable. Some of the Jamaican instructors began to refer to Marcus as Babylon. When he got to hear of it, it embittered him into policing his kingdom more oppressively, thus becoming self-fulfilling.

Up to now, Candace had taught only two groups and so had occasioned no lasting worry. She had a spread of qualifications similar to Marcus's but also a growing list of conference presentations and articles in good journals. She was in an unimpressive institution but had a full-time, tenure-track post there, and even if she seeped across through tutorial hours and summer classes into some other programme and made her way into the linguistics or literature programmes, that was neither here nor there. If Marcus suffered by comparison, it would be indirect and transitory. But what if she left ITS and took root right there in the AFP alongside him? Well. He had neither forgotten nor forgiven the fact that the initial idea of a self-funding accelerated programme had come from her.

"So. What you working on now?" She had come back to drop in a document, and he drew out a box of Lindt chocolates from his office fridge to wave it mischievously before holding it out.

"Usual thing." She accepted and popped a truffle into her mouth quickly to account for her terseness.

"What's that? We haven't exchanged notes on our work for a long time. Four years, girl? What you doing?"

"Discourse analysis."

"Yes, and if I ask you what you're analysing, I suppose you will say 'stuff'. Honestly, Candace. What's the secret? I need to be able to support the next contract to the Head."

She thought quickly. "To be very honest, Marcus, the secret is I'm kinda . . . at a standstill right this moment." She made her voice as confiding as she could. "I'd published enough to apply for the post in the first place, but I can't say I've anything in the pipeline to talk about. Perhaps it's this changing jobs and relocating." She leaned forward and looked soulful. "But tell me about you."

The lines that had tightened between his brows smoothed, and he relaxed visibly. "Crushed by all the work but hoping for a little leave, and – I don't talk about it, but as it's you – I'm thinking of taking up book I had started, and getting the damn thing done. It's all there, of course, but for a little editing, only I had to stop so as to keep a grip on AFP, as you can imagine. But there has to be some limit to the sacrifices UWI can expect. I feel I have to do something for *me*. You know?"

"You're so right, Marcus. High time you thought of yourself." With which bracing words she pressed forward the sealed envelope with the vitae he had asked for on behalf of the Head, and took her leave. It was addressed to the Head, but he might sneak a peek. He won't like it, she thought, but she couldn't have refused to supply it.

Three articles had come out in the past year, and once he laid eyes on the sketch of work in progress, he would try to figure out whether she had lied to him or falsified the vitae. He would hope it was the latter, so time would show her up, but it was too late now to retract his recommendation that had prompted the Head to call for the updated vitae to accompany the proposal to Appointments.

The following week, Candace explained. "Having got a paper or two out and begun this last project, I just faltered to a stop. It's true an analysis is in progress – just not . . . progressing." She had a happy thought and added, "I suppose it must be a little like what you were talking about – your book, you know? One is into a project and then gets overtaken by . . . events? Honestly, Marcus, I don't know how you juggle it all."

Candace came to date his hostility to her from that exposure of her vitae. But at the time, he gave a sad smile and squeezed her hand.

"You could have been forthright with me, though. I'd have spoken up for you to the Head, whatever the circumstances."

No further feedback came about her reappointment to AFP, until the following semester, when the timetable showed her teaching rescheduled from Wednesday to Monday, which, she had told Marcus, was her heaviest teaching day at ITS. He had allocated her two groups in writing for the Faculty of Medical Sciences, which she had never taught before. But she dared not part with the UWI teaching. Silently she accepted the twelve-hour day, because of a sensation that unsettled her as she stepped back among the corridors of ITS. A disconnect between her own values and those she had picked up around her unsteadied her, so that – however she pressed forward during the working day – at night the suspicion that she had made a hideous misjudgement cast a lengthening shadow that took substance and weight, pressing her deeper and deeper into the bed, as if to smother her.

That was what it was like. That was the way it began. Then, some-where after the hours had worn by, a point would come when it would sink into her – the realization that the night would never end, that the darkness was not just outside but inside and not just an alternating thing, not something balanced in the inevitable passage of night and day, not something structured in any relation to light at all, but a massive cloud taking form inside.

She forced her eyes open and willed herself to move, shoving her feet out of the bed and stumbling towards the computer. As it booted up slowly, she flicked on the wall and ceiling lights, the desk lamp and even the tall standing lamp at the far end of the room. A few pages of her own work, before going back to tackle that of unprepared students whose fees ITS had accepted – criminally, she was beginning to think. Another page, one more before having to untangle whatever remarks Dudley delivered or Dexter contrived, or to help administer the conference without decoding Francine, Courtney or Sat more than she felt able to bear.

Yet there was no avoiding involvement, nor could she hope or wish to be excluded from their toils.

One morning Francine glanced up from the conference file, inserting a finger to hold the place, and after a perfunctory comment about the shadows under Candace's eyes, reminded her how essential it was to keep in mind the individual gifts of staff members, even those who were unlikely to shoulder obvious tasks. Take Olatunde, for example, Fellow of CSSGDS. The magnificently attired scholar, who had come to ITS from the GKIA, had already provided his abstract and offered to chair a session. Francine was not expecting him to plan room management or juggle the programme against dizzying manoeuvrings of participants.

"Keep him involved, though," she said to Candace. "Such a positive addition – atmosphere, you know."

They shifted to the coffee room, where Francine turned to Sonja with that whole different expression that overcame her in Sonja's presence. Candace could not help comparing it with the transformation in Cassidy, when the rare person in whom the dog recognized true superiority entered the room. Then Cassidy would drop her normal insouciance, lowering her head and flattening her ears foolishly.

"Sonja," Francine crooned, "anything you'd like to do for us?"

It came to Candace that Francine was terrified of Sonja ignoring the conference, for how would it look – contempt from a scholar of Sonja's eminence actually located at the centre. How could Francine ever bring it off, if it sustained a blow like that from within?

"What's it called?" Sonja's voice had a wary tone.

"The suggestions to date are so tentative. I was hoping you would help us think up something appropriate." Francine's meek demeanour was a revelation. "What would be a good time for you to attend a little meeting?"

"I'll let you have my teaching hours, Francine, and you just schedule it." Sonja scooped up her bag and files but turned back at the door. "And if you need a hand scheduling the actual presentations, shout me."

Francine was ecstatic. "Give me a few good women every time."

She brushed aside the question of talking to Theo Philbert, the American (marking time on the way to greener pastures, she said), or Curtis Martin, who attended and gave papers at every gathering but never officially registered and paid the fee, let alone raising a finger to help. Stolid and totally lacking in gallantry, as Francine pointed out, but, of course, he made up numbers. Percy Stone might not even do that. Candace barely recalled Stone's existence, when he was not in front of her. But yes. Arms thin and dry-skinned, eyes expressionless and unblinking, an unprepossessing man a few years older than herself. (Was she imagining it, or had she seen a pencil stuck behind his ear?)

"No depending on Percy," Candace noted.

"Only to take the line of least resistance," Francine replied. "Now, we can rely on Courtney. No problem there, once you like the sultry primeval type."

Candace did not.

"So, right." Francine charged on. "We're on the road." Forget the old men, she decided, except, of course, for Dudley, who had to get the application through the Grants Committee. "In fact, forget the papers themselves for now," Francine reasoned, as Courtney and Sat came into the room. "Those will shuffle into shape. What we have to nail down at once is the stuff that's going to catch attention, the moves that will attract the money. And it's no point rolling up your eyes as if I'm just being crass. No money; no conference. Keep that in the front of your heads."

"You look as if you need cheering up," Sat said in Candace's ear.

He had the ability to make the most harmless string of words seem loaded with obscene intent. She would have been annoyed, if unattractiveness hadn't rendered his cockiness ludicrous.

"Right," Francine was saying again, as the two men left with their coffee. "Let me see what Master Sandiford'll do for us. Dudley's an old dear, really, once we can get past that dragon, Mackhail."

A strange pair, Sandiford and Mackhail. Some of the younger people entertained themselves by wondering whether Dudley had ever been young, his mind flowing fast and clear, before the innovative ideas dried up and original insight ossified into pedantry. And more unimaginable still, whether Mackhail had ever been young and limber in outlook and bearing. She may well have been striking, if not handsome – however raddled and angular now, braced as if under siege against corrupting forces. She was indomitable, though, the way she positioned herself between Dudley and the faculty.

". . . intellectual rigidity." It was the youngsters who would make a difference as far as the work was concerned, Francine was saying, and she was probably right. Francine went down the list in her head, calling the names out and assessing them as she went along.

Nadine Lashley was one of those Bajan troublemakers, it was true, but she was bright and frenetically hard-working. A little too much of the revivalist Christian for the twenty-first-century stomach, but temporary – and near white, so she was super sensitive about job security and desperate to make herself indispensable. "Of course, she's spiritually conceited, you know – an absolutist." Francine was not sure about Nadine's long-term usefulness to the centre, considering that the young woman was hardly in a position to understand the real concerns of Caribbean persons. "And so inhibited, quite the opposite to Anthea, who is such an advanced thinker. But Nadine will certainly be helpful as far as legwork where the conference is concerned."

Francine counted on Anthea's absolute loyalty and watched her with some affection through the window of the lunch room, crossing from CSSGDS to the Cultural Studies building. Candace's critical expression caught Francine's eye, and she shook her head.

"Yes, Candace. Anthea cultivates the dishevelled look, but you must admit it gives her an air. The aspiring scholar careless of appearances, and all that. No harm in it."

Candace wondered whether the affection was returned; she suspected that Anthea's layer of loyal-student disguised a somewhat chilling detachment from the interests of Francine.

"And Laura Chai?" Candace asked, not quite sure what to make of the temporary instructor, an intense, chain-smoking young poet whose work Francine promoted, "although she is such a repressed person – not at home with her sexuality, if you ask me."

Francine considered for a few moments and then added, "We need every single body we can get, but she's not the type to be satisfied with the mundane stuff alone. She'll do the donkey work, but she'll have to feel there's more to her responsibilities than that. You know what? Let's have her run an open mic."

"What about Nicholas?"

"Who?" Francine seemed slow on the uptake for someone so loud in her opposition to homophobia.

"Nicholas Sylvester." Candace figured she must have imagined the hesitation.

"Should we be careful?" Francine pondered it. "Insults from the unenlightened, don't you know? I can't think why I always have this impulse to protect him, poor fellow."

And hopefully from some of Francine's own friends, Candace thought, offering only a slight nod. Courtney and Sat delighted in baiting Nicholas – mainly, she thought, to flaunt their own rampant sexuality.

"Now Percy simply can't handle responsibility," Francine continued, and Candace could only agree. In a smooth shift from the quietly competent Nicholas, Francine confirmed that Percy Stone was not to be entrusted with any essential task. Percy would promise and had the capability, but more often than not he would never deliver. His conversation was like that too, Candace reflected, talk that veered and pitched and veered again. "Like a battimamzelle," Candace had remarked a few days before in a light-hearted characterization of staff discourse styles. "The Trini name for a dragonfly," she added in explanation.

"Batty what?" Courtney had grinned. "No, I thought this was Percy. You mean we were talking about Nickers?"

"Off to class." Candace snatched up her files. The two men were routinely and blatantly offensive, as if they knew themselves to be a protected species.

Perhaps they were. It was common knowledge that complaints about Courtney's behaviour at a conference in Washington had reached the

Provost. Courtney had attended without paying for activities that were billed separately from the regular conference fee. He had even incurred costs for drinks and voiced a raucous protest when a conference organizer discretely slipped him the bill. The Provost, like anyone else, had seen Courtney in action at ITS events. Staff were never expected to pay for drinks at these functions – alcoholic drinks were either served, or they were not – but staff were expected to attend only functions to which they were invited. Courtney drifted into any assembly he pleased and found the bar at once.

Sat, on the other hand, was quieter, more inveigling. Yet of him there were more worrying stories that must have reached his Provost – student whispers that if you were nice to Sat, he might hint upcoming test questions. Students in the final-year class confided to Marion that Sat said being nice to him was an investment in one's future: when he was CSSGDS Fellow, teaching assistantships for graduates would be practically within his gift. The Provost wouldn't object. Sat had smiled slyly. Earl Rider couldn't afford to insist on protocol, when his own daughter had been appointed without the subcommittee being called.

When the snippets came back to Candace's ears, she was furious, but Francine regarded none of the stories as any obstacle to collaboration with Sat. "Nonsense." She laughed. "Staff appointments are a free-for-all, anyway. What procedures are there to follow, and who would put them in place, just so we could tie ourselves up?" She patted Candace's cheek. "As for you, you have to lighten up, my dear. Did you know that the fellows have nicknamed your office the Priory? Listen. Men are the most prolific of gossip-mongers; but if they talk, if they make a little fun, and it goes a bit far – they are men. Nobody cares."

Candace cared. Care tightened her forehead and thickened inside her, slowing breath and weighing down her limbs.

Now, as she made her way back along Old Hope Road after a UWI class on writing process analyses, she tried to fasten her thoughts on Randall.

"How long has this gone on?" Randall had asked, years ago during one of her milder invasions by the fog. On the way home from a calypso tent, he had discovered that his belief that he could cheer Candace up was a simplistic one; achieving this required more than consistent good nature on his part, or an act of will on hers. So he reached deeper – for whatever triggered her reaction, and for some story submerged under their talk, even beneath memory – far, far down where words had never penetrated.

The fog had floated in long ago, but she was not born with it, she told him, surprising herself by acknowledging it at all. Like any child, she had felt sad from time to time. Then something had changed: it began to cling. At first it came with trivial disappointments – an outing to Dunn's River cancelled, or a test result driven down by careless reading of the question paper. Then, one Friday evening when her father's meeting had run late, she waited with her mother outside the gates of the zoo, while Hope Gardens emptied of its visitors. The dusk rushed down during the seemingly endless trek to the gate along a deserted road, and the bushes crouched gloomy and threatening. An approaching car sounded promising, until her mother's body tensed beside hers against the possibility of it being wrong, very wrong, and darkness shrouded them in those last terrible minutes to the gate.

Worst of all, her father, furious about leaving work to collect them eight minutes from his office and not finding them where they were supposed to be, vented his contempt for her mother's ineptitude, while her mother explained, excused, placated. With so much on his mind, he berated them, they had him running around on a weekday to fetch them, then having to look for them? What would his position have been, if anything had happened on the road? What would people have said but that he had forgotten the two of them there? The dusk that had seeped inside of Candace along the way began thickening into gloom and adhered to her brain. And after a while, as things went better, as she did well in school, it would recede. But it stayed floating there, until something set it off again, drawing together and forcing its way forward, a dark tide in her head. She had never told anyone but Randall.

"How do we make it go away for good?" he asked.

It sounded so easy that she smiled, quoting the raven in the corner of her mind, "Nevermore."

And now, in case longing set it off again, she pressed Randall from her thoughts, even though he was everything her father was not.

At nights, though, small trials warped into encroaching shadow, and when she felt it circling, loitering between her thoughts to obscure the scripts she was trying to mark for her UWI class, she e-mailed Randall. "Fog again. Almost afraid to lie down, lest I'm too crushed to get back up. I dread the night."

He telephoned right away. "You need something for it. I want you to see someone, a doctor."

"I need to take charge of my mind; I must be strong enough."

"No," he said. "You survive because you're strong, but you'd have taken charge long ago if it were that straightforward. There must be medication."

"Good Lord. A cycle of popping pills?" She had a thought and laughed. Mercifully, laughter could penetrate the fog, before it became too thick. "Watch yourself with your unsettling advice, or I'll report you to the ASO."

"What the hell is that?"

"One of our campus societies. Have you forgotten the Association of Significant Others?"

"So I can take it that I'm an SO?"

Her voice turned gruff. "Skype you tomorrow."

"Wait. You're on the verge of something more unpleasant than medication. See someone."

He spoke in the old matter-of-fact way that conveyed a sense of an ear turned without an eye, as if he were sparing her direct scrutiny. It came back to her, his ladling a mixture onto a hot pan while dropping offhand comments amid the hiss of salt-fish fritters crisping. Talking to him held at bay sensations that were threatening but had not yet closed in.

That night, she fell off to sleep trying to work out how many years it had been since she had fritters.

⇀⁄ι⇃⤙

She woke in a frame of mind to face a nine-thirty planning meeting for the conference – which was just as well, because the other members of the committee put forward a request they had obviously agreed on in advance. The funding application must go through the required channels, they said, but they could smooth the way by interesting the Provost in advance of the Grants Committee meeting. Everyone knew the Provost decided such matters in advance of the meeting anyway, if indeed he convened one. Candace shrugged. Let them lobby if they liked.

Then it was carried, almost unanimously, that Candace would be the one to approach the Provost.

"I have the budget right here," Percy Stone said, startling her into awareness of his presence, into instant realization that he had been added to the committee, not for any work he might conceivably do but to swell the numbers of people who agreed with Francine.

Disorientated by the impossible situation into which she was being bundled, she stared at Percy and the pencil he wore behind his ear (no one had ever seen him use it), like an oldtime grocer's boy.

"It would be utterly improper." She managed to keep her voice down.

"How so?" Francine, at her most urbane.

"Ent you say the two of you not close?" Sat asked.

"Practically strangers," Courtney chimed in helpfully. "The two of you land up here by chance, and you have no relationship." A wolfish grin.

"If he *does* harbour some fatherly feeling for you, Candace, as he must, after all, this might bring it out. So much the better for the application and perhaps for both of you." Francine took a moment to contemplate Candace with concern. "This might build something. Don't you think?" She smiled softly, almost misty-eyed.

"There is no connection between the Provost and me that can possibly benefit you. Even if this doesn't turn him against the application – which it might – my getting involved in a financial request will look, will look . . ."

"But to whom? Think. Either you care deeply about his attitude to you, or you don't."

"I don't. I mean, I don't care how it will look to him."

"Then to whom? Not the staff, not us. We're sending you. You won't support us in seeking funding for this crucial project of the centre?"

The pointlessness. One more opportunity for her father to deride her; then it would be over. They would have only themselves to blame.

"Why don't I see if he's free now?" Candace shoved a copy of the budget into her case.

⌐≻⏜≺

He made a point of having her sit in the waiting room for forty minutes. It was to show he could, to get her edgy, so he could fluster her once she got into his presence. Ms La Mar, the lush assistant in the outer office, showed her in and seated her with meticulous care. Candace braced herself as he ran his eye over the budget. Then he flicked a glance at the hard line of her mouth and rigid set of her shoulders.

"They cornered you, eh?" He smirked and bent again over the document. "I'm noting on the proposal that it must go by a proper route, through the Master of Studies to the Grants Committee." Relief washed cold sweat down her spine. "Mind you, I'm not sure when I'll find time to convene a meeting. I may have to deal with it administratively and copy to the committee for its next meeting, for noting. Actually, I'm sympathetic to a bit of a splash at this time." Now she froze. "We always need some good press, especially with the accreditation exercise coming up. In fact, I'm inclined to be rather generous."

He was almost purring. "I'll note that subject to the correct procedure being followed, this has my full support. I'll call the PM myself about Vale Royal for the welcoming reception, and – I tell you what – let me give a little dinner after the finale. We must find money for musical entertainment. No clear line item here, of course, because you can never get definite information from . . ." He swung back to her. "Isn't it always the way? Bloody artists and their cohorts so incompetent when it comes to money? Carrying on in song and dance and paint and print with their iconoclastic attitudes to officialdom while trying to milk the system for whatever they can get. Well. Off you go, and tell your colleagues the good news."

She was bereft of words, undone. He had compromised her by responding with a generosity no one would have expected, had anyone else approached him. No choice but to return to the centre, where the meeting was unfinished but had broken for coffee.

There, as the group crowded around, she delivered her news stiffly.

"Good God! Committed himself in writing. And giving a dinner? At The Habitat?" Courtney stared at her. "What a beloved little daughter you've turned out to be, after all. We must get to know you better."

"Much better," Sat agreed fervently.

"I knew you'd be marvellous." Francine flung an arm around her shoulders and turned a triumphant face to the group. "Didn't I tell you?" She turned back to Candace. "And to think you said you weren't close. You sly thing." Francine hugged her again.

Candace was mortified. Her embarrassment weighed her down into the thick of the fog. Work was her only way up: analysis of verb phrases for the role of transitives in conveying power distribution. A chat group for CuSt240.

The students of her CuSt240 class varied in competence, underqualified or merely underprivileged – youngsters whom life had cast aside just before their final school examinations, scrabbling for a toehold on a steep, slick slope. For their sakes, Candace objected to cancelling class so as to attend meetings for conference organization, although Sat insisted that students were adults and, given appropriate readings, could very well catch up. For once, Francine objected that he was cold-blooded. "Yes, you can give them work to read, but at least drop that topic from the exam. Good Lord, Sat. They're adults, yes, but youngsters. People's children, man."

How far, Candace wondered, was the management of ITS aware of this dizzying topography of sinkholes and shallows? The Provost, as a real academic, must surely know. Candace had registered, without him ever telling her, each stage of her father's ascent from temporary to permanent positions, through the contracts and crossings of merit bars, the trauma of securing tenure, and then the arduous climb to Senior Lecturer. She had picked up details in his bitter exchanges with her mother and irate telephone conversations with colleagues. His appointment to a Chair in Texas came shortly before her mother's death, and Candace could not recall how she had heard of that last elevation. But the long shining track of his scholarship was indelibly imprinted on her mind.

Now it was all summarized in *ITS Newstime* in bold font, under the handsome face above "Message from the Provost". Those achievements at least were genuine. But it had been a protracted day of increasing unease about how many of her colleagues might now regard her as a direct conduit to the Provost's ear. Waylaying her on her way from the building that evening, Dr Curtis Martin had congratulated her on being Professor Rider's daughter. He explained he had not realized it before. He unburdened himself of this earnestly, almost plaintively, as one clearing himself of blame since the thing had been kept from him. He had noticed Candace at once, though, he assured her, and – now that he had sent off the paper that had tied him up earlier in the semester – perhaps they could make up for lost time. Did Candace like Italian food?

Candace faintly recalled hearing something about Martin never paying conference dues and chuckled inwardly at the idea that he might mean to stick her with the bill. She reined in her amusement so as to thank him bleakly and mumble an excuse before giving him the slip. But as she walked off, she found herself wondering what she actually knew of him. Perhaps she had been hasty. Uncharitable. So forbidding, she chided herself. So not warm. So likely to spend her life alone.

At the entrance to the car park, Marion Bailey-Brown greeted her. "You look done in, girl? Who could blame you for leaving a little early?"

Well, not Marion, when she was just coming in. But Candace responded pleasantly to what was kindly meant, for everyone knew time spent in actual teaching was practically negligible in contrast to demands outside of classtime. Even without extra teaching at UWI, class preparation and marking alone could have gobbled up Candace's week, leaving little time for the research on which careers rose or fell.

"Got to grab a shower and get back for my six-to-eight," Candace said. "AC's off in the water wing."

"Oh no. After alternately freezing over and flooding all week? Gone?"

"Hell – reconvened from Náströnd to the Inferno. But this evening I'll pull those drapes and open whatever windows they've been hiding on the side to the sea."

Under the sign that said, "The Lifestyle Society Cares about *Your* Environment", Marion took Candace's hand with the air of one braced to deliver bad news. "The windows don't open, girl." She nodded at Candace's patent dismay. "Like, they construct these places for air conditioning? Those windows are just for effect." She squeezed and released Candace's hand. "Going to give my two-to-four and get out. I was to have tackled those files piled on my desk, but I guess the students are already waiting?" She waved distractedly and strolled off, while Candace fumbled in her purse for car keys.

The soft trembling sentences and febrile sensibilities of Marion Bailey-Brown tended to unnerve her. Candace would have been terrified to bare her uncertainties in the way that Marion shared, even flaunted hers, but Marion would confess mournfully that she was indecisive, that she procrastinated and dithered. Even a little thing like her always being late for appointments showed that, didn't it? Marion would turn her palms up apologetically.

Marion came habitually late for class and meetings, loitering over scripts or correspondence. Inevitably she turned up, just as she ultimately delivered work so sound as to make the delay more frustrating. "Me woulda do the frigging paper different if me did get the comment-dem before me done write," one student had complained bitterly to another in Candace's hearing. "Bailey-Brown say fe consult her, and me send the plan, but me never get nothing back until the day before the something due. Is now I must re-write i' when exam pon me. You see why student a foreign pick up gun go a school and mow down teacher? You know why it don't happen here? Is good Jamaica people good."

Everyone knew Marion's little shortcomings. When the Cultural Studies secretary requested staff to clear uncollected scripts, these were almost all Professor Bailey-Brown's – students having no interest in feedback on a course already done and examined. Gillian dispatched group reminders rather than singling out Professor Bailey-Brown, a kind soul who brought her cookies on Administrative Professionals' Day and forwarded alerts on new books or films about the Royals.

"No one's perfect," Francine would say wisely. "Marion's a good sort. You pin her down and get her talking, then you take it all down, and it's gold. Only, don't send her off promising to write you anything or send in an abstract by weekend. Hold on: epiphany. We'll have her moderate the panel on material culture." Then, as an afterthought, "And forget an abstract. If she turns up with a paper to present, we squeeze her in."

The mystery was how Marion had published so much. No one doubted the genuineness of her vitae, but the question was how she had pushed work out or responded promptly enough to publishers. Not that it mattered now. At her stage of life, ITS provided a comfortable environment for someone of Marion's leisurely style. She had a respectable profile and a secure pension supplemented by ITS's handsome stipend. Like Sonja, she described the ITS contract as iffy but as making no difference in her case.

"Iffy?" Candace repeated, making a mental pledge to cling to her UWI hours, whatever crap Marcus dished out.

"Don't notice them." Francine flipped dismissive fingers. "The system here is so much more nurturing, so much freer that UWI and UM and the rest." Francine pointed out that if those places were going to survive, they would have to overcome their outdated notions about the bases for academic advancement. "This whole publish or perish thing that leads to student neglect and to an endless number of worthless papers being churned out instead of good solid team studies like they do in Tropical Sciences – all that simply has to go. It's been sucking the blood out of the older institutions for decades, and we just have to put a stake through its heart. You draw your students into your research, and your CV takes care of itself. Collaborative research" – Francine thumped her right fist on her left palm – "and on topics relevant to the community. That's how you make a difference."

They seemed agreed on that, Francine, Courtney and Sat. When the conference had come off, and the papers were out, they were going after the system itself, Francine said, going for academic freedom at the most personal level and a shift in balance to student learning.

Candace's minute observation took in the bemused tilt of Sonja's head as well as the thrust of Francine's neck and set of her shoulders. Francine was a powerhouse – solid, determined, impossible to deflect from whatever purpose drove her at the time. Francine Forbes-Garcia had been on contract at a university in Florida (some said a minor college, but she always referred to it as a university), and she had taken leave from it for one year at Mona to replace a member of Literatures in English on sabbatical. Francine had been intent on returning to Jamaica, where her mother was bedridden, so here was her chance to bewitch the faculty. But blood was not to be got out of stone, and when UWI had no post for her, she had allowed herself to be wooed by ITS with an offer of tenure as Senior Lecturer. There must also have been at least some delicate implicature about a Chair. Francine recalled it as an overt promise.

Francine had presence – not the unselfconscious resonance of Sonja but something more deliberate, cultivated. In any case, she was not a figure to be overlooked, tall and full-bodied with bright appraising eyes. But they were eyes that conveyed hurt, and together with a somewhat dissatisfied set of her mouth, they gave her a wronged expression, while a determined jaw signalled that the wrong would not soon be forgiven. Not enough to put off anyone. She was handsome, and decidedly elegant in business suits of dramatic cut and a hairstyle silkily bouffant. Nevertheless, her direct, unflinching gaze conveyed that though there were people who disliked her – she knew that – and would try to prevent her advancement for no other reason but malice, she was a match for any of them.

Francine recognized but dismissed with contempt somewhat older heads, like Barham. "Living in the past," she pronounced. "You know the computer in his office has never been turned on? And now it will all be worse, when Dudley goes and Dexter replaces him, if they bring in someone from outside to head our centre. In confidence, Candace, I'll tell you that people have spoken to me about putting myself up as Fellow, when the time comes, but I don't know. I'd rather immerse myself in my research, but I'm torn – I mean, we just can't allow ourselves to be cursed with some amateur at the helm." She leaned closer. "And then you know if Courtney or Sat gets to be CSSGDS Fellow, we'll work well together, and with two of us on the Committee of Fellows, I think our funding requirements will be in the bag for several years to come."

"What about all the talk? About those guys and their students?" Candace spoke quietly too. "Are they okay for positions like that?"

"Candace, listen. You can*not* pay attention to every malicious rumour. And don't worry – the students are well able to take care of themselves. Adults, remember? What it is? You been listening to Mackhail?"

It was true Candace turned a fascinated ear to the Administrative Assistant who guarded Dudley, when she unfolded her caustic view of all that lay in store for an institution that condoned Sin even briefly and even to facilitate accreditation. Candace had heard Francine attempting to reason with her. "One has to be practical, after all, Ms Mackhail. No one's perfect, and we all know how a man is going to weigh another man's personal weaknesses against the bigger criteria in advancing his career."

"That's as it may be, Dr Forbes-Garcia," Ms Mackhail had responded icily. "But if he's not held accountable in one world, he will be in Another." And even Francine could see no fruitful way of pursuing her point.

As always, the sea lapped and churned when Candace walked out of the building to the car park, but on windy nights like this, after a late class, the ghosts of the Middle Passage whispered to each other and to her almost as if she were one of them. Sometimes they broke away singing, *We don't give a damn, we done dead aready.* Sometimes they gurgled more politely, in the rhythms of Eddie Baugh's poem.

Chapter 6

The Project

Togidres han thise thre hir trouthes plight
To lyve and dyen ech of hem for oother
As though he were his owene ybore brother.

Right. Time to lobby." Francine frowned over her notes. "Thanks to Candace, the Provost bought the conference, but now there's the whole project. We have to check who's on the Grants Committee and nail support."

"Won't the Master see it through?" Candace asked. "Or what if the application were broken down? Would we stand a better chance of getting funds for separate, smaller amounts?"

Francine smiled tolerantly. "You'll get accustomed," she said. "The scientists get all that money because they ask for it – a request big enough for people to take seriously." Francine's eyes narrowed, peering through the weeks ahead. "If we play this right, we'll get digital cameras and stuff for the centre – in the name of fieldwork, don't you know? And money for research assistance. Dexter loves us for that, so that's the Fellow in our corner all the way." Francine thought some more. "But you know what? Candace, you're right: I'll go see the Master. Poor Dudley is so pressed right now, he'll probably promise anything just to be left in peace."

"Lots of luck." What else to say? Francine craved enthusiasm over the project but clutched it tightly to her and the rest of those named on the title page.

The study attracted Candace but gave off bewildering vibrations at every approach. Only a week before, Nicholas had remarked admiringly on the title. "'Unstable Skins'? What does it cover?"

But Francine was tired. She said this thing was just consuming her, and she didn't feel she could spare another word or thought on it that day. Candace could tell him about it if she liked.

"Well." Candace felt her way. "I don't know that much, though the potential seems limitless. I suppose Unstable Skins explores conceptual delimitations of body and self. I haven't seen much on the specifics. Oral literature people might follow up myth and folktale – like ole haig or soucouyant. Others might go after metaphor in the idiom of different territories ("the first skin on you body, not yours" – that sort of thing). But most obviously, I guess it will focus on social constructs of ethnicity – and gender issues like penetration . . ."

". . . and why not economic exploitation, as in the *skin trade*?" Nicholas broke in. "Fascinating possibilities, even in literary characterization."

"Now Chariandy's *Soucouyant* demonizes old age." Francine suddenly regained her strength. "Or at least strips it of humanity."

"No, no." Led away from the project, Nicholas plunged into issues of the book. "It laments that burning away of . . ."

"But it was not *about* the old woman," Francine objected. "It was that cyclical thing: the young rejecting the old as Other, lose themselves and . . ."

Their voices faded to background noise, blocked, through Candace's inattention, from signifying anything – for all the world as if she were working out a conundrum with her back to a menagerie. The project itself so gripped Candace that her eyes remained on the file Francine was sliding silently, smoothly into her case, locking them out. So despite warm words of encouragement and generosity, Unstable Skins was never to include Candace. She must devise her own research base.

Yet how to do that without seeming to challenge someone who had openly set herself up as confidante and mentor? As the road before Candace buckled, a lull in the discussion brought her back to it; the talk had wilted as

Courtney came in sight through the louvres, making his way towards the door.

"By the pricking of my thumbs . . ." Nicholas murmured, picking up papers and coffee mug for an exit.

"He better keep it in his thumbs too," Courtney proclaimed, before the door swung in. "Restrain those burgeoning ambitions and all that." He rounded on Francine in time to chorus with her, singsong, "Really, Courtney. How can you be so backward." Then he sniggered.

"You really are Stone Age," she began, then halted. "Oh, be quiet. Quiet." For all her fervent affirmative action, Francine was grinning widely. "Such a sin. And that young man is so good-natured. A little out of his depth – and what can one do for him without one's motives being questioned? The thing is these people are so sensitive."

"You sent in the application for the money?" Courtney zeroed in on what mattered to him. "Can we rely on Dexter?"

"He's a bit slippery," Francine confided, with the air of one giving voice to an original thought. "But there's stuff in it for him too, you know."

It had long dawned on Candace that members of the centre operated on self-interest in a vacuum of administrative apparatus that enabled anarchic funding arrangements. If only she had Randall's gift for functioning on his own terms, not only unsoiled but unfazed by whatever he passed through. Or Sonja's unruffled balance above the conniving and turbulence that churned beneath her notice, as she intersected chains of events and set off entirely new ripples. Yet this air of detachment dissipated abruptly at Francine's retelling of how Candace had won support from the Provost.

Sonja drew Candace out of the room, into the passage. "Wait," Sonja exclaimed. "*His* daughter? Rider's? You don't mean you are Patrice Clarke's child? I thought she said the name was Sheena. No, you and I would never have met, but Patrice and I were in school together in Tobago – Buccoo R.C. – and used to get into all kinds of mischief."

Candace searched her imagination for her mother as she might have been before all the mischief was wrung out of her.

"When I heard she had got married, I was already in London," Sonja said.

Verging on the topic of Patrice's marriage, the reminiscences petered out. Sonja tossed a sad sort of smile at the deep past. "She was my dearest friend," she said. She shot a glance back at Candace, sudden, penetrating. "What brought you *here*?" Her gift for unanswerable questions.

"Needed a job," Candace mumbled, as they made their way in the direction of the conference room for the Master's meeting.

"You never thought of a good secondary school? As a start?"

"Well, but there was always something on campus, however small: part-time hours, short assistantship, eventually the occasional temporary replacement for someone on leave. And now it's been so long . . ."

". . . that you're hooked. It's the life you want? Academia?"

"I suppose this is only the edge of it."

"One can't let go," Sonja sighed, as if remembering. "But what is *this* really the edge of?"

Candace said nothing. She slipped into a chair in the meeting room, her mind whirling. Hell of a thing, irony.

She had quarrelled with Randall six years ago for clambering over the horizon of social relevance in choosing his PhD topic: "Leman – The Politics of Sacred-Profane Passion in English Medieval Lyrics". "Dumping the Caribbean," Candace had said. She had not added, *and me with it*. "What new insights can you offer *them*? And not even grounding it in anything connected with yourself, current or local."

"Such as?" Nothing sarcastic in his tone. Only curiosity.

"How would I know? Oral argumentation in developing societies: flytting and kas-kas. Or something."

He considered. "No. It would take a discourse turn I'm not up to. If I had a grounding in semantics – perhaps. If I'd done the double major like you, instead of just a minor in linguistics, I might have gone on in semantics." So there he was in London, clinging to the fringe of his department, writing verse at night and muttering about a novel, while applying for posts in traditional literature, as a medievalist, as a generalist, asked at interview after interview whether he couldn't teach a little Naipaul or Walcott.

Little by little, she had adjusted her gaze at the world he was exploring, and when she peered through his eyes, it was distant yet somehow parallel to theirs. "How can that be?"

His quick intake of breath at her question went along with the fleeting, arrested expression, as if she had touched a special place in his innermost mind.

"That is exactly what I want to know," he answered, in a tone that resonated so deeply, she began to listen for that timbre every time his voice came through the microphone and to feel cheated when it was not there.

At least *he* had interviews. She, on the other hand, had let go of one margin to clutch at another – an offshore campus of an institution no one had ever heard off. Nice conference room panelled in mahoe, but what the hell?

Cutting across these soul-searchings, the Master called his meeting to order, but little impacted on Candace before the end, when an item came up under Any Other Business and set the faculty grappling with a directive from the Provost that scolded about bad press. An environmental group called PROTEC (whatever that stood for) had complained about behaviour on CWiLS field trips, goings-on that were potentially damaging to the environment. Mostly, PROTEC identified outings that involved too many beers and turned into rowdy carousing that disturbed avian nesting patterns. But a stranger accusation nudged Candace from silence.

"Hunting? On field trip? But, Master Sandiford, isn't CWiLS a con-servation group . . .?"

"Ah. Yes. But not infrequently, members take friends of incompatible outlook or values, and I don't think I'm going too far in revealing that so-far-unidentifiable persons on these outings have (perhaps not entirely by chance) encountered crocodile eggs and been unable to resist gathering them – whether for sale or personal use, one can't say." Personal use? Dudley was obviously being delicate, and his manner forestalled further questions, so Candace saved them for Francine. Percy Stone was there too, staring in equal bewilderment, but Francine waved him aside impatiently.

"No, he's not looking for answers, child, he's just right up there in the ether. But the crocodile business? Oh, you must have heard about the much-bruited properties of croc eggs, Candace." Francine's voice was clearly audible from the door, as Sat sauntered in.

"You don't need *that*." He raked Candace with a stare that was bold yet crafty. "You just need someone who know he business."

"The letter from PROTEC," Francine explained, quelling Sat with a glance, "came up under AOB?" Then she turned back to Candace, who was already on her way from the room.

"Got the picture," Candace assured them. "Sorry I asked."

She forgot it all, as Monday evening kicked in – the traffic to UWI, the excuses for late submission of scripts, the labour of dragging students towards logical organization and academic register. Only later did she recall the exchange and go online, tracing not only the benefits of crocodile eggs to the libido, but menus for preparation and anecdotes about successful use. "Me did have was to sleep pon me back for a week," bragged one interviewee.

In a few days, it appeared that someone may have been overindulging. A headline about sexual promiscuity in an ITS centre broke first in the *Star* and then rippled into briefer columns in the inner pages of the *Jamaica Observer* and the *Gleaner*. In the more restrained papers, "a source" had reported improprieties regarding staff and student relationships. Two days later, the CSSGDS's secretary, Monique, complained that a journalist had called to ask for her thoughts and later waylaid her and the Master's Administrative Assistant on their way from the car park. In response to a direct question of what position the institute should adopt regarding the report, AA Mackhail had responded (with the air of one stating the obvious) that the righteous would reject fellowship with the unfruitful works of darkness and reprove them.

In the coffee room, the atmosphere was lighter. "Like the fellows not sticking to omelette, man." Courtney jabbed an elbow at Sat's ribs. "You don't see PROTEC say they hunting and thing?"

"Must be two good croc tail they ketch in a soup, you see them there," Sat reflected. "Tail is a hell of a ting," he added, eyeing Candace soulfully.

Francine intervened swiftly to cajole Sat into easing up. "If Candace is bashful, you must give her time. No, really, my dear, if you press her, you'll just drive her off. Listen, you guys are liberated: let the girls chase you. Strong and blasé, that's it. Courtney, you tell him."

But Courtney was sulking, because no one would go with him to some body-building contest at Fort Clarence, so he had nothing to say.

Francine took up the proposal. "We have the students in place, but we must finesse those graduate course descriptions and package the programme attractively. Provost is gung-ho about the accreditation exercise, so we press his graduate programme buttons."

But Courtney's attention had flitted again. He and Sat were griping about the need for teaching assistants to relieve them of marking. Had their interest in the project wavered?

"You know what?" Francine's voice sang out insistently. "We must do lunch, fellows, and talk all these things over. I mean work is work, but we're all *friends*." She became expansive, her tone rejoicing. "Like Derek says: *Give wine, give bread*."

Much as Candace loved that poem, she could conceive of no advice Derek Walcott might want to offer about securing one's foothold in academia without a healthy research agenda. The fast track to tenure that Morgan Shade had fluttered in front of her – not to mention her lingering hope of decamping to UWI, should a post there magically materialize – required evidence of research. She had begun charting a project but had faltered, haunted by the spectre of pure rage that might be unleashed if she betrayed wavering commitment to Unstable Skins. Nevertheless, at around two in the morning, when the darkness pressed in on her, something beckoned, irresistible. Flirted almost. She clambered out of the doldrums to flood the house with light and pound furiously on her laptop, until the sun slanted in on the screen, and she had to get up and yank at the curtains.

Print. Print it out before she found time to think about the position Francine might take, after a congratulatory few words and smiles, regarding Candace's declaration of scholarly independence. Both the thrust of the project Candace was proposing as well as her own impudence prompted the title: "Forbidden Words". Submit the proposal with its modest request for funding straight to the Master but copy it to Danraj, for the upcoming centre meeting, in case of some vague protocol regarding support from her peers – as a courtesy. For noting.

The Forbidden Words project had the potential to ripple through multiple topics. It could address linguistic taboos in the Caribbean regarding race and gender, or draw in intersecting disciplines, like literature and medicine, in relation to community crises. AIDS leapt to mind, feeding as it did off perceptions of sexuality and of masculinities in particular – most of all feeding off silence. Forbidden Words might probe beliefs that inhibited expression, interrogate dogma or dismantle time-worn fixations through discourses of empowerment. It toyed with her mind, whirling it giddily over the papers she could produce, luring her into a dream of assembling a research group with critical mass. Rope in a contingent from UWI? Fat chance. She ran her mind over the linguists and then launched off to scholars in Cultural Studies. But why would they notice her?

Then it swept over her again, the craving. Forbidden Words opened up a whole dimension for analysis of disobedient discourse, like Jamaican kas-kas and Trinidad robber talk, as well as offensive signals like suckteet (steups, the Trinis called it). Or what about behavioural and non-verbal expressions: cut-eye, skirt lifting – that sort of thing. The challenge was pinning down topics narrow enough to cut deep. Hold on. Literary applications taunted her – hedging in Caribbean narrative, unreliable narration. But something more? Teasing from the shadows. Something in institutional dialogue, but nebulous. When she tried to stare directly, it retreated shyly, and then as she looked away, it beckoned.

She cast her thoughts elsewhere, over the range of possibilities, and her mind swam. The thing was limitless. Social applications, cultural dimensions, critical value. Linguistic operations and discursive strategies. It hooked her obsessions. Forbidden Words. It was provocative, it was seductive, it set her alight.

Candace circulated hard copies of the project proposal the evening before the meeting and left campus at once. She turned off her phone and huddled over her two stacks of scripts, UWI and ITS, and then she shoved them aside. She was too high, too edgy.

Next morning she drove around Portmore to avoid arriving early in a quiet room, where she might be tackled, urged to withdraw the project and goaded into some disastrous utterance. The car rattled over the scrubbing-board road, some of it on reclaimed land not properly settled, sunken areas making the top uneven. In other places, it was an unfinished surface that overlay good hard limestone. Then the traffic closed in abruptly. She had barely pulled into the car park, when one of the few Trinidadian students waylaid her. In accounting for a late assignment, the young woman omitted no revolting detail of the stomach disorder that followed on her bout of chikungunya. When she got to how her stomach *did operate*, Candace scribbled her mobile number and thrust it forward, so as to disentangle herself. And she hurried inside.

Students. They sparked or nettled you, or reminded you why you were born, or made you wonder why you had been. Staff goaded or reassured you. Some of them freaked you out, and some were what you wanted to be. Then there were some who postured on their own distant planet or stepped down from it, secure in the belief that you were waiting to genuflect when they did. But students – never two of a kind.

She walked into a full room, where Dexter had pounced on her paper as yet more evidence of research in the centre under his stewardship, and he hauled it up higher on the agenda.

Excited suggestions raised the noise level of the meeting to painful proportions, before subsiding to orderly comments.

"What I like," Sonja reflected, "is that the aims and objectives are clear and distinct. Have to be narrowed, of course. Right now it's all over the place. But I can see what the project is for and what the outcomes are likely to be. Best of all, I can see how they are to be achieved. The methodology is elegantly set forth."

Francine was livid, but with her usual brilliance at character demolition at once began lauding the attractive features of the project, while she betrayed a trace of sadness at whatever had motivated its author to hold back these suggestions from the officially established project of the centre, to which she believed all had expressed their loyalty. She hoped it would not deflect the graduate student cohort who had committed themselves to Unstable Skins (committed themselves as young aspiring professionals, Mr Chairman).

Under her baleful gaze, the student representatives at the meeting hastened their reassurance. Except, one of them said, so tentatively that her voice was almost inaudible, it had occurred to her that the two projects might usefully complement each other. But she stood no chance, for Anthea charged in with the sweeping conclusion that this new proposal was entirely derivative, a predictable path of enquiry shooting off from the original and not a viable independent investigation at all.

So the likelihood of research assistance for Forbidden Words withered at the root, what with the dependence of so many graduate students on Francine for supervision, or, in the all-too-probable future, as Francine moved up in the administration, for opportunities in part-time tutoring.

The truth was that although she habitually devolved much of her work on graduate assistants – so they sulked and blasphemed accordingly and referred to her as ole haig – they supported her every whim. Often they went unpaid, because, unless one was beforehand with such arrangements, funding for students to assist staff did not find its way into the budget. But the same students were painfully aware of the shortage of paid part-time work to be had and of Dr Forbes-Garcia's pivotal role in distributing it and, in the first place, even inventing it. So they clustered around her like so many chicks evading inclement weather.

On her own, Candace could still make something of her project; she saw that. She worked best alone, intensely organized and silent. Boring too, she supposed, with her flair for cataloguing facts and retrieving them years later; unusual in summoning exactly the ones required in each instance and networking them in new patterns of thought. But she knew she did not shine in a group; she was quick-witted but too cautious for scintillating repartee, too disinclined to reveal herself. She knew Francine described her as repressed and was probably right.

Well, now that the balance of goodwill and hostility in the centre had shifted, bracing advice and positive criticism were no longer all that must be expected from Francine, who was likely enough to be Fellow in the next dispensation. The whirl of observation and reflection prompted as few words as possible.

"We just have somewhat different research interests, Francine." Candace tried to keep her voice as conciliating as she could.

"Well, clearly. And that's all right – depending, of course, on what one means by *interests*. The individual naturally seeks self-satisfaction, the right to follow her own particular academic *interest* and to further self-development. And you're young, a beginner as far as scholarship is concerned, so that's natural."

Words, Candace reflected. Golden and poisonous as alamanda, slicing like razor grass.

"Forgive me, Chairman," Francine continued, "but there's a crucial philosophical issue here. Those of us who actually are scholars recognize a duty to the larger issues: the needs of the community, the requirements of the discipline and its interplay with other disciplines (we cannot condone tunnel vision here) and, also, the profile of our institution itself. I suppose I want to address these more far-reaching issues and bring together like-minded colleagues in the endeavour. It may be a little sentimental of me, but these are my *interests*."

When Candace opened her mouth, Francine held up a forbidding palm.

"If I may, Chairman, a minute more. I think as a senior staff member, I have earned the right to complete a thought? Thank you, Chair. Yes, I just want to add that my ultimate concern (beyond my own enjoyment of indulging in the reading of verse and fiction) is – look, I have a goal. I want to dispense with all this miasma of second-ratedness that is hamstringing our academic community at ITS. Or we're never going to compete with other institutions around here, let alone abroad, and we won't do it without single-minded mutual support. Scholarly collaboration, Chair. The success of this centre's existing project is already in evidence: one need only glance at the list of names involved." She read out a few from the provisional programme of papers to be presented, including Sonja's. "Chair, stack this against individual *interest*. I commend Dr Clarke for . . ." (here she paused to visibly search her mind) ". . . for being true to herself and producing a fascinating document, and I thank you for your patience and unfailing support." She tucked away her list of participants, with a flourish.

"I am become a name." Sonja emitted a histrionic sigh, setting off an uneasy chuckle of relief.

Then a lull fell, as the Chair turned from the gathering to scrutinize a message Ms Mackhail had brought in, and Candace's mind roamed.

Sonja, now. Sonja offered some distraction from confrontation, but even she had already found herself in Francine's displeasure, ostensibly because she had again forgotten to return two books Francine had pressed on her. And it was very true that Sonja forgot such things habitually, just as she could never quite recall to whom she had lent her own books and was always enquiring for them vaguely – sometimes even a little uncertain which books, precisely, had gone missing. Trifling – if only Francine had found herself able to depend on Sonja's unquestioning support, whatever the issue. As it was . . . "Perhaps," Francine had recently remarked in a voice sugared with sympathetic understanding, "she's just getting to that point."

But Sonja basked unaware of belittling excuses for her, and the consuming envy from which they oozed. "I probably need to eat more fish," Sonja had reflected, when the subject of her forgetfulness came up. "And here I am, you know, where it's so available. Nowhere cooks fish like they do here – mmm-hmm – steamed with okra and pumpkin, and the bammy infused with the flavour. Lord, Lord. It's like curry crab and dumpling at Pigeon Point; it would be sacrilegious to go to the place and not pay your respects."

Candace's mental wanderings broke off, as a new eruption from Francine jolted her back to the meeting. The message Ms Mackhail had conveyed to the Chair declared that the conference would take place in Florida instead of Portmore. This decision emanated from the highest level of the association's hierarchy. ("There's an association?" Candace had not known, not that anyone heeded her.) Portmore could have the next biennial conference, in 2013, the e-mail had announced airily.

Francine received the news as if it were the ultimate act in a regional conspiracy to undermine her professional advancement, and she glared at Candace as if Forbidden Words had been a central strand in this whole web of betrayal. Candace went back to New Kingston too exhausted for more than a bowl of tinned soup and a couple minutes in bed before showering. She closed her eyes against the overhead light she dared not switch off and contemplated the ghetto principles that governed Francine's project and became aware of Francine bending over her and flourishing a nine-inch blade. *See ya*, she said, *dis ya project garrison. Nex time you push you dutty self inna ya, me go chop you belly open.*

Candace awoke with a jerk and reached for her laptop to dispatch a plea for advice from Professor Crichlow. Would it damage her vitae to seek a new situation at once, at the risk of making her record yet patchier? Or would it be less risky to hold on and build up the vitae, whatever the profile of ITS? An out-of-office response set her turning over other names in her mind, picking one almost arbitrarily and sending off her query; but she was cagey enough about ITS to draw a cautious, even evasive reply on looking before one leapt and then making the best of things.

Francine's reaction to Forbidden Words presented a quandary for Candace and Sonja to work out over bammy and fish at Port Royal.

"What can she do me, anyway?" But Candace was startled when Sonja paused, seeming to seriously consider what Candace had meant as a purely rhetorical question. "Well, what?" The wind slapped her hair over her face, and she boxed it way impatiently. "If I do the job – teach, research, publish, everything – what can anyone say to endanger my progress here or an application to somewhere else?"

Sonja eyed her as if she could not believe anyone was that naive. "Even praise can be fashioned into a lethal weapon." She speared an okra and took her time with the central bone system of her parrot fish, before continuing. "We're talking about character assassination here. A studiously kind word, a hesitating and then patronizing recognition imbues your work with an odour of mediocrity. Then rumours are easy to start – a hint of unoriginality, that perhaps the publications are derivative, or even a remark about lack of independence on the job market – an implication that you got the job because of your father rather than any impressive record. But the good thing is that it's a basic appointment. Lecturer, you know. Just needs proof of recognized output and sound work underway."

Candace absorbed that, as she poured coconut water into her glass with her usual intense concentration, as if what was flowing from the jug had come from the last coconut on earth. "And the PhD? How do they talk away my doctorate?"

"They could say your father wrote it for you."

"Well then, I'm safe. One thing to be said for Earl Rider – perhaps the only thing – is that his scholarly integrity is intact."

"Ah." Sonja scraped a mass of bone and fin to the side of her plate and uncovered a thick chunk of fish that had eluded her. "So tell me – you never go back to Tobago? Oho. I did hear when your grandmother passed away. One amazing lady. Were you there?"

Candace nodded. She could hardly speak of it even now, although at the service she had read a Jennifer Rahim poem, "Walk Like Trees" – in thanks, but also as a sort of promise to try.

"I saw Patrice only once after she was married," Sonja added, "although we wrote for quite a while." Arriving at the usual point where her recollections of Patrice dried up, she seemed to gaze straight into Candace's mind. "Why, coming from Rider's household, did you choose this life?"

"It chose me." Candace could not get out any more, having wrapped herself in years of silence.

"You look as if you're walking a tightrope," Sonja remarked.

"Well, now I've alienated Francine," Candace blurted it out. "I can't believe I was wrong to define a research path for myself, but she takes everything personally, and then you can never stop it escalating. It's as if she just goes for interpersonal conflict."

Sonja nodded affably. "Like an addict for cocaine. Didn't you know?"

Chapter 7

Deadly

Ther cam a privee theef men clepeth Deeth

*I*t have a type of person can cripple you without laying a hand," Randall reflected.

Candace set out not only to avoid engaging Francine's attention but to dwell on her sparingly. So it was months before the subject of Francine came up again between Candace and Sonja – not until May of 2011, when Candace asked what Sonja made of some strange expenditure on graduate assistance. Sonja brushed aside a rumour that Francine had knowingly supported an extortionate claim for data collection.

"Dishonesty with money? Francine?" Sonja regarded Candace almost haughtily. "Nah."

"I only wondered how Courtney's application got so far." Candace sounded defensive even to her own ears. "Dexter off collecting his honorary degree in Delhi and Francine acting for him. Courtney doesn't stand to gain a cent from any claim for a research assistant. You questioned it at the meeting, and I thought perhaps you knew something."

"I ask questions when I *don't* know something," Sonja returned, "in this case, whether a breakdown of the RA's work was attached to the claim form."

Candace recalled Francine's face after the meeting, when Courtney exploded in the coffee room. "The issue, Courtney, was what the RA did to earn such a sum."

Francine had gone studiedly expressionless.

"It's a joint project," he retorted. "Everything needn't go through you." Then he reset his voice to comforting, with an undertone of mockery. "I have things covered."

Francine wheeled on him in scarcely contained fury. "You had Dexter sign the claim before he left for India; then this query lands on me." The whiff of financial misdemeanour had disturbed her, but much more was going on. "It's our project, right? Were you going to tell me about her data?" He declined to discuss it in the coffee room and swung away, but Francine positioned herself in the doorway, following him implacably with her eyes. In the brief lull, Nadine shot a nervous glance around, while Ravindra Sumra turned a dispassionate eye to as much of the sea as was visible through the nearest window. Graduate students who were marking Francine's last test loitered nervously outside the door for a word with her, and one stepped forward, but Francine turned a cold eye on the hapless tutor, withering her where she stood.

"A misunderstanding, surely?" Marion intervened in so pained a tone that one could hardly help feeling sorry for this blameless soul who found herself in the midst of unpleasantness. She batted her hands helplessly at the problem, as if that might shoo it away.

For once Francine ignored Marion, oblivious to everyone but Courtney. "As I have nothing to hide myself, I don't care where I discuss it," she shouted.

Courtney regarded her with maddening good humour. "You're suggesting I would exclude you in some way?"

"Perhaps not from the data, Courtney." She thrust aside a few elderly mangoes someone had abandoned in a bag on the table and slammed her palm down on the laminated surface. Then she turned on him with the savagery of a wounded beast. "You bastard."

In Candace's mind, a question hovered on the rim of consciousness. She blocked it, but it circled persistently, jostling other issues pressing for attention – scripts, of course, a dress to be found for functions that cropped up in the evening, a pot or two of ferns for her living room. Or a bromeliad if she found one she could afford. But however adept she was at distancing herself from bickering, there was no evading the open war Francine waged unremittingly from then on – on Courtney and, by extension, Sat. Neither the mid-year vacation nor, after that, the new academic year witnessed any reconciliation between the co-authors of Unstable Skins. Academic emergencies paled in comparison. Nearing the end of Semester 1, Percy Stone's disappearance just after exams (along with seventy-five examination scripts) went practically unremarked, beyond Marion's tentative recollection that he might have been a little high and was probably lying low somewhere. Exam scripts were important, though, Marion commented.

In between such searching remarks flared the exchange of fireworks between the most vocal members of CuSt and CSSGDS. Against cryptic observations by Ms Mackhail regarding the sharpening of ploughshares, mattocks, axes and sickles, a tirade from Francine to the Master had been copied to the Provost, but Dexter said it was unlikely that either that has-been, Dudley, or Earl Rider would find time for in-house bickering when they were so caught up in the accreditation exercise. Dexter's turned out to be a sound prediction, because by early 2012, the Provost directed the Registrar, Harindra Baldeosingh, to meet with the offended parties and shut down the barrage of correspondence.

Candace was mildly surprised at the urgency with which the accreditation exercise was being addressed. "I can see the importance of an accreditation thrust, boring as it is," Candace said in the special meeting of the Academic Committee that the Master convened. "But the place has been producing graduates for some years, and ITS Newstime insists they've been an adornment to the labour force. So why is this exercise suddenly overshadowing all else?"

Dexter dropped his voice. "Market value."

"We're for sale?" Barham demanded, his wiry grey eyebrows as threatening as a thundercloud.

His dry, curt question drew a general laugh, followed by Dexter's good-humoured response. "We sell knowledge, and people want to know they're buying from the right place."

In March, Dexter dropped in to see Candace and picked up the discussion as if it had not been in abeyance for six weeks. "But you remember when we were talking about it, eh? I didn't want to say this in front of the whole of them," he said.

She regarded him suspiciously. Why would he talk to her about anything remotely confidential?

"You probably know what's in the wind," he continued. "The negotiations?"

She knew better than to believe Dexter took her seriously. She had overheard him heckling Sat for pursuing her. "Bottom flat like bammy" was Dexter's inspired comment, and she doubted he had a better measure of her mind. So she looked at him blankly, until it dawned on her – and she wondered why she had taken so long. He assumed she had information he wanted. She was the Provost's daughter.

"Lemme fill you in," he said. "You too discreet to repeat anything I tell you."

Now he would reveal some of what he figured she already knew, so as to draw her out. That was it. Fascinated, she watched him pretend to share inside information.

"The Provost and the Board of Trustees are discussing the modalities of some measure of independence for ITS." Dexter's eyes took on a faraway look, conveying that they were not really in conversation, and she was not learning any of this from him. "I don't know whether you've heard about discussions with certain agencies?"

"Well, approaches to the Rockefeller Foundation have been in *ITS Newstime*, and all the Provost's recent speeches." As harmless a remark as she could manage.

"Nah. That's about funding for higher education and research. I'm talking equities."

"Aah." She was actually lost, but a protracted vowel and downturned pitch could convey such profound understanding that he seemed content and opened up.

"The talk is about landing some huge investment from a private firm. You'd have heard about Antillean Investment Group and a much bigger organization, LMV Private Capital, getting into discussion along with ITS parent organizations, about making this an independent private institution.

That would bring it into competition with the other tertiary places around here, not just in Jamaica, like UTech, but in the region, like UG, UTT and UAG."

"You don't mention UWI."

He shot her a keen glance. "I haven't heard UWI mentioned."

"Odd."

"I wondered whether you had heard why."

His eyes fixed on her face for any telltale expression that might flicker there. They grew bright and intent like a cat's, and she almost felt that if she peered deep into them, she would see a mouse or lizard reflected there, impaled on his gaze. But she did not look, in case she glimpsed herself.

He asked, "You think UWI might want to annex us as another campus?"

Startled, she stared back. "Why would they want to do that?"

"Outreach and all that crap." He slung in a couple obscenities before adding, "I didn't reach where I reach and come here to be part of any campus of the Mona campus."

"But how could that be?" She had been so low in the system at Mona that perhaps she had no real idea of how the place worked. "Surely that's what the Open Campus is for – I mean, what you said." The lame ending seemed to relax him in the assurance that she knew too little to be keeping anything back, and he slipped seamlessly into his usual offhand, jocular self.

"Well, Mona expanding, you know. Ent they set up a colony in they so-called Western Campus? For all anyone knows, they might want us for the St Catherine overflow." He threw her one of his winning smiles. "Ent Portmoreself develop through overflow from Kingston?" On that flippant note, he shuffled together his files. "Nah, Earl go tell me what happening. He's my good pardner. Right now this accreditation thing have he head hot, but when we clear it up, the rest will sort out. He go call on me."

Dexter had barely left her office, before a young woman in a slate grey suit looked in and asked Candace if she had a moment. The visitor's mid-thigh skirt was bandage tight, and a briefcase swung to the level of the hem by a long shoulder strap. A forefinger kept place among the leaves of a stenographer's pad in her left hand. She introduced herself as an investigative reporter, Elizabeth Woods, who needed just five minutes of Candace's time.

"I'm on my way to class." Candace regarded her warily. "And I'm sure I can't be the person you need to speak to, but how can we help you?"

"Is that a royal *we*?" Ms Woods flashed an endearing smile. "I did *Henry V* for CXC."

"One of my favourites," Candace assured her. "But my *we* was meant to include ITS. Tell me what I can do for you, then."

"Well." Elizabeth Woods rolled her eyes volubly, indicating that the visit was about something challenging that she had bravely girded herself to meet head-on. "It's this sex scandal thing."

Candace regarded her silently, her fascination muddled by an impulse to run away.

"I've been approached by . . . let us say, an interested party." The reporter smiled primly at herself for pulling off a particularly discreet form of words. "I don't say by anyone involved in any way, but someone . . . interested."

She paused, obviously waiting for Candace to offer something, so Candace said, "Do go on."

"But you're aware of a . . . situation?"

"No."

"But surely your position here . . ."

Candice interrupted her. ". . . is a very lowly one. I took up my post recently and have no administrative duties, so I've no more knowledge of what goes on than anyone else on the ground. Why in the world did you choose to see me?"

"Well, of course, we know your connection with the Provost, so it stands to reason . . ."

"Is *that* a royal *we*?" Candace stood. "Look, I'm running late: let me point you to the Provost's office. No? Well. Good afternoon." Candace grabbed a folder from her desk, any folder, and headed for the door, hustling the young woman ahead of her.

Afterwards she heard from Monique that the journalist failed to penetrate the Provost's office and came back to sniff around staff offices. Monique was slinging mail into staff boxes, and for emphasis as she spoke, she tapped the table with an envelope addressed to Dr Satnarine Nagassar. An eye-catching logo with a banner imprinted *Acadamentor* appeared from beneath Monique's thumb, as she tapped on while relaying Ms

Mackhail's blighting response to the journalist's efforts at the Master's Office.

By next morning, Professor Rider requested Dr Clarke's presence in his office and demanded her observations on staff relations.

"How could you do this?" Candace asked. "How could you drag me into it? I have to work with these people."

"The Provost may summon any member of staff to throw light on a problem in the institution." He reeled this off righteously like canon law.

"They'll say I'm spying for you."

"Immaterial." Then an abrupt change of tack. "This Sonja Palmer – what's a Visiting Professor's interest in the running of the place?" Palmer's questions about an internal financial matter were just the sort that might prejudice decisions on a staff member's tenure. "What this institution needs now is to enhance its research profile, and here's Courtney Straker showing steady output with good impact levels. I'm not putting up with some loose cannon in the discussion," he said. "The woman could cause untold trouble, if her comments reached the wrong ear."

"She asked a reasonable question. If you're concerned about the institution's reputation, what about the unsavoury rumours flying abroad? I thought that was why you called me. Some woman from the press, named Woods, is following up a sex scandal, but no doubt she's had the insight to come straight to you."

"I've no time for non-issues. Right now, identifying funding is everything, and I'll have no questions about financial accountability. All ITS needs now is to have auditors distracting the accreditation team. *Is there careless talk of that kind?*"

"Employ a spy." Candace caught up her folders and left.

On reflection, she had not conducted herself as one should to the head of one's organization. But to hell with that.

⁓⁊⸜⸌⁓

That night sleep eluded her, as the darkness inched into her skull, whispering of defeat, of how pointless it was to resist the current rather than give way and let it sweep her downstream. She awoke in the roar of a torrent sucking her to the verge of an abyss. Then she was bolt upright, remembering the first time.

She had been a child with no words for the darkness cascading in her head, and she had read that poem to her grandmother, about what Dickinson called a funeral in her brain, and Silver's rebuke came back to her about "just dawdling around watching a thing like that going on in one's head. Lord have mercy." Waste, Silver had pronounced. Waste of time, waste of life.

She could see herself, a little girl with yellow ribbons in her hair, clutching Silver's fingers on Sunday, every thought in her head about good and evil absorbed from Silver as a sort of nourishment for which there was no other source. Candace could still hear her grandmother warbling over her work, "My hope is built on nothing less." Silver's straightforward directions oversimplified things yet rendered others clear. "Get up and make your bed, so you won't get back into it, and for the Lord's sake, child, wash off that long face that's dragging you down." But Silver had also said, "If you find yourself in a place with a bad smell, back out." The thing was, where *to*?

UWI? If only. It got back to Marcus Walters that Candace had made enquiries about full-time positions in the programme, and then it got back to Candace that Marcus had gone into high gear.

"Dr Clarke is one of our most competent and qualified people," Marcus had told his department head in the hearing of a technician whose partner taught in the programme and knew Candace well. "But Candace is committed to her own discipline – as she should be – and can't give our programme her full energy." She was often absent or late, he added, and disinclined to give students her time. They didn't like her. He didn't think they were being fair, but they insisted she wasn't dependable.

From that time, incomprehensible things began to happen in the UWI dimension of Candace's life, things that at the outset could have nothing to do with Marcus. It began in her mail. A worm tunnelled through her trash and fired off to a range of her contacts obscene messages that the UWI system diverted from her inbox. The sort of thing that could happen to anyone. But two days later an e-mail message came in: "You're hacked. Resign, or your credit card info and bank account numbers go on Twitter." A prank, no doubt. Not inconceivable.

But then, one morning around two, the phone shrilled, and a deeply muffled voice said, "Is this UWI AFP Instructor for Group 7?"

"Who the hell is this?" Candace shouted.

"A student who hates you. Die, bitch!"

Candace had no students who hated her. She was certain. Not a single one.

Then? No, she thought. He couldn't sink that low in an effort to drive her off. Could he? She didn't know if he would. But he could. He could get away with almost anything. He already did. She had not believed Marlon, a particularly cantankerous AFP instructor, when he said that Marcus had demanded lecture notes from him. Then she noticed that Sophie and Jeanette routinely sent theirs – *for the AFP manager's files*, as they put it. Sharlene refused to word what she suspected him of, but Nickie insisted he had appropriated research data she had left unguarded.

It might all amount to the college equivalent of urban legend.

But Candace knew that Marcus had assigned onerous workloads to Tony and Jessie-Ann, when they confided that they were trying to finish their theses, and Jessie-Ann had eventually resigned, because, she said, it was the only way to preserve her marriage. And speaking of marriages, he had crushed Carissa, an outspoken young mother in the Blended Learning arm of the programme, by piling on unnecessary face-to face night classes, until she too withdrew.

Complain, Candace had urged. But they shrugged. To whom? There wasn't a relevant Head or Dean to whom Marcus had not made himself indispensable. You couldn't expect them to make out the secret operations of the machine at work deep beneath that opaque surface Marcus kept polished to perfection. Marcus himself was the connection to the upper administration. As for the Principal, he depended on his Deans and lowly Heads. He was someone part-time teachers saw on TV or had shaken hands with on stage at graduation. Yes, there was a chain of administrators able, even willing to help, but the link to these was Marcus, and if the device ran smoothly and productively at department level, what would prompt anyone outside, above, to pry into the workings of minuscule parts.

No. It was a matter of holding on blindly, until one could clamber deeper in. Or of just letting go. Candace clenched this last hold on UWI. Then Ariana Ramirez happened.

Ariana Ramirez had signed up for her programme at UWI as a native speaker of English who had grown up in Venezuela with a Spanish-speaking father and Trinidadian mother – both, it seemed, dead. Because she was bilingual, Ariana could not sign up for Spanish language like most English-speaking students, but neither could she benefit from some English as a Foreign Language alternative to the regular Foundation language courses. She fought the university over each course offered in lieu of Spanish language and over the English Language Proficiency Test that every student had to do. When she passed the ELPT, she declared herself to have satisfied the language requirement, and from there on, semester after semester, she avoided the compulsory composition class. She went down as *Failed Absent* in the composition course, until she had completed every other requirement for her degree.

Then, protesting vociferously, she landed in Candace's late class on Mondays, all her belligerence now concentrated on her instructor, and she proceeded to write English that demonstrated interference from both Spanish and Trinidad Creole English. She took an instant dislike to Candace – which was so unusual that Candace had no idea how to react – and Ariana remained impervious to all advice.

Why was she in Jamaica? Why had she flown over the Eastern Caribbean to come to Mona rather than the St Augustine campus? Marcus said she had applied to St Augustine originally, when her mother booked their return flight to Trinidad, but then she suddenly requested a transfer to Mona for undisclosed "domestic reasons", and Ariana now declared that she would never set foot in Trinidad again. In a bid to advise her wisely, the Registry at Mona consulted the Registry at St Augustine and learned only that there had been police enquiries regarding her frequent flights between Trinidad and South America, subsequent to her mother's death. Ms Ramirez had taken offence at people questioning her movements and demanded a transfer to Mona. At this point, it might be best to have her complete her studies and end her connection with UWI as swiftly as possible.

Meanwhile, Ariana Ramirez worked her way into the soft spot Candace kept for misused students and lodged there as a thorn in the flesh. Unable to graduate without passing the course, unable to support herself adequately for another year, unable to work legally as a non-national, she focused on her instructor as the sole representative of UWI and this particular programme and held her responsible for all the undeserved and protracted suffering she felt forced to endure.

Ms Ramirez was not without alternatives, as Marcus reminded Candace when she applied to him for advice. The student could request to register for the examination only, pay a lower fee and go her way until the exam; but Candace pointed out that this student would not pass without instruction.

"Then it's up to you," Marcus concluded and took himself off.

Perhaps, Candace thought, it was time to apply for a job in the civil service, in a travel agency, in a daycare.

Impossible. Academia, she admitted to herself, does more than get under one's skin: it recalibrates the mind as surely as a drug interferes with brain function. Of course, a career change had occurred to her from time to time, but it was no use: the craving for the intellectual life made her unfit for any other. At any rate, it had strengthened her resolve to avoid even a domestic one. For all *this*, she could pass her whole life alone – or she could do worse.

If for a minute she paused to reflect on what might have transpired had she had risked letting Randall in, it was easy to dismiss the thought by arguing to herself – wildly, as she well recognized – suppose this place, this ITS could come to something. His work was the one thing her father took seriously, and with his efficiency, mightn't he make something of ITS, after all? Every institution began somewhere.

She knew ITS had been established by its parent organizations essentially as a commercial undertaking. It recommended itself to Jamaican school-leavers as offering more accessible tertiary education than UWI or University of Technology, but the truth was, it accepted applicants with blithe disregard for qualifications, raking in the fees. Then, to avoid disappointing results, the Global Knowledge Institute of the Americas had advised their offshore teaching staff to be realistic about the capacity of third-world applicants for higher learning. GKIA warned that student evaluation must proceed along generous lines, with an understanding of student quality in such circumstances. Unrealistic standards would produce poor throughput, and this would discourage the clientele. Teaching staff with habitually poor results should not expect their contracts to be renewed. Student friendliness was to be the watchword.

This ideology that Candace found repugnant, not to mention insulting, had been absorbed uncritically from the parent institution and applied willy-nilly. Now it slid out of official reports and the odd pep talk, leaving trails of irrational policy on student centredness, and filming everything – from routine correspondence to applications and discussion papers – with unctuous slime. Olatunde, the CSSGDS Fellow, quoted these sayings reverently, as he rearranged his robes to ensure that the exquisite borders showed to advantage.

Yet something in his pronouncements of mission statements and pedagogical policies – or rather in his pronunciation – triggered an alarm in Candace's head, jogged a subliminal awareness that had been pressing upward for some time. Then she realized there was something odd about his accent. She listened to the memory of voices she knew well, relived her undergraduate days studying African literature in English. She recalled the lecturer's voice in her head; and Olatunde, supposedly from the same area and linguistic background, sounded nothing like him. She thought back to conference presentations on consonantal systems and on syllable structure, by scholars in and outside the region, linguists versed in the phonology of various West African languages, and she could not account for Olatunde. If he were from elsewhere in Africa or from a different cultural group, why would he pretend?

On the way home, she had grabbed a patty and a box juice, and she sat at her desk nibbling the pastry and congratulating herself on choosing beef this time rather than seeking out the Ital stand where two rasta brethren prepared and sold strictly vegetarian food. At the same time, she retrieved scraps of phonetic transcription she had scribbled when listening to Olatunde, and she made a note about whom to write for opinions on a linguistic oddity. Could something in parental speech account for the difference in Olatunde? In his own inconsequential way, he made a point of his rootedness. (If you sell your father's land to buy a trumpet, he had reasoned, where will you stand to blow it?)

Realizing she had slid from what she should be about, Candace flipped mentally to the stack of scripts before her. Having found herself at ITS, she must negotiate her own way between compassionate grading and acceptable academic standards. The parent institutions had done their bit, as far as they were concerned. The Provost's magnificent salary was appropriate to the challenge of resolving conflicting demands, and the GKIA funded a skeleton staff of well-qualified academics, supported by a cadre of temporary assistants, to ensure satisfactory results. Some of these indentureds, as Sonja called part-timers, were well qualified but habitually out of permanent work. They had been grasping at straws so long that their CVs were tattered and their choices outside of ITS drying up.

ITS maintained an impressive staff profile in its handbook and displayed cordial staff relationships at surface, despite hints of an evolving caste system based on staff background. Some of the older, well-established academics who had retired with honours held onto their status with the clench of rigor mortis. With no mandatory retirement age or review process, nothing was in place to loosen their grasp. As long as they supported their Provost, he rewarded them with his brilliantly strung encomiums at graduation and matriculation exercises.

By dispensing with middle management, Earl Rider had pronounced a whole system of bureaucratic delay eliminated, making feedback on important issues swift and direct. From the beginning, with little money expended on infrastructure, most of the proceeds had accrued to the GKIA. Graduates were listed as part of the GKIA product as well, and distinguished lectures and publications were noted under GKIA output. Everything ITS actually produced went back, except for the graduates themselves. They somehow had to find work in Jamaica, where competition was fierce even among UWI graduates.

Now the word was that Earl Rider contemplated running the place on its own earnings, buoyed by a subsidy to begin with. He would proceed cautiously towards self-support while forging links between ITS and other Caribbean institutions. At first the parent bodies had rejected the idea; but then, as the pickings diminished, the GKIA was graciously giving way to the proposal for autonomy. Even then, ITS management below the Provost held out nervously until Rider – well, rode them down. The Registrar, Master and Fellows resigned themselves (rather than resigning their positions) to give it a try if the Provost could bring it off.

But now, throughout the institution, baseless supposition sprouted up alongside rooted distrust of the system, to propagate an almost superstitious jumpiness about the future. In the widespread scepticism, all sorts of speculation flourished, as the general sense of external control faded. So now a new skid began to make itself felt through exorbitant claims from the more competitive staff members. The possibility of ITS sliding towards bankruptcy without the safety net of a loving parent institutions had prompted a concern (fed by hearsay) to get everything possible out of the place before the collapse. However, the Provost plugged that drain by promising to suspend all disbursements beyond basic salaries, if he encountered any further distractions of that sort. Rider insisted he could hold it together once he had the support of a few governments, but to do this, he must get ITS accredited. He could allow nothing in the way of this exercise.

Against this administrative ferment, the academic centres maintained a somewhat flat profile, brightened by superficial good humour. The investigations by Elizabeth Woods were now common knowledge and sparked laughter. Risqué wit circulated about the idea of sexual liaisons being illicit between consenting adults. Dudley, however, was not laughing. He could not, he said, take anything but an other-than-frivolous view of whatever non-constructive remarks found their way, however unconfirmed, into the public sphere. He pointed out that there was no telling what might be deemed inimical to the accreditation process or at least fail to further it. What most concerned him were chance implications that might seem to undermine the integrity of the exam system, if left unrefuted.

"So he's saying that the problem is really a grades scandal behind the sex thing? Or what? What's he saying?" Sonja asked.

"He's not."

"Not what?"

"Not saying," Candace replied. "Dudley never actually *says*. Just for fun, I'm making a study of his declarative sentences that never quite declare."

"Damn linguists," Sonja muttered. "I'm asking *what*, not *how*."

"You'll never know what unless you watch how. Not fully."

"Damned blasted linguists."

Despite the welter of gossip, innuendo and concrete information, it dawned on Candace that building the place as a scholarly enterprise might have been the basis of a common interest with her father emerging at last, a shared passion. Then she laughed at herself, there at the bottom of the academic food chain, for picturing herself in league with the Provost. For that was who he was to the core. Useless trying to excavate some long-overlooked vein of fatherly fervour.

What had she to offer that he could possibly want? If he kept ITS under the GKIA, he was probably guaranteed a major post on that home campus after, say, a second term of office (and to hell with Clyde Seuraj). If he contrived a separation, ITS had no system for replacing him, so he could stay in charge indefinitely on his own terms. But if he saw it sliding, he could jump clear, for he must still be tenured at the Texas College of Arts and Culture, even if it was by holding on through one protracted leave of absence after the next. He was back and forth to Texas, delivering the monthly Special Lectures on Caribbean Letters – the series he had put in place before taking up the post at ITS.

Yet surely a desire to safeguard finances and raise standards should draw the provost's eye to anomalies in expenditure and examination security. And conferral of tenure must give him pause, when the staff member's professional conduct was the subject of newspaper scandal. Those considerations alone might halt a moral collapse. But nothing so straightforward was operating.

The announcement of staff promotions threw little light on the Provost's thinking. Olatunde's Chair evoked no surprise; he had been with ITS from the outset, a find under the aegis of the original institutions, and he had served as CSSGDS Fellow for the past two years. Francine's professorship seemed to have stalled, however, pending publications in the pipeline. Her fury was predictable, as was the length to which she went to mask it in congratulating Olatunde. It was possible to admire her dignity and sympathize with her disappointment. After all, Candace had read Forbes-Garcia publications and attended presentations by her – not earth-shaking but enlightening enough. But no one could boast of having witnessed any actual contribution by Olatunde. He bowed graciously in Francine's direction and then came across at his leisurely pace (he processed rather than walked) and took both her hands in his, with the expression of one who recognizes the selfless goodwill of another whose heart is full. No doubt hers was.

How did anyone who walked with such slow stateliness find time to write? Candace had asked Marion about Olatunde's publications and heard that he had produced substantial material through oral addresses and presentations, and the only thing else Candace could gather was that the criteria were different in his case. One had to be flexible. Marion had it from Dexter, who had chosen his words carefully, as if being careful not to seem racist. People can be so cruel, can't they? Marion reflected. Candace came back to herself in time to hear that Laura Chai had a renewal of contract for two years, a warning to strengthen her scholarly publications. Creative writing did not, apparently, carry equal weight.

It turned out that the Provost had whittled down the assessment exercise by excusing invited experts like Sonja from actual attendance. They were merely to submit written advice to the Provost under confidential cover. So Courtney's tenure went through on the basis of scholarly merit, although it leaked out that Master Sandiford had felt himself obliged to raise in the meeting some questions on other professional comportment. Barham's barely suppressed revulsion when the award of tenure was announced contrasted ludicrously with a range of other responses – Olatunde expansive, Sumra inscrutable, Clyde Seuraj scooping up his papers and stomping out, the Master downcast about scolding from all sides regarding his part in the discussion.

"It can hardly be argued by anyone that I attempt to block the progress of my colleagues," he said plaintively. When he stood up, the further slump of his shoulders caved his chest and bellied forward the bottom-shaped bagginess of his pants. "An undeniably good academic profile isn't negated by comments pertaining to administrative, ethical or other criteria, but such considerations can't remain undisclosed." He heaved a sigh, because his suggestion that other issues be addressed at least for the record had not been well received. It would not be too much to say, he reflected, that the Provost now held him in disapprobation.

"Dudley's not a bad sort," Barham concluded afterwards, easing a foot out of a dilapidated rubber slipper and grating his thickly encrusted heel against a chair leg. "He can actually think pretty straight in his own constipated way." But the precise nature of those misdemeanours Dudley had in mind remained unstated, and it was clear the administration had more urgent concerns. Only Administrative Assistant Mackhail declared that whatever honours were heaped on the unrighteous, the truth would come out into the open, and the light of their candle would shine no more.

"So you hold out no hope for certain of our colleagues?" Marion enquired in a horrified whisper.

"For those who contaminate the innocent?" Mackhail shook her head and bustled away, muttering obscure promises of wound for wound and stripe for stripe.

To the surprise of all, the Master announced a visit by the Provost to attend what was to be a specially convened meeting of the Academic Committee, what he termed an "Extraordinary Meeting". Even Courtney was attending – but only for the snacks, if Barham's assessment was correct.

Snacks?

"You didn't see refreshments pledged on the invitation?"

Candace refrained from admitting to Barham that she had not read it through.

But sure enough, there were side tables spread with spotless linen and piles of tea plates and napkins. Trays of sandwiches and pastry arrived, and a colourful fruit plate balanced on three fingers.

In the conference room, Master Sandiford woodenly introduced the Provost, who congratulated Courtney'nSat on achieving tenure, a signal of their professional development. Exemplary, the Provost summed it up. This had suddenly become one of his favourite words. Candace scrabbled around in her head to make sense of it but only came up with the conclusion that ITS remained an imaginary college, dreamed up rather vividly but never put into effect.

This idea of being part of a fantasy faculty was unnerving but confirmed by day to day experience. Communication between academic staff and management, for example, although a much-bruited idea, remained cosmetic. Official statements enhanced the institution's profile; most others were unwelcome. Academic performance or other display of worth must not be undermined by drawing public attention to spurious rumour. Wild talk could bring the place down.

Perhaps because the institution was a mental fabrication – the stuff of words – any discussion of its operations proceeded in an easy, weightless way. Scandal, or intelligence of scandal, was waved aside by dismissive humour. Talk of sexual relations between staff and students was brushed off with contempt by several of the more serious staff members and trivialized by the light-hearted. It was clear that while frothy allusions abounded, heavier rumour regarding questionable allocation of grades was to be squashed. Even staff members of unquestionable ethical principles somehow found themselves in a web of evasion and euphemism, and the idea that anyone, especially a mere functionary like Dudley, could question a decision being weighed on academic excellence was generally felt to be inappropriate. Somehow it seemed acceptable to regard Dudley, with his non-academic background, as a functionary, while other administrators' backgrounds of university teaching and research imbued their posts with real value. Or perhaps it was because Dudley was Dudley that it seemed impertinent of him to intervene in the academic advancement of a faculty member.

No one, as Francine remarked, could fault either Courtney or Sat on their publications – which was as well, considering the institution's needful effort to arrest this creeping mediocrity that seemed to be overtaking ITS. (Here, she allowed herself a speaking glance at Candace.) Whatever those fellows' ethics might be, everyone was aware that nothing counted in staff assessment but publications. As for Dudley, everyone loved him (I mean, who could help it?), but he really was a handicap now, poor fellow. Francine stroked the highly varnished surface of the table in the coffee room as if it were Dudley's face and reflected that he was obviously without any real influence, and it was surprising he did not feel this to be the case and get out while he could still do so gracefully.

What Dudley did or did not feel was never to be discovered, however, as he next came to general notice in an intranet circular of April 1, 2012, framed within a double border of heavy black lines, announcing *Death of a Colleague*. Widely respected Master of Studies Dudley Sandiford had suffered a mild cerebrovascular accident at his home on Thursday night, the announcement explained, followed within hours by a further massive stroke that proved to be fatal. In a feigned slip of the tongue, Dexter dubbed it the master stroke.

Chapter 8

Of Chambers Long

And ech of hem at otheres synne lough

A week after Dudley Sandiford's private funeral, staff offices emptied for the memorial function at ITS – which Sonja (drawing from a favourite television comedy) wryly dubbed a working memorial, because it enabled what the Provost termed timely professional interaction with colleagues who poured in from other institutions.

Candace had begun the morning in two minds about what to wear. She pushed aside the black skirt and jacket she had set out the night before. It might look ostentatiously mournful, especially as she hardly wore black. Or the white with the black stripe? A bit flashy? She settled at last for navy, without the light mint shirt that normally relieved it – very plain as it turned out, in the shadow of Olatunde's splendour (the deep hem of each sleeve bordered by a procession of zebras), yet almost tastelessly colourful against the unrelieved black of Francine and Anthea, who came in arm-in-arm, clearly bent on supporting each other in this time of trouble. To Candace's relief, Sonja slipped into the row behind wearing a light grey linen.

The Provost's remembrance skilfully extracted the real deceased from their minds and replaced him with a distinguished scholar that few people knew but that had lurked beneath the scimitar-sharp administrative mind and the great open-hearted father-figure to so many students. This led perforce into a passing treatise on current thinking regarding higher education and the centrality of student-centredness in it all. Dizzied by the circularity of the oration, Candace found herself forgetting all about Dudley in pondering the delusional politics bequeathed by the parent institutions and, subsequently, practised ad nauseam.

Francine offered an affecting tribute. "We are a family touched by Death," she announced with a faltering movement of a hand in the direction of the urn, and she went on to define the loss of Dudley as irreparable. Afterwards, congratulated by a fawning student, she gestured it away depreciatingly. "I don't know," she said. "I was at such a loss, nothing seemed to be adequate, but somehow the words just came – as if they were sent."

Candace wondered what it must be like for words to be sent. Producing her own always seemed to mean gouging each out of her inmost gut. She supposed what her father had once termed her "pedestrian intellect" must account for that and almost giggled before remembering where she was. Then, a BBM from Randall distracted her further. He had landed a post, he said, entirely thanks to her. She was to see a longer e-mail message at once, so she slipped outside and strolled down towards the sea, reading hungrily.

His last article had clinched it, Randall said. He had managed that extra twist outside of mainstream medieval criticism, just as she had urged, although not the Caribbean connection she had suggested. He had been meaning to beef up his semantics for years, then he had; and now he had applied possible world theory to medieval verse that portrayed the otherworld. References to his argument had come out in journals on medieval literature and on narrative theory. Even a real semanticist had found something encouraging to say about literary critics who engaged seriously with the technical issues of meaning.

When he presented the original conference paper, Randall said, some of the traditionalists had sulked, but even they had admitted this article shed new light on the old topics. The narratologists who normally focused on contemporary or recent literature turned "The Wife of Bath's Tale" over on their tongues like an exotic food, while those who were familiar enough with Chaucer's well-known tales but less clued on other medieval poets went for the intersections of Hell, Hades, Paradise and Fairyland in *Sir Orfeo*. "Just wait till I hit them with the next instalment." Randall planned to focus on a few lyrics, turning inside out the dialectic of substance and accident so exhaustively argued in medieval exegesis. He would bring concepts of real and illusionary (crucial in medieval thought) alongside cutting-edge semantic theory regarding the actual and possible.

"Hope Skype holds up this p.m. Can't wait. No one else to tell," he said.

Candace was ecstatic. She had no colleague but Sonja with whom she could celebrate a friend's breakthrough in verse nearly seven hundred years old. The others might play with buzz words like semantics or hybridity, but then the medieval poetry itself would induce a glazed look, before they began raising snide questions about who would bother with that stuff nowadays and where Candace had dug him up. On the way back to the jovial atmosphere that had taken over Dudley's memorial reception, she tucked Randall's elation deep inside like a secret treat wrapped and stored but accessible for a taste later in the evening.

Meanwhile, Anthea had picked up some drop in temperature between ITS management and the distinguished visiting professor. "Eh?" she said, "Who you saying the Provost don't like? Sonja Palmer? The Swanton Visiting Professor?" She bent in two and laughed more loudly than the occasion seemed able to support despite having relaxed to light socializing. "Nah, nah. Not to disrespect the dead, but you can't give me joke and tell me don't laugh. Nah, is all right – I can't wake Dudley. But it sounding like a change of prospects for Professor High-and-Mighty. So when she bad-talk Courtney at the meeting, that was she swansong or what?"

Curious how many ways people reacted to Sonja's mild and (to Candace's mind) disinterested comments. In her research, Sonja Palmer had always dissected established trends of thought dispassionately and unwittingly initiated new ones. Her gift for zoning in on essentials, while dismissing more popular peripheral issues, gave the impression that she sent things flying off at a tangent. Francine concluded regretfully that the venerable Palmer was becoming befuddled by irrelevancies, and, indeed, Sonja increasingly shrugged aside matters high on the centre's agenda and occupied herself with whatever seemed important to her.

Against the drone of a centre meeting next day and still preoccupied with Randall's success, Candace began to sketch an article he had suggested – largely to preserve a conscious look on her face. A peculiar timbre in Francine's voice caught her ear, a muted urgency regarding Dudley's replacement. Francine, who was chairing the meeting on behalf of Dexter, said the replacement must, at all costs, be appointed to CuSt, at however basic a position.

"We have to keep our eye on the ball here," Francine said. "I'm authorized to tell you that there's been an emergency arrangement for Professor Danraj to act as Master, and in view of this institution's whole patriarchal apparatus, it can only be a man appointed to the post – so they must be going to confirm Dexter." Her tone conveyed that such ratifying of male leadership amounted to some subtle onslaught on her, even as she went on to affirm the mutual esteem and comradeship between Dexter and herself. "And, I mean, Dex is an international figure – they can't bring in someone over his head. So members of this centre will have to come up with some plan for leadership here. There needs to be a unified voice on this." She lowered hers confidentially. "I understand there may be a play for the post of Fellow from *outside*."

"Outside where?" Nicholas leaned forward and so, consequently, did everyone else, reinforcing the atmosphere of an exchange of secrets between intimates. "It's been advertised?"

"Well no, for it's not vacated yet, not officially. On paper, Dexter's still Fellow. But once he moves up, there are those in another centre who feel themselves qualified to make both a lateral and a vertical shift." She sat back, making it apparent she would not be calling names. "Remember everyone thinks he is an expert on culture. People spread themselves thin to cover areas they know nothing about, then claim expertise and set themselves up as leaders in the field." She stacked her papers with an air of finality and gathered their attention with a last fiery glance around the room. "A word to the wise is enough."

By morning, Dexter dropped in at Candace's office to enquire how her research was coming along and to offer his thoughts on avenues for publication. Actually, a pardner of his in the United Kingdom was getting together a collection of papers on West Indian poetics, Dexter said, and if Candace had anything with a literary application, he would pass it on.

Then, as he got up to leave, Dexter mentioned that the Provost would be consulting members of staff regarding the position of Master, but it probably wouldn't be right to ask whether she had been contacted yet.

"After all, whatever you and you Daddy have to say to each other – that is all you business, right?"

"I suppose it would be, if we had anything to say," she said. "You must know we aren't close."

"That's a pity." He stood in the doorway a while, extrapolating on the relative absence of father-daughter bonds in Caribbean writing. Then he reminded her to let him have her article to send forward, and he took his leave.

In a matter of days, Francine's subtle remarks regarding appointment of the next Cultural Studies Fellow had given way to a rampage in which two junior staff members who had not yet declared allegiance were psychologically gored and trampled. The replacement of Dexter as Fellow became a topic for coordinated and mounting hostility and unrest. For Candace, this atmosphere brought back memories of family life in Portmore, on certain days as an irritation at the surface of her thoughts, on others as an open wound in some deep place almost beyond consciousness of pain, yet tingling so that she worried it incessantly.

"Repression in Mother-Daughter Communication: Dysfunctional Dialogue in the Fiction of Two Caribbean Writers" – the title of the paper she had started – sent her mind reeling back. Back. Her own mother reached for her from the past, and alongside Candace's lingering contempt and consequent guilt, there arose again a tenderness and pity for what was probably Patrice's true terminal illness, her addiction to Earl. Had Silver been alive, she would have muttered that everything was an illness nowadays rather than a moral failure or flaw of character. But perhaps it *was* an illness, that insatiable longing that made Candace's appeals to good sense useless. Patrice's fixation proved incurable, despite expensive sessions with a psychologist – which was precisely why Candace distrusted the lot of them.

Every effort to detoxify Patrice had failed miserably. Earl's hold on her (even when he had tossed her aside) was overpowering. The fact that her devotion bored him all the more traumatized her further, until, like one watching a loved one through the prolonged agony of a terminal illness,

Candace found nothing left to pray for but release. It had all lain safely under the slab of silence over her past, and when she shoved against it, the memories skittered roachlike across her mind. Yet in giving it a wide berth, she sometimes circled back unconsciously and found herself there, again, at the dark mouth of it.

In the foreground, the centre hummed with rumour. Dex assumed his most forthright manner to report that he would advise the Provost about the next Cultural Studies Fellow on the basis of a strongly affirmative outlook: no one was going to be ruled out on the basis of race, gender or sexual preference. As to the possible takeover of CuSt by CSSGDS or any of its members, that was a lot of hot air – according to Candace's virtuous translation for Sonja of what Dexter murmured reassuringly, as he made his way around the offices. He had not been able to control a furtive glance in the direction of Francine's open door.

Sonja was collecting her files from Candace's desk, when a pretty but distraught graduate student dived into the office and sank in a heap on one of the chairs. Sonja cast up her eyes and left, closing the door behind her.

The girl's wide dark ackee-seed eyes were red under puffy lids, and she was still mopping up with a worn wash rag.

"You're Lindy, aren't you?" Candace shared out tissues. "Well, what can I do? Try to calm down."

How could she, Lindy whimpered, when her supervisor refused an appointment to discuss the current chapter? Strange, Candace thought. Francine was unusually accessible to students. Yet Dr Forbes-Garcia had described the quality of Lindy's work as too disappointing in its present state to merit attention.

The student admitted she had been distracted by demands on her as a research assistant, and Dr Forbes-Garcia had advised her to give up the assistantship for the sake of her own scholarly development.

"Well, perhaps you should," Candace said, trying to ease her way out of a conversation loaded with potential for future confusion. "I've never known Dr Forbes-Garcia to be unreasonable in this regard." In fact, Francine was a bit too soft on students, in Candace's view. But the girl seemed so wretched that Candace probed further. "Lindy, is it the money why you need the assistantship so badly? I thought you were on scholarship."

"Well, I postponed the scholarship because I had the assistantship this year, and that was offering me so much more." Lindy added sulkily, "They wouldn't let me keep both." It turned out she was the research assistant for whom Courtney had claimed extensive payment, and her sorrows were many. She bewailed the failure of that payment to come through, the coldness of her supervisor and the ruin of her most cherished dreams. There had been this . . . this relationship. Everything to her. Now she had lost him.

"Dead?" Yet Candace felt her sympathy unaccountably drying up. She began wondering how she could get the girl out the door before learning anything more.

"No. He's taken up with someone else. Everyone tried to tell me, but I refused to listen. I didn't believe them about *her*. I was young, and she was even older than he was – I said she didn't stand a chance against me, and I was right. Only, now he's taken up with this little undergraduate tramp –"

"So he's on staff here?" Candace interrupted. "That's horrible. You're well rid of him."

"No, no. I love him." The girl dissolved, clinging to the sodden wash rag she had been rubbing and wringing between her fingers since the last tissue disintegrated.

"Why?" Candace insisted. "How is it possible to go on loving someone who is no good?"

"But one loves people even after they've died. You know how you keep on loving them, even when they're gone? Well, I love the person I thought he was."

Oh, please. Assuring her she would recover, Candace hurried the girl out of the room, before she could reveal horrors Candace could do nothing about. God forbid that she should take Francine's side on just about anything, Candace reflected, but Francine was not known for neglecting her students. Candace also harboured a lurking sympathy for Francine, whose marriage, according to Marion, was unravelling.

Occasionally Candace had met Francine's husband, a tall, thin, preoccupied man with a slight limp on the right from childhood polio. To Gillian Carpenter, the CuSt secretary, Courtney had remarked that all was not *right* with the poor chap, though recently Courtney had added that marriage to Francine might be guaranteed to throw anyone off balance, and it wasn't surprising the old boy was listing in the storm. Candace made no remark on anything Courtney had to say, partly because his wit slid smoothly into more slippery innuendo, but mainly because he was a wild flirt, and she had had her dose of the type. Even Dudley had been heard to confess that Courtney was not known to have ever limited his, er, pleasantries to those not ineligible to receive them.

But the incident called to mind a final-year student who had dropped out a month or two before, refusing to work under Courtney's supervision a day longer. That young woman also refused a change of supervision requiring slight tweaking of her topic, and this caught general attention. She proved impossible to help, because she refused to step outside the original framework of her thesis. She was rigid with a sort of intellectual agoraphobia, which made it unbearable for her to glimpse any possible change to her topic or open discussion of it. Even talk of adjusting her theoretical slant drove her into panic. So change of supervision would have been difficult, had she even been willing, and she dropped out, leaving the scar of some intractable but unnamed problem.

This recollection nuanced the plight of the somewhat gormless Lindy. Though it did little to stir Candace's sympathy for grown women collapsing in tears all about the place, it did raise ramifying implications.

"Did you ever learn how that RA work on Courtney's claim was broken down?" she asked Sonja afterwards.

"Why would I?" Sonja seemed surprised. "Wasn't my affair. Once I raised the question, it was up to others to follow it up. No doubt the Provost has investigated and is satisfied."

Her intonation – not entirely that of a statement nor yet of a direct question – carried just enough upturn to leave the matter unsettled. Candace felt somehow tainted by the way it hung there, as if she might be in a position to resolve the mystery if she cared to.

"I can only conclude he must be satisfied, since tenure has been granted, but I'm not privy to his thoughts." Candace must have spoken abruptly, because Sonja raised her head and surveyed her attentively before bending again to her papers.

Rather more quickly that anyone had expected, by late August of 2012, when Dexter was confirmed as Master, ITS made an appointment to cover the duties he left behind. In due course, the new man wandered in, clad in elegant pants from beneath which peeped highly polished and pointed Bally shoes. The shirt, a misleadingly loose cut of some material that hung and clung in such a way as to set off a well-proportioned yet somewhat fragile frame, lent him an air of one visiting the staff lunch room on the way to a society watering-hole.

"Dr Xavier Wright," Gillian said, with an arrested glance at the shoes.

But the new man intervened. "Well, no. My dissertation's submitted and the defence done, but the official letter is yet to arrive. So, for now, plain Mr Wright."

Oh, surely not.

His smile was little more than a mocking spasm, as if he had eavesdropped on her thought. "Ms . . .?"

"Dr Clarke." That sounded petty, and she added quickly, "Candace." His glance swept by rather than over her, a little wearily, but by a force of will, she thrust out a hand and said, "Glad to have you with us."

The glance stopped and settled on her in mild surprise. "Oh. Why particularly? I mean, we haven't met." He thought a bit, lowered himself languidly onto a chair, and then he went on as if trying half-heartedly to unravel a mystery. "And you can't have heard of me, because I'm not anyone in particular."

"Well, we were naturally interested to see someone come to replace Dudley."

"Dudley?"

"Dudley Sandiford, our late Master."

He sat up a fraction, eyes widening. "Good God!" Then he closed them again faintly. "Not Dithering Dudley. Master? The scions of Trinity College must be turning in their graves at the misnomer." He searched her face. "I encountered him once at . . . at something I've mercifully forgotten. No, but surely he died decades ago. Perhaps no one noticed." He pondered further and then recovered. "Oh well. I'd never have thought he'd have left a space, but I'm glad to have it." He watched her with interest, as she snatched up her papers. "I've offended you? But I'd be grieved if I had."

"I don't care to make fun of him. He had his shortcomings, but he was a decent man, and he's dead."

"But wasn't he also sententious? An affliction to any conversation? Do I have the wrong Dudley?"

"Bye, then." She bustled to the door.

"Dr Clarke," he called, and she turned. "Do you practise it?" From Sat the question would have seemed obscene, but Wright's voice infused the words with a smoke of mysterious ritual that made her stare at him, startled. He said, "I mean, this air of rectitude with which you carry yourself? Though, on second thought, I sense it's quite genuine." He put out a hand again. His fingers were long and tapered, like a pianist's. "I'm Lex."

"Which is not short for Xavier. Is there an Alexander in you somewhere?"

"No. They named me Lex at Jamaica College. Short for Lexicon."

"You must have been an intriguing child." She parted with him more pleasantly than she had expected.

Nevertheless, he continued to jar on her even when she got beyond that first wave of distrust and irritation. It was clear from his inexhaustible supply of barbed witticisms that he held no one in any particular regard and that his main delight lay in skewering as many victims as possible at each verbal thrust. He was unlike any academic she had known, going about his classes with a thoroughness he seemed to find amusing and attending to all else fastidiously but at a tempo of one merely passing the time.

"Why is your name Wright?" Candace had determined that only the most direct attack was likely to get sense out of him.

He fell in with her line of enquiry, assuming the concentration of one grappling an existential problem. "You think it should be Wrong?"

"Bother you. Can't you answer? Or is it private?"

"Oh, nothing's private." He shuddered at the thought. "Next thing you'll imply something might be sacred. No. I only paused to wonder what you had against my name." He raised a reverent palm for hers. "What's in it? You think there may be some *Romeo and Juliet* something operating here?"

"You referred to your Lebanese extraction. Wright's not a Lebanese name. That's obviously what the question meant."

"Right. But then, I'd never want to suggest you might be obvious. I actually quite admire your mind." He was like a splinter in the sole of one's foot exactly at the place one could not see.

"Bother."

"And I've never before met anyone who said *bother*. Don't you – at least as a linguist – know any of the more usual terms? Or are you being studiedly repressed? Oh, very well. Wright. My father's side is not as pure as they would like to make out. Sometimes I wonder why he didn't take my mother's name, but he was not enlightened. Nor, it seems, particularly intelligent. Once he was out of her hair, my mother did well, but she never seemed inclined to dispense with the name. I've wondered why."

By the time he deliberately sought her out in her office, she knew more. The ITS grapevine had supplied background: A successful woman from a well-to-do Lebanese family had indulged her son in his surprising bid to leave the world of commerce for one of scholarship.

Yet he projected a decidedly cavalier attitude to the job, which, if his people were as rich as was rumoured, he did not need for bodily survival. When he dropped in to see her in her office a couple weeks after his arrival, her face must have conveyed something of the thought, for he slid back in a chair he had appropriated and regarded her lazily.

"I was born to be a drone." He turned both palms up helplessly. "Only, the role was too boring to support. But tell me – for I crave entertainment – is it true you all have a tame journalist running around the place investigating lack of accountability and possible links between sex and grades?"

"There is certainly such a journalist," she admitted. "How tame she will remain I can't predict. I actually know very little about it all."

"Then I must make enquiries far and near." But he settled in even deeper. "Or rather, I'll have them made." As an afterthought, he assured her that he knew better than to ask Professor Forbes-Garcia.

Francine had established her contempt for whatever might or might not be happening as far as the whispers about unprofessional behaviour were concerned. She remained superbly uninterested, intimating that there was serious work to be done, and she was there to do it. Leadership alone could pull the centre from this slough of sordid tittle-tattle, she declared. Personally, she preferred to focus on her teaching and research, but she had come to see there was no alternative to some intervention on her part, and she was not one who would refuse to make a sacrifice.

She was writing the Provost, she assured Dexter, on his dedicated service to the centre and of her certainty that he alone could have shouldered that responsibility with such grace and brilliance. And she did write, her words becoming common property in no time. She commended the institution on the selection of the new Master, the illustrious Professor Danraj. The gap he would leave in the Cultural Centre itself was one nobody could be expected to fill, but she was prepared to undertake it and believed she had wide support from students and staff alike. This was the level at which she chose to operate. Even in the coffee room, she did not descend to comment on rumour, as that would only be dignifying trivia when there were crucial matters demanding attention.

In the background, of course, there was talk, and most of all, there was talk about talk, about revelations on Facebook and spreading gossip on Twitter. Everyone knew someone who had seen or heard something improper between someone and someone else, but no one admitted to having seen or heard anything themselves. Francine maintained a scornful silence, and Wright murmured there was a communication studies paper in it somewhere, perhaps something on how salacious details wholly irrelevant to intellectual life took off in an institution of higher learning and went viral.

"It's one of those novels people feel they can never write," Randall said, when he and Candace chatted on Skype.

"I'd write it," she said, "but not as a novel." She glanced at the papers on her desk, neatly stacked but mounting. "When does one get time?"

"My problem isn't the time," Randall said, "it's the dialogue, especially where characters are unwilling or unable to speak."

"Sounds like a paper for my project – which has not precisely taken off." But after that, she began to note her colleagues' more circuitous modes of expression. The question was: Was there anything beneath these layers? Or was there only nakedness beneath the cloaks of apparent secrecy?

"Is there stuff really going on?" Candace asked Marion at the secretarial station.

Gillian hastily suppressed a mocking chuckle, and Marion took Candace's arm and drew her aside.

The driver of the van that took students and staff on field trips would know of the van being borrowed for fieldwork by a group of two, wouldn't he? And wouldn't students notice, when friends posed suggestively on Facebook with their lecturer at a beach party at an area of the coast where snorkelling (on the track of environmental issues) would never be undertaken? A strip of shoreline notorious for deadly currents? A lecturer in social rather than environmental studies?

And what about cleaners, who drew their own conclusions about finds in staff offices but denied ever having heard about a bra turning up under the cushion of an armchair? Most people skirted outright acknowledgement of knowing anything along such lines, in the vague horror of being identified through the spreading haze as having glimpsed something concrete, as being able to testify about any actual event, as possessing verifiable information.

"Raatid," Candace muttered, when she caught up with the tidbit about the bra. The cleaner who was said to have lodged the bra complaint rigorously denied even hearing of any such allegation, let alone making the report. Later she was identified by a former night watchman, a recent retiree, as having once been pursued along the corridor by Courtney's wife, a Jamaican who screamed obscenities unusual (especially at that intensity and pitch) among even moderately well-behaved women. She demanded to know why the bumboclaat he had needed to put up curtains over the glass panel in his office door, and she had punctuated her views on this with a range of other telling expletives. These were all old tales, of course, said to have taken place (if indeed they had taken place) under an earlier dispensation and, like others who proved versed in the stories of the past, the watchman denied knowing anything to be wrong now.

"You can't be serious," Candace said after further details from Marion. "What could be in doubt? A cleaner must know a bra from a scouring pad. Oversight what? Who could forget behind any item of personal clothing? I mean, not a sweater or umbrella. A woman who fits herself up in a bra with hot-pink rabbits (was it?) must know when going out of a man's office door whether she has on all she went in with."

"But perhaps the euphoria . . ." Marion's voice trailed away under the onslaught of deliciously shocking speculation. "Unless . . . you know, a trophy?"

Oh, not another snivelling child, Candace thought, as a worn face edged around her door one morning. She had barely had time to put down her case. But when she shoved the box of tissues forward, the face that was raised to her shocked her in its extreme youthfulness and dry eyes.

"You can't be a student here?"

"I won't be after today."

"You'd better tell me everything."

It was pointless, the girl said, but she supposed she would, as it made no difference. It was why she had come anyway. She wanted one person to know.

Her name was Michelle, and she had three younger brothers and no father. Her mother, a messenger in the mailroom, had put every cent she had saved into getting Michelle started in a programme that would qualify her to take care of herself and then help get the boys started. One by one, each would launch the next. Michelle had been doing well, although she had no money for books or a laptop. In any case, there was no electricity where she lived. She had passed every course with A or B+ and was set for Honours. So one day she would get into a postgrad programme.

But now there was this one course, Dr Nagassar's, which would be compulsory next semester. He would offer sessions in the coming vacation to prepare for it, but she had no money for extras, and he said she would never pass the obligatory course otherwise. When she explained her circumstances, he said he understood, and if, instead of registering, she let him have just half the sum, he would consider it an incentive to get her through the course. She knew from other students that there was no real alternative, but her mother needed every cent if her brother was to write CAPE.

"You would have paid money to pass an exam?" Candace demanded.

"No. Just to have the chance of being fairly examined."

"You have to report this," Candace said. "What have you to lose?"

The girl's bold stare reminded Candace of how often Silver had told her not to watch big people in they face. Michelle was not afraid of anybody, just pragmatic. She dragged a prolonged suckteeth from the depths, relegating

Candace to the ranks of clueless and useless academics. "Don't I tell you my mother is a cleaner? They can replace her overnight." No, she knew Dr Nagassar didn't employ her mother, but who knew who knew who? People like herself and her mother couldn't afford to cross a lecturer.

There rose in Candace's mind a side of Sat she had seen for herself. She had watched him attack a student presentation with a savagery distinct from Harvey Barham's ruthless attacks on approach or accuracy. Sat fired merciless questions unconnected with each other, and at times, it seemed to Candace, even with the presentation, all the time his eyes were alight as if with a ghoulish satisfaction in the despair of the student. And it was his own student, whose work he should have vetted before the presentation; but he swooped down and eviscerated it.

This girl was strong, though. She must fight. But Michelle waved away Candace's arguments. No use. It was done. She'd de-registered. The car fare from Kingston, the examinations fees – fi what? To fail course she had no money to repeat? How she could do her mother that? Her final suckteeth as she stormed out of the room hung there, refusing to dissipate, then sank with crushing density. All that yearning, effort, capability – crushed. The girl had only wanted everything Candace herself had fought for, and the few minutes with her had presented a mirror roiling with deformed reflections.

Marion had the misfortune to encounter Candace in the staff bathroom and took the full blast of her views. "Don't you think you're taking this a little hard?" Marion asked.

"What? That Sat's a monster? Who devours children?"

"Well, what is it you want?"

"His blood. His professional life. He should be hurled out in a way that precludes him from ever working in an educational institution again. He should starve in the gully."

"Isn't that a bit . . . extreme, girl?"

"Extreme? He has mangled the life of that young woman and God knows how many others. Not like a serial killer or child rapist or terrorist – so no one bothers, because his trail is bloodless, and people don't notice broken minds. But he's a destroyer."

"Candace, you need to get away. A little weekend in MoBay?"

Perhaps Marion was right, and what sense did it make to expose all one felt? It was not to say UWI staff displayed unrelieved virtue; nor did Randall's colleagues, from a recent, rather racy account. Any institution was vulnerable to such vermin. Nor was it just that she had never herself encountered anything like Sat – but she had not foreseen tolerance of such abuse, a lack of outrage that set her thinking about ways in which people got through an academic year peacefully. Perhaps it had to do with being what they called *laid-back*, pleasant enough to students but casual about detail.

She suddenly caught sight of how the way through academia might be paved with disinclination to intervene and tiny denials of accountability – a script inattentively skimmed, an exam record hastily compiled, then approved unscanned – one trusted one's colleagues, after all, and there were all too many scripts. A deadline disdained, a dazed student wandering the corridor unquestioned, a testimonial postponed, then let slip – little oversights, life-altering – flicked under mumbled references to *student responsibility to follow up*, or *loyalty to one's colleagues*. Her persistently ground-level view gave on small collusions in ruin and young lives frittered away. *Don't you think you're taking this a little hard?*

But if students felt unable to come forward, what then? "It's not to say the authorities don't know all of that already," Marion had said. "But if the injured party won't speak up, what to do? Like the man says: *The world is what it is.*"

And, yes, pockets of madness opened up even where one felt safest. Candace's late group at UWI was taken over more and more by the Venezuelan Trini student, Ariana Ramirez. After studying her second essay, Candace had realized that Ms Ramirez's writing problems could be solved, but the student had bristled with hostility. As gently as she could, Candace agreed that the outstanding requirements were straightforward, some few but important issues of diction and logical organization; if the student preferred working with someone other than her instructor, she could attend a writing lab. And Ms Ramirez exploded. UWI was multiplying its hurdles – every day it was another course she had to do. She had passed their stupid proficiency test; she had been prevented from doing English as a Foreign Language, because she had native-speaker competence – yes, her bilingualism had been held against her, *held against her*; and now another programme was being foisted on her to prevent her from graduating.

"Fine," Candace capitulated. "All I suggested was an option." From then on, she marked and returned assignments with detailed written comments, never meeting the student alone.

But Ms Ramirez continued loud and furious, and she did waylay Candace in the corridor after class to dispute a C, which, she pointed out, would not raise her mark to a Pass if she went down in some other essay. "Do you know where I live?" She pushed her face forward an inch away from Candace's. "You don't want to know who I live with or where." She named a street Candace did not recognize. "You keep on give me a hard time, and he find you where you live."

As Candace hurried away, she heard her New Kingston address hurled behind her at the top of Ariana's voice.

"She's mad," Candace thought, first compassionately and then anxiously. For how would Ariana ever pass the course, and, if not, how would they ever be rid of her? Then it occurred to Candace that she at last had a student that hated her. Her anxiety gnawed a little deeper, when she Googled the street Ariana had named. Lex Wright made enquiries and confirmed it.

"Garrison," he told her. "Nowhere you can go."

Yet it was so unthinkable that a student could want to hurt her that it fell out of mind in all that was unfolding around her. At ITS, against bad press for CSSGDS and ensuing ripples of speculation, the centre devoted to Cultural Studies maintained a surface of normalcy and lunchroom chatter, conveying that serious CuSt people were oblivious even to rumours of impropriety. Francine argued earnestly that no one in ITS had any business setting themselves up in judgement against others. ITS should focus on marketing itself as the intellectual pulse of the nation. Indeed, as a whole, the institution should be on the media all the time – speaking out.

"But who could possibly want to hear what we have to say?" Lex Wright possessed the ability to lift one eyebrow without disturbing the rest of his face.

Incredulous at his insensitivity, Francine launched into an exposition of the intelligentsia at the hub of social awareness, seekers after truth who had denounced the plantocracy and identified with the folk. "*We concretize a whole new concept of the estates.*"

"But then, that might prompt someone to term us post-estatic." Wright yawned, touching a delicate hand to his mouth. "How wearisome – not to mention confusing for those few students who could spell when they got here. Promise you won't introduce the concept at your conference – next year, is it? Two thousand and thirteen? Lest it catch on. I don't think my nerves could stand it." He watched with interest as Francine flounced out and then grinned slyly at Candace. "Actually, *she* is post-ecstatic." He smiled more broadly at Candace's bewilderment. "Never mind. One day when you get big, I'll explain it all to you. Meanwhile, I'll commit my thoughts to limericks – oh, definitely the right form for such topics, and very restful," he insisted.

He was engaging when he liked; Candace would give him that. She could not agree with Francine that his appointment to *dear Dudley's* post was a travesty. But Candace was not in a frame of mind for light-hearted banter. The troubles of Sat's student clung and weighed down on her.

"Does no one understand? He wiped her out," she told Wright.

He studied her with unusual seriousness. "But in her place, you wouldn't have given up like that," he said.

"I wouldn't have been in her place. I did have some resources."

"Sat's as nasty a piece of work as I can imagine," Wright admitted.

"Francine wanted me to go caving with them. They were going to take care of me. As if being underground wouldn't have been enough."

"I don't mind a cave," he reflected. "Different world altogether. The problem is that all these different worlds are interdependent." He began to sketch it for her – only a little way in through the openings, that twilight zone where mosses, ferns and liverworts flourished in the steady temperature and humidity, and the walls were green with cyanobacteria. Some areas had stream caves that supported thick rootmats in which life thrived underground, out of sight; but in drier areas, thin roots reached down between cracks and hung in the cave, minerals adhering and hardening until rootites extended between the other stone formations. "Either way," he continued, "it's the cave water that enables rootmats and guano and other detritus that sustain them. And then these attract cave creatures, or support plants even on the upper surface. But when these plants drop their leaves and other debris, they make the water more acidic, and that corrodes the rock. Infinitesimally."

"Then we load tons of concrete on top." She smiled at him and added simply, "I could never go inside a cave. Just in case the light went out."

"And Sat would be the one to ensure it did."

In a brief CuSt meeting the following day, Francine was forthright on ethical considerations. "Whatever stupidness goes on in other units cannot be *our* concern," she pointed out. "On our part, we shall maintain the scrupulous professionalism that has been the hallmark of our own centre. I trust the new infusion of frivolity in our midst," and here she glanced at Wright, "won't influence us in the direction of the cynical and shallow."

"Oh, never cynical," he protested, wounded, "though certainly shallow. I trust – profoundly so."

Francine went on to announce that she had put in her request to take forward Unstable Skins as a project purely within the purview of CuSt. She had a strong cadre of committed graduate students who must be groomed to take over from their elders. Francine declared the economic and socio-logical dimensions of the original proposal to be peripheral considerations, which their proponents had not had the gumption to take forward. Some other unit could follow up those side issues, she said, should anyone ever get up enough interest in them.

Wright reflected afterwards that Francine operated her graduate students as a ventriloquist would, only she contrived that her puppets intoned her thoughts. Yet she seemed to get no satisfaction from such toys. In the midst of the unfolding politics on the intersections of CuSt and CSSGDS, it was clear that mysterious grievances rankled and grew more toxic.

"Perhaps it's her husband making her so miserable," Candace pondered.

Lex Wright shook his head in wonder at Candace's expression of concern over someone who never hesitated to undermine her. He also raised his brows at the assumption that Francine's husband must be in the wrong. "What do you suppose the embattled Mr Garcia says to himself?" he riddled, before supplying the answer: *"O full of scorpions is my wife, dear mind!"*

"Beast."

Randall laughed too, when she relayed it over Skype, but he seemed preoccupied. "At the risk of defending Francine, she may have a point about this new guy, though," he said. "Does he do anything but lime?"

Which irritated Candace, until she reconsidered and found Randall's tone quite gratifying. Then he shifted the talk back to Francine and company.

—⁄⁄\~—

"I thought the three of them such good friends, though," Candace protested a few days later. "Francine and Courtney'n'Sat, I mean. Not that the others quite compare to Sat."

"My dear girl, you really are clueless, aren't you?" Marion sighed. "Should I tell you a fraction of what I got from Francine?"

"Please."

Well, people said Courtney came to ITS because UWI had given him the boot, but was that strictly true? Even the best universities found it hard to discard predatory staff, for legal advisers insist on hard evidence, and how was one to wring that from the victims? So an institution mightn't be within its rights to block normal advancement. A lowly part-timer could be headed off, though. As a graduate student, Courtney had cozied up to girls in his tutorials, and it was easy enough to withhold teaching hours the following semester. The course had only a few tutorial groups and a host of would-be tutors desperate for part-time employment. Later, he applied for a tenure-track post at St Augustine among thirty-six other applicants, and a set of random events had kicked in. The Head of Department turned out to be the very staff member, relocated from Jamaica, who had been first examiner for that course Courtney had tutored at Mona.

A point system on the university's form prevented young Dr Straker from getting on the shortlist. But the new Head made sure by taking the Campus Principal into her confidence. She didn't want anyone on the subcommittee enquiring whether a special case could have been made for this bright and deserving young graduate, right? So Courtney had never got into UWI, and ITS opened up just in time.

It seemed common knowledge that he married and sank his wife's savings into a sports car for tooling back and forth over the causeway, but Courtney's marriage turned out to be a casualty of any number of student liaisons, not only conducted in full view but flaunted as publicly as he could contrive. In class, he leaned forward to gaze into girls' eyes, and in his office, he bent over to peer down their bosoms. He retrieved waste-paper from the floor of the department office so as to brush his arm along their legs, and he eased among them in the lift, so the front of his pants would squeeze past the snug backs of their jeans. He offered personal help after hours and brought along costumes and toys. His smirk assured them that he knew what they needed and was qualified to deliver. The more bashful girls sat in the back row and far corners of the lecture room to avoid catching his eye.

Nor did he confine himself to students. A junior clerical assistant, pressured by her partner to leave the job, actually approached the Association of Significant Others with a convoluted complaint in which no names were called. After wrangling over it for hours, the ASO had no solution to offer.

A few students actually complained, one or two weeping copiously enough to produce a new Salt Pond for Portmore, but none would go on record. Instead, makeshift responses gradually developed around the intangible issues and calcified to routine. To collect assignments, some girls came in groups to Courtney's office, and some brought a burly brother or boyfriend. Others took a strictly businesslike view, dressing provocatively while making the necessary basic and private precautions, and onto campus they came, well prepared to face the next test. Some students, Courtney liked to observe, were performers, and some were not.

In fact, proud of his own performing skills, he had managed to rig up a camera in his office and take home souvenir recordings. It was after one of these got into the Céline Dion jacket in his wife's CD collection that she had blown in screaming like Wild Gilbert along the corridor between the CSSGDS offices. Marion's account of how she had yanked down the offending curtains – *whup, whup* – while yowling Jamaican curse words substantiated the night watchman's testimony to BEAM, especially as Marion too conveyed that the vocabulary of Courtney's ex-wife was apocryphal, without going into linguistic detail.

As Courtney was not inclined to engage with his wife seriously on the matters that interested her, she applied her own technical skills (which turned out to be considerable) and circulated the film by dropping DVDs in selected dips. But she also managed to install it on the intranet for staff and students to click on, and the site registered multiple visitors before the web manager could intervene. This last scandal had broken the year before Candace came on staff, Marion had said, casting a bewildered glance over Wright's shoulder at verse he seemed to be roughing out as they spoke.

"Limericks," Candace explained absently. Apart from a reflection, sotto voce ("*fib* and *glib*, I suppose"), Wright had nothing to add, and Candace was left to her own thoughts. Without engaging with why Francine should only now be outraged by the history everyone seemed to know, Candace was struck by how it could all have proceeded unchallenged. Take Barham, she said, the most senior member of CSSGDS. He refused to consider accepting any administrative appointment so as to clean things up. He was fed up, Marion said, but like everyone else, she stopped short of defining what he was fed up with.

Francine, always forthright, declared as she passed through that responsibility for just about whatever mess they were debating lay directly at Barham's door, because he had been there all the years and done nothing but complain. What he could have done she did not say. The truth was that she had come along midway through the discussion and had no context for any of her comments – only some whiff of resentment in the air had gone straight to her head.

Chapter 9

Fields of Enquiry

Radix malorum est cupiditas.

The only funding for Forbidden Words came nailed to graduate support. But which graduate student would be fool enough to sign up with Candace at the cost of Francine's favour? Next thing, Candace thought, a future Fellow of the centre might shaft any claim Candace put in for payment from the grant, or manoeuvre to get the grant withdrawn altogether. With a determined suckteeth, she hunkered down to speed up output and tighten her hold.

Spinning her mind over potential subjects that offered a fast turnover, she sidestepped ideas that called for interviewing or transcribing. Written data might well be lying around, ready-made. Narrowing to two or three topics, she roughed out the dimensions of a paper on literary exploitation of linguistic taboos, with Anthony Winkler for a case study. Winkler was a bit of an obvious choice regarding forbidden words, though, so she turned her mind to language attitudes in relation to dancehall lyrics, and she noted linguists and critics at Mona who might take an interest.

Then she groaned. The whole project would take off if she could collaborate freely with UWI people she knew, but could collaboration flourish in the face of negative attitudes to ITS? Then again, the dancehall topic promised wide appeal, but she would not deliver it as quickly as the first. So, fire off an abstract for the sociolinguistic study on dancehall for the next conference on Caribbean linguistics and finish the mother-daughter thing for the Cultural Studies conference. But what if, in the end, Francine left Candace's paper out of the publication? Francine could always say the press had insisted on a word limit that had forced her to cut a few chapters. Depending on her temper at the time, Francine's story would either run that there were chapters she would have liked to include, or that there were chapters that would have carried the publication down.

Never mind, Candace decided: one through the old Dextrous to his pardner and the other to Her Majesty; they might not both fall through. She polished up the almost-spotless mother-daughter paper, while jotting odd notes on Winkler that cut across her thoughts. Yet, another option ranged on the outskirts of these, eluding her. Or was she evading it? She made a note to focus on non-literary written data when she got back that evening.

But, then, the thought of leaving her desk to nudge her way through the traffic to Portmore made Candace burrow down more deeply before the screen and rub her toes against Cassidy's chest. Writing enfolded her in that sense of community with like-minded others that she had always yearned for, but she knew that driving back under the metal archway to ITS would dispel the magic. Perhaps, she reflected, still curled in front of the laptop in Silver's old fringed wrap, but a little flippantly as she prepared to disconnect from the paper – perhaps what she needed to do was turn the whole thing to fantasy. What was it Randall had suggested in his offhand way? Fictionalize the office. More his thing than hers, though. So alongside her proofreading, she toyed playfully with the idea of ITS as a field for data collection.

Then, the mother-daughter paper shifted to a sort of automatic activity chugging forward almost on its own, and from the back of her head, another possibility that had been teasing her from the shadows shimmered into view – that she might lace the institution's incoherence into her research project. And then, under the onslaught of data regarding suppressed, disguised and otherwise distorted discourse – data from her memory, stored in occasional notes and just out there everywhere apparent – the stream of other parallel considerations fell away. She got in the car without even writing the big idea down, for there was no need. It had taken over.

By the time she had parked and walked into the CuSt building, she was thinking out the design. One had to build on something that was neither sliding nor likely to dissolve, as the foundation went down. Yet the dysfunctional discourse that interested her was produced precisely to destabilize meaning, to defer certainty, to evade responsibility. Only – her mind quickened again – if the slipperiness served the speakers' ends, was it dysfunctional? Two students paused and regarded her strangely, and Candace realized she had been chuckling to herself. Her particular focus in the Forbidden Words project would be (dys)functional discourse in ITS. The data was all around her, limitless – from coffee-room chat to debate at board meetings. A ceaseless flow.

It had naturally been supposed that after the nine days' wonder associated with each outburst of confusion between CuSt and CSSGDS, participants would return to their routines. This might have happened but for the Quality Audit Initiative that the Provost set up to satisfy accreditation requirements. Terms of reference for the exercise required members of the Quality Audit Initiative Liaison to come from three other tertiary institutions; and, to avoid the cost of international fares, ITS drew from local campuses – UWI Mona and the University of Technology. The third member had to come from some institution outside the region, so the advisory team from the Caribbean Accreditation Agency suggested Professor Sonja Palmer, because she was only a visitor to ITS. To the Provost's relief, she refused, on the grounds that her current appointment, though temporary, rendered her anything but objective. So the Provost borrowed one of UWI's Visiting Professors.

At first QAIL uncovered little besides perennial complaint about understaffing and overwork, and some consultations dissolved into haggling over hours of part-time assistance that Courtney and others claimed to deserve. It also emerged, to the surprise of the visitors only, that Barham regarded students with distaste, as a not-precisely-necessary evil. Then, the audit moved on to discuss individual perceptions of scholarly and pedagogical standards, and Candace registered the old unease inching up. Misguided expectations about humanities research could wreak such havoc when it came to topics no one could tie down, in advance, to concrete social outcomes, let alone quantify in dollars and cents. Candace admitted to Wright that she had found QAIL's introductory discussions of staff research annoying, even insulting.

Patronizing, he agreed. As if the inclination to blue sky research was a harmless neurosis demanding some show of sensitivity from normal academics but little genuine consideration.

"And certainly not significant funding," Candace concluded.

The worst part of it was lip service from colleagues – Francine, for example, recapping how she had held forth to the team on the academic's duty to the community.

Wright, with his genius for ignoring what others viewed as the salient issues, had zoned in immediately on a fraught situation, by seeming to wake up suddenly and blurting out, "What community? Where?"

Anthea's prolonged steups as she leaned next to Courtney had no effect on Wright beyond a few muttered half-lines (*a prater, a hater – hmm*). Afterwards, he wandered into Candace's office with coffee for her exactly as she would have made it, and, in the other hand, a file folder with which he fanned himself.

He sank into her armchair and drew out his notes. "On Anthea," he explained. "Not coming together yet, though. *He'd date her, and later would probably mate her.* Trash." A grand sweep of his arm propelled it to the waste basket. "But she's putus-potential, in her own view at least. Lacks the ideal form but has an eye on the main chance." He wafted his manila folder back and forth regally.

Candace supposed she should be glad he had not produced an actual fan.

"Don't look at me severely," he pleaded. "My nerves are already lacer-ated. On and off this week, Francine has lectured me on my laissez-faire approach to the institution's profile." But he smiled sleepily as if soothed by the attack.

"And what had you to say?"

"What was there to be said? She approached me with the usual forthrightness calculated to paralyse even the strong at heart – among whom, you must know, I do not number myself. And as always when she is involved, debate becomes a pitched battle in which she has to annihilate her opponents." He regarded Candace and purred. "And I have so much to live for."

"You delude yourself. Anyway, it's reasonable for her to wonder why you stay."

"Ah, now you disappoint me: I don't expect you to pause over easy questions. Still, all that is required is brief autobiography, so I shall do my poor best. I can't begin by claiming I was born of poor but honest parents, so we shall start at the next chapter. I was brought up mainly by my grandmother, who, in earlier days, was one of the Manley set, tight with Edna and that crowd, though younger. Grandma's only son, my father, was inept but had enough sense to die early in the marriage, and I spent my days with said grandmother – an avid reader – while my mother took up the family business where my father had left off, and she ran it brilliantly.

"Mother was amused by anything I did and threw herself behind my predilection for the world of letters – which I mistakenly supposed to be a leisurely place where one pottered among one's favourite books, expounded pet theories, was entertained by bright young minds and, for all this fun, was paid a modest stipend I knew Mother would supplement. To her, culture was just another commodity to buy and sell, but she wanted nothing more than to support my tastes, once I stayed around and visited her from time to time – which presents no problem, because she really is, though exhausting for long periods, quite remarkably entertaining." He regarded Candace helpfully. "Does that answer your question?"

"I've forgotten what it was," she grumbled. He invariably made her peevish.

"And I suppose you won't tell me all your own past? You know you're quite ravishingly unfathomable, my dear. And the thing is that your most secret fear is *too* baseless. But never mind. I'll disclose to you all my own . . ."

"Wait. What secret fear do you suppose I have?"

"Terror of being ordinary – so unfounded. Anyhow, to reveal my own dark secrets: I've got off on the wrong foot with your father. Aah. Now I've said something to make you like me."

"Get on with it." She came from behind her desk and drew a chair close to him.

"So I was in this caving club, although I hadn't gone on a field trip for years, and I did happen to know the Hellshire caves rather better than most people. The cavers hadn't worked much of Hellshire, but in the course of some graduate work on petroglyphs, I found myself a decade or so ago inside a cave not far from here, with a bit of a mixed group. I remember there was a geologist whose delight was limestone caverns, an anthropologist panting for Taino remains, even a botanist whose specialization was the underside of Dry Forests. And of course there were kids who just wanted to see inside a cave.

"Well, we came upon some pretty impressive petroglyphs, which just about made my master's thesis on the Taino presence in St Catherine, and I got to thinking – what is that soupy phrase people use to seem community minded; what would Francine say? Yes. I got to thinking I should give something back. So I went along with some conservationists who wanted the site protected. No one took the slightest notice. Nothing to be seen from the outside. No government official would go inside, and, with no other known caves nearby, the authorities questioned whether what we talked about existed at all.

To be fair, all there is to show on the outside is an overhang with what appears to be a flat wall of rock at the back. In fact there are two slabs of rock at the back overlapping by a foot or two but a yard or so apart. The opening between them widens as it tunnels forty feet under a hill before narrowing again and opening to the outside. Light gets in here and there through holes from above, and, of course, there would be water when it rained."

"It's deep?"

"Not particularly. There's a way down to a much lower level, but that's pitch black and only accessible by worming one's way down a narrow fissure. I never worm. Those who have done so say that lower level is often under water, and the floor, when dry enough to see with a strong beam of light, is unstable. The limestone appears corroded."

"But that's not where the petroglyphs are."

"No. That level had nothing to offer. Above, in the main tunnel where light gets in, you see stalactites – singly and in clusters. One of these clusters is heavily carved with glyphs. I only went that once and suddenly felt I was being watched, and when I looked up I met the stare of two huge stone eyes.

The nose was this high straight ridge, axe sharp. When we looked more closely, we made out carvings on other stalactites here and there, but those had been eroded. Even that upper level showed significant water damage. I took the most wonderful pictures, because the holes in the roof let in light at exactly the right angle."

"Did the government ever take you on?"

"Certainly not. We insisted it was an important centre, probably the site of significant rituals. We urged it should be officially protected. The fact that Portland Bight was already declared a protected area made not the slightest difference. In no time, some land developer had cut up the area and sold it off in residential lots."

"And that was that."

"Essentially. Up on the surface was an elevated site of substantial residential value. The backhoe came in. The more zealous conservationists (of which I am not one) received threats, and the developers made a killing. The geologist was horrified and came out in a rash of papers on land safety, which no one read."

"I've often wondered about this whole site of ITS, built up on reclaimed land."

"The geologist had much to say about that too. The developers were too busy drilling into rock and sharing out incentives to officials, left, right and centre, for anyone to read papers by an unknown academic. Or even a known one, come to think of it."

"What did that have to do with Earl Rider?"

"Well, the Provost is the official Patron of the Conservation and Wild Life Survival Society, our ITS group of conservationists – CWiLS, as they call themselves. Quite active. But anyway, Patron or not, the Provost was one of the first to snap up a property advertised for sale: large family home with stunning view. This may have been 2009. I'm not sure when it was actually built, but Rider did a lot of work on it, from installing the sunken patio with its Jacuzzi, right up to the balcony projecting at the top on fat pillars. He couldn't have been expected to know about the Taino remains or consider the effect of nearby drilling on the petroglyphs, but when I heard he had begun negotiating for a large neighbouring piece to develop and sell himself, I brought the site to his attention. All I said was that it might save him later embarrassment if he distanced himself from anything that could threaten the environment or the cultural heritage in this particular area."

"He did not thank you."

"The Conservation and Wild Life Survival Society, our Provost declared, was a highly professional group with which he was pleased to be associated. Amateurs claiming an interest in the environment should think twice before imputing base motives to his own deep commitment to the area. There was a little stir about it from two UWI historians afterwards, and I suppose Rider thought I put them up to it."

"And you're sure you had the right place in mind? You couldn't be mistaken about the location?"

"I'm thoroughly familiar with the Jamaica Cave Register. I've been in and out of groups involved in these arguments over years, and specifically those debating external land use. I don't claim to be expert on the hydrological status of caves, or to rejoice in bat infestation and guano deposits, but I know pottery shards and petroglyphs when I see them, and I don't forget where."

"And he's Patron of CWiLS. Do they know about . . . about all of it?"

"Can't afford to. He's generosity itself. Funding for all sorts of exciting trips." Wright smiled engagingly. "See? I know something about him that you didn't. Everyone has some secret deep down and thinks no one else knows. Someone almost always *does* know. The question is – whether to tell."

"Another communication dilemma. On my side, I'm beginning to feel that everyone wants *me* to tell something." She paused, but as he refrained from saying anything outrageous she continued. "Our centre seems to feel I'm their ear in the Provost's Office, not to mention a hotline to the financial hub of the place, while the Provost expects me to be his personal spy."

There – she had said it. There was silence for a while.

"Nasty box to be in." He did not seem to be laughing at her. Then he added, "Perhaps the scandal-mongers will bail you out. By offering a distraction, I mean."

"What shall it be? A juicy spread in the papers about sexual harassment? Or an accusation by our parent institutions that we've been holding back their profits?"

"I vote for the latter – not as luscious but in the long term more effective. Busy giddy minds . . ."

". . . with foreign quarrels," she finished, chuckling.

⸺⁄⁄\⸺

As it turned out, the Quality Audit Initiative Liaison did express the wish that Dr Candace Clarke would more clearly demonstrate the significance of her work to pressing social issues in the real world, because it was clear that she was a promising staff member. Also, as one of the older men on QAIL added (with the air of one driving home his most telling point), a particularly charming one. Nevertheless, they had not grilled her. Culture had been last on their agenda, and they saw no need to drag things out. After consulting academics, administrators, students and maintenance staff, the team made an exhaustive report with clear recommendations and then broke up.

And there the matter would no doubt have rested, had not the distinguished Swanton Visiting Professor Emeritus, Sonja Palmer, asked what the recommendations were.

It turned out that one recommendation was an enquiry into professional conduct in the institute as a whole and the Centre for Small States Governance and Development Studies in particular. Professor Danraj, crisply supported by the Provost, intimated that one would have expected the audit to cover *all that*, and made as if to move on. Only, Sonja pointed out that the team's remit had been essentially academic, while the concerns underlying the recommendation spoke to other dimensions of professional comportment. By the end of 2012, for the sake of smoothing the way to accreditation, the management of ITS grudgingly set up the enquiry.

"Another investigation." Francine spread her hands in disbelief. "Enquiry into enquiry, while staff behaviour becomes more and more unrestrained. When do they pick up a few of the findings, and act? You know, it's going to take a woman to sort out this place." But all that was surface irritation that diverted attention from a persisting fury Francine vented on anyone who got in her way, especially on Courtney'n'Sat. She even defended Wright, when they sniggered about him being appropriate fodder for Nickers. She demanded an end to homophobic insults, vouching for Wright's straightness on the grounds of his penchant for "little Dr Clarke," as she had taken to calling Candace.

"I do believe she has glimpsed my true worth." Wright contemplated his impeccably manicured nails with satisfaction. "But I doubt the truce will hold, for she *must* be jealous of my unswerving devotion to you." True enough, he soon reported further rumblings. "Francine continues to emit signals of volcanic activity," he confirmed, having presented himself at Candace's door, after Francine had slammed hers behind him.

Even when things seemed uneventful, Candace found collegial relationships a minefield to negotiate. "And I don't think it was like that when I arrived. What happened to the meeting of souls over Unstable Skins?" she asked. "Those three made up this tight group of like-minded scholars. Surely it must mend."

Wright said, "Come, child. It falls to me to unfold the facts of life to you. Sit. *Sit.* You've not seen what has been in your face for some time." In answer to her blank look he continued. "Have you completely wiped from your mind old adages we were made to learn in school, so we could be rebuked for resorting to them in adult life? Clichés, my innocent, and specifically, hell hath no fury . . ."

"Oh, nonsense. Can men think of nothing else? And how could you have wind of such a thing, were there a grain of truth to it, when you've just come, and I know nothing of it?"

"Because you have a pure mind, and filth passes you by without adhering," he surmised. "Courtney's young, and, although admittedly not so personable as I, he's got an air about him some women like. Sat Nagassar is just a vulgar lecher and blackmailer, but Courtney has a sort of dangerous address . . . Haven't you felt it?"

"Not at all," she replied truthfully. "He wouldn't address me anyway. I'm not his type."

"He has a type? Aah, he would. We must work up a profile."

"But Francine? You really think there was a . . .?"

"Oh, decidedly a . . ."

Before Candace could properly take in the idea, though, a story broke first in the *Star* and a day or two later in the *Gleaner* that the ITS accreditation exercise had turned up dirty linen regarding sexual impropriety and financial fraud that might compromise examination security.

Randall began to grumble that Candace had landed the job with all the action and provoked her into laughing at her situation. But he also complained about things that entertained him less.

"You seem to tolerate this fellow Wright with some amusement. I can't help thinking you'd have run a mile if I had betrayed so much as a spark of other-than-intellectual fervor."

It came as a shock to her that he did not know it was *because* his mind spoke to hers so poignantly that she was wary of anything that might intervene. And, yes, because of . . . old scars. She mumbled something inaudible and signed off.

By October 2012, in bold font, a *Gleaner* article demanded: *What are you doing to clean this up, Mr Provost?*

The *Star* was more forthright regarding the rumours themselves and less sententious about the example being set for the nation's youth. Wright was heard to murmur, "Steadfastly said 'nope' when he started to grope," but Candace reminded him sharply that this was about abuse of power by predatory staff. So he found the grace to apologize.

Two weeks later, when the audit seemed safely faded to a vaguely recalled unpleasant dream, the Provost's personal assistant called Candace, on Professor Rider's behalf, with his invitation to serve on a Board of Enquiry into Alleged Misdemeanours in CSSGDS. It was a well-established practice to gratify unwilling members of a paltry subcommittee by designating that body a board, and this group was already being called BEAM. With a view to achieving the broadest possible representation, the audit had stipulated there must be at least one person at Lecturer level, and all members had to be drawn from outside the centre named for particular investigation.

It had been raining for days, but Candace's umbrella had snagged and broken two spines, and she had been forced to dump it, so she was bedraggled by the time she had crossed the campus from the CuSt offices to that of the Provost. Her father's presence stirred the usual queasiness in the gut, but she was too horrified to modulate her voice.

"There has to be someone else," Candace snapped. "Everyone will say I'm a plant. Who would tell me anything?" Then she pulled herself together and continued more quietly. "It can't be proper for you to put a relative . . ."

"I feel confident you'll do a good job, and fortunately it will look fine on paper, thanks to your forethought in disposing of my name in favour of your mother's."

At least *that* rankled.

He swung his chair to the other arm of the vast L-shaped desk and threw a dismissive afterthought over his shoulder. "If anything exists, it's documented somewhere. We must be seen to search for it."

"You can't expect me to snoop into staff correspondence."

He whipped around. "The institution owns its computers and everything on them. It owns staff working time. Its network is its own. As Provost, I am entitled to gather up hard drives, I'm privy to e-mail correspondence on the system, and I can authorize whomsoever I please to muck it out."

And much he cared how much he smashed in the process. Not for the first time, she wondered if he inhabited a different world, one almost exclusively tangible and material, so only physical violence could cause pain. A world immune to viciousness of the stealthy, cumulative sort that did not threaten flesh or bone but scoured away at the spirit with invisible ferocity. But she knew he was one of the rare ones who straddled both worlds, thick-skinned himself but sharp-eyed for the tender places in others.

The appointment to BEAM loomed in Candace's imagining to the proportions of a nightmare. She closed her eyes and swallowed hard against a wave of vertigo. Questioning staff relationships would alienate her not only from members of CSSGDS but from colleagues with whom they collaborated in CuSt, even from those they fought. Almost everyone was senior to her and might one day be an administrator who could injure her substantially. Feeling around in her mind, she found no footing, as if she had stepped out of one life but not into another and hung suspended in a vacuum, fixed yet floating.

"You're either working here or not," the Provost concluded.

Outside, she got to her car and leaned on it a few moments before getting in. When anger got the better of shock, she pressed her foot on the accelerator, roaring out of the gate. The mirage of clear water over the hot asphalt swirled, vanished and reformed on her way back to the causeway and over it, to Hagley Park Road, chaotic at the lights, people sprinting or strolling across the roads, careless of life, between buses, motorbikes, handcarts, street boys popping up to wash windscreens and slapping soapy water on the glass in defiance of all signals to desist.

On through and out of Kingston towards Stony Hill and a small restaurant beside a river. Normally the rocks were strewn dry alongside, except where they offered footing in the low clear stream or support for waders in the deeper areas. But now, after days of rain, the Wag Water River came brawling down from the hills, dark with mud and leaves, and slinging stones and branches on either side like abuse hurled at inquisitive bystanders. There was no approaching it, and the restaurant was closed, for the caretaker said nobady wouldn' sit pon chair round de tabledem fe watch *dat*. Was ongly he one come out to work, and that was because he live pon the premises.

So she sat in the car watching the river's display of wrath from a respectful distance and wondering why she was crouching there alone, with this problem of her father running things so as to put her in one hell of a fix after the next. And now she asked herself why she had no one to take this home to besides Cassidy. Then she stopped, because she had pushed Randall away – essentially for investing his future in the British medieval. And what business had that been of hers? Fear, she thought. Fear that a shift from the interests they shared would begin the end of the one true friendship she had known.

It was not as if he had committed to the life of starving poet or would-be novelist. Viable or not, that wouldn't have taken him away. Most artists struggled until they were discovered, or died banking on being discovered posthumously, and even if they left the Caribbean, they remained connected. But Randall threw himself at worm-tunnelled volumes few people on earth would approach or be able to read if they did, at electronic facsimiles of manuscripts and editions of verse in obscure thirteenth- and fourteenth-century dialects. He browsed the current journals and online musings on grim exempla and ecstatic mysticism. He relocated himself in a world that had seemed to Candace as far removed from the Caribbean in its understandings of life, in its beliefs and values, as it was distant in time and space. He embraced a life almost cloistered in its orderly exclusion of everything outside his studies.

His daily routine would have horrified the Life Style Society, Candace had written to him. "If you wake to the alarm on your cell phone, it's only because no tolling bell can be arranged." He ate what was necessary for life and hurried in his almost threadbare coat through the subway to the library, where he spent the day. At night he paced the corridors of his mind, gathering, sorting and assembling the day's data. Candace could see him as if she were there, quite apart from the odd selfie he sent by WhatsApp.

Then she paused in mid-thought, for, before this nightly review would come the luxury of a glass of wine, while he wrote to her. A few words almost every night, but also in nightly jottings that he drew together and sent on Saturdays, a long, letter-like e-mail. And so she felt him far away yet immanent.

As the roar of the river settled to background noise, she began to wonder in a dispirited way whether Randall could, still, enter into her dilemma, this entrapment in the BEAM enquiry. Then she realized she had unconsciously scratched a few words on a pad that had come to hand, and she began to write more connectedly. Not like the brief nervous responses to his mail, but a slow uncomfortable probing of the pen on the notepaper she kept in the glove compartment of the car, in case she was delayed somewhere and could set a test or outline a conference presentation to pass the time. This was not something dashed off the top of her head but dredged out from inside. Then she thought, If I go on with this, I'll never get around to transcribing it for e-mail, so she opened up the laptop and invested its last hour of battery life. "While I wouldn't imitate her approach, I confess to a deep chord of sympathy with Woolf and her pocketful of stones," she concluded.

That evening, after she had sent it, his response came instantly.

"Alone? I'm mere hours away. A phone call. *You* cut yourself off; *you* flagellate yourself. And what about this woman Sonja, who sounds like a real human being? You're not alone in some backward place with no plane out. You're not trapped. Instead of tormenting yourself, you should think about seeing someone." She slammed the delete button without reading to the end and shut down the wireless.

He telephoned, and his voice enfolded her. "Forget the messages. You know how tone goes brutal in e-mail. Listen," he continued. "You live and breathe and have your being on a plane of existence unknown to most. Joy and pain for you penetrate levels far removed from the awareness of many people around you. I'm not belittling either physical or mental suffering, just distinguishing them. Wounds at every level require healing, sometimes specialist care."

But even if she *were* a little mad, she thought, she had seen enough of therapists, what with her mother. Still, his euphemisms touched even as they bruised her. Only, he was beyond touch. To hell with Skype.

She flicked open a book on her Kindle, reading and then allowing herself to be pulled into the operations at work under the surface. By midnight, if Ms Mackhail had been around, she might have reminded Candace that much study is a weariness of the flesh, but without deterring her for a moment, because Candace operated on the basis that much study was what flesh was for. She plunged deeper into the expressions that yielded up plural meaning, often contradictory, a crisp outer layer cracking to an inner smoother one with more subtle, more delicate effect, but not the core at all, a layer that gave way to something else, that the writer may not so much have intended as betrayed.

The alarm on her phone startled her into awareness that light was streaming across the bed. She must have found her way automatically beneath the sheet. She bathed Cassidy and passed the mop on the tiles before showering and settling back at the laptop. Then, for a few minutes while she dressed, she turned up the sound system that her flash drive fed with an unlikely mix of Neil Diamond, Bob Marley and Andrea Bocelli. But she hardly heard it and was almost back at ITS, before wondering whether she had turned it off.

When she got in, Gillian was stuffing herself with Godiva chocolates purporting to mark Administrators' Week.

Who cares about the official date? We can schedule our own personal Administrators' Week, said the card Gillian pushed towards Candace with a coyly disapproving shake of her curls and a giggle that became breathless as Courtney passed by for his mail.

Gillian tut-tutted in response to Courtney's declaration that he too loved chocolate, especially milk chocolate blended to just about her complexion. When he whispered that he personally didn't like his chocolate with nuts, but smooth and melting in the middle, she emitted a little squeal and said he was a bad boy. Then she made a great show of bustling away, but Candace recalled that Marion had quoted Gillian as saying one couldn't altogether blame students for being taken with Dr Straker.

Courtney intercepted a glance from Candace and asked, "Not a Godiva person, Candy?"

She churned out the required grin and shook her head. "I lean more to Endangered Species." He returned a wide-spectrum smile that showed he didn't get it.

Meanwhile Francine had been collecting handouts at the laser printer. "Another admirable turn of phrase, Courtney."

"Leave it alone," he advised briskly. "Copyright."

The brisk exchange between scholars had thinned to scattered deposits of wit over a base of animosity. Yes, there had to be some play of minds revelling in disagreement and dissent. How else would a new thought ever emerge? Candace expected confronting views to break out in argument and speculation that was boisterous or biting. But the exchanges had become a cover for hostility. Disagreement on teaching methods or theories on cultural diversity provoked irate crossfire or more muted disgruntled muttering.

Then, in between those fractures in academic relations ran a different pattern: a counter-force shifted alignments among lecturers, students and the administrative, technical or support staff. And some of these interfaces destabilized professional life. Unsteady connections mushed into a slough of rancour and favouritism that mired even those trying to stay clear of the centre's politics. Once Courtney kept Gillian supplied with chocolates, Francine would give her a wide berth. Then Gillian would shore up support from other members, in case Francine became Fellow. But how would Gillian offer evidence to BEAM, if she had any?

Feeling jumpy and irritable, Candace ducked out of an evening meeting so as to drive over to Mona for a public lecture. The university's grounds and their presiding mountains comforted her, but at the lecture, she glimpsed few faces she remembered. Afterwards she met a past lecturer and a secretary with whom to exchange a couple words. The topic, truthfully, lay well outside her areas of interest. She had come to escape ITS and keep herself in the consciousness of anyone who might know of an upcoming vacancy.

A brief meeting with Marcus Walters before the address had not helped. Ariana Ramirez had not passed the course. Regardless of the anonymity of student identification numbers on examination scripts, Candace had recognized the Ramirez script at once. Even if she had not known the handwriting, it stood out as a mass of unsolicited complaint about the writer's mistreatment at the university, unconnected with any question on the paper. The second examiner had given it an even lower mark.

"If you fail her, we'll never get rid of her," Marcus warned.

"Read the script and moderate," Candace snapped. "Your decision is final, isn't it?"

"That's not how I operate," he objected virtuously. "Examiners must be able to perform objectively. I'm only pointing out consequences."

"Just don't put her back in my group," Candace urged. "She's dead set against me and refuses to learn." Candace knew that in arguing with him, she was doing nothing for her own future in the programme, and she went home to New Kingston with a sense of finality.

"I suppose there's nothing else for it but to serve out my time at ITS," she told Sonja the next day.

"My own is drawing to a close," Sonja said.

"Your contract finishing?" Candace heard the note of panic in her own voice. "You're going?"

"I let them extend it for one year," Sonja said.

Guilt followed hard on relief. Sonja would gladly have moved on, Candace knew, but for a reluctance to desert her in what Sonja discreetly termed *her predicament*. For the news of Candace's inclusion on the Board of Enquiry into Alleged Misdemeanours had fluttered out through Twitter long before there was any formal announcement, and while the matter remained strictly confidential, speculation and theory regarding the Provost's intention behind putting her on the committee spread, in Lex Wright's delicate phrasing, like AIDS in a whorehouse.

Thanks to one moutamassy or the other, there was just no point being coy about it at this stage. Lex agreed it would have been banal even to comment on the insidious release of information that was supposed to be restricted. The fact that it was general knowledge before she mentioned it reinforced popular perceptions of her secretiveness, and remarks were dropped about a need for openness with colleagues. Francine disclosed that such comments were being made, and she (for one) dismissed them as entirely unreasonable. Whatever took place within a family between parent and child, Francine said, had to be recognized as a private matter in the first instance, and no doubt a public statement would be made when father and daughter considered it appropriate. Such connections within an institution were always sensitive, and fortunately (she hurried to say), the Provost was a man of proven integrity on whose discretion she – for one – was happy to rely.

Bracing words, belied by the look of disdain she flicked at Candace. Or was it something in the air? Something like a change of wind direction that blew in an unpleasant odour – the sort that rose when one brought down one's shoe heel on the green mitre-shaped beetle popularly known as a bishop. More disheartening was the dismissive glance thrown Candace's way by Professor Clyde Seuraj. It was crushing for a scholar of such standing to view one as a pawn. But at least she did not see him often; Francine was a constant.

Candace trudged to class disoriented by the maze of contradiction released through the blatant innuendo at which Francine excelled, aching to complete the day and get home. When she felt herself becoming undone, Lex Wright sympathized and diverted her, while Randall went some way to ravelling her up again. But did she open herself to Randall despite or because of his being out of reach? Even when she had stopped shutting him out of her mind, she had kept the rest walled off, and, whenever his warmth penetrated, she shrank back into the cool shelter of ideas. Yet even there, between mind and flesh, a glow spread, a yearning, so she was in danger of unfurling like a fern frond involuntarily oriented towards light. It took an act of will to curl herself back tightly around her feelings and address herself to her class.

A student in the front row pointed out to Dr Clarke gently that her hands were clenched. She laughed it off, but thinking about the rest of her person, hidden behind the desk, Candace realized she had resumed an old posture of crossing her legs so tightly as to wrap them around each other. If she could have examined her gut, no doubt that too would be knotted. *Secretive*, even her body hissed at her.

Chapter 10

Long-Time Story

For lewed peple loven tales olde;
Swich thynges kan they wel reporte and holde.

*I*t was the first Monday of the new academic year, and there was Ariana Ramirez again, seething with resentment.

Her fury became hypnotic, impossible to look away from. She broke into Candace's teaching with angry questions, interjected accounts of all she had had to bear. Class time became clogged by complaint after complaint, a baffling bitterness that frustrated the other students, made progress impossible. Ariana seemed to fill the room with her umbrage, the heat shimmering around her as if it were something she gave off, dazing the others with the monotony of her rage. The rest found it unbearable and began to stay away from class, the group thinning. Fearing for them, Candace thought of contacting each individually to make an alternative time and run a parallel class. But, of course, that would not work. Yet, if she did not act, the Monday night class would shrivel to Ariana and Candace, alone together.

Then, suddenly, Ariana Ramirez disappeared. Throughout the first class without her, the tension persisted, the unspoken sense that she could come in at any time. But she did not. The diminished class breathed a sigh of relief, and, as the news spread, those who had fled began to return. One by one, the students dropped back in, at first looking around tensely and finally relaxing.

Meanwhile, at ITS there was nothing for it but to put on one's blandest face and dispose one's limbs as if perfectly at ease while asking colleagues to speak out (for no reason at all) about things they had been at pains to conceal over years on end.

The BEAM Chairman, Dr Colin McGregor, was a retired UWI professor – not emeritus, because his appointment to a Chair had come too close before retirement, following which ITS had engaged him in the Centre for Tropical Sciences. His appointment as CTS Fellow over the more distinguished Professor Clyde Seuraj had been flattering, however fraught with discomfort, and he had fitted seamlessly into the almost uniformly masculine profile of CTS. With the significantly higher ITS salary added to his UWI pension, he had gladly retired at sixty instead of sixty-five, choosing financial benefits over the status of Emeritus Professor that he might acquire if he remained longer at UWI. In any case, everyone continued to address him as Professor – except on pension statements from UWI. His letter of appointment from ITS and all subsequent communication from his new institution acknowledged the title. Candace had heard snickers from a neighbour who lectured in natural sciences at UWI, but McGregor was a decent chap as far as she knew, and a solid scholar, however outshone by Professor Seuraj. She had more serious irregularities to think about in her own corner of ITS, so she addressed McGregor as Professor without reserve.

Professor McGregor opened the first meeting, on October 30, 2012, by zeroing in on the issue of how the committee would get anyone to talk. He sought their views as a facilitator rather than a chairman, he said, and suggested that BEAM was there to listen to those who had something to tell, rather than to pry. Still, he admitted their committee's major challenge might be finding something to report at the end of the exercise. He couldn't foresee them turning up solid evidence of anything, but BEAM must direct its light into the remotest corners to demonstrate that every effort had been made. "I don't think," he said, with a reassuring glance at Candace, "that it will involve too much unpleasantness."

The ITS Registrar, Mr Baldeosingh, had resisted inclusion on the committee but in the end given way before the iron will of his Provost. Morgan Shade had only five years ago wooed Harindra Baldeosingh away from administration in the University of Guyana, and Hari was very clear on his wife's position, that if he found himself returning to Guyana, it would be without her and the children. So he was treading with the caution of one walking through a cow pasture in the night. He knew very well, too, that if the Provost was going to put his own foot down, he would have to be on firmer and cleaner ground than the committee was likely to establish.

Professor Danraj expressed his disdain for the situation that had brought them together, but he couldn't see what this group could do – coming as they were from an entirely different set of professional standards – about the sort of blatant slackness some people at ITS seemed prepared to live with. His flicker of attention in Candace's direction, with a phrase of acknowledgement about her only having been there a couple years, at once exonerated and dismissed her, besides underscoring that years of part-time employment at UWI counted for nothing. (In case she had not noticed.)

The final member of the committee was an elderly emeritus professor of a university in Australia who had come to ITS for two years and was in the last month of this appointment. ITS had suitably celebrated her in a lavish function the week before. Professor Waterman, already packed up to return to her memoirs and grandchildren in Queensland and snatched, as it were, from the shadow of her departing plane, seemed uninclined to say much at this time.

"Where do we begin?" Candace asked, blunt as ever.

"Well, Chairman," the Registrar said, "why don't we hear the ideas of a fresh young mind?" Hari Baldeosingh smiled encouragingly at Candace.

"To interview members of the centre individually, we'd need a staff list and contact information –" Barely in time, Candace stopped short of asking whether there would be a secretary for the enquiry, as her own eminent qualifications for the role flashed on her. She was, after all, female as well as younger and more junior than the rest.

"As the material will be too sensitive to expose to anyone outside the group, Mr Chairman, I suppose you will be keeping your own notes?" Professor Waterman's question demonstrated that she had aligned herself smoothly with Candace.

The Registrar hurriedly fell in with this understanding, before the note-taking devolved on him. That left the Chair with no alternative but to nod and move on to the modus operandi.

"I should think," the Registrar remarked, "that we would want to avoid offering opportunities for mud-slinging, and that group interviews would control that."

"But without confidentiality, Hari, who would say anything negative about a colleague?" The Chairman's face was a study of perplexity.

"And if it's confidential," Professor Waterman went on, "what good is it? How will we report? Anyway, to begin with, I suggest we meet them individually and then in groups. In the group, we could raise for general discussion things we had learned in the individual sessions – but without calling names."

"Well then, of course, they'll all clam up." The Registrar threw up both hands. "I mean, we know the type. I can't believe I agreed to do this." He thought morosely for a while and then added, "There are groups we may need to see anyway. The societies associated with the centre, for one."

"Let's begin with Mr Barham," Candace suggested, "and work our way through members of the centre, until we reach the Lifestyle Society."

"We simply have to get this out the way before Christmas," Hari Baldeosingh agreed. "I spend the holidays in Boston with my in-laws. That's set in stone."

"Thank you, gentlemen." The Chairman dismissed the meeting.

—⁄⁁~

Barham was to have a root canal on the day proposed but promised to be available in the following week. Olatunde accepted their invitation eagerly and surged in with a lavish swirl of bronze fabric edged with black and rust red. He was an enthusiastic interviewee, firmly supportive of his colleagues and the institution as a whole.

"Do not call the forest that shelters you a jungle," he cautioned. He could not imagine how any story along the lines published in the papers had got around. People misunderstood things, he surmised. Demonstrations of collegial goodwill and student friendliness must have been erroneously interpreted.

"I wondered what sort of administrative structures for dealing with staff-student relations you might be familiar with," Candace said. "Tell us about guidelines or precautions in those institutions where you worked before coming to ITS. In fact, where were you before, Professor?"

"Many places. Wide experience at home and more recently in the States."

The Friday before, Candace had enquired at the Office of the Master about how other institutions dealt with professional impropriety, and Ms Mackhail had assembled a hefty folder on guidelines UWI was currently reworking and on policies in North America, Europe, India and Singapore. So Candace asked the CSSGDS Fellow about approaches at his alma mater. But Olatunde had never encountered problems like those reported in the Jamaican newspapers. It was an important investigation, he agreed. One frog can ruin everyone's water. But in his experience, ITS maintained the highest level of professionalism, which was why he suspected some deep misunderstanding of motives underlying the reports on staff and student interactions.

Candace would have liked to get home directly to her laptop, but it was her AFP evening, and it was now possible to enjoy class again.

This sixth for the semester was proceeding smoothly. The students were light-hearted, and Candace felt almost playful. A holiday atmosphere prevailed. Then Marcus arrived and drew Candace outside.

"Have you heard?" he asked. It had come on the five o'clock news. The body of a UWI student had been found, and identified as Ariana Ramirez.

Candace made her way back in and told the class as gently as she could. Then she dismissed them and went home. She tried to work, but it was impossible to mark scripts or word a paper, her mind a tumult of images – Ariana arguing fiercely about a grade; Ariana devoid of fury, her tense shoulders sagging, as she turned to Candace a face shattered by an emerging bullet. If only she could shut down her imagination, Candace thought. Switch off memory and supposition. If only something genuinely important could sweep her thoughts elsewhere.

The next day, with Ms Mackhail's assistance, Candace got hold of Olatunde's personal file. "If you're investigating something for the Provost, you must have unlimited access," the AA said.

On the way back to her own office Candace stopped and held a door frame and thought again that Ariana Ramirez was dead; and there was no explanation.

That evening, beside the AA's folder, Candace laid an e-mail response to questions she had addressed to a West African university about a former member of their faculty. In a terse reply of November 8, 2012, the Director of Human Resources had responded that the institution did not release information on staff members, but, in any case, there had never been an employee by the name Dr Clarke had sent. Within days, a rough assortment of other data, gathered through Dogpile and scattered in ITS records, began to pool together.

It seemed Olatunde may never have completed his doctorate and had probably not been born in Africa at all. A glance at the employment policies of the Global Knowledge Institute of the Americas, which specially welcomed applications from *veterans, women and other minorities*, led her to online comments about indiscriminate filling of quotas. On the other hand, she reflected with a sigh, perhaps outstanding Afro-American scholars had been too discriminating to apply. However that might be, Olatunde must have talked his way to the attention of the Global Knowledge Institute, oozing proverbs he had acquired randomly on the Net, among other verbal flourishes. At any rate, his accent was unfamiliar not because of a parental linguistic mix but because it was faked. Could he talk his way out of this? she wondered.

Then the other imponderables of her life jarred on her. For, how could all this be of importance, when one of her students was dead? Had been *murdered*. But what was there to do? Ariana had been shot point-blank. No one knew why. Well (a shiver down the spine), someone did. But Candace could not, must not dwell on it.

The following week, Candace brought her findings on Olatunde to the attention of BEAM. The consensus was that his identity – or, more accurately, that of Clarence Stewart (born and bred of American parents) – was not the remit of the committee. Since it had leaked through in the course of their data collection, they would inform the Provost, but it was up to him to proceed as he thought fit, while they returned to their own mandate.

"Who next?" Hari was anxious to move on and went for the door, and

Barham loped in dragging the inevitable rubber slippers that Sonja had described as pre-Columbian artefacts. Indeed, they were deeply worn into smooth depressions under his heel and built up around the edges with a grainy residue of apparently ancient provenance.

BEAM had now trundled well into the second month of its investigations. Air-conditioning had failed, and the windows stood ajar, shuddering against a lively breeze. In passing, staff and students glanced curiously at the group in the meeting room. From beyond them came the gurgle of the sea between the stones under the wall that rimmed the property and, between the slosh of water a noise of gnawing, or so it sounded to Candace, of foundations being eaten away.

Ariana Ramirez was dead, and Candace tried to take up her UWI class that Monday where they had left off. Her students treated her with gentleness, as if she were bereaved.

"And I am," she admitted to Randall afterwards.

"Of course. How could you have foreseen that Ariana's absence, when it came, would bring no relief?"

Meanwhile, BEAM's questions regarding sexual impropriety all met with denial or with impassioned demands for confidentiality. Individual student testimony brought back to Candace's mind the tale of the bra mysteriously forgotten by its owner in a staff office. Euphoria, Marion had speculated – but not according to most accounts. Students offered muddled reports of victimization. "I failed because I refused to cooperate," one said righteously. "Then he offered another way. It was play or pay." This student refused to testify that she had turned over fifteen thousand Jamaican dollars, nor would she say to whom. For how might her payment be construed? People might not understand what she had been going through, she explained.

A female graduate, who had finished her degree two years before and could be expected to speak fearlessly, denied all knowledge of any scandal, but a week or two later a retired technician named her as an ex-girlfriend of Courtney. But how was the committee to prove whether this young woman's child was really his, without a paternity test? The real problem was that the mother might not want her child tested. The committee asked why the interviewee thought the father's information would be more readily offered. Well, not offered, of course, the technician said, but perhaps available. Hadn't they heard about the condoms in staff trash bins? No? Well, perhaps that wasn't happening again, then.

Another thing that wasn't happening was the solving of Ariana's murder. One newspaper had described Ariana as riddled with bullets. Another reported a single bullet wound to the back of the head. How could there be such different versions of a death? Ariana had sat in the classroom with Candace, loud and flushed with resentment. Everyone had wanted her gone. Now that she was, she had left a rent.

"You really didn't know her," Sonja protested.

It was impossible for Candace to grasp that only students physically present were part of one's life. "You mean I can't miss her? I don't miss the trouble she gave, but I miss a student I've . . . lost. Your student disappears, and you must want to know what happened."

"Present in the flesh or in print or soft copy," Sonja insisted. "You think me heartless, I suppose."

"Of course not. You're an outstanding teacher."

"When a student walks away from one of us, it's her affair," Lex explained. "When one walks away from you, they take a part of you with them. Which makes you either unusually suited to the job or painfully unsuited. Not sure which."

"She didn't walk away," Candace whispered. *Gunned down.*

⁓⁓⁓

Candace tried to apply herself to BEAM. Christmas and New Year passed, and BEAM interviewing was well advanced before classes resumed. One or two staff members made circuitous references to implied threats. Breathlessly over the phone, a secretary repeated innuendos about job security. If anyone quoted her, she promised, she would deny it. Coffee-room talk half-heartedly dissembled as open discussion.

"What do you all think about this enquiry business now?" Marion asked the room at large.

"Think?" Wright arranged his brow in a pained furrow, like one faced with an abstruse concept. "What do you mean 'think'? In this context I mean – not that I generally indulge myself."

Marion regarded him in bewilderment. "Indulge in what?"

"Thinking. Wasn't that what we were talking about? Mr Barham?"

Barham had popped in to hand Marion a file with student proposals for graduate topics.

"But all this talk about improprieties? You've been here from the start, Harvey. Good Lord – you practically built the centre. You must feel it so dreadfully?" Marion looked at Harvey Barham as at one tending a dying relative. "So, is any of the talk true?"

"I know tutorials and discussions of student scripts go on in my office," he said shortly. "Outside of that – I can't comment on what happens behind closed doors."

"What about if people kept their office doors open?" Marion said. As usual when discussing matters of principle, she took on the forlorn tone and posture of a second-year graduate student not only devoid of a research plan but without even a couple tentative thesis topics to rub together.

"Perhaps if others weren't so fast, *they* would keep *their* doors shut," Francine retorted. "Anyway, mine is warped by the damp and can't shut properly; and right now, with the conference coming off at last, I have no time for nonsense. So I suppose that lets me off. Marion, why don't just we two go out to lunch?" She put an arm around Marion and led her off.

"Damp?" Wright assumed his most befuddled expression, his eyes straying over the arid landscape. Then he bent again to his task: "A young scholar in hasty retreat." He sighed. "I'd be inclined to pass over *meat* for *heat*, don't you think?"

⌐ノ\⌐

"Finished marking already, girl?" Marcus accepted Candace's packages of essays with an admiring glance. "Deadline is end of the week."

"I had to," she replied, and went on unthinkingly. "I've a paper to finish for the conference."

"Go straight home," he responded. "You should be careful, you know. We can't tell whether Ariana invented that boyfriend or whether he's real. Or what state of mind he's in. Don't be too late on the road."

In January 2013, before teaching kicked in and just as the conference was to begin, BEAM, which had dimmed for a couple weeks, flickered on again to interview Morgan Shade, not because he seemed pertinent to the investigation, but because he had called to say that he was leaving the country for a couple months and must be invited soon, should they want his thoughts. Reminded of his existence and reluctant to say that they could think of no conceivable use for his thoughts, they met with Shade. He dodged in, looking more cadaverous than ever, and delivered a treatise on the integrity of the Provost and (by association) the institute at large.

Alongside this inauspicious progress, the glitz and fanfare of the Cultural Studies conference revived interest among more jaded faculty. Sat voiced a last-minute objection that there was no East Indian plenary speaker, and no woman either, so Francine dramatically announced that the hunt was on for a female East Indian – preferably lesbian and disabled war veteran as well, to keep a balance, don't you know. Francine had documents, should Dr Naggasar be interested, to confirm that she had attempted to bring Naipaul down, though that did not come off, and she would have thought even Dr Naggasar would be aware that you couldn't pull an East Indian luminary in Caribbean Culture out of a hat last minute in Jamaica – unless Dr Nagassar was suggesting himself, which even he could not be so foolish as to . . . And – you know what? She was too damn busy bringing off this whole thing by herself to stand up and listen to stupidness.

The opening of the conference was preceded by a well-meaning trickle of volunteers in the early morning, setting up trestle tables sulkily delivered by Physical Resource Management, and scurrying about so as to round up tablecloths Professor Bailey-Brown had forgotten to drop off the evening before. Then the participants rumbled in by shuttle from the New Kingston hotels and the Portmore Grand. Imagine paying costs like that, Francine had lamented. With a whole resort lying derelict right there in Portmore – the towering tourist hotel that had been started and then dropped, and now lay dead and empty. Waste, Francine moaned, sinful waste.

The bright colours of Americans in the tropics lit up the white stone and dull green cactus landscape and complemented the sea lashing blue and white beyond the rocks. And here and there, the grey, navy or khaki British participant put in brief practical questions about venue and programme.

"Stereotyping," Sonja rebuked Candace for her profile of the visitors, but she spoilt it by crumpling in laughter.

Marcus Walters materialized and embraced Candace. "I'm depending on you to come to my paper and ask easy questions," he said. He gave Sonja's hand a friendly tug and turned back to Candace. "No, it's a nice set-up. You don't mean you really thinking of leaving all this?"

"Not at all," Candace returned stiffly, measuring the distance away of interested ears.

"What are you talking on, Marcus?" Sonja intervened, flagging Lex Wright over.

By evening, the reception gathered in a mixed bunch of academics who attended conferences for all sorts of reasons – some for exposure to new ideas, some to expose their own theories to the comments and questions of their peers, some to cut another notch on their CVs by adding a further title to their list of papers presented. The odd participant, like Courtney, combined any or all of these motives with the hope of getting lucky. And he was very much in evidence among the younger women, assuring them that he had read their abstracts and that nothing could keep him from attending their presentations, were it not for a seminal panel he had to chair himself.

Dexter was there for that surge of gratification at being recognized by everyone and the assurance that his attendance enhanced the status of the conference. Earl Rider arrived in an aura of combined charm and authority, eager to shake hands with new people who might one day come in handy. Among these bustled the many who simply delighted in encountering others of similar interests to themselves and keeping up with developments in their disciplines.

Greetings and laughter swelled the noise level, as colleagues who only met at such events renewed acquaintance. One or two confided matters that concerned no one but were entertaining enough to seal goodwill and seemed unlikely to do harm if shared with strangers one wouldn't see again for years. Drinks flowed into those to whom drinks were important, and trays of cocktail patties and jerked chicken wings, borne aloft by plump women in national costume, emptied and were replenished.

In between and occasionally parallel to the conference presentations, members of BEAM went on meeting with interviewees drawn from academic, technical and secretarial staff; cleaners, groundsmen and drivers; students, presidents of societies and ex-presidents of unions. Outside the meeting room, ITS faculty pretended politely that the enquiry was not happening, or referred to it out of context with blunt good humour, as if they were above subterfuge. One or two visitors (Marcus being one) asked Candace whether it was true that there was this enquiry underway that people whispered about, and an elderly admirer enquired what the findings were to date.

Francine was genuinely too busy to care, lavishing overseas calls on Lady Saw, whom she had thought a convert to her cause – good for a performance in the finale – but who was not convinced about cancelling a prior commitment and was no longer communicating with her. Meanwhile, conference papers were delivered, questioned and defended, while fragile participants panted in the heat and the more belligerent complained about the icy temperature of the meeting rooms for people who had thought they were coming to the tropics and dressed accordingly. Most were blissfully unaware of genuine hitches in the conference arrangements.

As usual Curtis Martin withdrew from the programme at the last moment, on the grounds of unforeseen circumstances, and declined to register or pay fees, but he remained very much in evidence, chatting with the dignitaries who passed through, consuming the limited snacks set out for morning and afternoon breaks and, at last, delivering his paper as originally scheduled. By now it was routine that this would happen, that Dr Martin would manage to have his entire presentation published in the newspaper in the next few days and that he would, on receiving a reminder about the conference fee, return a copy of his earlier communication to verify that he had in good time notified the organizers of his withdrawal .

As was the way with so many conferences, all this unfolded along with fainting air conditioners and consequent shifts of venue unnoticed by all who heaped praise on the conference committee and congratulated Dr Francine Forbes-Garcia on a splendid gathering. Provost Rider made some very kind remarks, and Professor Danraj confirmed that it was no more than he was accustomed to from his colleagues.

So at last the conference wound up. Student assistants, whom Sonja termed the Weeding Gang, scuttled back and forth gathering conference detritus. Shuttles set out to collect those who had not yet flown out, and maps were distributed so that the unshuttled could find themselves to the Provost's elegant home, Hellshire Palms, which his colleagues liked to call The Habitat.

—ᐟᐟᐧᐟᐠ—

Hellshire Hills looked down on a sea of postcard aquamarine and waves tumbling onto a glorious beach, a view broken only by occasional silk cotton, alamanda or coconut, riotous with bougainvillea and made rugged by occasional huge rocks eaten with holes or strangely veined with red earth. Along the Provost's driveway, the palms were picked out by solar-powered lights, and soft reggae pulsed on the grounds. Tents sheltered food, drink and tables for eating. It was all on fine polished tiles, because Professor Rider had long decided that he had better things to do than maintain a lawn in Hellshire. Palms fountained up, and bougainvillea cascaded from huge pots, and only the cactus was planted in the ground. It was a fine dry evening, cool even for January.

"Delighted to welcome you to my home," he said to Candace, "and I invite you, not for the first time, to make it your own."

"Thank you, no," she said, not for the first time.

He greeted Wright coldly and kissed Francine. "Another coup. Congratulations," he told her before wondering away with her at his heels.

"So this is The Habitat – his, at least." Wright swept his eyes over the grounds and house.

"What do you mean?" Candace could not help her own curiosity but was arrested by an unusual quality of anger in his voice.

"I don't suppose much trace remains of whatever else lived in the vicinity, before he joined in the so-called development."

Having no reassurance to offer, she drifted around the grounds like the other guests, peeking along a corridor past a half-open door, as she exited the bathroom and returned to the grounds. When Marcus appeared and attached himself to her, she drew him over to introduce him to Morgan Shade. She left as soon as she decently could.

As the dazzle of the conference wore away and post-mortems gave place to the routines of lectures, scripts and student consultations, a thick lethargy became apparent, almost aggressive, as if the conference bustle had been overtaken by sullen lassitude. Photographs spread through the papers – government ministers at the opening of the conference, visiting dignitaries at the Provost's reception, Francine delivering her paper, and, right on time, the full text of Curtis Martin's presentation.

Regardless of BEAM's note of concern regarding Olatunde's past, nothing had changed in the good professor's demeanour. Whether or not the BEAM Chairman had actually sent the note to the Provost and whether or not the Provost had read it, once again there was Olatunde, rolling out tattered yellow notes from his own undergraduate years. In the same vein, as everyone knew, Percy Stone would again be shuffling and rewording the exam questions he rehashed year in, year out.

Marion Bailey-Brown peeled off those few bits of correspondence that absolutely demanded immediate response and resolutely pushed aside essays for her final-year course for another fortnight; but she taught, and fretted about her students with genuine concern. Francine plotted and bullied, but she too guided and defended hers. Barham insulted any of his who crossed his path, glowered at everyone from behind a bush of brownish grey overtaking his face, published nothing but gave meticulously prepared classes.

There was valuable research and devoted teaching taking place. Giving the arms of her spectacles a particularly violent whirl, Sonja said that the sad thing was, the place could have been viable.

"But it isn't, is it?" Candace asked in a small voice.

Meanwhile, a sort of pact had grown up between Lex Wright and Candace. They never spoke of the enquiry or the rumours that had prompted it. When she said she had a meeting in the afternoon, he simply sighed as though exhausted at the thought of another session of directionless talk. Against it all, there was Ariana Ramirez, dead, with no one to receive condolences and little trace of her ever having existed anywhere but in Candace's mind. And there she remained, taking up more and more space, while no one else seemed to notice. But then, even the news that a major scholar in cultural studies had died merely provoked Francine to say "Well, we can kiss that possible connection goodbye," before breaking into an encomium on the Father of Multiculturalism.

Campus routines closed in. Weeks later, an arbitrarily slung-together Joint Sub-Committee for Staff Advancement argued over comments by a peer reviewer. One camp said the reviewer demonstrated less expertise than the staff member under review and expressed loud distrust of outsiders; the other group, led by Barham, held forth on the evils of inbreeding.

Then Francine described that particular reviewer as notoriously insensitive to the postcolonial aesthetic. In any case, she said, celebration of the Caribbean in his work was entirely exotic.

"Cultural studies." The leader of the Dengue Project turned it over on his tongue. "What *is* that, anyway?"

Francine rounded on him savagely. "Nothing clear-cut like environmental studies, you mean?"

Candace mentally applauded.

"Okay, nah," Dexter said. "No need to be touchy, folks. We all tired here."

It was a meaningless exercise in any case. Joint sub-committees could advise the Provost all they liked, but in the end, Rider was a law unto himself.

The pointlessness grew painful. It became impossible to sit still. Candace's chair grew increasingly, illogically hard and lumpy, as if her every limb had to be distorted for her to remain on it, and she eventually excused herself.

The drive home was unending, the traffic boisterous, the sun unremitting, every joint sore. Her knees buckled, barely supporting her through the door. She made it to the couch, lay for an hour feeling steadily worse and then scrabbled in her purse for paracetamol and swallowed it dry. Clutching her phone she punched in Sonja's number.

"Chik-V," Sonja exclaimed. "I'll drop off fluids, and get you to a doctor if you like."

But it was easier to stay home, gulping coconut water.

After a few days, she could walk but not get her feet into shoes.

"Some people are going to work barefoot," Sonja confirmed. "But you needn't. I've organized for your classes."

It was a mild bout of chikungunya, and despite Randall's warnings Candace limped out a week later. The rash never showed and the fever stayed low.

"You've been lucky," Sonja warned. "But Randall has a point; he must have been reading it up. Don't risk a setback. They say the relapse is from hell."

For another two weeks, Candace skipped meetings, taught her ITS courses and went home. The UWI classes required two weeks' leave, however, because there was no one to drive her, and she was utterly spent after the few hours at ITS. Marcus was heard to tell the Head that Candace might say she was ill, but he knew she was staying home to work on her publications.

The chik-V visitation meant she missed the BEAM interview with the Master's Administrative Assistant, Ms Mackhail. Professor Danraj had dismissed in advance anything the old harridan was likely to say; and when Candace returned, the Chair, Professor McGregor, confirmed that the AA had had nothing of substance to contribute. Surprising, Candace thought. Yet the notes of the interview quoted the AA only as remarking that whatever puny mortals might attempt to conceal or reveal, the iniquitous would drink the wine of the wrath of God, poured out without mixture into the cup of His indignation. And what could Mackhail know except from the confidences of others? Candace reflected that the whole committee was being packed tighter and tighter into the same box.

BEAM plodded more slowly. Some invitees persistently failed to meet with the team. Ravindra Sumra had offered his apologies, but that was understandable. Having landed a post in some minor college in the United States, he had given the required notice, but the Provost had been incensed about this lack of loyalty to ITS, so Sumra had left at once. Other staff members who were visible on the compound offered one excuse after the next.

In April, Professor Waterman pointed out that only the Provost's intervention would force anyone else to attend. The Chair recalled a similar situation at UWI – well, not similar, of course, he qualified quickly under the expectant eye of the Registrar, but not absolutely different, in that it had been an enquiry, such as all institutions have at one time or the other. A comparable situation at UWI had been more or less grinding to a halt, when they had had to ask the Campus Principal to intervene, and the Principal had promptly sent out a strong statement of his support for the team. Actually, he had more or less threatened the job security of anyone failing to comply.

"And that brought the desired result?" Professor Waterman enquired.

"Oh, immediately."

"But with what result?" Candace's question seemed abrupt to her own ears, and she added quickly, "I wondered what we might expect."

"Those who had been hanging back came tumbling out of the woodwork, as if a torch had been applied."

"Our Provost won't," Dexter said with a finality that bespoke insider's knowledge.

The other members waited respectfully for him to continue but waited in vain. His manner made it clear that he could say much if he chose but that his lips were sealed.

"Let's disturb the Provost only as a last resort," McGregor concluded.

Even when the committee reworded its invitation as a summons, Sat declined it, because, he said, of an urgent and potentially tragic personal emergency. Courtney did eventually appear at the end of a long day but poked his head around the door only to confirm that he had no information with which to assist anyone and would therefore not accept the invitation for the interview next morning. He wanted to make clear, however, that he wished the committee well in its deliberations. After he left, Danraj said that he understood Courtney and Sat were committed to a croc hunt the following day, in any case. Professor Waterman announced that she had wasted enough time and would withdraw from the committee and leave for home, if they did not request the Provost's intervention. So the Chair conveyed the request.

The Provost, however, responded that he would be reluctant to taint their report (which must be submitted to himself) by meddling in the process. Reflections prompted by this bracing message gathered oppressively over Candace's left temple. Yet she understood that other matters occupied him to the point of obsession. To realize independence from the Global Knowledge Institute of the Americas and the International Consortium for

Borderless Education, and yet to remain viable – this was a complex process, fraught with opposition from beyond and within ITS. Sonja had heard nervy comments about job stability and had observed that it would take just a few of the more recognized members of staff landing positions elsewhere to upset the already precarious equilibrium.

At the next BEAM meeting, Professor Waterman left early, but the others stayed back, and Dexter opened up regarding his take on the ITS situation. "Much more serious than the fellows letting on. I can't blame chaps who can't see what's going on, when the Provost himself refuses to articulate it. Listen. The more Rider separates from the GKIA and company, the more dependent he going to become on a set of impoverished governments in the region. And then he's going to need recognition from competitors like UWI." Dexter pushed away the file in front of him. "I try to tell him, but he ent listening; he just watch you until you done talk. He's a helluva cold fish."

He modulated his tone to one of admiration, glancing at Candace. "I'm worried about my pardner – that is all. He will find himself going the way of joint degrees with places that want to see him fail anyway, and in the end he going have to sell out to them. Or, as they say here: You fatten fowl to make mongoose take him. One way or the other, though, he has to keep the place looking good. For all our sakes. Not one of us would want a fiasco on his CV." He bowed in Candace's direction. "Or hers."

Professor McGregor, as the other UWI retiree in the room, nodded regretfully even as Dexter's snidely sympathetic smile in Candace's direction seemed to her to convey mysterious insight into her most recent job enquiry to UWI. The Registrar directed a vague nod at a cactus beyond the window, little more than a grimace that committed him neither to agreement nor disagreement with Dexter.

"I suppose you've all heard about Clyde Seuraj." Hari's input was a statement rather than a question.

"What's happened to him?" Candace registered a pang, unwilling to hear whatever catastrophe might have befallen this man she did not know but respected.

"Resigned. This morning."

"Basis?" Professor McGregor's voice betrayed nothing of the relief he must feel.

"On a principle."

No one enquired further. *The P word*, Wright would have said sagely. But in the room, the only sound to be heard was the deep gurgle of ridicule and the prolonged belch of the sea in the hollowness beyond.

When they had drifted outside, Dexter pounced on Candace in the corridor and took her aside to let drop his assumption that she had heard about the UWI vice chancellorship. He supposed she knew it was coming up for grabs, because her daddy would have told her whether he was considering the chances of his appointment. Candace gave not a flicker of reaction, as she thanked him for keeping her up to date and for paying her the compliment of always imagining her to be in the know. She strolled back to her office as if untouched by any but restful thoughts.

Her impassive look was well practised. As a child, she had inscrutably played out in her mind stories of her life as it could have been, should have been, might yet be – multiple versions in parallel. As she grew, the intersections between her mother's pain and her own cut deep, seeping emotions she had continually wiped from sight, suppressing sensation to a degree that gave an impression of coldness. But always the rawness, smarting, welling up. Then, contained again.

After a while, she could tell Randall, especially when he had gone far away. Here, well. Lex Wright was simpler to deal with, but they talked of the present rather than the past. He made no secret of his interest but seemed neither offended nor surprised at her somewhat sister-like response. Lex's direct and irreverent comments brought relief from the innuendos of CuSt and the circumlocutions of BEAM interviewees. He had stopped needling her at every opportunity, and his whimsical delight in *seeming* to torture her actually lifted her out of herself.

Yet when she bumped into him that day, she paused, trying to pin down some difference. Under her critical eye, he looked worn, and he shifted restlessly.

"Don't dawdle," he commanded. "I've nothing against frittering away time myself, but it does not become you."

Something in his voice, a weariness, made her look again. He seemed weightless, and his eyes darker. No, larger.

"What riddle are you currently unravelling?" he demanded.

"You don't look yourself. My imagination?"

Lex swatted tiredly at the idea as at a mosquito, and she did not persist. She agreed readily when he invited her and Sonja to lunch on Sunday at a restaurant in the mountains above Kingston.

But Sonja seemed uncomfortable. "He hardly knows *me*." She bobbed up to hand Candace a glass of coconut water and sat again briefly, pleased that Candace had at last come round for breakfast.

"I won't go on my own," Candace said. "No, I don't need a chaperone, but I want to stop short of anything like a date. He says the lunch is part of some cure he requires, and we must not deny him."

"Oh, very well."

When Candace got up to leave, Sonja said, "You must come again. You can bring What's-his-name, you know. What is it again?"

"Cassidy. Ms."

The following Sunday's escape to Strawberry Hills was healing, perhaps more so for Candace than Lex, lolling at a table spread with crisp linen, the mountains folding away around them, mist rolling down bright then deeper green slopes and streaming in silky wisps into the valley.

But by Monday, there was Elizabeth Woods again at Candace's office door, asking whether Dr Clarke had reconsidered her reluctance to grant an interview, now the issue of financial accountability had arisen. Candace gave no inkling of the interview she was about to attend, but the journalist dogged her as if smelling out BEAM's upcoming meeting with the Finance Officer.

As usual, this interview produced little information on what the committee was there to find out but much about the state of ITS. The Finance Officer was amazed that anyone could be unaware of the massive financial difficulties they faced. Once the parent institutions stopped funding, and no new system of support replaced them – where was the money to come from?

Curiously, Candace found that each question she put to the Finance Officer elicited from the Chair or the Registrar some other enquiry that deflected hers. Afterwards the Chairman apologized. He had taken a while to see where she was going with her questions, Professor McGregor explained, and now he realized that in trying to help, he had got in the way, so they would have a follow-up interview with the Finance Officer to air Dr Clarke's concerns properly.

"Thank you, gentlemen," he said, when they had agreed on a date, and the Registrar held open the door.

"Chivalry in the twenty-first century?" Dexter tossed a malicious grin, before strolling with Candace back to the coffee room, where Francine, after a swift nod to Danraj, returned to the conversation underway.

"Of course, enquiries get us nowhere," Francine said. "People like to *talk*, but only informally. Sure, they'll complain in whispers, but only real leadership brings the problems out into the clear light of day so that action can be taken and ethical standards upheld."

"Throw in a couple negatives, and you will sound just like Dudley, gyul." Dexter flashed her a cheery grin, before hoisting his coffee mug and setting off for his office.

"You know, he means no harm," Francine observed, when the door swung closed, "and Dexter's as good a Master as the patriarchy may be expected to produce, but he could show a bit more respect. For those who have gone before – don't you know? I mean, Dudley was a *faithful friend* to us, and he gave his life, his *life*, to building the *académie*." A quiet and gracious reflection, before she made her way brokenly from the room.

Chapter 11

Crooked

And here is gold, and that ful greet plentee,
That shal departed been among us thre.
But nathelees, if I kan shape it so
That it departed were amongst us two,
Hadde I nat doon a freendes torn to thee?

Sometime after midnight, a staccato of gunfire in the distance triggered the recollection that Ariana Ramirez was dead and that her death meant nothing to anyone else Candace knew. She too must lay it down and move on, if she was to pick up her own life. After an uneasy sleep, the BEAM data stirred in her head at about three in the morning, rubbing alongside day-to-day events extruded on the surfaces of ITS. As her attention shifted, small incidents long sunk in her past pushed their way up. When her eyes popped open, her mind bared its strata, fault-lined by the ongoing problem of how to arrive at what BEAM's informants regarded as, at best, confidential and, at worst, self-incriminatory.

Then, with an almost physical jolt, the illusive nature of the BEAM discussions came to rest against the Forbidden Words project.

She sprang up and flicked on the notebook for those general guidelines she had written at the outset in designing her project: . . . *may well include*

analyses of repressive . . . or of narratives of resistance . . . or of discourse for
suppressing information under the guise of revealing it. . . . She caught her breath.
BEAM could be her major source for investigating (dys)functional discourse
in ITS.

She jotted down a title for a possible paper through which she might
draw directly from the BEAM data: "Undermining Discourse: Guises for
the Keeping and Breaking of Silence in Three Professional Contexts". She
mentally stroked the ambiguity of the main title before setting it aside as
less applicable than its subtitle. Then she settled down to identify her three
contexts: institutional requirements of confidentiality, collegial reticence,
and evasion of personal involvement.

It was all well and good for Randall to say there were things best
fictionalized if one was ever to make them manageable; she worked best
with data from real situations.

"I expect you'd produce something fast and gripping on ITS," she told
him. "I don't have that sort of thing in me."

"Like a murder mystery? Gruesome gang epic? Or something chilling but
not so gory? You'll never get even that from me. Mind you, there are many
bloodless ways of taking a life."

"And your research? Scholarship is my trade, and I thought it was yours."

"Why not two trades? Divided to the vein, ent? And, academic or
creative, the intensity is the same for me."

Fiction and criticism made the same demands on him, he said. "I'm
working on a situation related by a narrator who won't look at it directly.
But I must manage it without intervening."

"Like trying to arrive at findings in one's research without warping them
with one's own pet theories," she mused.

"Exactly. So – issues of narration are tantalizing. I love that part. For
me, the nightmare is dialogue. Voices that filter through the mind of the
narrator but keep their individuality. So far, I can't hear anyone in my head
except the narrator, let alone work out how to represent the rest on a page.
And then some voices aren't, well, forthright."

It did not sound that fictional to Candace. More like the sort of
equivocating mess she worked in every day.

Only a few of her colleagues seemed *not* to be twisting or suppressing anything. Lex Wright was one of these, but he persisted in approaching matters from a set of values entirely alien to hers. He made less of Sat's predations than his attire, "those vile shreds of denim"; while Courtney irritated him by being offensively rambunctious. "Shouldn't there be a study of valid and invalid effervescence?" Lex moaned. "What are you working on at present, Dr Clarke?"

"Forgotten words," she said absently.

He regarded Candace with an unexpected expression of disfavour. "Will you never stop hedging?" he protested. "Your evasions riddle conversation with cracks, which you fill with gnomic utterances preserved in brine from your grandmother to the present day, regardless of their dwindling relevance. I'm thinking of calling it the salt pond effect. To go down in the books as Wright's Salt Pond Effect. Or perhaps Clarke's, for what claim do I have to it? Well? Why stare – apart from my obvious charm and appeal?"

As Candace's silence lengthened, Sonja mused, "Remapping? Hers is a labyrinthine mind." They were in Sonja's office for a private discussion of weird programme changes that Francine had put forward but was probably passing on from Althea without scrutiny. "I too have corridors I've cordoned off and edge past nervously."

"I didn't think. . ." Candace's voice trailed off. Around corners loomed well-lit objects (like the fact of her own evasions) to which she had closed her eyes. The reasons why she closed them swept up, gleaming near and then fading as she turned on them. She might glimpse things that had lain covered for years, like her old sense of the universe as a magical place where her father charmed and punished whom he would, but, in the end, might . . . "I have to work," she said, her words thick with urgency, and she turned away.

Sonja's worried voice followed her. "I'm not sure her eyes are open."

Lex responded, "Aye, but their sense is closed."

Candace wandered to the lunch room, only to find Francine holding court in high spirits – but with a brittleness, as if this vivacity would snap under the slightest pressure. Their centre seemed held together only by its tensions. When Lex arrived and Francine made unpredictable overtures to him, he responded with more of a wince than a smile.

"One doesn't dare let her in," he explained to Candace fifteen minutes later, when he followed her back to her office. "She wants only the narrowest opening for one of her terrorist attacks." At her glance of surprise he said, "Her whole purpose is to create fear; everyone must quake before her. I have more compelling things to be afraid of." He placed reverently on Candace's desk, as on a shrine, a pale blue-green rosette of echevaria he had purloined from one of the stands in the outer corridor. "You know I would not intentionally cause you pain," he said softly.

"My pain is from elsewhere. It adheres to an inner lining of my mind and sometimes lets go at one corner to take hold in another crevice. It's not from you."

As he parted with Candace at her office door, however, he encountered Francine accompanying around a Dr Halifax, just returned from his year's leave abroad with the air of one who has expanded his horizons and must now try valiantly for a niche within the old confines of local endeavour.

Thrusting out his hand graciously, Halifax said, "You're Wright, aren't you?"

"Almost invariably." Wright rubbed forlornly at a crease in his shirt, sighed, then drifted away.

"How did he get here?" Halifax asked Francine plaintively, tucking his rejected hand in a pocket.

"I can only suppose Dr Wright's mother made a sizeable donation to the institution," Francine returned in honeyed tones. "Otherwise our Provost could hardly have foisted on us anyone so patently uninterested in everything we stand for."

"Oh, but isn't Lex a nice chap?" Marion said as she passed by, drawing a tolerant smile from Francine.

Only Marion seemed comfortable about being befriended by Francine, who had, hitherto, been mildly critical of her – and perhaps with cause, as Sonja noted good-humouredly. Marion did always seem perched on the verge of the vapours, a posture naturally provoking to a woman like Francine, who felt the need at all times to flaunt independence and strength of mind.

Block them out. Candace flipped on the desktop in her office: the Power-Point introducing language variation in the Caribbean; a chat group on forms of address; BEAM data for evidence of staff impropriety and BEAM notes for analysis of equivocation in staff discourse. The balancing act demanded dexterity and concentration, leaving no room for the dismals.

Yet how much could one accomplish, where the institution's few administrative procedures led not to ways out of its problems but to dead ends or sinkholes? ITS management drew at will on its limited infrastructure or arbitrarily dismissed it, and this fraudulent bureaucracy spewed out meaningless routines that made discussion purposeless and frustrated planning. The frittering away of time rubbed Candace raw. Directionless meetings grew unbearable, however carefree a deportment she adopted to avoid seeming petulant. So the grey mist curled in, thickening to a humid presence. Even under the shadow of the covered walkways, the Hellshire heat scorched like the hot breath of something stalking her mercilessly.

That evening on Skype, she could see Randall reading her, catch questions flickering across his face before he rethought and left them unuttered.

Finally he said, "Gone, then. I'm getting into the most recent of *A Song of Ice and Fire*; but you look as if you'll need to work tonight instead of reading. When we talk tomorrow, you should be brighter."

She tried to put up a better face, without success. "My name is Bleak," she quipped. "It rhymes with *geek*."

That took them into a few more minutes of argument about the author's convoluted storylines and radical transformations in character, before they hung up. But he was right about work; she plunged into it, and it bore her up.

She gathered around her the second paper she was currently fleshing out for Forbidden Words. She called it, "Discourse of Useless Testimony: Epistemic Modality in Refusals to Commit". Sorting through notes from interviews of CSSGDS staff, she catalogued speech that revealed silences, gaps, circumlocutions, equivocations, waverings. Some data she put aside for another article, tentatively titled, "On Not Pronouncing Sentence: Hedging in Testimony Regarding Professional (Mis)Conduct". When she was fairly sure of her design for "Refusals to Commit", there were a few hours left for sleep, but she was too alert. So lying down waiting for sleep, she turned her mind again to a set of observations she called "CuSt

Narratives" – everything the people in Cultural Studies (and especially Francine) had said about improprieties in CSSGDS. This set of reflections had driven her unwillingly to conclusions that did not pertain to CSSGDS alone.

In particular, an implied account of Francine, Courtney and Sat had come together from scraps through elusive testimony, as well as gossip, confidences and odd fragments of documentation. A tale had assembled, as comment after comment from Wright, Marion and Sonja fell together with chance revelations from others (Dexter, Barham, Nicholas) and became superimposed on each other. Then the different versions filled in each other's gaps. The result turned out to be a three-cornered history rather like some composite but contradictory quest. Sort of thing Randall would love.

As she saw it, the progress of the three colleagues must have amounted to a fellowship fraught by subtle but corrosive conflicts of interest, and it seemed now, as Candace mentally reviewed what she had heard, that the three together had been searching for different things – one for love (of a sort), one for money and one for unlimited sexual opportunity. The fraternity had gone sour at exactly that point when their interests converged on the road to professional advancement. Each had declared a common interest in the Unstable Skins project, an interest that was genuine but secondary to the separate private greed in which each was absorbed and which each fed like an addiction. They were not at one after all: once Francine and Courtney'n'Sat found themselves with a common goal, nothing was left but to destroy each other so as to keep the whole mess quiet and get exclusive control of the Unstable Skins publication.

She got up and slung these scraps into an e-mail for Randall, nuances of narrating being one of the things that grabbed him. Candace had a different interest: How had the tale got through to her despite her colleagues' best efforts? How was information suppressed even as this evasion was betrayed in the discourse? Snippets of testimony and informal talk came back to her, and she reached for a notepad beside the bed. *Don't call my name. This doesn't go outside this room, eh? I just talking to you – is not for the record.*

Widespread anxiety to avoid responsibility for whatever had happened, or even direct knowledge of it, had spawned phrases like *my understanding is that, I've heard it said, the word on the corridor is, everyone knows that, is not me say so,* and *you can ask anyone . . .* Even while refusing to commit to their personal knowledge of anything, speakers hastened to underscore their own honesty with *actually, in fact, let me be straight with you, if truth be told,* and *I would'n lie.*

But what could BEAM *report,* when it was manifest that the rest of her colleagues were already clear on what this report should include but must never say? Interfering in their business of leaving facts unstated, she might block her own professional advancement. And her father must have suspected what he was mandating BEAM to investigate. Her mind paused over the mesh of contradiction with a sort of fascinated horror. What was she for? Surely not to ensure a report on what he already knew and kept silent in the interest of the institution's reputation.

"What reputation?" Wright demanded the instant she consulted him.

As he enlarged on the question, Francine put her head round the door in search of an e-mail contact and picked up one of his choicest comments.

"So why do you stay?" Francine snapped.

"But, my dear" – his voice conveyed mild surprise – "who else would have me? Admittedly I'm not a Percy Stone, whom only ITS would employ" – he paused to scribble *babble* and *dabble* on the palm of his hand – "and I cannot, like him, boast a palsied mind, but I am *so* politically incorrect. I mean – all my iconoclastic theories of Caribbean Culture?"

Francine having gone in a huff, Wright had settled back on the cushions and now became expansive. "So how's your Ralph Ellison fellow?" He seemed carelessly bent on leading Candace away from the ideas she was trying to work through. "Your invisible man, Randall Jefferies."

No point telling Wright to mind his own business, because, as he would readily point out, he had none.

"I can't banter with you now." Candace pressed her thumbs to her temples. "My whole career – which is, of course, not whole – is on the line. As well as in shreds."

"Must have been to begin with – or you wouldn't be here," he said, though not unkindly, and scrupulously ignoring the mangled imagery. "What has further lacerated it?"

"Tenure," she said. "Or, rather, lack thereof. Everyone is slicing up everyone else to get ahead – and where do I fit in?"

"Perhaps you are asking the wrong questions," he reflected helpfully. "You may need to be thinking of how best you can wriggle out."

His suggestion was lingering in her mind, when she chanced to encounter in Tropical Plaza a former colleague, Cheryl Grandison – a loud young woman with whom she had taught part time at Mona.

"You mean a full-time position?" Cheryl shrilled. "But I mus' bawl it out. After I *green* with envy. How you manage to land that? I never see that advert, and God knows I comb the papers every day. You knew somebody in the system?" Candace parried swiftly with a question about opportunities at UWI, and the young woman regarded her in shock. "Trade in a tenure-track position for some one-off post? You mad or what?" But Cheryl was eager enough to exchange e-mail addresses and agree to link up on Facebook. "If they not publishing the posts, best I really have someone on the inside. Or how the hell I going get to hear?"

Perhaps, Candace concluded yet again, she had best bide her time rather than advertise her unease. UWI was worth the wait, although (like anywhere else) it harboured its own pockets of unreality.

The AFP instructors, in what was a largely virtual programme, did not really exist in any tangible way – not so much because of the level at which they were employed as because of what they taught. This was not assistance with the rats for an Alzheimer's project in a Med Sci laboratory, or measurement of sewage in a field project on viable marine environments. It wasn't even gang member interviews for a Criminology study led by some high-profile sociologist. This was academic writing, which was something anyone could do, or something everyone should have done already, or something no one needed to do. To get on the payroll or stay there without Marcus Walters's support had become impossible. Not only was he cherished from above, but his underbelly was invulnerable.

Randall had begun to ask why she didn't give it up.

"But AFP is my only remaining link with UWI," Candace said.

"Is it even a link?" Randall asked. "Is it worth the harassment of working with Walters? I wish I could do something about him for you."

"A short story?" She lit up at the thought of Marcus happening upon himself in a book, but Randall's questioning of her AFP hours as a viable link to UWI throbbed on in her head.

The ongoing BEAM investigations did nothing for her spirits except insofar as they churned out new data for her research project. Rather than hard evidence for disciplinary action, most interviews produced speculation and moralizing.

"I know the type of thing," Lex said. "You feel the hairline fractures in your sanity multiplying wildly."

"And yawning wider."

"Just so."

Still, although few would say anything specific about sexual impropriety, some had much to say about money. Not in their mandate, the Chairman argued, but Candace insisted that where questions about one aspect of professorial behaviour kept leading to another aspect, there was a connection that made it one discourse. Besides, however confidential such matters regarding financial corruption might be, a trickle of documentation showed up greedy claims for reimbursement on field-trip expenditure, research assistance and extra teaching.

Then it came out that whole courses had been mounted at Courtney's home, a sort of tertiary extra-lessons initiative. Some students appeared to have paid fees privately and others not. Candace wanted these students' names, to urge statements from them, but the Registrar asked uneasily whether she was being a bit premature.

"And what about Sat's classes at Courtney's house?" She pointed to records of claims and payments. A technician said students had grumbled about having to sign up for Sat's module to be sure of gaining a pass the following semester.

Candace's heart lurched at the memory of Michelle dropping out. But still no document, no promised testimony. Nothing concrete.

Allowing her mind to play over odd comments that seemed peripheral to the issue, she recollected a couple of interviewees mentioning that Percy Stone "knew stuff". But Percy? Ever since Percy had reappeared with his examination scripts, he had seemed much chastened (it appeared to have been an exceptionally bad trip) and looked more than ever like the gecko in a TV advertisement. Dexter said that putting the most harmless question to him might send him racing off again at a speed likely to put Usain Bolt to shame (and probably clutching another set of scripts). As the discussion dissipated into congratulatory chuckles over the possible meanings of *speed*, the committee remained undecided about calling Stone at all.

Outside the window, a female student paused, ashimmer in overstuffed tights and short top held up by frail straps straining against gravity. The overflowing top barely reached down to the low-cut tights, as she stood holding her phone to her ear. When her book dropped, and she leaned forward to retrieve it, the top rode up and the waist of the tights down, proclaiming that underwear was no longer a private matter and that indeed one should be grateful for it or wish for more as protection for what was sliding fully into view –

"Dr Clarke?" The Chairman's voice broke in on her reflections. "Are we agreed about Mr Stone?"

"Gi' she a chance," Dexter crooned. "She taking in the sights."

"I was thinking there's a reason why some institutions have a dress code." Candace sighed. "Forgive my inattention, Chair. Old-fashioned notions of propriety die hard."

"I couldn't agree more," McGregor replied icily, and he closed the meeting.

⌖

Only the financial leads seemed traceable, but Candace could hardly follow them without a bureaucracy of the sort she had often cursed at UWI. Worst of all, there was no ferocious Bursar at ITS. Any system for monitoring expenditure existed largely in the heads of administrators, and whatever had dwelt in Dudley's head had died with him. Mackhail would have turned over whatever she had to BEAM.

The thought of the old man doubled over mounds of papers on his desk made Candace wonder what guidance Dudley might have offered. And what had become of his files? Dexter, having moved into that office, could have disposed of anything Mackhail had not seized. On the other hand, Dexter had beaten out his own path in traditional university systems. He said things like "Chaps must find ways to get rid of all this rigmarole", but he knew the value of records. Perhaps he had not dispensed with Dudley's papers. Perhaps they were stored up in his cabinet. In case.

When she voiced the thought to Lex, he scolded her for playing hysterically with the idea of raiding the Master's drawers. "While you would actually do nothing so unseemly," he said, "it is troubling that you can't resist the fantasy."

Fantasy? The word sent them into peals of laughter. Only last week, Marion had spoken of leaving ITS and holing herself up in the mountains – Newcastle, she said, or at least Irish Town – to write fantasy fiction. Francine and a gaggle of cohorts had applauded. Follow your dream, girl, Francine advised.

Lex had preserved an unusual silence, until he found Candace and recounted it.

"Fantasy?" Candace had asked. "Surely not. I mean, I've got to love the speculative stuff but . . . but surely not Marion."

"No, really, she can't be serious. Marion's not the type of writer to create a new world, however perceptively she analyses the failures of our own. But the real spectacle was Percy – you should have seen him come alive, the cold reptilian blood visibly pounding through his veins. Percy became enthusiasm itself. It was just what he had always intended to do, he shared with us. Projected himself as the Tolkien of the Caribbean, and it's too foolish. He can barely work over the leftovers of his own limited experience to serve it up in whatever verbal garnish he thinks will fool the consumer's palate."

"You beast," she exclaimed. Yet his tone belied his words, conveying little malice – more a surgical precision and scientific interest. He enjoyed poking around in other people's brains.

Indeed, Lex in his keen but indolent way had even extracted some sense of Randall, more from what she didn't say than what she did. For some reason, this connection had begun to interest Lex and prompt probing remarks.

"But surely even our current technology doesn't handle basic bodily functions?" he argued. "I mean – though I'm woefully behind in such things – the electronic exchange of bodily fluids isn't quite worked out yet, is it?" He leaned forward to deliver a provocative whisper in her ear. "Tweet, tweet."

"Get out of my office," she said, but without hostility. She had grown quite accustomed to him. "And why are you looking at me like that?"

"You mean, lustfully?"

"A few years ago, you would have been arrested for that look."

"Aah, the distrust of the flesh. But then, only a couple centuries before that, if you were rumoured to engage in some relationship with an unbodied scholar – a liaison that was other than fleshly – you'd have been burnt at the stake. Dear me. Such a waste of fine flesh."

She held the door open and closed it behind him barely in time to stifle a chuckle. She had stopped short of describing Randall as just a friend – only, she told herself, because she was reluctant to encourage Lex.

To her horror, though, her father introduced the topic of her personal life, when she waited in the Provost's meeting room for the other members of BEAM to arrive.

"So there's a significant other in the UK?" he asked. "I was almost persuaded you'd given yourself to scholarship – like a nun married to Jesus, you know? Still, a guy thousands of miles away is hardly more substantial, even less so than the delicate Dr Wright. Actually, it doesn't say much for your powers of discrimination to cuddle up here with someone who would probably prefer your boyfriend."

"Wright's actually straight, not that that's your affair – or mine, since he and I are not having an affair."

Only a week later, Lex mentioned that he had met the Provost. Rider had actually accosted him in a friendly way. "Your dad – well, I'd hesitate to say he had given us his blessing," he told Candace, "not a metaphor to apply to inimical characters. But I'd say he conveyed his approval. I hope that doesn't put you off."

"It does, rather," she admitted. She contemplated Lex with a sort of objective curiosity. "How can one man be so annoying?"

"You refer to your father, I trust, and not to my poor self."

"I refer to you. I mean, how? How can you be this way? How can one human being. . ."

"Perhaps because I was to have been a twin," he surmised and then looked serious. "You know, you've not only gone silent now; you look quite pale. Come, come. Stop pretending to search for words. I know the concept of two of me is fearful to contemplate, but you'll be reassured to learn that my counterpart mercifully strangled in the birth process. Just the cord, though – nothing sinister." Then he cheered up. "Tell me more about your demon lover – you did say the relationship is conducted in cyberspace, didn't you? This other-than-human dimension fascinates me. Do you adhere strictly to verbal play, or do you use video? The questions this raises are limitless. Like – how far can one go on Skype? I mean, I'm trying to understand what seems to be an essentially mystical something in one sense but has to be fraught with . . . like interventions from the spirit world – a tiny bit creepy for my taste, but no doubt truly stimulating if you like that type of thing." He seemed to give it a thought and then shook his head. "No. Really, you ought to balance things with a stint of the physically erotic. Why don't you let me lead you through the basics? We should give ourselves up to the current temper, for what times we live in – the campus rife with naughty rumour . . ."

She stemmed the torrent firmly. "Have you heard the news about the Unstable Skins publication?"

"There is one?"

"Going to be. The book proposal has been accepted."

"How d'you know?"

"Francine sent a copy of the contract to the committee that's considering her application for the Chair." As his questioning gaze continued unwavering, she added, "Marion's on the committee."

"So she told you – of course, in confidence."

"Yes. But I also heard it from any number of other people she told in confidence before that, so I'm at liberty to spread it wholesale. There. It's accepted. They've struck gold."

"Who gets to keep it?"

"Who, indeed?" Her attention wandered, as it came to her that everyone had their own hoard to safeguard. Secrets, sometimes. What was her father covering under the enquiry? She knew of no job-related misbehaviour in his case. Yes, he was unrelentingly self-serving, but his flagrant infidelity to her mother had nothing to do with his professional life.

Randall had never bought that. "Nothing? A relationship with a student under his supervision? In a system in which the supervisor is also an examiner?" That role of the supervisor was changing, but examining had been part of the supervisor's duties in UWI history and at TCAC, so there was no gain-saying Randall's point. And what had become of that student, anyway? Allison. Candace remembered a storm that broke over her head once, as a result of a chance remark; but she could not recall the surname. Wait. Allison was the surname. What *had* become of Ms Allison?

Candace found her through Google by combining the name with Earl Rider's and with TCAC, to which she must have shifted following one leave of absence after the other from UWI. The whole process must have stretched over twelve years. Dr Allison currently worked at a minor college in the United States, and her thesis had come out through what looked like a vanity press. The blurb on the back cover, of the sort so often quoted from a reviewer, was identified as a comment by Earl Rider.

So he had peer-reviewed a book based on a thesis he had supervised. For this press? Something shifted at the bottom of Candace's stomach, but she stilled it. She searched for the press and confirmed that the publication fee was not straightforward subsidy, such as many publishers required in order to make ends meet in a difficult market. Nor was it a variation on respectable self-publication by authors who had undertaken to go it alone. This was a set-up, a chink in his professional integrity (his breastplate of unrighteousness, Silver used to say). Which brought her mind back to circle, obsessively, the question of why he had forced her into an investigation of professional decorum.

No one was going to say anything forthright, except perhaps Harvey Barham. Questioned for a second time by the committee, Barham slung around obscenities with unbridled fury. Nothing would happen to the guilty, he insisted; nothing ever did, which made each enquiry a farce. From the deluge of profanity he let loose regarding ITS management, it was clear he, at least, was unafraid of reprisal. And Barham's posture was well known. "Anything could fall out that man mouth," Dexter liked to say.

And it did. Barham pointed out that the Provost was as lawless as the rest. Why else would he unilaterally appoint his own daughter without even a pretence of procedure. Oh, yes, a fine young woman, and he intended no slight on *her* – but in bringing her to a place like this, Rider was obviously acting in his interest rather than hers.

Then she knew. So obvious, it was ridiculous not to have seen it at once. She stretched for her BlackBerry and fired off a BBM to Randall. She was on the committee to block disclosures regarding her father that might snowball to the point that *she* would find embarrassing. From conclusions that would ruin *her*. The Provost was taking cover under his daughter's need to protect her own good name.

Chapter 12

Endowment

This tresor moste ycaried be by nyghte
As wisely and as slyly as it myghte.

So many paths along which events unfold – criss-crossing even more in factual report than in fiction. Randall said what mattered in a story was which path had brought a character into trouble, and which led out – or deeper in. But character itself had to be the thing, Candace insisted, whatever Aristotle had to say: a speaker's profile was as important to meaning as the speech itself. But over the years, Randall fretted, his characters had not crystallized enough to produce a clear strand of events.

He had grown restless. He barely squeezed this writing into little pockets between his research in possible world theory and the medieval otherworld, let alone lectures like the one that currently occupied him, on the exemplum in Chaucer's *Tales*. Of course, he had had miraculous good fortune in landing the position he held, but he was certain he would write fiction more easily in the Caribbean.

"Because you'd be living in the setting?" she asked. "Don't expect more time to write." In response to his somewhat wounded silence, she said, "Obviously I'd be glad to see you back, you dope; I'm only warning that what people insist on terming the creative *streak* – as if it's a cosmetic highlight – hardly draws more than lip service in assessment of scholarship. At least, where I am now. UWI may be more enlightened." It seemed almost a fault line to some, she added, as if it involved time and effort that could have gone into real work.

It was not only the odd taunt by Courtney or dismissive comment by someone more serious, like Professor McGregor. There were actually artists – like that poet, Ronsard, who had delivered a distinguished lecture recently at UWI before going on to his tour of the French Caribbean. Ronsard described creative writing as something an academic toyed with – as if one could never be a real artist unless one had pined in a garret. He dismissed the tug of both impulses, the interplay of the academic and creative, as little more than indecisiveness, an unwillingness to commit. But the result of Ronsard's line of argument was a professional artist setting aside all else but art, and (till that art gained enough recognition to make a living) starving as a badge of honour – and starving out there in the world experiencing *real life*, not nestling in some cosy, leisurely academic niche.

"Starving as an active rather than passive demise, with a bit of heroic flourish," Candace said.

"Original sense of the word." But Randall's smile seemed somewhat distracted.

"You see, I know to my cost." Candace continued, hesitantly at first and then picking up momentum. Confidential ponderings of assessment meetings quickly became common knowledge at ITS, and she had listed on her vitae experimental poems published in a good print journal, later hearing these items had drawn fire.

"Well, I don't want to be unkind." Marion had quoted another member on the panel. "I wouldn't want to imply that Candace is just in denial about her mediocrity as a scholar, but how else is one to account for the propping up of one's résumé by little publications of half-baked verse in the odd magazine? I mean which of us hasn't a few pathetic poems or what have you hidden in a file somewhere – it's part of the humanities thing, isn't it? – this forlorn hope, but then when you realize you're up against Walcott and the rest, you say, Let me concentrate on what I've come here about. I'm not in some attic in London or Toronto trying to scratch out my living with my pen, staking my life on it, don't you know, huddled away in the damn cold and taking the racism and other rubbish instead of snuggled up here in a comfortable university with the sun shining all year. See, I'm in a faculty claiming to be a scholar, and I need to get out of whatever fairy tale of myself I dreamed up and settle down to serious research."

"So much for confidentiality, when all would have been the better for it," Randall grumbled.

He showed admirable forbearance in not adding that Candace had never told him she wrote poetry, let alone published any. Perhaps he wondered whether any of it was about him, she speculated hopefully. He went on to talk as if she had concealed nothing.

"Your academic publications alone were strong enough to carry you, so what motivated this snide attack? The fact that you *came out* rather than remaining a closet poet?" He pondered for a while. "No. This was an assault – the attacker had been waiting there for an excuse to strike. Who and why?"

Candace set her mouth mutinously and stared into the screen. Before Skyping, she had powdered over the tear track on her makeup.

"You could work you tail off," Randall grumbled. "Somebody will call you wutless, because what you doing ent real work. Plot and character," he continued. "What else is there, even in the *real* world?"

"Which doesn't necessarily include sites of intellectual activity. Even some academics locate the real world 'out there'."

And whichever version of the world one was dealt, Randall reflected aloud, it shape-shifted as one advanced, spawning choices that looked innocent. Besides, what lurked along the paths one did not take, waiting to branch off and intersect with the chosen way? Events and the motives that prompted them, he said. "For look at your father." A glance, and he proceeded gingerly. "A history of neglect and manipulation – from which at last you're breaking free – yet isn't he showing signs now of setting up some sort of dependence on you? That is, if you were less resistant."

When he had signed off, she turned from her laptop, glancing up from the screen, and caught her face in a mirror, under the tangle of curls. Shadows had deepened beneath her eyes yet perhaps withdrawn somewhat from her mind. She turned to a box with random notes on her table, doing so almost with distaste, as if her research gave off the chill of a cold case, but from that descending spiral that sucked her in from time to time, her exchanges with Randall on their separate projects offered fissures for escape.

Still, questions that crystallized when they were talking often remained unanswerable. Why, for example, would staff misdemeanours be side issues to someone in the position of Provost? Her careful notes of Earl Rider's instructions and responses to BEAM's interim reports recorded hedges that made her track his qualifying phrases more intently. Why he should hedge remained a mystery.

As usual when coming up against a blank wall, she allowed her mind a detour. She thought of Courtney and Sat apparently brokering reconciliation with Francine to keep their names on the Unstable Skins project, and Francine responding with icy disdain. On the other hand, both Francine and Courtney were, separately, treating the Provost with elaborate deference, to which he responded graciously. But these scattered observations brought no insight into the Provost's mind.

Candace swept aside the glossy *ITS Newstime*, with its mission statement, strategic plan and sappy slogan – all in the end for the aggrandizement of Earl Rider. He flashed a smile above the announcement that one of the world's first-rate universities would be awarding him an honorary degree. The image captured purpose, brilliance. But how did the scholarly integrity he projected beyond that smooth hard polish coexist with what he tolerated in others under his watch?

The air conditioning had gone in mid-August, and the need to equip classrooms in time for the 2013 to 2014 academic year had taken precedence over the condition of meeting rooms and offices. Of the heat-hazed investigations by BEAM, the most recent had been a meeting with Anthea O'Connor, who stared malevolently at Candace and answered with as much insolence as she could generate.

Candace struggled to repress her memory of quarrelling with Lex over his inappropriate references to Anthea's unfettered breasts. He had enquired plaintively whether they shouldn't be subject to some Dangerous Weapons Act. Or something. "One day," Lex had prophesied darkly, "somebody will get knocked down." Candace had scolded him for sexist stereotypes and evicted him from her office, but she was not as offended as she should have been – or would have been, had it been anyone but Anthea. Which was inexcusable. Candace fell to wondering whether there was some way of packing Anthea off to work for Marcus. Then she realized she was smiling foolishly instead of attending to Anthea's diatribe on traitors to the centre, and the Chair was eyeing her severely.

The Provost had routinely embarrassed Candace by short-cutting his own arrangements, summoning her arbitrarily for updates on the committee's findings. He bluntly rejected her request to be removed from BEAM, even when she sent it properly through the Chair, and the Chair betrayed growing unease about the tension between her and the Provost. McGregor even wondered, audibly, whether he should recuse himself from the exercise. Then, suddenly, he relaxed. All at once, Professor McGregor was there to stay, though steadfastly avoiding private discussion with Candace.

The week after BEAM's session with Anthea, Candace arrived for their second meeting with the Finance Officer, only to learn it had passed, brought forward by an hour and a half that morning, when the Registrar had found it impossible to contact Dr Clarke. This second meeting had added little information in any case, the Chairman assured her. The interview with what cleaner? Ah, the one said to have discovered that . . . item of clothing, yes. To be sure. That had been scheduled for later that day, but a technician had cancelled at the last moment, when Miss Monica was sweeping the corridor outside their meeting room, so they had invited her in right after the Finance Officer. She denied ever making any report of the sort, so, again, little had been gleaned. All very disappointing – or reassuring, depending on how one looked at it. The Chairman and the Registrar both hoped, naturally, that there would be no support for aspersions of unprofessional conduct at the institution in which they were employed.

Meanwhile, the gap Dexter had left in assuming office as Master filled as expected. ITS announced Francine Forbes-Garcia's elevation as Fellow of the Centre for Caribbean Cultural Studies. She showed herself increasingly anxious to nail down her professorship – promised, as she insisted, when Morgan Shade recruited her. If she had needed administrative stature before, what was the hitch now?

For the sake of the centre, she deplored Candace's involvement in the enquiry. Not that Candace's teaching load was reduced; only, there were now areas of operation outside of Francine's supervision. More invidious was Francine's unceasing reference, so subtle it could never be pinned down, to Candace's position on BEAM as a favour bestowed by a powerful relative. Francine stopped short of pronouncing nepotism. Yet she must know, Randall surmised, that Rider had no concern for his daughter. Francine was clearly unafraid of offending him by undercutting Candace.

The long-term view at ITS was no more encouraging than the current atmosphere.

"Frankly, I see no basis for recommending your tenure at this time," Francine had said. "And what's the rush? You've not been here long."

"Nor has ITS."

"And you haven't been in academia long. Part-time hustling in UWI's Foundation courses doesn't count for promotion there or anywhere else."

"Oh, right. Longevity." Try as she might, Candace could not help exploding. "Mr Barham ought to get his chair before anyone else then." Unwise, Candace admitted later as she thrashed it out with Randall, but one could stand just so much. She had stalked out angrily through the general office, in time to see Gillian gazing up at Courtney, wearing on her face a heart yearning to be broken. Strength, Lord.

And, all the time, Candace's appointment on BEAM lay there in full view like a gauntlet thrown down. Worse, the Provost's new and insufferably stylish assistant adorned every meeting to which he summoned Candace, and he spoke in front of this Amelia La Mar with a freedom that flaunted their intimacy. Perhaps it was to goad his daughter but, with her mother gone, Candace cared nothing about his women – except that this one was eight years younger than herself, and the La Mar's curves made Candace feel like a bamboo stalk. Still, such personal irritation was nothing to the inroads being made on her professional life: Francine's underminings and the Provost's demands wore her down, as if the foundations of her world were crumbling away.

Dr Critchlow's caution a decade or more before circled back to mind: registering for that doctorate had fixed her in a way life. It might have been different in IT or dance, or more flexible in a huge city abroad that harboured career options beyond her dreams. But in her world it was definitive. Now, to be pushed out of the only life she was fitted for would be . . . beyond contemplation. The magnitude of such a personal calamity loomed all the vaster for being beyond the imagination of most people, even of many in academia. She belonged in a university; it was constitutional.

To get Francine out of her mind, she headed for her car and drove off for the countryside. A roadside sign announced a restaurant that turned out to be little more than a mean shop cluttered with barely identifiable goods. It was riddled with dark corners like a Dunkley painting, in which unexpected creatures might be expected to lurk.

A bored girl dragged her slippers over the floor to see why she was being disturbed and, when Candace asked for a cup of tea, rewarded her with a long-suffering nod, before wandering away at a languorous pace into the dark fuming bowels of what must be the kitchen. The place was so contrary to the accustomed cheer and friendliness along the Jamaican roadside that Candace wondered if she was the problem, whether she was exuding some atmosphere carried over from ITS, some negative mist: *As if the darker forces there have possessed me.* Perhaps she said it out loud, because the young woman who had returned now shoved the tea forward on the counter and backed hastily away. Sipping it, Candace searched her mind for a way though her current circumstances and found herself cataloguing her colleagues. ITS seemed peopled with members who had invested their lives in academia yet not made it in the institution of their choice. They had either fallen short or overflowed from well-established places with limited posts. No one outside the institution could distinguish one of these groups from the other, so even ITS's promising scholars must partake in a general impression of ruin.

This reflection softened her attitude to some of her colleagues. Sumra had got out, but there were Nadine, Nicholas, even Francine. And an unwilling sympathy crept up, for what was ITS in reality but a sort of halfway house or limbo for the academic wounded? A natural impulse prompted these wounded to distinguish themselves from the rest through malicious or, more often, snidely compassionate remarks that left a corrosive residue on relationships.

"But I should go back to my cage, shouldn't I?" she asked the waitress. Then she walked to the entrance followed by the woman's eyes, narrowed with suspicion. Trying to escape ITS was pointless, if not impossible.

So, in the midst of this intellectual wreckage Candace felt herself propelled forward with BEAM, despite glimpses now of the committee's own proliferating irregularities of conduct.

Lex had repeatedly told Candace that he had never witnessed anything along the lines of the sexual impropriety so hotly rumoured. She believed him unreservedly, knowing how fluently he would have expounded on any atrocious tidbit that came his way. "On the other hand, it could well be unfolding in front of me but escape my notice," he had warned one day, "for, generally speaking, the mating eccentricities of pseudo-academics fail to arouse me. Howsomever . . ." His eyes gleamed.

"Out."

"Well, let it go this time. On a different topic – I hear your father has a pit bull named Turnitin. It was called Sadam for a time, then for some reason renamed. It doesn't matter, of course, because it answers to no one. I pass this on, so you won't go tripping carelessly into The Habitat on your next filial visit."

"A pit bull? He would. What does he care who gets mauled? Anyway, I shouldn't think he needed one."

"I take you to mean he does his own mauling, but he probably did care when Turnitin took a turn at the secretaryputus who exited The Habitat in the wee hours to get something from her car."

"Good Lord. Is she badly hurt?

"No. L'Amelia managed to get into the car. Barely – she was in a somewhat diaphanous negligee, it is said. The dog flung himself on the flanks (of her vehicle) and ripped off the licence plate, a door handle and various rubber whatevers. I think she's in hospital but just traumatized. External fixtures of her car were rubbished, but the long, well-oiled legs remain intact."

"You're heartless. Don't you care about anybody?"

Lex considered. "Apart from yourself? Only from time to time. I am, however, genuinely attached to my own person – which may be more than can be said of your monk."

"By now you know that marks the end of our conversation, and, as I can't physically evict you, slam my door shut when you leave." She unslung her purse from the back of her chair and waved to him.

"But you are so conversable," he protested, his voice following her out the door. "And most especially, I expect, in older senses of the word, *conversation* . . ."

Outside, the sea's flatulent rumble drowned him out, but she made the mistake that night of repeating a single word of his remarks through WhatsApp, Skype having collapsed in bad connection warnings alongside weird clucking sounds.

"Monk?" Randall demanded. "That's how you picture me?" When she paused, flurried, he hurtled on. "I can't believe you've mistaken me for some impassive recluse content to live in mind and spirit only. Because *you* yearn to let go of the world, you refashion me into a bloodless disposable version . . ." As if his rebuke had been pent up for years and unplugged by careless reference to Lex Wright. She shook her head in silence, stunned, then cut the connection.

Her response took days to form and, even then, it welled up like blood against the pressure she applied to keep it down. How could he have been so brutal, she began; then she paused. *Had* she been trying to deny part of herself by dematerializing him? For the thought of complicating her already fraught existence with a relationship beyond friendship frankly terrified her.

"How's the monk?" Lex Wright demanded next day, after a searching glance at her demeanour.

"Stop calling him that."

At her obvious annoyance, he stared, then changed track. "Did you tell him about the pit bull?" Ignoring her silence, he said. "For myself, I'm all for doing away with him once and for all. By all means, let us lay this ghost, so we can get on with our own life."

"*We* don't have a life," she reminded him, and again he regarded her thoughtfully.

"Just so." After a silence, he continued with the air of one who had not hesitated. "Not that you should consort with anyone so depraved as I . . ."

She walked wretchedly out of her office and left it to him. Randall had not contacted her since she hung up on him.

Nor had he weeks later, when BEAM concluded the last of the interviews on its original list. That was when BEAM decided to see Barham and Marion yet again, especially Barham, because he was the most longstanding member of the centre under investigation and was in no way implicated in any wrongdoing – except, perhaps, failure to intervene. For what had he done about any of it? All very well to say he regarded unprofessional behaviour as beneath his notice. His intellectualism was almost fundamentalist, Dexter remarked wisely.

"Still, we'll talk to him again," the Chairman said to Candace, adding in his kindest tone, "if it will ease your mind."

But it was at about this time that the Board of Enquiry into Alleged Misdemeanours more openly took on a life of its own and began to spawn its own misdemeanours. Candace sent a brief query to Randall about whether he planned to remain silent forever, because, if so, he was missing out on the action, and he returned a sullen reminder that it was she who had hung up. She didn't bother to bring up any of the crap he had said before that, but just launched into the latest on BEAM.

It appeared as if, at the very least, the Chair must be sharing essential information unevenly. At first Candace thought he was concealing findings from her, because he considered her a straight line to the Provost. Then she perceived it might be because information was not to reach the Provost, because the Provost did not want to know. Oversights in communication began to come together into what she could only regard as a cover-up. After receiving a stern telephone call from someone in possession of BEAM's list of proposed interviewees, a secretary had cried off from an interview. A student letter of complaint regarding Courtney, which Mackhail said she had described in her testimony and had sent to the Registry months ago, as Mr Baldeosingh had directed, was reported destroyed by mildew and damp, after spending three years scrupulously filed in an arid environment.

This was all overtaken by the third meeting with Barham. He was coldly polite for half an hour and then began to stutter with rage, tearing his fingers through his beard. "Complete waste of time. What is there to say? Who is the final arbitrator, and how can he speak to anything with his live-in secretaries, self-allotted executive salary and CV woven from thin air? What you want me to say?"

She could feel the blood draining from her face and steeled herself to shut up and wait on someone, anyone else, to say something. And no one did.

But his work was the one dimension in which her admiration for her father remained intact, founded on bedrock. She boiled with defensive rage at Barham for denying Earl Rider's single redeemable quality. Not that Candace was ignorant about unscrupulous practices in academia, but her father had done his own work, damn it. Give the bastard that.

She had cooled down by the time Barham left and Marion arrived. But Marion seemed too unwell for an interview. Indeed, she gave the impression of being on the verge of some sort of spasm and was hastily excused, Candace assisting her out to the admin lunchroom. Being summoned into this whole unpleasantness again, it turned out, was a challenge to Marion's fragile nerves.

"Palpitations," she whispered. "I try not to let on, but quite often, well . . . I mean, I don't want to cause worry."

Apparently too fatigued at first even to retrieve papers she had dropped in the meeting room, Marion began to revive with the steaming cup of tea Candace placed gently in front of her. "How in the world do you stand up to this?" Commiserating with Candace, she was bright-eyed now. She leaned forward confidingly. "Then, you hear Francine's been sending out applications, girl?"

Candace struggled between the need to get back to the committee room and eagerness to hear more. Then she gave up the fight and sat down, pouring herself a cup and ladling in the condensed.

"Tell me," she said.

"Well, you know she hasn't got the Chair? I don't mean Fellow of the centre; we all know she has that. No. The professorship. And the Provost isn't taking her on, is he?" Marion was one of the few who spoke of him naturally to Candace as, simply, the Provost. "He's totally tied up in the keynote address he has to give at the Professional Integrity Conference in Brisbane, because the award of his honorary LLD will be at the convocation there in a few months. So Francine says she has to stop making this sacrifice of her professional life and see about herself. She's not burning any boats, of course, but she must be really trying to get out, eh? Applied to UWI, I think, but she can hardly say that, can she, even if it turns out that they have no post. When she says she's stigmatized by her employment here, I guess that's in case the applications all come to nothing?"

Candace went back to report that Professor Bailey-Brown was recovering and would come in to talk to them the following day.

"Another Anansi story to look forward to from Marion." Dexter steupsed. "I suppose we have to go through it."

So they packed up, their appointment for an interim report to the Provost having been cancelled. An acting administrative assistant had explained that the Provost was required for media interviews leading up to his departure for the Professional Integrity Conference. By afternoon the wide flat-screen in the Tropicourt Restaurant – which normally, for reasons that mystified Candace, flashed mute pictures of sporting events, international disasters and local soaps – was full of front views and profiles of the Provost, concluding with him getting into his car and the BMW receding in the distance, and then the whole coverage playing all over again.

"Show-aaf," a groundsman muttered, following up with an extravagantly protracted suckteet.

"No, man. Is advertise him have fe advertise the place."

"Fe wha'? Is a shap?"

"Shap, yes. Nah degree dem a sell?"

Indeed, Candace reflected. It occurred to her that in recent years he had become primarily a businessman. And what else? After her evening class at UWI, she fought her way through the traffic to New Kingston, then got onto Google and looked up a certain Gerry Ann Shipley, whom she recalled as a particularly glamorous graduate student of her father's. (Graduatestudentputus, Lex would have corrected her.)

At first, nothing. On a whim, she had opened her father's web page and run down his vitae to the list of successfully completed theses he had supervised, cursing herself at the same time for being fatally obsessed.

Then, there she was: Gerry Lynn Shipley. Candace had misremembered the middle name. Google's lead on Gerry Lynn Shipley took Candace to an open-access journal, *Online Publications in English for New Scholars*, which invited submissions from less-experienced academics who might need mentoring in relation to their publications. A second journal came up with an almost identical name and description. The first was situated in India and the second in the United States. Gerry Lynn Shipley appeared on the Board of Governors for both journals, and neither listed an editorial committee.

Camouflaged between well-known publications, this was the type to slide through unchecked on a CV, making up bulk. Scholars less clued on the gulf between creditable and worthless online publishing might miss the discrepancy. A surge of something (curiosity or déjà vu) sent her back to her inbox, where she recovered the e-mail that had recently called on her to submit an article:

> Papers are invited for *Caribbean Network*, an intellectually liberating, peer-reviewed journal devoted to critical rethinking of limits and borders that are geographical, ideological or disciplinary.

Caribbean Network, a spin-off from *Online Publications in English for New Scholars,* focused on work relating to the region and encouraged submissions from young scholars unhampered by traditional prejudices and single-minded in pursuit of new forms of thought. Academic studies on a wide range of topics and eclectic in methodology would be accorded sensitive consideration. The journal invited radically designed investigation and devoted itself to Caribbean self-discovery and representation. The invitation concluded with a promise to contribute to the future of knowledge.

Whoa. She grinned.

But was this coming from inside or outside the region? Some mutation in an unfinished trade in the Caribbean – from flesh to more intangible artefacts? Amid the swirl of inanity, something indefinable sparked her interest, and she read on.

All submissions would be confidential. Because of the dynamic nature of advanced knowledge in our complex Caribbean space, the journal guaranteed responses to all submissions within two weeks, with a view to tight turnaround. A chuckle edged its way up Candace's throat as she read the inevitable next line: The journal required a modest submission for such prompt consideration in the first instance and, later, following acceptance, a more substantial publication fee.

By spawning *Caribbean Network, Online Publications* clearly prompted and embraced Caribbean investment in the global problem of academic skullduggery but, so far, she could see nothing of personal concern beyond that old reference to her father as a reader of Gerry Lynn Shipley's publication.

Forcing down the questions churning beneath that, she turned resolutely to her data on Forbidden Words.

—⁄⁄\—

In an analytic moment, Lex had once remarked that Candace could only appear as controlled as she did if she had much to repress, and that her deepest responses probably bordered on hypersensitivity. She knew very well that while she locked down some thoughts, other parts of her brain irrepressibly went on picking up clues on related and different matters and storing them to network days or years later. But she had assured him that if she wanted a shrink, she would choose one qualified in psychology rather than archaeology. He insisted the disciplines had enough in common for him to proceed.

It seemed a part of her wanted excavation, for she missed unburdening herself to Randall. Since her call some days before, he had neither e-mailed nor Skyped her. The silence tore at her, until she flipped the lid of the computer savagely.

"Why does it always have to be me to reach back out?" she demanded, when he answered the Skype call almost on the first note.

"Because it's always you who cuts off."

He sounded no more conciliatory than she did, but after a pregnant silence, she muttered, "All right, all right."

As their late-night talks resumed, first tensely and then more naturally, she found she found herself touching on an unshapely array of memories of her childhood and anxieties about the more outrageous aspects of ITS – in no particular sequence. However much Randall insisted that order was crucial, there were some memories Candace could reshuffle only vaguely. The untravelled paths of her potential relations with her father, intersected by the actual past, looped and contorted around her – a labyrinth she had carried for years without properly examining.

"Seems unfair to saddle you with it," she told Randall.

Yet, unruffled on the surface, she went on to revisit harrowing sensations from life with her father, or rather, life in his presence but without him. Afterwards, however excruciatingly the memories had carved their way up, she said she felt emptied of their toxic residue.

One night when the video quality for Skype was unusually clear, she slid back in time and stopped responding to his account of the day's trials with his dean. His voice trailed off.

"What?" he asked.

Swinging in a chair on the porch, so deep in *The Wind in the Willows* that the chair had ceased to creak back and forth, Candace must have been little more than an extra lump in the throw cover and clutter of cushions, when her father opened the wrought-iron gate for the lady who had driven up to the front step. She was young, stylish, her white linen pants pressed so crisp the seam down the front was sharp and straight from belly to instep.

"But it's pleasant out here," the lady said to him. Only, her supervisor preferred to work in his study, so they went inside without a glance at the child, only a hint of perfume left hanging.

The book had come to an end, and Candace was turning over in her mind a cool dim home in the earth and being furry all over with sharp claws for digging one's way farther in, and she closed her eyes and wiggled her nose, trying to decide whether she was Mole or Ratty. Perhaps Mole smelling the way, she thought. Then she caught the whiff of perfume again, somehow spoilt now. She opened her eyes a fraction, and her father was letting the lady out, but the well-ironed pants were rumpled. No. Only from the knee up. Below the knees, they were still smooth, with the seam sharp.

While burrowing through another book (*Doctor Doolittle*?), Candace had turned things over in her mind, but it was no point asking her father about anything so mundane as an issue concerning the ironing or crushing of clothes, so at supper, after they sat down, she asked her mother why it was that a lady's pants would crush partway and not –

Her father exploded, saying that after he had listened to students and staff talking rubbish all day, Candace should shut her mouth, if she had nothing worthwhile to say. She should just get in her bed, because he didn't want to hear anything else brainless she might come out with. And when her mother looked shocked and bewildered by the outburst, he said he was tired and that they should have a quiet dinner at last, just the two of them. Her mother was so flattered that she never questioned Candace being sent away hungry, tight-lipped.

The next day, he told Candace that perhaps he had been a bit abrupt, but his work was a very separate thing from his home life, and he didn't want her mentioning work he brought home or students he had to meet with when he needed to relax, because it would set her mother off, and that would be the *end*. Of what? Candace almost asked – but she knew: he meant the end of any use he might ever have for her. So she said nothing.

Even later, what was there to say? As his womanizing became more open, her mother slid into a languishing mental collapse. She stopped reading. Then her conversation lagged and broke up, her husband goading her further and further towards the edge of reason. The slow intellectual dispatch seemed to Candace like some unspoken murder/suicide pact that any comment from her could only accelerate. And all the while, Rider's career soared in one scholarly achievement after the next and that organizational genius through which he pulled off deals and projects. Yet the events of Candace's childhood had so shifted and reshaped under her mind's eye that she could not tell whether she had been a participant or a prop, a culprit or (no better) a victim. Then, as she took her eye off her father, she caught sight (at the edge of her field of vision) of an Earl Rider she had never noticed before. He sparkled, but the glitz was little more than dandified thinking above a thin layer of underlying substance. Or was that dross? Otherwise, the thought intruded, why was he Provost of ITS?

Yet there *was* that genuine administrative flair with which he negotiated the separation of ITS from its parent organizations, and financial support for it as an independent institution. She heard he had begun marshalling an impressive group that might take it over as a functioning business. People who knew about such things were discussing equities, and others were admitting that the successful accreditation exercise had been of value, else the transaction would never be going through.

And now Francine *was* ecstatic, for she had been given to understand that funding of her chair was part of the full package the Provost was negotiating. Venting their fury about the rumoured endowment, Courtney'n'Sat called it the CuSt Chair. Francine intensified her vendetta against them even while re-sketching a more subtly ruinous picture of Candace. Francine, Sonja had long pointed out, was the world expert in damning with faint praise. "Candace Clarke," Francine had explained in dulcet tones to a visiting colleague who said she believed she had read a fine paper by Dr

Clarke but had never met her, "is still at her best in her upper-middle-class setting against a background of china and silverware. You know. Civilized. You mustn't blame yourself if you find her . . . a little off focus. Right now, she's fighting valiantly for a place in the real world of the Caribbean. To come to terms with our revisioned space – don't you know? I've faith she'll get there, eventually." In passing this on, Lex had remarked that for all her tone of sympathetic tact, it was Francine who had grown up in precisely such a setting as she had described. But by the following week, that was all behind Francine. It was confirmed she would be Professor of Postmodern Studies in Caribbean Culture. So much to feel gratified about, at last – even up to the ultimate small detail of news. Francine's voice had a kind of exultation in it, when she announced that that awful man they had brought in as a replacement for dear old Dudley was on his way out.

Lex Wright had resigned with immediate effect, offering no reason whatever.

Chapter 13

~,\~

Balade

The world hath mad a permutacioun
Fro right to wrong, fro trouthe to fikelnesse

Candace was curious, and then angry. (He *could* have called.) Finally anxiety set in.

It was three weeks before Lex came in to clear out his office. When he arrived with a supply of cardboard boxes, he looked in at the coffee room and eradicated Francine, Sat and Percy by emitting a deep, rattling cough. Candace was unperturbed, having practised fake coughs often enough as a child to get around her mother, until Silver cured her by standing a bottle of castor oil on the bedside table.

Having sufficiently cleared the room, Lex settled down opposite Candace with his mug. He seemed thin and not as tall as she remembered. The sun shone through his hair – or it was a shade lighter? One of his affectations? But no, for it had lost its sheen. The brightness of his eyes was not so much sparkle as agitation. They seemed larger, luminous, intense in a face unaccountably drawn, his pale skin stretched over the cheekbones. It hit her that he was gaunt.

Yet he was coming along, he said. Some tingling still but mainly the fatigue – which was passing. The muscle spasms had stopped. No more than another flare-up, as it turned out.

244

"Some variant of chik-V?" Candace asked, every chord of sympathy awakened. "But couldn't you have let me know?"

He shook his head and said gently, "Multiple sclerosis."

Her breath hitched in her throat, as at a twist in some fundamental rule. Or, no. Sudden awareness that it was an altogether different game, the joker in the pack operating under constraints, wild card or not.

Lex looked out at the sea, which the rain, moving in, was systematically erasing. "Before I quite leave the premises, let me tell you something I've heard." He seemed to weigh her up. "You are so often the last to know quite obvious things." Through his family's business connections, he had learned that moves for ITS to reinvent itself as a private institution had brought increasing financial disarray. "That's why I didn't bother to apply for medical leave. If all goes well for me, and I'm here in a year's time, ITS may not be." He took her hand and squeezed it urgently. "Try to get out."

After that, they talked in a haphazard way about everything except Candace's future and his health, and for the first time, they exchanged phone numbers. He shared a few of his most recent lines: "Would have failed her exam / For avoiding a slam / Were it not for . . .'"

"And that's where the thing gets especially demanding," he complained. "What rhymes with *honorarium*? Or do I just buckle under and go for *bribe*? Not as rhymable as one would expect."

"Had you thought of changing topic?"

"No. Like you – yes, I'm haunted by the proprieties of my grandmother. But that's fatally coupled with a horror of the obvious. Otherwise, I'd go for 'A plump little duck in his class . . .' and so on."

"What about the article you were submitting to *Caribbean Quarterly*?" Candace persisted. "Did you come up with a title?"

"I thought: 'Stone Cold: Shards in the Indian Ridge Burial Caves'."

"That may carry you further in the world of letters." She reached for his hand and wound her fingers through his. "Apart from being in better taste."

After he left, Candace locked her office door for a few minutes and prayed. Then she e-mailed Professor Critchlow. His swift response touched her, but when they met, he had nothing encouraging to offer. No vacancy he knew of. The department was fighting for a new post but really to safeguard the one he would vacate when he retired the following year, to forestall any decision to freeze that.

The thought of the department without Critchlow jarred her – visibly, apparently, for he leaned forward, his usual affable, earnest tone warmed further by affection. "There is nothing I would like better than to see you appointed."

But all he could do was advise her about strengthening her publications and supply her with references. She should look out for the advertisement of his post, as it would be set at Lecturer level. He said not a word about ITS or its prospects.

The next afternoon, at the Master's planning meeting for the following academic year, Francine was on the warpath. "They give me the centre to manage and truncate the budget," she proclaimed. And what was this about Lex Wright's post being in question?

Courtney put in helpfully that the post would be no different frozen to what it was with that dead-and-wake in it, but Francine continued as if he had not spoken. She could not believe that CSSGDS – despite everything members of that centre had put the institute through – retained line items that had been deleted from CuSt's budget.

"But all you do is to apply for the same things, calling them something else," Dexter soothed her. That was how you handled this sort of thing, he pointed out knowledgably.

"Is that quite straight?" Candace blurted it out, and Francine turned on her in outrage.

"I would think a junior staff member whose position is by no means secure would think twice before intervening in an exchange on policy between a Fellow of the institution and the Master, let alone dictating on ethics." She turned her back. "Anyway, Master, I comfort myself that if we lose one post we can always redeploy another that is less than satisfactorily filled."

Candace forced a smile at this sally and maintained an air of nonchalance until the meeting broke up. In the tutorial that followed she found herself divorced from the students, unable to attend to anything they said and, midway, she cancelled it, murmuring that she was unwell and would make it up. She had to get home.

The parking lot was in chaos, vehicles backed up from the gate, students crowding round a van to listen to a harangue from a young man perched in the tray with a microphone that delivered incomprehensible fragments of his address. But she hurried to her car and turned the radio up, finding no music she could listen to, only a call-in programme with an angry voice protesting the closure of the causeway. "But, caller," the host interjected, "what would you have the authorities do if the foundations are insecure?"

Candace cast an eye around for Sonja's car and, not finding it, she turned off the engine and walked back towards the Master's office. "Ms Mackhail, you hear anything about the causeway?"

"Nothing more than the news flash an hour ago. I got a notice onto the intranet, but you may not have been on your system. The guard at the gate is warning people as they leave." It appeared that fishermen had been dynamiting fish and damaged the foundations of the causeway that linked Portmore to Kingston, and it was now closed for repair.

"So what happen to those students now?" Candace asked.

"They want us to supply transportation to Kingston." The AA glanced upwards for strength. "Two years now they've been asking for a shuttle."

The Master wandered out. "UWI, UTech – everybody have bus. So now this thing happen."

"What thing?" Candace demanded impatiently.

A student looking for an alternative way home had gone astray and found himself on the Dyke Road, where his car had broken down. Thugs had descended on him, stripped the car and dragged him away, but he broke free, alternately running and hiding. A taxi man had picked him up and brought him back to campus for free, because, the driver said, he had a son that same age.

In the carpark, the students began to chant, louder and louder. "*Mus have a bus.*" Candace stood at the window with the Master and his AA and watched students surround the BMW in the Provost's lot and rock it back and forth. "No ride for Rider," bawled a girl in a red top. While the rest took up the strain, two stalwarts blocked one lane at the main gate by relocating the pots of cactus, and they sent the guard home. In an hour, the students had shut down the campus and dispatched a statement to the press regarding their demand for a student bus. Then they marched on the

Provost's Office, where an urbane assistant told them he had left for a meeting two hours ago. As their voices rose to a crescendo, Ms Mackhail plucked Candace's sleeve, and they nipped downstairs to Candace's car.

Ms Mackhail seized the keys from Candace and planted herself in the driver's seat, racing the engine, even before Candace was properly in. The students at the gate stared, but the bolder ones had gone to the Provost's Office, so these were clearly at a loss. Ms Mackhail headed for the gate slowly but implacably, her eyes fixed ahead. The students parted before her.

"Where do you live?" Candace asked meekly, as they drove away from the campus, determined to take Mackhail to any part of the island, however remote.

"Oh, I'm not going home," the AA replied. "It's Mission Week." A block or so away, she stopped and returned the keys to Candace and alighted in front of a white tent, where buses from Kingston and more remote areas were pulling up, one lively with choruses and clapping.

"I don't know any way over but the causeway," Candace called after her desperately.

"Go by Bernard Lodge," Ms Mackhail replied, and a sister beside her shouted not to take the Dyke Road.

But it was an hour before Candace found her way onto the Bernard Lodge Road, not least because she made wrong turns, as her mind kept going around the idea of ITS being unable to put out for a school bus.

⁓⁊⁊⁊⁊

In a day and a half, the student shuttle was running and the students themselves had settled down, but Candace told no one except Sonja and Randall what Lex had said about ITS finances, so she was one of the few who knew what to expect when the Provost called a staff consultation at the beginning of May to apprise them of challenges facing the institution as it moved to full independence. They must brace themselves, he warned.

"It makes no sense coming out from the governance of foreign institutions by giving the reins to bloodsucking financial houses. When that lot impose their repressive measures, we'll find academic and pedagogical decisions being made entirely on monetary considerations." For members collectively to take control of their destinies, they must tighten their belts for a while. That meant dispensing with the luxuries to which they had become accustomed.

What *that* meant, as the Master made clear at the emergency meeting he called afterwards, was that the part-time budget was slashed with immediate effect. So a number of the temporary staff would have to go, and chaps must discontinue small-group teaching in favour of mass lectures. Tutorials were abolished, and – a word to the wise – it was time to think about replacing essay assignments with multiple-choice quizzes.

It was a matter of days before large lecture rooms were being fought over for the summer programme and a few weeks before some walls between small classrooms were knocked down. The upheaval in venues triggered a timetable war, and every subsequent discussion of scheduling dissolved at once into pure vitriol. Equipment that had grown faulty beyond the capacities of the institute's own technical staff had to be packed away until funding became available to send it out for major repair. "'Rain a-fall but dutty tuff,'" Francine quoted wisely.

Two months had not passed before tradesmen who had gone unpaid refused to deliver printer cartridges, stationery, coffee and toilet paper. In late June, water was not being replenished in coolers, and sanitary bins in ladies rooms were not carted away. The Institute of Tropical Studies at Portmore transformed under their eyes to become, indeed, the PITS – as some smartass UWI professor had named it to begin with. Hold on, though. Surely that was Professor Danraj, himself now a denizen.

Candace and Sonja shared a laugh – a little shaky, after conveying Cassidy to the vet. Cassidy had taken Dr Machado in violent dislike and made every effort to maul him. Already old for a ridgeback, she had nevertheless required their combined strength to prevent serious injury. Indeed, so far from conducting herself with her usual restraint and dignity, Cassidy had displayed an uninhibited savagery that had been in every way embarrassing.

"I was afraid they'd tell me to put her down," Candace had confided as they drove away, still in shock.

Having dropped the dog home, the two exhausted women were recovering at Devon House by way of exchanged anecdotes, fortified by beef patties and june plum juice.

Even on the ITS campus, there was still laughter, but mostly shrill and false to Candace's ear, camouflaging hostility. In what Sonja called a desperate attempt to rally institutional loyalty, the administration sent around alternative mock-ups for a logo, to be discussed by staff.

"Shouldn't we have a library first?" Candace realized she was growing more recklessly candid by the day.

Francine eyed her with the disfavour due to a youngster taking a frivolous attitude to the sacred. She indicated the crest suggested by CWiLS – a blue galliwasp encircled by its own preternaturally long coiling tail, on a green background.

"Lovely," Francine said, "one with the environment and all that. Mr Chairman, I for one support this incentive. A logo is the visible brand of an institution, and I can't think how we've managed so long without one."

Despite the urgent adoption of the logo, however, as staff went through the motions of teaching in increasing discomfort, collegial relationships disintegrated, leaving a sense of vacancy, so that the flitting between offices and classrooms began to seem phantasmagorical.

"It's fallen into a state of collapse, hasn't it?" Candace observed.

"Already sunk, when you of all people give way to tautology," Sonja answered. "But yes. Yes, yes. 'Why, this is hell nor are we out of it.'"

"You make a convincing Mephistopheles," Candace replied lightly.

But on further thought, Sonja's quip seemed applicable. Candace's quandary regarding her father, combined with the inexorable deterioration of her workplace, hazed her day-to-day routine with unreality. A sudden but familiar plunge in spirits, a sense of sinking into a grey trough, rendered it difficult to work on. She confessed to Randall that when she walked along the corridors of ITS, venom seemed to ooze back out of the walls.

As to the future of ITS, it seemed Lex had been right. (Ha!)

"And a gratifyingly large number of people quite hate Rider," he reflected when he dropped in for coffee two days later. "Someone approached a don – who owes my mother a favour and talks rather more freely to her than is good for either of them – someone actually approached him to take out your father. And no, I don't know why. But again I say it: Back away."

Randall had a different angle. "You can't divorce goings-on at ITS from your father's self-advancement," he reflected that night. "Nor is his academic progress irrelevant to yours, for – what prompted you? You'd rather not dwell on that, but better to think your way through and beyond it than have it haunt you for life." So Randall encouraged her to strip off whatever protective layers she had evolved. "It's a wound, to clean before it festers any more."

Yet what did he know about how deep it went, or of the miasma curled beyond the brim of sleep to mist down, seep in and fill the spaces in her throat, lungs, belly, limbs, dulling thought and sensation.

Still, each immersion in the past turned up misplaced details and unsettled conclusions. Quite apart from the impropriety of Rider's intimacy with particular students, how could he have supported a friend's promotion while recognizing fraud in that colleague's publication record? Not relevant to the central issue, Dr Rider had argued. Again this trick of definition: compartmentalize to bring out the admirable qualities and background the rest. Allow the rotten bits to drop from view.

So now it came together. This was the same person overlooking so-called peccadilloes of predatory staff members and maintaining a studied unawareness of Olatunde's fraudulent vitae. But if that were so, he must have been flagrantly dishonest all along, as she continued to work with him. Even if she escaped the taint of widening institutional decay, would the odour of unethical practice have rubbed off on her?

That was when an ecstatic e-mail arrived from Cheryl Grandison, Candace's erstwhile colleague in part-time teaching in the UWI Foundation courses. Cheryl's contract for a post at Cave Hill had come through, and she was so glad she had *waited*, as she termed it, instead of clutching at straws in some inferior place. She knew Candace would be glad for her, and she would be sure to keep Candace up-to-date regarding opportunities on the Cave Hill campus.

Cheryl was a Barbadian and was naturally overjoyed to land employment on her own island, so it was a little surprising to read on Facebook, within a week of her message to Candace, bitter recriminations about appointment only at the level of Assistant Lecturer. And it did seem unfair, Candace thought, for the PhD was granted, and Cheryl had taught and published for several years. Then she remembered the clutching-at-straws phrase and said to herself, "Serve her right. A-good."

Nevertheless, it grew clear that Candace's outlook at ITS might not brighten. Having had no offer from elsewhere, Francine obviously looked forward to Dexter's retirement so as to be Master herself. (Would she accept the title or try to revise its gender? As Candace toyed with it, she realized Francine had not demurred regarding Fellow.) Meanwhile, Francine had done everything possible to get the Unstable Skins publication to herself, to obliterate other names from the book before it could come out, and to contrive, delicately but unremittingly, the academic demise of Courtney'n'Sat. But the two men needed to lay the groundwork for one or other to be appointed CSSGDS Fellow, so they worked tirelessly to double-cross her. The Provost demonstrated sympathy both with Francine's claims and with the complaints jointly submitted by Courtney and Sat. So he kept them all, on surface, placid. Only a well-running institute might land massive funding.

Which might have been why his response to the BEAM report was incendiary. The Chair and the other members had distanced themselves the minute it was printed and left it for Candace to take in. It was, the Provost shouted, exactly what he needed at this time, an official record constructed to make the place look bad, just when solid financial backing was in the air.

As if to confirm this view, Elizabeth Woods published a saucy account on how an elusive sex scandal at ITS had led her to investigate claims that money was an alternative currency to flesh for extortion in the sale of grades. She announced that her tracking of shoddy financial records had led to substantial evidence regarding lack of accountability. She demonstrated mad expenditure on research assistance and entertainment. She listed excessive claims for extramural teaching, recorded exorbitant spending on routine travel and threw in pictures of cheques, credit card slips, cell phone and restaurant bills, together with letters of authorization to banks. Even in the somewhat fuzzy image in the *Gleaner*, Candace could make out Sat's signature on two of the claims, and they were dated before the award of his tenure.

This was one for Lex.

"The question is, what power could Courtney or Sat wield over my father, or is he really that blind?" Candace asked.

"Well, that's two questions," Lex observed. "The first is the real issue, and the second not an issue at all, because our Provost can not only see clearly but has seen a hell of a lot on which he prefers to stay mum."

"Seen what?"

"Well, it's X-rated."

"Don't dawdle."

"Very well. The Provost has the video."

"*The* video?"

"Yes. It is not given only to linguists to rightly determine proper use of the definite article. I say *the* video, because it is the definitive video to hold over someone's head, and the Provost has one of Courtney's."

"Get on with it."

"Very well. Before her installation as the Provost's recent secretaryputus, Amelia La Mar was one of the choicest morsels to fall into Courtney's lap. Or was it the other way around? Surely it was he . . . Anyway. She was inspired to entertain your father in one of their informal moments by running a video of herself and Courtney at play . . ."

"They made a film?"

"Indeed. You must have heard he likes to. Well, with admirable fore-thought, the Provost impounded it the minute she showed it to him and made a backup copy."

"How could you know that?"

"Because his technician is my old friend – though decidedly avaricious, for he confessed he also sold a backup backup to Courtney's wife as evidence for the divorce. He actually showed me a bit, before I could stop him. The shot of her wearing Courtney's belt and boots and nothing else was particularly fetching. If we could get the film out to the Cannes Festival, I suspect we might garner a rather significant award. Well?"

"Well, *what*?"

"Well, do you want to see it? Shall I arrange a full screening, or just clips of the more athletic parts?"

Candace clapped her hands over her ears.

⚜

"In truth?" Randall demanded.

She had at last upgraded her mobile – not, she admitted to herself, for unbroken availability through e-mail, or for camera or multiple apps – but for the comfort of knowing herself only a fingertip away from Randall. Now their conversation flowed unbroken, muted for lectures or library but resumed at will on either side, veering, returning, hesitating over whatever else one or other was doing at the same time, consulting, and breaking up in laughter. "You still there?" she would ask, and Randall might say, "You think?"

This time, the gossip from Lex had intrigued Randall. "You mean blackmail? Why would the Provost need to blackmail Courtney?"

"Perhaps a grip on the power base – preventing credible academics jumping ship," Candace surmised. "The ITS staff profile is delicate."

As newspaper reports unfolded, the administration of the campus seemed at first naively trusting and then irresponsibly slipshod, but, eventually, suspect – not of clearly profiting from dishonesty but of looking the other way, perhaps to safeguard the accreditation process.

So it was not long before pictures of the Provost's house and car began to appear in one of the papers along with copies of a salary statement and a bank withdrawal slip. These, however, together with references to the Provost's stunning bank account, came out in a small gossip-mongering paper with limited credibility among those rare readers interested in fact rather than sensation. In any case, nothing in the press pointed to financial gain by the Provost or his high-ranking officers; only a few members of ITS management seemed to call for investigation.

But a spin-off of media interest was that one article called Olatunde's qualifications *bogus*. As ITS played it, however, Olatunde had perpetrated his deceit – if, indeed, there had been deceit, and there was no evidence of such in their possession – on the Global Knowledge Institute of the Americas. He had been unconsciously inherited by the innocent local administration of the offshore campus.

Soon his wife and two other spouses of ITS professors were moaning self-importantly about harassment by paparazzi. They lamented the institution's failure to support their husbands by rejecting with disdain whatever mischievous implications of dishonesty had emerged in the media. They complained to their respective Societies without any immediate feedback. Lex theorized that this delay stemmed from the fact that the Association of Significant Others had recently amalgamated with the Lifestyle Society, and the organizations had not yet agreed on a mutually acceptable title. As a merger of their original acronyms would have turned out to be ASOLS, he argued, no statement was likely in the near future.

In mid-May, the Provost called a final meeting with BEAM. This came at the height of rumours about unravelling deals and mounting expenses. The University of the West Indies, Dexter had been whispering, had withdrawn its offer to work out the modalities of a relationship with ITS; the financial houses that had earlier expressed interest in discussions were cold-shouldering all advances; agreements that had been in train regarding an investment deal were withering up. And there was no turning back from the separation – their being steeped in so far, as Dexter remarked. The institute was no longer firm under them. The Registrar had no coherent answers for anyone. In fact, Hari seemed on the verge of a nervous collapse, unless it was that he was belatedly coming down with chikungunya.

Earl Rider dismissed it all with a sneer, because (thanks to the precautions he had introduced in good time) he had a safety net of such proportions that he could probably buy UWI when all was said and done – what with the chronic financial challenges that plagued the place. A few loose ends remained to be cleaned up, and this brief meeting with the BEAM committee was to lay that particular set of issues to rest. He expressed disappointment and surprise that the committee, having found little or no hard evidence, had stopped short of a clear statement that scurrilous tales in the press had been baseless.

Every mention of the BEAM enquiry turned Candace's mind back to the Forbidden Words project. What the data supported was not just a series of papers, Candace recognized. This was coming together into a book, for which she had effectively written four chapters. The title of a fifth crystallized as her father gesticulated: "Equivocation and the Mandate for Investigation: Ambiguity and Contradiction in Administrative Directives." And there might be more there than one chapter could accommodate, she reflected.

Then the meeting took a turn that drove the chapter from mind. Professor McGregor, the BEAM Chairman, joined energetically with the Provost's expression of disappointment. Perhaps some members of the investigating team had been insufficiently committed to dispassionate enquiry, more at the mercy of preconceived ideas. So valuable time had frittered away, for how did one *act* on the fabrication of a fevered imagination?

But there were circumstances that had hampered forthright testimony, Candace urged. More formal and stringent investigation could override staff reluctance to speak out. But, even as the Provost raised his palm to block that, the BEAM Chairman broke in to protest that enough time and resources had been invested in a wild goose chase by a committee that had, in any case, perhaps not been ideally constituted – if he might be permitted to say so. The Provost waved a hand to generously indicate this permission, and McGregor went on to explain that it was difficult for a member prejudiced against a certain type of male, popularly described as macho, to contribute objectively to such an investigation.

Thinking McGregor such a decent man, Candace had not seen that he was going after her – pinning blame on her for inconclusive evidence by invoking rumours that twisted her connection with Lex Wright. McGregor even went on to refer nebulously to how persons betrayed their own repressed yearnings in unguarded observations of students. Whether one was gay or straight was not the point, Candice realized, any more than who got hurt. The bottom line was that staff members' personal relationships and professional behaviour offered fair game or were off-limits, according to the Provost's convenience. And the Provost, having taunted her about Randall months before, allowed free rein to the professor's innuendoes.

Randall. The thought of him diverted her. He had messaged her that morning to say he had sent in an application to UWI Mona. And this buoyed her – a ridiculous hope about what she knew to be a long, long shot. She might have cared what members of BEAM thought of her, if she had not glimpsed a possibility of the world transforming into something of light and promise, where McGregor might take his committee and put it in a dark place. She switched back to them, watching attentively so as to relay a vivid account to Randall.

McGregor was on a roll. He was by no means unsympathetic to the gay fraternity, he assured them, but he would not have such sensitivity cloud the recognition of another type of man, whose traditional normativity was surely nothing that he needed to hide or apologize for. A team member's sympathy with alternative orientations might well have rendered her, or him (he allowed generously) unfit to make judgements in certain cases. McGregor could not say. His appreciation and respect for his colleagues on BEAM were boundless, but he felt sure that reopening a spent issue with the same team (however impeccable) could take them no further.

He for one, he announced, turning to face the Provost sternly, would have to refuse to chair it. What was needed now was a general statement that extensive investigation had produced no basis for the allegations published in the papers. The report in its final form would conclude with such a clarification.

The Provost thanked him for this forthright statement, commended all members on their selfless sacrifice of time and effort and stalked off to his next engagement, for which, he intimated, he was already late. Brusquely he directed Candace to walk with him as far as his office.

Along the way, he made no mention of BEAM, in which he had no further interest. What he required, he said as soon as they entered his office, where he shut the door and started talking about his research without preamble or glance in her direction – as he had no time (there was a plane to catch) – what he required was for her to do some superficial tidying up of his CV and then to e-mail the document, so it would be waiting for him when he landed. As he shot out directions, a chill rippled along her skin, with the realization of why he had not called on an administrative assistant. He needed an academic to concoct this delicately.

No. She was *not* going there. "Leave me out of it." She backed away from him and grabbed the door handle, leaving the building and getting into her car before he could send after her. Candace already understood her father's vitae to be more than an impressive display of learning: it was designed to intimidate. Rather than a purely private matter, any vitae was created for display. His was to make clear that he was unassailable professionally – not to be tangled with as a scholar. The rumour that the vice chancellorship at UWI Mona might come vacant replayed at the back of Candace's mind, yet her father wanted the refined document urgently on the other side of the world. He was throwing a wider net. Trepidation shivered over her: How did he plan to entrap her?

Beside this thought, McGregor was no more than an irritant. Tension sent spasms through her gut. Her father's inattention to her over her lifetime was turning out to be less painful than his determination now to force her support, twisting, reeling her in. She recalled something Randall had said about her father rethinking his neglect in favour of her usefulness. But why wasn't the Provost more concerned about the financial future now, rather than strutting about and flaunting his invulnerability as a scholar? The gaps in her comprehension of him brought back another chance remark by Randall, that the Earl Rider she had described left him with a sense of a character insufficiently worked out.

It was that evening when she returned to Portmore an hour early for her six-to-eight class that a BBM from Randall sent Candace tearing out of earshot of her colleagues for an emergency call to the United Kingdom, and he confirmed that he had applied over two months ago to the Mona campus as a generalist in British literature, although he had only told her that morning. And now he had just got word that he had made the shortlist. Two other applicants were unlikely to settle for the salary offered, so the chances looked good. Candace knew there was still no full-time opening for her even in AFP, since Marcus would block any application she sent in for an instructorship, but she could not help a superstitious shudder of relief: Randall's progress had to be a sign. Of what she could not say – but he was coming back. Had to be.

She had ended the call, promising to message him, but she hardly knew what to write without seeming overeager, and she was more than eager. She felt infused with hope, and there was nothing abstract or tenuous about that hope – it was so patently shining out of her that, afterwards, strangers grinned at her in the street, and a cyclist waved enthusiastically and called, "Beautiful lady, is me you smiling for?"

Yet what could she say to Randall that would not be too much? How could she risk expressing a fraction of what she felt? She began a message so lame that even after several rewordings she deleted it.

But. Floating. And the sensation frightened her into trying to press herself down to earth. The prospect of Randall actually moving to Jamaica was too heady for her to allow her mind to play with it. If she began to follow up with imaginings of where it might lead, she would be completely taken in. She told herself that he would never get the post. Or he might, and then continue their friendship along its present lines, until he found a suitable wife, and they could all be friends. When she realized she was overflowing with animosity towards a woman Randall might meet in the dim future, she admitted to herself that she had allowed her thoughts too much rein. Randall was a nice man. Okay, he was an amazing man. But she was very well off on her own. Only, when she tried to itemize how she could possibly be better off on her own than with Randall, she ran dry.

He was openly elated enough for them both. More and more ebullient. Boisterous. In short order, Skype conversations collapsed into hilarity.

"What if I get the job," he said, "and your father really does become Vice Chancellor? It looks like one of us is doomed to work for him. One way or other, I'll get to study him first hand."

On May 24, 2014, the Vice Chancellor of UWI announced that he would indeed be leaving, and Candace was at last certain of one circumstance that had put the ITS Provost on high alert. The closing date for applications would be July 28, 2014. Midway through the month, riding the wave of curiosity regarding Earl Rider's chances, she set off to a book launch on the campus and, over the snacks, angled for opinions on the vice chancellorship among UWI staff. The responses included a number of shrugs, a puzzled and somewhat offended stare, and at least one knowing look that reduced her to abject embarrassment. Of course, Dr Goldman thought she had come fishing on behalf of her father.

Now that it behoved her to avoid her few remaining UWI connections, she slunk back to her car and found the way home, oppressed by an inclination to crawl under the bed – until the Skype melody thrummed.

"I remember Goldman." Randall broke into a huge grin after her account of the evening. "Wasn't he at St Augustine for a few years? Nobody could sit in the front row? Remember Jenine opening the umbrella before class, only for him to walk in early?"

And there it was again. He had pointed her back in the direction of life.

—⁄ι∖‒

In the first week of August, Candace learned Professor Rider had withdrawn his application for the post of UWI Vice Chancellor, having come to understand that a very valued colleague and friend was under consideration – someone, he let it be known, who had his absolute support and good wishes.

The better part of valour, Sonja remarked, convinced that their Provost had recognized he stood no chance and was withdrawing in good order.

In any case, Rider was quoted as saying, he had taken note of alternative and more compelling opportunities, in the event of his deciding to leave ITS, which he was by no means inclined to do.

Probably didn't know *one* of the applicants, Sonja said, "and the idea of someone being dear enough to him to prompt so selfless a gesture – hell, no." He was shifting lanes, she said.

She stretched her feet obligingly on Candace's porch, so that Cassidy could rest her head on them. Their Provost, Sonja said, was modulating his tune in order to land the post Down Under quickly enough to demonstrate a choice of his own making. But it didn't mean he was going anywhere, Sonja warned. Perhaps he was only showing he could. No doubt it looked good to be in demand.

Over cocktails after the launch of a glossily illustrated *ITS Newstime: Decade of Excellence*, Dexter came right out and asked Shade whether he thought their Provost should have pursued the UWI vice chancellorship more aggressively and how it was that he, Morgan, couldn't help he pardner at all.

But Morgan just bared the grin and shook his head. "Wasn't his time," he said.

Chapter 14

The Scourge

Arys as though thou woldest with hym pleye
And I shal ryve him thurgh the sides tweye
Whil that thou strogelest with hym as in game,
And with thy daggere looke thou do the same;
And thanne shal al this gold departed be,
My deere freend bitwixen me and thee.

*E*arly August was supposed to be a quiet time, when one could get on with one's own work. But it was after ten in the evening that Candace's cell phone jarred her out of her data bank on equivocation. She had taken cover from another abrupt instruction from her father on what she regarded as the laundering of his curriculum vitae. By now he was boarding his flight, and she had deleted the e-mail without fear of a follow-up for some time. So the call was not from him.

It took a minute for her to comprehend that it was his neighbour, complaining that Professor Rider's dog had been barking and whining for days but was now raising an indescribable racket. The man said he had been ill for a week now, and it was hard enough to sleep with the fever and joint pains and rash. Could she please contact the Professor – he seemed to be away from home – or come in and do something about it? Something.

Please. It was making a goddamn noise, and he couldn't sleep. Nor his wife, and she had been up nursing him night after night.

Candace assured the caller politely that she had nothing to do with her father's affairs, but the voice at the other end rose plaintively. They worked together, didn't they? He wanted to sleep; do something about the dog. And she said she did not know the dog but had heard it was a pit bull, so she obviously couldn't go near it. Well, he said, something had to be done. People needed to sleep. Candace apologized for Professor Rider and rang off.

Was there no escape from her father?

The next morning, she got to ITS early and turned to Sonja in despair. "Can you believe he actually wanted me to polish his vitae – even the bits that were only dazzle anyway? He bestowed a list on me."

"Good thing you were the one he asked," Sonja remarked calmly. "And very stupid he was to choose you. Others would have complied eagerly in return for his support. I always thought he wasn't half as bright as you made out."

"Others?"

"You're not the first to ask my advice this morning." Sonja thought a bit. "I think I'll tell you, for I never promised otherwise – although confidentiality may have been taken for granted. I've had both the Francine and the Courtney'n'Sat asking directions from me. Not together, of course. Francine was here first thing, as I arrived. A bit later, Courtney'n'Sat found their way hither. But all breathing fire, Francine for her rights – which means instant advancement, and death to the male cabal – and Courtney'n'Sat for what is due to them on the grounds of hard work and solid scholarship. I assume the two fellows to be driven by lust and concupiscence, but they spoke of the recognition of their peers through the Provost's Prize for Exemplary Staff Performance. They also look forward to being elevated to CSSGDS Fellow – what with both Olatunde and Marion potentially out of the way. I asked Courtney'n'Sat if they saw themselves sitting on the same Chair, but they said whichever of them got it would be fine, as they could trust each other."

Sonja got up, went to her cabinet and brought out a battered manila folder. "I had little to offer any of the three that they would listen to," she said. "They will just keep going till they self-destruct, and the sooner the better. But I hope to do something for you. Look. You already have two sets of documents – your BEAM findings and your father's CV and dazzle list. You may illuminate those by reference to yet another file that I'm sure I should not show you. But I shall." She handed Candace the folder.

Sonja's office door swung back with a leisurely groan, and a nervous student poked her head around the door frame, mumbling about the late submission of her script. She knew she had passed the deadline and apologized again and again for the inconvenience.

"Put it on my desk," Sonja said. "At least you've had the manners to come to me personally rather than wedging it under my door."

"You sure it won't decompose you?"

"Well, no. But perhaps it is not yet quite time." Sonja responded with only a hint of a tremor in her voice.

When the door closed, she and Candace slumped back in their chairs stifling laughter as best they could.

"What a good thing I came to you," Candace said. "I wouldn't have missed that for the world."

"You may not be so glad you came, when you consult that file."

But first, they took stock. Their available information up to that time indicated a CSSDGS financial scam under the sex rumour and, under both, a meshwork of examination breaches. Against this background loomed a gathering financial insecurity which was, at least to some measure, a result of inadequate accountability. Nothing improper could be tracked to the Provost except inaction.

Could he survive a charge of negligence? Candace wondered. Wait. He could let go of administration altogether and maintain his international standing on the basis of publications alone. At worst he could pack it in for a home campus of the Global Knowledge Institute and the Consortium for Borderless whatever, or he could go back to the Texas College of Arts and Culture. (One of the things he had wanted her to fiddle on his vitae was the degree to which he was still officially on staff at both institutions.) He still had his record of academic excellence and scholarly integrity. Only the play to embellish his vitae called any of this into question, and, perhaps, not seriously. Everyone with a scrap of sense shaped the most attractive CV possible, Candace admitted; she was probably just being squeamish.

But for this new (old) file, Sonja insisted.

Candace's hand hovered over it, but the thought of discussing it later over Skype sustained her, and she began rifling through the contents. Sonja's documents included a record of appointment as external examiner for an doctoral student named Vanessa Allison over fifteen years ago.

"Allison." Candace looked up startled, and Sonja sat beside her and took her through.

Sonja had found the Allison thesis curious in a number of ways. The student had shifted from UWI to TCAC along with her supervisor, and an effusive opening acknowledged Dr Earl Rider. Still, students with supervisors they appreciated tended to be eloquent on the subject. The real red flag was uneven language – elegant academic prose in some places and awkward, amateurish style in others, while the level of academic argument varied from trite to profound. Ideas that seemed original remained surprisingly underdeveloped. But with no proof of dishonesty, and some quite respectable parts, the dissertation was not weak enough to require resubmission, let alone outright failure. After minor revision, it passed – and TCAC awarded Vanessa Allison her degree.

A few years later, in 2001, the Texas College of Arts and Culture invited Sonja to serve as an external reviewer for a professorial appointment, the case of Dr Earl Rider. Paying no attention to a name she should have remembered, Professor Palmer agreed, received the package of works and vitae, and scrutinized the papers. Vanessa Allison's name appeared on the vitae under the heading of research degrees successfully supervised, so Sonja wrote the university to explain that she had examined one of the candidate's graduate students and might not be a completely independent reviewer. TCAC did not require her to withdraw, but by then, she had remembered that this man was the creep her friend Patrice Clarke had married, so she preferred to back out.

She never got around to posting back the package, because something from the vitae haunted her, and she followed up a few titles. Read some of the articles. From a back row of old theses on a lower shelf, she retrieved the Vanessa Allison dissertation. (She had never been good at returning stuff, she admitted.) How else would she have seen that some of the Allison chapters were identical with parts of Rider's articles?

Each of these articles had come out before the student submitted the thesis. "She obviously copied his work." Candace's voice was a little faint but cross enough for Sonja to stare at her.

"And he didn't know? Didn't he read the thesis as supervisor, and eventually as examiner? My assumption at the time was that he wrote bits for her. However," Sonja added stiffly, "if I'm offending you, I can stop here."

Candace steadied her voice against the tremors Sonja had set off. "No. Please. Go on."

She ran her eye down the articles on his vitae that appeared as joint publications with students, and this looked good – valuable mentorship and all that. But the Allison thesis invited speculation about a different level of collaboration. It had prompted Sonja to glance back at Rider's vitae and pick commonalities between titles of student submissions and the supervisor's publications. Not that this was improper in itself either: sensible graduate programmes allocated supervisors with proven expertise in the areas students proposed for research.

"In any case, I'd already withdrawn from the review and had no *locus standi* in the matter," Sonja said. "Besides, if I took it on myself to send an unsolicited report, I'd have been tearing open lives with accusations of serial plagiarism, and set off . . . other repercussions."

She had contemplated most of it remorselessly, she assured Candace, quite unmoved by the weakness of students or supervisor; but she kept coming up against the damage that would accrue to her oldest friend. She knew Patrice was already shattered by her husband's betrayals and clinging desperately to her pride in him as this distinguished scholar. Even the limited correspondence between Sonja and Patrice made it clear that Patrice's fragile hold on herself could never survive such a blow to Earl, especially by someone close to her.

"The truth is that I hesitated over it," Sonja said, "and the time slipped by." She added with a forced smile that AA Mackhail would have declared her a muddied spring or polluted fountain.

Candace was startled. "Why?"

"For such is a righteous one who gives way before the wicked. I'm not proud of having kept silent."

Sonja told Candace how she had eventually stuffed the material into a folder and put it away.

After a while, Patrice stopped writing anyway, as she let go of one thing after the other. Over the years, the folder of notes, the thesis and the envelope of articles worked their way to the back of the lower shelf on the bookcase against which she placed her desk, and it had come to Portmore in a box with other stuff from that shelf that she had not had time to weed before packing up. And now she had drawn it out because Patrice was dead anyway, and her daughter in another kind of mess altogether.

"It was unprofessional to let it slide. Even if he wasn't writing parts of student chapters, only closing his eyes to their copying – why would he do that for free? And do you realize," Sonja continued, with a desperate glance over her shoulder as if pursued by an incubus, "this man could have ended up as Vice Chancellor at UWI."

"No," Candace hurried to reassure her. "He withdrew, remember? As if he ever had a chance. I suspect the process is pretty rigorous and would rule out the lord of such a petty fiefdom. And now applications are long closed and the matter under consideration."

"Well, that's a mercy, at least," Sonja said. In the silence that yawned, she asked, "And what about your young man in London? Definitely coming out?"

"Looks likely." Candace kept her voice bland, but Sonja grinned at her. "The young." She sighed. "And looking younger every week. I hope he gets here before you're under age."

Back in her own town house, keeping her finger stuck in the relevant page of Sonja's folder, Candace searched for papers by graduate students who had worked with Rider between 2004 and 2008. A few were published by the same journal she had noticed earlier, *Online Publications in English for New Scholars*, or by its offshoot, *Caribbean Network*. Clicking the former drew an instant invitation to submit, wormed promptly to her ITS e-mail address. Her intake of breath was answered by a movement under her desk, Cassidy raising her head to cast a look of concern. "Spam attack," Candace said briefly, and Cassidy dropped her head heavily with a groan.

It was a campaign of the sort that recruited articles through Facebook and personalized e-mail, gushing praise for a paper she had published three years ago in a thoroughly reputable publication and urging her to submit something current for a proposed new collection. *Caribbean Network* guaranteed peer review within seven days and notification about acceptance within ten after that. For this prompt service, the Board of Governors was forced to exact a modest submission fee, to be sent to a Hong Kong bank, although the publisher's address was in Denmark. None of this Googling turned up anything about Earl Rider; though, one familiar name popped up.

Sat?

Candace paused to burrow her toes under Cassidy's chest and commit Sat to a compartment of her mind for future consideration. Inspired by Cassidy, she switched to Dogpile, slid into a back issue of *Caribbean Network* and found papers of mixed quality: some credible but packed with mundane information, others making exciting but unsubstantiated claims. Many offered up conclusions through shaky argument or inexact methodology. Flinging a few key phrases from some of the better papers on the Net, as she would with suspect undergraduate essays, she discovered a few articles filched whole and others cut and pasted from websites, online journals or e-books.

One, she forwarded. "Just look at this, R," she wrote. "It's a novel waiting to happen. Sending to cheer you up, now you can't look forward to ER as your VC-in-waiting. By the way – UWI contract arrived yet?"

A warble announced a new message, a follow-up invitation assuring contributors that *Caribbean Network* required only 20 per cent originality of content. Young scholars at the cutting edge should not be held back by inflexible traditions of the past. The mission statement of the journal, an increasingly vague and flowery effusion, culminated in a promise to enable new constructions of Caribbean realities through an interrogation of hegemonic normativities. None of this reflected the smallest trace of Earl Rider, except by the odd contributor's reference to his work. Although Sat's name had appeared in the earlier issue as a member of the Board of Governors, she never found it listed again. Names that recurred were those of a couple of Earl Rider's students, publishing in this crappy journal.

By now she could hardly hear herself think against the thunder in her head, her brain hemorrhaging its past – her mother's ineffectual tears swept aside by his impatience and contempt. Then, her mother's retreat, even from food. Cocoa was all she would swallow – sweet, thick with sugar, so she would not get too thin and embarrass Earl. Cocoa bought by the case. And the scorn curling his lips, as he eyed the cup at Patrice's mouth, her eyes over the rim, more pleading than rebuking. His distaste intensified, until he stormed out of the Curepe flat to the house in Valsayn. "To give her space to get a grip on herself," he had said.

Her mother had begun to sprinkle cocoa over the kitchen counters, the table, chairs. Candace registered her mother's collapse not as a physical falling to the ground but as a heaping up of cocoa, clogging the sink, dusting floor, skin and hair, the smell clinging to the walls, clouding Candace's thoughts. She had sensed it hazing her, in her father's consciousness, to an irritant – peripheral and cloying. Six years later, along Trinidad's Eastern Main Road, Candace had stepped off a sidewalk to avoid an overturned bin and kicked a cocoa tin in the gutter, and a tremor from the loss of her mother slammed through her.

A warm, velvet tongue on her elbow roused her to prise her chin from her hands and force open her eyes. Cassidy gazed into them, brow furrowed so the wiry white hairs that were taking over lifted and stuck out, shoulders hunched forward tensely.

"You're right," Candace said, reaching for the laptop, and the dog dropped to her haunches. "That's done. And Randall will soon be here. But let me call on another of your fans."

She e-mailed Sonja. "You said there was more?"

Sonja phoned back at once. "Tomorrow? Saturday breakfast at eight?"

How to survive till then? However lightly Candace spoke, she held at bay a beast materializing in her thoughts and straining against control. It had been one thing learning to avoid her father after years of unrequited longing. But now here was Sonja viewing him as a charlatan who enabled students to engage in academic fraud so as to extend the list of completed doctorates on his CV, or even in return for actual favours. His shape-shifting literally sickened her, and she packed a glass with ice before splashing on water, and drew out a notepad to sort her thoughts before the next morning. She began by acknowledging to herself that he fitted somewhere in a scale of unprofessionalism: ignorance, negligence, compliance, collusion, fraud by fabrication or plagiarism.

His proven competence ruled out ignorance; unfailingly, he knew what he was about. And he was sharp; even professional negligence seemed unlike him. At the other end of the spectrum, his work ethic made plagiarism or even support of it unlikely. Mostly he fell in between, tolerating dishonesty where convenient. Compliance. Or was it more active? Collusion? She sucked a bit of ice and felt calmer. Then her stomach clenched again.

For what did all this demand of her? If she found it in her power, would she expose him? Of partake of his compliance? Her fingers loosened nervelessly on the pen at the thought of a public stripping, of embarrassed colleagues averting their eyes. Of scholarly value gradually leaching away from one's body of work. Of erasure from the world of letters. To bring that down on her father? She could not engage with the thought. But then, by silence to be implicated and wiped out herself before she even made her mark? Better to be dead. To cease upon the midnight with no pain.

She put aside her usual reticence about medication, swallowed a quarter of a tablet and crawled under the covers. Her last thought was foggy. "Lord, if that is what is in store, let me not wake."

The next morning, they sat on Sonja's compact back porch over plates of hard dough bread with avocado pear, and saltfish that had been pickled in vinegar, onions and peppers. The attraction of easeful Death had dissipated through a good night's sleep. Four mangoes and a sharp knife waited in a corner. Tiny blue flowers peeped in here and there through the latticework, and the porch was shady and quiet. Suddenly, though, the blue flowers started to disappear, one by one, snatched roughly through the lattice, and on investigating this extraordinary phenomenon, they discovered a goat eating away from the other side, demolishing the flower bed. Sonja shouted and gesticulated, but it gazed at them with its uncomprehending, incomprehensible eyes and munched on, until they gave up and resumed their own breakfast.

"Just as well I didn't bring Cassidy today," Candace said. "Imagine her fury?"

"One less goat."

Sonja seemed untroubled, sending Candace's mind off in contemplation of what life in her town house would have been like without Cassidy. From there, it was a short step to thinking about Randall's arrival and berating herself for daydreaming like a teenager. Life had reasserted its hold on her.

"... but hardly establish proof," Sonja was saying. She handed Candace a dissertation, articles and essays, a copy of Earl Rider's old CV with its list of publication dates. "Do whatever you think best," she said. "Burn it all, if that is what works for you. Only, don't give me it back."

"Wait." Candace said. "Tell me more about the Vanessa Allison thesis. Everything. And where it led you."

The student had shifted from UWI to TCAC in 1998 to complete a thesis entitled "Bodies of Writing: Commerce in Flesh and the Evolution of Caribbean Literature". After a long bit on the socio-economic background, the critique turned to the kept woman in eighteenth- and nineteenth-century literature about the Caribbean and arrived at the twentieth century through connections between prostitution and literary angst in the life and works of Jean Rhys. The first chapters were strong, Sonja said, but contextual rather than literary. The rest were weaker: thin literary interpretation barely linked to all that social background. Of course, Sonja acknowledged, she never did see the revised work.

TCAC had sent the thesis to Sonja because of her strengths in literary and cultural history. Other examiners might have been chosen with an eye on gender theory. Sonja was certain the first three chapters were not the student's own – rather than the fourth and fifth, which were not worth stealing – but tracking down the original source proved impossible. Also, nothing seemed to justify so much economic history. It may have been thrown in as ballast, Sonja said.

"What got me when I went back to the thesis after receiving the Rider package was something else: some of the material in the Allison thesis overlapped with an earlier and better written paper by *another* of Rider's doctoral students."

This was called "Loose Links" and considered Rhys's gaps in productiveness, the descents into despair, the recurrent helplessness, victimhood and "wallowing alcoholism" – against the crisp clarity and sustained coherence of her prose.

"The style attracted me, so I read it pretty carefully," Sonja said. "But then, that paper questioned what it termed *singleness of authorhood* on linguistic grounds that seemed pretty thin to me, little as I know of the discipline." That 1997 article had been submitted to a minor literary journal, a print publication that paid lip service to peer review – hardly the sort to inflict stringent requirements on writers, like strengthening principles of discourse analysis or applying those of psychoanalytic criticism. "So out the paper came, and became a published thing to mislead naive students."

"But it could be one student copying from another. What makes the supervisor culpable? Why are you sure he knew about the publication?" Candace asked.

"Well, reference was made to it in one of Rider's own papers," Sonja said patiently.

"The Kept Woman Writer" came out in 2000. This tracked the influence Rhys's husbands and lovers had wielded over her life, the baseline of exchange – sex for money – that provided the physical conditions under which she was able to write even while (in Rider's estimation) disabling her as a viable, independent person. Rider's paper gave special consideration to Ford Madox Ford, who published, supported and encouraged her into public recognition, actually giving her the name Jean Rhys. Ford was the one who introduced her to an agent who would manage her on his way to becoming her second husband, before dying and leaving her for the third as well as for an unknown quantum of other lovers.

Sonja paused and then threw herself back into it. "For Rider to reference paltry work by his own student was to dignify it, Candace. You can't be so blind as to not see that."

"No. Not that blind."

"Go on?"

"Go on."

"This is the next document I highlighted." Sonja pulled out a yellowed copy of a student paper that claimed to be based on field study and on perusal of Rhys's papers. It was entitled "The Suppressed Author: Who Wrote *Wide Sargasso Sea*?"

And Candace distinctly remembered hearing her father talking on the phone to a student about this work. They were in Toronto for Patrice's funeral, and her father was on an overseas call. The student paper (so far anonymous) took up the issue of Rhys's unknown lovers and proposed that the true author of *Wide Sargasso Sea* was a black man – a strong young descendant of slaves dispossessed after the burning of the estate in Rousseau, Dominica, where Jean Rhys had grown up as Ella Gwendolyn Rees Williams.

Everyone knew that in 1936, Rhys had visited what was left of the estate after a more recent burning and had roamed the ruins, but this paper claimed that a single letter, hitherto unknown to Rhys scholars and undocumented in the official collection of her papers, recorded her relationship with a man who had been born on the estate and hinted at his part in the novel. In fact, the paper described what could have been a sketch for the story, later discarded. The provenance of the source was shrouded in mystery, and even its possible categorization remained unclear – whether, for example, this belonged to what, in Sonja's experience, an official collection would have classified as Series 2 (Correspondence) or Series 4 (Personal Papers).

Anyway, the writer opined that Rhys was thirty-six when she met Sandy, and he was twenty-eight, with the body of the Young Bull in *Wide Sargasso Sea* but a good mind and persuasive tongue. He was an English teacher in a reputable Dominican high school. Thirty-six or not, the woman who had become Jean Rhys had still about her that forlorn and dewy-eyed quality that made strong men feel stronger, so there was a steamy affair that alternated between fiery exchanges (about arson and the whip in their respective family backgrounds) and tumbles in the soft grass behind fallen walls.

"You know, linguists are a coldblooded lot," Sonja remarked. "So I don't know how this grabs you. Our boy Randall would probably be more stirred up by it."

"Oh, he's *our boy*, is he?"

"I have come to trust your judgement."

"Look, he's a friend."

"Aha. But to get on. . . ."

In these brief meetings – so the argument went – Sandy revealed that he too was a writer but could never be published because of his social circumstances, for which he suggested she was somehow to blame as a descendant of a slave-owning family, and she could only make reparation by assisting him into print. He compared her family to the characters so familiar to them both from the English classics, people like Austen's Bertram and Brontë's Rochester, who carted away the wealth they had amassed on the backs of people like Sandy's ancestors, so as to live in splendour abroad. Gwendolyn, aka Jean Rhys, was outraged. The idea that she should be accused of living in splendour in England provoked her into a racist epithet she did not mean, so that they parted in hatred – he actually threw a stone at her, as she left – but his ideas were already carefully laid out in three exercise books of notes she had recorded from their conversations. These had not yet been found but were referred to in the newly discovered source, which also revealed that she had actually begun to write the novel as a dually authored work, when she heard of his death. Her final production of the novel made no mention of him.

This student paper had been delivered in 1998 at a huge conference but never published. Sonja said she had written the conference organizers (one a past student of hers) for a copy of the paper, in view of what followed next.

Candace braced herself.

Earl Rider had set up his own interrogation of Jean Rhys as a credible author of *Wide Sargasso Sea*, so as to reflect a bit of that glamour and notoriety of the circle (scattered down the centuries) who persisted in doubting Shakespeare's authorship. Candace had long known that her father had strong radical views on Rhys's prominence in the formation of a Caribbean canon, and she had actually asked Randall what he thought about it. The idea had turned out to be particularly offensive to Randall, this effort (as he saw it) to rob writers of credit for their own work. Bad enough that, for years, Rhys had been listed as an English rather than a Caribbean writer – but that was a different quarrel from this vile attempt to discredit a brilliant artist.

Refocusing on the file, Candace saw that Earl's Rider's stunning conference paper (which had at once been scooped up for inclusion in a book called *Disobedient Critics*) had been titled "Pale Copy: The Issue of Black Male Authorship for Jean Rhys's *Wide Sargasso Sea*". Here Rider took up the innuendos of the student study and met questions regarding credibility head-on in a powerful attack that questioned Rhys's status as a revered writer in circumstances of uncertainty regarding the authorship of her most significant work. Arguing an inescapable autobiographical connection between the Sandy and Antoinette of *Wide Sargasso Sea*, and the Sandy and Gwendolyn of the elusive document discussed in the student field study, Rider's essay acknowledged the autobiographical thrust of other fiction by Rhys even while arguing Rhys's dependence on the men of her life for her (eventual) literary success.

It was not a popular picture in these days of affirmative action, Rider acknowledged, but truth was truth. The greater part of his article was on possible black male authoring of the *Wide Sargasso Sea* core story through a sort of private oral performance that Rhys had done little more than inscribe and develop. (Here, Rider inexactly referred to concepts of creole and oral-scribal continua, with a vague flourish.)

In the end, Sonja pointed out, the essay sidestepped available biographical work, apart from missing more recent studies which were, at the time, mercifully unavailable; the comments of friends and critics; and the findings of those scholars who had pored over and annotated the Rhys archive in the McFarlin Library at the University of Tulsa.

"But he covered his tracks," Sonja said. "Rider did stop short of explicitly claiming that Rhys had plagiarized the novel, but only by pointing out the necessarily delicate status of the evidence."

Rider had explained his student's extraordinary discovery as having been acquired under circumstances that could seriously incriminate others, so full source information could not be published in the present circumstances. Negotiations with a view to rationalizing this were underway, according to an endnote, but proof of authorship, one way or the other, was a substantial research project away.

"You know he is the master of innuendo." Sonja glanced at Candace, who nodded. "There was the shadow of a hint about vested interests in preserving the Rhys opus intact, leaving a conclusion to be drawn that if no more was heard of the topic, it was because witnesses had been muzzled or the relevant scholars loath to expose the innocent to censure."

"There are people who love that sort of thing," Candace said. "Doubt of authorship and so on."

She and Sonja stared at each other, before Candace sang out, "Percy Stone."

Having readily accepted that there had never been a Homer, Percy Stone (even in his undergraduate days, to hear him tell it) had been well on the way to a conviction that Shakespeare was a fraud. He accepted with alacrity that Jean Rhys had plagiarized her best known work and probably others. Walcott was so abstruse he had to be genuine, but Bob Marley, Percy had said darkly, was a front for something. Big business of some sort. It was the sort of irresponsible speculation, Sonja said, that had always made her wonder what motivated the renewal of Percy's contracts.

"But I suppose Percy is the sort who creates a distraction when people are focusing too carefully," she reflected. "At any rate, he comes out of suspended animation to make up numbers, when one needs a support base. Against all odds, Percy has his uses."

"But back to Rider on Rhys," Candace insisted. "Where were the references for all this? As far as I know, my father thoroughly documents his work."

"There was a massive bibliography with primary sources making up the better part," Sonja said, "but these pretty well mirrored the catalogue for the McFarlin repository. There was no actual indication that the works listed had been read, let alone drawn on for conclusions."

"Probably just what Rhys was afraid of," Candace mused, as Sonja set down a plate from which emanated the unmistakable smell of coconut drops. At Sonja's questioning glance, she continued. "Randall saw somewhere that she was dead set against biographies. He said her editors suggested it was from some 'dread of inaccuracy'."

"Well-placed, as it turns out." Sonja said, adding under her breath, "*Randall says, Randall says.* When do we get to approach the oracle directly? But I won't tease you. What I want to know is what you made of the examination irregularities suggested by that stuff in the folder I turned over to you."

"Well, but if all of that is as it . . . as it appears" – Candace was feeling her way – "where were the other examiners of these students? I mean, in a system where the panel of examiners must include independent assessors and even examiners drawn from outside of the student's and supervisor's institution – how did no one pick up this, this . . ."

"There's a word for it." Sonja encouraged her. "And it's not *intertextuality*." She grinned at Candace's prolonged suckteet, then resumed. "'Loose Links' was just a conference presentation by a student from TCAC. You ask about examiners: those relate to theses and would have been orchestrated quite carefully. Rider could have got some crony to advise on selection of an external – *if* they were operating in a system high-minded enough not to turn the whole choice over to the supervisor."

"Some perfectly good institutions leave it entirely up to the supervisor and even the student to select examiners," Candace reminded her, "excellent systems founded on the belief that the student best knows the subdisciplinary dimensions of the work. That's where examiners are part of a supervisory team. There are a host of other possible checks and balances."

"However that may be, if the supervisor is a law unto himself, wild and wonderful things begin to happen." Sonja continued to eye Candace expectantly. "Well? Aren't you interested in the student author of the Rhys exposé?"

"You mean you have a name?"

Candace watched mesmerized, as Sonja ran a finger down the list of works cited on Earl Rider's "Pale Copy" paper.

"The author of the inspired student paper," Sonja announced, bringing her finger to a halt. *Stone, Percival.* "Authorship and Plagiarism in *Wide Sargasso Sea*". A paper presented at . . .

"Lord have mercy." Candace closed her eyes and swung away. "I've always heard Percy knows more than he lets on, but . . .'"

". . . but the mouth is always muzzled by the food it eats to live."

"I suppose." After a minute, Candace reached across to the plate Sonja turned in her direction, because the day had barely started, and it was clear that it had a long way to go. She ate with a sort of wonder that she even wanted to eat.

Earl Rider's tolerance, indeed validation, of manufactured data forced her awareness of something that had, only hours ago, been unthinkable. Yet around her, the sunlight and sweetness, the soft strains of an old Frats Quintet collection, all remained untainted, and it could only be because she had long harboured suspicion subconsciously and it was almost a relief to relinquish stubborn uncertainty.

"Do you know," she said, "I'll be fine." How, though? Where did she go from here? "But I can't eat a thing more now. I'll take my mango home."

As Candace got into her car outside Sonja's gate, her phone rang – the blasted neighbour again, she supposed. He had called before 5:00 a.m., going on and on again about Rider's whining dog. But this was a wrong number. She was faintly surprised not to see the neighbour's number, not that she would have answered if she had. She had actually tried to contact the Provost's assistant without success and eventually learned from Marion, whom she phoned for the venue of a meeting, that Amelia La Mar had left the job in the Office of the Provost for one at a hotel in Ocho Rios. Marion confided that Ms La Mar had taken off from the Tinson Pen Aerodrome for Boscobel with the loudly stated intention of having nothing more to do with ITS or its Provost.

Knowing he would be away for several more days, Candace felt bound to make some enquiry about the dog. It occurred to her that if she was going to her father's house at all, she had to get there before his helper left. If anyone worked on Saturday, it might only be half-day.

At 11:50, Candace found herself turning into the entrance to Hellshire Palms. She stopped outside the gate and looked in, noting that the pedestrian door in the centre of the sliding gate was unlocked. And who needed a padlock, with a pit bull on the inside? At least, once the gate was safely closed. She cast her mind beyond Cassidy, who was already on borrowed time, and knew that she and Randall would never own a pit bull – however securely their gate closed. Her mind played with the idea of them having a gate, a bougainvillea hedge, a dog. (A friend, she insisted to herself severely. He's just a *friend*.)

Then she saw the gate was not quite closed, just lightly swung in. She couldn't assume the dog was still tied and would have been nervous about getting out of the car, even if it had been locked, in case of some hole in the hedge; but she edged out, pressed the bell and jumped back in the car. The wide electric gate slid open, and she slammed the car door hastily. As she drove in, she heard the gate sliding again and lowered her window a fraction to speak to a woman who had come out on the porch.

"Some neighbours have been complaining about a dog," Candace shouted. "But I don't hear it. Is tied?"

The woman called down, "I just come to pick up me tings. Two weeks I in me bed with fever and bad feeling and never come to work, and I still weak can hardly stand pon me foot – to come land up in this thing. You could let him know – I not coming back here. Me don't want dis ya wuk."

"But is true the dog tie?"

"Tie, yes. Watch." She pointed at a post from which sagged a length of chain. At the end of the chain was a dead dog. It was gaunt, flesh drawn back tight from the hollow face, so the teeth bared huge, out of all proportion.

"My God." Icy sweat trickled down Candace's back, and her stomach rushed up.

"When I come yesterday, and I see it still tie, it bark for a while and howl. Then it start whine. A so it whine. Then it fall down. I had was to go back to me yard and lie down, because I couldn't just clean house with that taking place. I couldn't do nothing for the brute, after no food inna de house. And me can't walk near it, much less let it go. A say when I come today, I going bring bread to throw fe it and see if I could push the hose. And is so I find it. I only come in the house to pick up me things and go. Me nah come back." She regarded Candace suspiciously. "What you is to him?"

Candace had got out of the car and was doubled over, trying not to vomit. Only when the pedestrian gate clanged behind her did she realize the woman had left. And there was Candace inside the grounds with her car and the dead dog, no option but to walk out through the same gate and down the road. A student from ITS, whom she knew at sight, gave her a lift to a place where she could board a taxi, actually a minibus, which (like its identical twin, the Trinidad maxi-taxi) bore its passengers along a prescribed route at bone-rattling pace. She supposed she would be dependent on rides and taxis until her . . . until Earl Rider returned.

He had been away collecting his Doctor of Laws and engaging in mysterious meetings, and he would return in time for the celebration in his honour. His *honour*. Francine was to read the citation, and it was generally expected that he would formally announce Francine's Chair. His honorary degree.

En route she dialled her favourite medievalist to debate alternative notions of honour, but there was no answer. He was probably in class, but that was all right; she could switch on his voice in her head at will. She listened to all he would have said, as she made her way to New Kingston.

"You know what I thought was a cliché till today?" Candace said, after telling Sonja about the dog. Candace had piled Cassidy into the back of the rented car (probably against some fine print in the agreement) and headed over to Sonja's house again. Remembering how ashamed she had been, when the helper at The Habitat asked what she was to Earl Rider, Candace said, "I really did wish the earth would open and swallow me up."

Sonja twirled her glasses by the arm so fiercely she sent them arcing across the room. "Nope. You have more sense than that. I can better see where you might wish it would open and swallow him."

A chill rippled across Candace's skin. "No."

Cassidy caught up Sonja's spectacles gently between her teeth and released them into her lap. Sonja replaced her glasses on her face and rubbed a silky ear gratefully. Then she turned back to Candace.

"This man still has a spell over you?"

"Not a spell." Candace was irritable, tired of being misunderstood. "I grew up wanting this gifted, successful, respected scholar – to notice me, acknowledge that I . . . I too . . ." She gave up trying to explain, even to herself.

"And still?"

"No. Today I was revolted and so . . . ashamed. Then I realized he had nothing to do with me – he never had – and, more important, I had nothing to do with him. Only, now I have to respond in some way to what I know."

By Monday, Candace would have been even more repelled by the lavish coverage in the *Gleaner* regarding the conferral of the honorary degree on the ITS Provost had it not been overshadowed by another event. She was in Francine's office, organizing a change in venue for a lecture, when Gillian looked in to relay the news that Dr Wright had been rushed into hospital in critical condition.

Gillian also mentioned in passing that Anthea was making frantic arrangements to visit him. She *would*, Francine said furiously, and Candace nodded. She and Sonja had already noted how Anthea accumulated friends by ministering to their needs when they were at their weakest – the death of a parent or illness of a child, or the staff member's own medical emergency. Francine herself appeared unaccountably sympathetic to Lex's situation following on yet another make-over of affiliations in the centre.

"My God. Anthea must already be taking the mothballs out of the black hat she wears that makes her look like a Jonkonnu."

Candace had already learned from Marion that Francine, slightly mollified by Courtney and Sat's overtures regarding the project, had actually driven to Courtney's house for a frank talk about their past and future. After some minutes of knocking with no response, Francine let herself in with her own key, only to be faced with Anthea just emerged from the shower and wearing Courtney's T-shirt, one of those ghoulish modern patterns with fiendishly grinning skulls – not that that made a difference.

All that Francine revealed to Candace was that that girl, Anthea, was a snake and Courtney a vile blackmailer. Candace might as well know that Courtney had a hold over the Provost, and that was why he (and, by extension, Sat – or was it the other way around?) had got tenure. A travesty if ever there was one – while here was dear little Candace, the man's daughter, for God sake, lingering on contract. Rider had documentation in every medium there was (including, according to infallible sources, at least one obscene video) with which he could nail the bastard, but Courtney had this obscure data regarding the Provost and some graduate student business. If only Francine knew what it was, she would have Candace's tenure sorted out, and it was not to say that Candace held any brief for her father: she had said as much often enough.

Candace picked up on Francine's indirect invitation to join with her in negotiating a revised relationship and said, "You know what? This discussion is too important to rush."

"You're right," Francine said. "We must do lunch."

"And for now, I should perhaps try to see Lex, before Anthea saves him," Candace said brightly.

"Poor Lex," Francine agreed. "Now there's a man who goes about his job without fanfare and posturing. So many of them don't get it, eh? It's the performance, not the props. I mean, poor little Percy Stone won't ever look like an academic just by having *The Chronicle of Higher Education* growing out of his armpit, right? Give Lex my best regards, and I'll see if I can find out whether his post is frozen yet – perhaps from Marion, before she goes. Marion knows stuff," Francine continued, "however innocuous she comes across. But she's so hyper about not causing trouble that sometimes she won't talk. Of course, you've heard she's been making plans to get out? Some plum position at a Centre for Third World Masculinities."

—*)(*—

Lex managed little more than a grimace of appreciation, when the nurses cleared out of his room and let Candace in, but when she rose to leave after a short visit, he seemed reluctant to release her hand.

Two days later, though, he was propped up, pale but with something of his old poise and wry, lazy smile.

"Seems I'm to live. And just as well for you, as I have information you could not possibly have accessed anywhere else." He paused, studying her. "I wonder if it will offend you. It's about your father."

"Haven't one."

"Well, in that case." He settled back more comfortably and patted the bed. "Sure you won't join me? It would make our chat so much cozier."

"Get on with it. It's reassuring enough that you feel your old self."

"One tries everything. But first: what new dirt do we have on our Provost? You go first."

He proceeded to lie there entranced by Candace's account of Sonja's disclosures.

"And there's more," she promised.

"Oh, surely not. I don't know anything about Rhys beyond *Wide Sargasso Sea* – which I liked – and a few others which were mostly too depressing to finish. But even on the basis of my limited information, what you've told me strains belief."

"Well, drawing on Sonja's info, including the documents she produced, I fed strings of names, titles of papers and key phrases into cyberspace, and a very substantial operation emerged, but it is not our Provost's operation. Nor is there anything to suggest that he has something to gain. The key figure, as far as ITS is concerned, turns out to be Sat. For most of the past decade, Sat has at best been aware of and at worst part of a lucrative business in online publishing. Moreover, this press is far more convincing that your basic vanity press. Peer review is set up (although I expect the review process is "fixed") and money made from contributors through publishing charges. Yup, authors billed upon acceptance of their manuscripts. The website gives a New York address, which is a mail-forwarding service. And mail is forwarded to Dr Satnarine Nagassar at ITS. He may be a relatively small cog in the international system, but he is the Caribbean cog."

She told Lex how she had seen the envelope addressed to him with the Acadamentor logo. And how that had set her off on a tortuous path of discovery.

It was still unclear in her mind, she said, but she had noticed that brainwaive@acadamentor.com advertised itself briefly as the ultimate online student guidance service and scholarly support system; but as one read on, it became forthright about the nature of its services. She calculated roughly: US$500 to $900 per essay (depending on length), $3,000 to $4,000 per Master's project, $6,000 to $7,000 per MPhil thesis, and about $12,000 for a PhD dissertation with an accompanying Oral Defence drill thrown in for another $400. The details had not crystallized yet, but it seemed Acadamentor assembled panels to agree on requirements for a thesis, after which a writer would be selected from some pool of appropriate persons. One Dr Courtney Straker had held a consultancy in the past to network qualified people who might share their expertise in Caribbean matters. Sat's vitae, among the papers made available to BEAM, actually listed among his consultancies an online scholarly community for student mentorship with a web address that appeared under the Acadamentor logo. But there was nothing much one could prove, as yet, regarding Sat's involvement.

Candace explained that she had stumbled on this thing by chance: it was an international business with just a tentacle in the Caribbean. It seemed that for junior researchers, access to mentorship began with the website itself – a sort of free road map to helpful sites. Then it moved to what it termed a backpack offering brief synopses, outlines or basic designs for topics, at about $50 a pop. The next level of guidance (called Brainstorm) involved a detailed topic outline, and the next promised qualified feedback, which meant editing that clearly extended to rewriting. The highest level of assistance was sale of the finished product, as set out on Brainwaive. "Absolutely in your face. Almost jeering," she concluded.

"But surely that requires substantial technical expertise – I mean, ways of avoiding antiplagiarism programmes," Lex said.

At the risk of sounding melodramatic, Candace replied, it looked to her as if the organizers had worked out a sort of smuggling route via the Internet for acquiring, conveying and marketing stolen scholarship; and now among the arrangements that were region specific, there was a booth especially for Caribbean material.

"To put it bluntly, then," Lex summed up with his usual unabashed candour, "Sat's been operating as a fence."

"I don't know. I think it's more subtle. And I wouldn't be surprised if it's more far reaching. *And* one can't help wondering about Courtney." Candace grinned. "Even though Sonja says that in the parlance of two or three centuries ago, Courtney would have been dismissed as a *rattle*."

"And Percy?"

"My own feeling was that there wouldn't have been a Percy then, but Sonja doesn't agree. She says we exaggerate his unreliability and that, in fact, he can be relied on to do nothing when it most matters and certainly to shut up about all sorts of crap. She says he would have been Master of the Stool."

"Sonja is a most wonderfully knowledgeable resource." Lex gave it further thought. "When stoned he would prattle of a courtly young rattle, but otherwise pass as a fool." After a while, he probed again. "And the Provost maintains an aura of blissful innocence. Is it true his last secretaryputus has taken off?"

"Seems so. More to the point, I can tell you that one of Sat's least impressive students has completed successfully. The thesis drew rave reviews from its examiners. I attended the presentation she made a month or two before, which was, in design and execution, an insult to the discipline."

"You can say that, although it's not your discipline?"

"Insult to any discipline."

"Yet he managed to steer her towards some form of qualification?"

Candace nodded.

"What flavour?"

"Doctorate."

"God help us."

Candace shook her head, speechless. Then she whispered, "I still can't see how Earl Rider is involved, whatever Sonja says or Randall doesn't say."

"Well, we've seen Rider tolerate fakes like Olatunde." Lex's voice was gentle, not accusing her of wilful blindness. "And it would seem that both Courtney and Sat are protected species."

"But my . . . our Provost has always seemed so . . . meticulous."

"He must be, to maintain clean hands while operating with his eyes closed to surrounding filth. He must, also, keep rather a finely tuned system of student records and submissions, if they are conveniently porous enough for chunks of one person's dissertation to slip through into the work of another. He may even, in the past, have been aware of Sat orchestrating a pool of qualified 'mentors' to aid output – custom-built theses and such. Who can say? Our Provost is a formidable businessman. Carries all off with aplomb – even with everything collapsing around him." Lex grinned. "Moreover, my contacts in the world of commerce have much to say about Rider's confidence regarding his hold on ITS."

"Tell."

"He has separated ITS from the governance of its original parent institutions but not met requirements of the proposed funding agencies. So these agencies have signed nothing, and he's – as yet – unrestrained by them. Meanwhile ITS rakes in all the fees."

"Why shouldn't it?"

"Won't be enough to be worth alienating everyone. There's a spectrum of different takes on it. To start off, the GKIA is grumbling that however much ITS continues to resemble a regular tertiary institution, it's a rogue company Rider has set up, one that allows him to operate in a zone of impunity."

"Blouse and skirt," Candace said.

Chapter 15

Banquet

Now lat us sitte and drynke, and make us merie,
And afterward we wol his body berie.

The *Gleaner* and the *Jamaica Observer* carried pictures of the ITS Provost, first from the 2013 trip when he returned to Kingston after delivering the distinguished lecture in Brisbane and then in the ceremonial robes for conferral of Doctor of Laws on the more recent visit to Gallagher University. His return was scheduled for the evening before festivities in his honour on the ITS campus.

"I know all about it," Randall bragged. "A bird of the air shall carry the news and that which hath wings shall tell of the matter. It's Twittered hither and yon."

"You sound like an affable version of AA Mackhail," Candace said. But under the laughter gathered the pressure of awareness, the need to act on what was unfolding.

Alone in her living room with Cassidy at her feet, she tried to see her way. She could not contemplate playing along over the years, suppressing whatever her father wanted to keep buried. But the idea of denouncing him filled her with horror, especially since so much was still unclear. Yet to do nothing would implicate her in whatever transpired. She forced herself to be still, strung out between unthinkable alternatives. She could see herself falling over the edge, or pushed off. Then it dawned that there was no choice, after all, none whatever: only one step forward that she must make for herself. She stared at it, feeling ice cold for a few minutes and then, gradually, calm as she had not been for years.

Candace absented herself the day of the Provost's return. Summer classes (as they insisted on calling them) had wound up at the end of July, and in the early August respite before exam scripts came in, she wrote up another paper from the findings of her Forbidden Words project. Days and nights flowed by seamlessly in the glow of the computer screen, punctuated by the occasional swipe of Cassidy's tail or the dull echo in her wrist of carpal tunnel reasserting itself. She figured she could work on without getting to the stage of the wrist splint, if she iced it often and avoided driving. For two or three days, she went nowhere, although she had rented a car to tide her over until she retrieved hers from Hellshire Palms. She had postponed collecting it, lest any contact she made prompt the Provost to rope her into his celebrations.

She had staved off this eventuality (quite neatly, she thought) by sending him an e-mail to the effect that she had driven to his house because of an urgent call from one of his neighbours, and her car had got locked in. She added that she had alternative transport and would contact him early the following week. Meanwhile, she had left her keys at his office, in case he needed to move the car. Apparently he was no more eager to meet her, because a day or two later, Sonja reported that his new secretaryputus had driven the car down to the ITS compound and dropped the keys on Gillian's desk in CuSt. "Thoughtful," Sonja concluded. "Or perhaps your elderly vehicle isn't adequate to the décor of The Habitat."

The Provost's imminent return had distracted Candace, and her mind roamed over what Lex had said about Earl Rider being well aware of nefarious operations among her colleagues. Candace set up a new e-mail address unconnectable with herself and put out feelers to Acadamentor. While she waited on a bite, she set about Dogpiling what more she could find on Sat alongside all she had pulled together over the preceding days and connected with the vitae AA Mackhail had supplied.

Wheels within wheels; tales within tales. When she had reeled it all in, she woke Randall up and delivered herself of the narrative.

Sometime before appointment at ITS, Sat had, as a sideline, operated as a freelance ghost writer for anyone who needed help in writing up business reports, proposals, abstracts and so on. Absolutely open and above board. It helped get him through the difficult months of application and disappointment before landing the job. Sat's understanding of Caribbean affairs made him especially useful to those attempting to address decision-makers in the region, so he sought out that type of interest. He wrote on Caribbean matters, on behalf of those whose areas of expertise lay decidedly outside written communication – people in IT, finance, the occasional cricketer. Once or twice he helped with a political speech, but that was not his thing. He preferred to deliver a piece of writing rather than leave room for poor oral delivery that could drag down the worth of his product.

After a while, though, because he operated in the academic world, he began to specialize in academic writing. These were the people he was in touch with, and this was the context in which he was versed. So he became a custom writing resource for academics or would-be academics working on Caribbean issues, or sometimes, he spread himself a bit to assist people working more generally on postcolonial or diasporic topics. Only, academics were not usually clients who wanted to publicize their need for such assistance. To get this type of business, he had to agree to anonymity and to supply confidentiality. This was where his tracks disappeared, because he became more of a ghost. Presumably the more he dematerialized from the work, the less it mattered how far his assistance went, for it seemed as if all sorts of other lines his colleagues might baulk at faded and eventually vanished from his landscape altogether.

It was not clear just when he linked up with Acadamentor, but it appeared to Candace that by the time Sat had his post at ITS, he must have comfortably inhabited two worlds. In one, he was a flesh-and-blood scholar who taught, published and built his résumé; in another, he sold intellectual property on the academic black market – sometimes other scholars' work, sometimes his own skills. Under the circumstances, it would have seemed silly not to make a bit extra by selling grades to the odd student, but this was not enough, not secure. Silver would have said he sold his soul, while Sonja might say he sold himself; most of the people Candace knew would have said he sold his abilities in unethical practice. But there were those who privately admired his business sense and hastened to make use of his services.

In answer to wide international demand, several thriving businesses openly advertised online their sale of intellectual artefacts like case studies, essays and theses. But research being context-bound, it would have been easy for Sat to carve out his niche, a custom writing network designed specifically for Caribbean interests. While he found clientele within the Caribbean, he got more bites from those approaching Caribbean topics from outside the region. Within the company's protocol, however far Sat had moved beyond acceptable ghost-writing, he would still have partaken of their claim to professionalism. Acadamentor had fabricated a respectable front so that clients might feel comfortable, might feel untainted. They advertised completed assignments as plagiarism-free, because no one was stealing from existing publications, essays or theses, nor reusing papers, articles, case studies or chapters. There was no fear of Turnitin and the like. No, no. As in other regions serviced by the organization, Sat's products would have to have been originals. Acadamentor promised to supply unique compositions, custom-made according to the client's specifications and, once downloaded by the client, never to be used again.

The organization – including Sat's corner of it – operated at the highest level of professional discretion. Confidentiality and authenticity were its watchwords. *Its* – not *his*. Anonymity was now pivotal to the enterprise. It operated through no identifiable person or from any actual place. Everything was virtual. The more persons whose input the business required, the more disembodied they became – so discreet as to be altogether invisible, each little more than a caring presence that hovered over the needy, somewhat bruised academic who had sought sanctuary.

Even so, it was a business and had to support itself to stay aloft. Costs for services rendered were calculated per page and varied according to the length of time in which material had to be delivered. Costs for overnight and fortnight productions differed widely. On the average, chapters at doctoral level went for $41 per page. Most customers bought individual parts, like case studies, literature reviews or annotated bibliographies. Guidelines were clear and user-friendly. A client submitted detailed requirements, received an estimate and paid a bit down. Then Acadamentor assigned an experienced writer with whom to stay in touch, until the product was ready for download. The personal touch was everything. Acadamentor promised and delivered 24/7 custom care. The ghost transfigured into a sort of guardian angel.

Searching the website, Candace had found that a client could choose to download a whole work or, in the case of major scholarly writing, to receive it chapter by chapter. The former was fine for someone in a spot for a hasty article to shoot off to a journal or a vanity press. Chapter by chapter was strongly (it might not be too much to say *lovingly*) recommended for the student who needed to build up a history of submission and discussion with the supervisor. This had to be a successful business, if it could afford to offer free title and content pages as well as abstracts and other bits and pieces. There was also a generous revision policy – free revision (barring departure from original specifications) for twenty-one days after downloading, before payment. Clients might pay by credit or debit card or by wire transfer, in the happy knowledge of a money-back guarantee on satisfaction. The warranty covered the much-advertized confidentiality and authenticity.

Now, this guarantee could only be possible because of the cadre of professional writers in the organization's network – highly qualified, specialist competence in a wide range of subject areas, a large number of these writers capable of producing PhD-level material on demand. Courtney seemed to have been one and may have helped recruit others. When one thought about who these people had to be, clients could only be reassured that there was nothing unprofessional about accepting their guidance.

Or the thought could be hair-raising. Depending on who did the thinking.

The Provost seemed to be aware, and his hair appeared to retain its natural curl.

"And your hair?" Randall found his voice to ask.

"A little wilder than usual but no static to speak of." But she was faking it.

"You're totally freaked out," he said. "And who can blame you?" She wished she was less transparent. "I guess it will be hard for you to sleep. Call me anytime. Don't ever hesitate."

Yet she worked it out. She tossed until two o'clock and awoke at four, but in the certainty of how she would go forward. She was settled, as if she were sitting in calm salt water under an almond tree. Warm seawater, cool breeze. Waves little more than ripples, a barely discernible lapping. Okay.

—)|(—

Ferocious heat, unrelieved by rain for weeks, had whitened the stone finish, overcoming even the limited greenery that normally struggled for survival, so that the framework of ITS stood out starkly like bleached bones among desiccated spikes of cactus. Yet on the evening of the dinner in Professor Rider's honour, ITS sparkled. The area around the events tent had been garnished with lights, and pots of crotons glowed gold and burgundy under the flicker of citronella torches. One or two staff members speculated on whether there were fewer guests than expected, and, if so, whether this reflected dwindling public respect for the Provost or fallout from the chik-V epidemic, which was only now losing momentum. But the whispers dried up at a peek through the door to the dining area.

Inside was lined with palms and torch lilies. The tables fanned out in concentric arcs from the head table with its long centrepiece of orchids, the dendrobiums spraying lavishly against leather leaf fern. The aisle to the head table ran through a colonnade of potted ficus, low, plaited together at their tops and illuminated by pinpoint lights. "But how were they transported?" guests asked each other in awed whispers.

Sidling past the small talk, Candace left Sonja to circulate without her, and settled at a table on the row farthest from the front to sit and make notes, while the snacks were still warm. Scribblenibblescribblenibble.

It was coming together. It was going to be her first book. Campus talk of the sort that had infuriated her was transforming to a database from which she was drawing the chapters. Wafting them together, she floated in a weightlessness she could not account for or define. *Ineffable* might be the best she could come up with. Yet she felt substantial. Even hungry. What was this?

This – was everything that mattered to her. The book was coming into being, and Randall had signed the contract and had his e-ticket. He had called and said, "I'll be there in a couple weeks, and I'm going nowhere without you again. Ever." She had almost dropped the phone but then clutched it and cradled it in both hands. *Did* he say that? That was what he had said, and he was never casual with words. They bore her up.

She was afloat in light. The way motes of dust gleamed in a shaft of sunshine words beyond utterance swirled around and through her, yet she was solid, irrepressible. In the barrage of malice she sensed around corners at ITS, in the onslaught of foolishness, she was invulnerable – as if the warm glow of Randall's imminent presence and the heady surge of the book she was bringing into being were together pressing age-old aches and pains to the periphery of attention and then out of existence altogether.

A glimpse of routine annoyances wavered and gave way, as voices that had hitherto been irritants transformed into data that strengthened the book. And the best of it was that Randall and the book were not opposing or even distinct forces, but complementary, for he was enthusiastic about her work – not merely supportive (and what wouldn't most women of her sort give for *merely supportive*?). He was committed to it. He listened with an intensity and fascination she had not foreseen, even searching out material for her in his university library.

Perhaps – it popped into her head – she could raise a child. Then the shock at finding herself contemplating any such thing, the unwisdom of investing the idea in the bald fact of a friend's relocation to the same land mass as hers, sent her mind reeling – but the idea took hold. She had never had much to do with children, but she began to think that perhaps . . . An overpowering surge of deep and conflicting sensations rushed on her at the thought of gathering a small body against hers, of holding a slight hand on the way to school – and a flood of longing broke over her at the idea of leading a child into a book. Incredible that none of this had occurred to her before. "Arrested development," she said aloud and laughed at herself. But it was terrifying to think she might have missed it. Perhaps it was too late for the child, or too complicated. (She dared not speculate on how Randall might view it.) But what if she had missed the inclination?

Sitting there with her notes before her and the evening unfurling all around, she was lifted up beyond her old dark thoughts, so that everything she saw between the shimmer of possibilities became valuable or, at the very least, entertaining.

She chuckled at the sight of Clarence Stewart, aka Olatunde, shaking hands near the door, large as life and twice as expansive. He had relinquished the somewhat sensitive position of Fellow, as Sonja had gathered from the ITS grapevine, on the understanding that he would not be demoted in any way, since nothing had been or could be proven against him. Knowing how things worked at ITS, he must be aware that Candace had been the first to question his past. A pesky woman. On the other hand, perhaps he had comforted himself with one of his favourite proverbs: When a leopard is chasing you, do not ask whether it is male or female. And he appeared to have got away.

"So what is he to be? On what pretence does he remain?" Candace had demanded crossly a day or two before her new and unaccustomed featherweightedness set in.

"Special Adviser to the Provost. Don't you read your *ITS Newstime* every day?" Sonja had managed to maintain a straight face.

Now there he was at the door, clapping the well-groomed shoulder of some dignitary in welcome and accepting congratulations on his leader's achievement.

Candace unfolded a few sheets of paper from her purse and burrowed deeper into the notes that were her sole reason for attending. The cocktail patties were crisp and a little peppery, the way she liked them, and she thought, This isn't so bad.

"You look better," Sonja said, placing her purse on the table beside Candace's. "If I did not know you well by now or had not been standing beside you, while you let the waiters pass you by, I'd have said you were tipsy. I was worried at first, when I saw the dress. Oh, it's pretty but not of itself uplifting, though perhaps only I might take it that way. It's precisely that shade that was so in vogue in the eighteenth century – that colour they used to call 'stifled sigh.'"

"Go away."

"Nope. We're summoned to the feast. Let us to the fleshpots." Sonja sat down with a look askance at the notes Candace stuffed hastily into her purse. "You'll have to conduct yourself with propriety, because Marketing is to video the proceedings, and any inappropriate gesture may be immortalized on YouTube."

A fanfare at the entrance gave Candace a bad moment or two, but she was fond of Elgar's *Pomp and Circumstance Marches*, and once her father was ushered in reverently and seated, she managed to pretend he was not there. By the time the Bishop specially invited for the purpose had signed the cross, support staff had swarmed out with pepper-pot soup that reached the tables swirling up steam. Candace chatted with Sonja, Nicholas and Barham contentedly, as the meal evolved, but speech time rolled round inexorably, and it would not be possible to take notes during the addresses without inviting remark, so Candace prepared to record all she could mentally. The possibility that the speeches might contribute to Forbidden Words made even these surprisingly palatable.

Francine's encomium on Professor Rider's administrative brilliance, original research, genius for mentorship and example to students and young staff (a father figure, she said) took a long time to wind mercifully to an end. When she concluded with reference to achievements firmly grounded on professional integrity, the Provost rose in a storm of applause to make his response. The inevitable beginning – a promise not to detain his audience long – moved swiftly to expressions of appreciation, humble reference to the signal honour recently bestowed on him and a modest acknowledgement that he had worked hard to reach this point. He announced Francine's Chair and congratulated Professor Forbes-Garcia on her advancement, mentioning the insightful collaborative work in which she was involved with her colleagues in CSSGDS.

Dexter muttered a subtextual comment with his most blandly omniscient expression, and Sonja passed it on in a whisper: It was a deal. The Unstable Skins publication remained a co-edit; Francine had got her Chair; Courtney would be CSSGDS Fellow. Sat was disgruntled, but that was neither here nor there, as Courtney had dropped him.

Then the Provost swept on to the subject of the future. There were, he said, exceptional prospects for ITS. He spoke movingly of his vision, and of how this had shaped the mission statement and strategic plan. But there would be significant change. There must always be change, he reminded them severely. There could be no progress otherwise, but they were well prepared, thanks to the groundwork he had laid over the years.

Speaking of groundwork, he had heard the concerns about environmental safety, and even now, work was beginning to secure the physical areas close to the campus, as in rehabilitation of damaged pipelines, both those that had gradually become corroded and those that may have been injured by heavy equipment in constructing certain buildings on the campus. Some holes that had opened would be filled. The Provost allowed a tolerant smile to play across his face briefly before adding that anxieties had been voiced about burnt garbage residue that could ignite and emit poisonous smoke, and that these were quite unfounded. A dismissive chuckle broke out obediently and rippled through his audience before fading. Sanitary landfill was in place for the purpose of rectifying whatever unevenness the more scrupulous observer had noted in the grounds, the Provost added in the tone of one who knew his assurances to be unnecessary.

But there was a lot more than physical improvement to look forward to. His audience leaned forward. There was, in fact, to be an entirely new dispensation, because the separation of the campus from its parent institutions was now a reality, and he was proud to take this auspicious occasion to announce that ITS was in the immediate future to be a fully independent university. The Global Knowledge Institute of the Americas and the Consortium for Borderless Education would always have the gratitude of the new ITS, but they would be, in a matter of weeks, no more than resources for advice and encouragement.

"The son-of-a-bitch really pull it off." Dexter confirmed it under his breath but was instantly quoted in whispers, one to the next, until it reached the farthest row behind him, and Sonja passed it to Candace's ear, practically shouting over the applause that erupted and continued to reverberate after the Provost's announcement.

Earl Rider held up a hand both in acknowledgement and for quiet.

"Alas," he said, "I shall not be here to share this reward of our labours with you." Sudden stunned silence. "Of course, I shall continue, officially, as your interim Chancellor, while we work out the modalities of this independence, and while a search team seeks out some appropriate person to take you forward from that point." He lowered his eyes modestly. "The thing is that I am at heart an academic, and the world of scholarship, rather than that of administration, has been calling on me for some time. I believe there may be some small corner – if another institution will have me" – he waved away their laughter depreciatingly – "where I can immerse myself in my research and writing once again."

He finished with a gentle warning. "Regarding the details of those transactions that have just been concluded, I can say little more for the time being. My commitment to transparency is well known, however, and I shall be laying the relevant documents before the necessary committees and making a full statement over the next fortnight."

Outside, as they threaded their way towards their cars, Candace picked up an unusual odour and wondered whether it was her imagination prompted by a growing outrage that threatened to deflect the upturn in her spirits. But Sonja too wrinkled her nose.

"A Drain Runs Through ITS," she quipped, glancing at Candace. "Are we beginning to read each other's minds or just to share neuroses?" She waved vaguely to Candace and drifted away to her car, muttering, "Does nothing stop him?"

Nothing could stop Candace from visiting Lex the following morning with an account of the festivities, but she was not the only one with a tale to unfold. The indolent and irreverent Lex Wright had actually telephoned Randall and had a long chat. The sheer impertinence of the man, alongside his physical vulnerability, rendered Candace speechless. Yet her relief at having Randall out in the open between them prevented her from trying to suppress the telltale glow. She couldn't have, anyway, she realized, writing herself off as shamelessly besotted – and with a man whose very absence had made him materialize beyond their intangible bonds. She struggled to come to terms with this . . . this enfleshment.

In the resulting lull, Lex confessed that Randall had been very short on the phone, no doubt recognizng him at once as a potentially dangerous marauder. "I assumed my most caressing voice," he assured her, "even though I've been able to contemplate him only with loathing and have always considered his e-mail and Skype communication with you as acts of assorted piracy." He sighed. It was clear, he said, that – not content with sharing some years of Candace's past – this Randall person might well be plotting inroads into her future. "On the other hand, it began to occur to me that since I had little future of my own, it might be churlish to . . ."

Her face whitened. "What do you mean? I thought you were better?"

"Oh, nothing immediately fatal. But 'tis enough. 'Twill serve." He digressed from the account that was of more interest to him, so as to sketch his prospects; then he continued. "So, in view of my own nebulous circumstances, I felt I should set my record clear with the phantom lover before he arrived." He shifted his tone to plaintive. "Did I do wrong? Again?"

"Bother you." She took his hand affectionately. "Damn fas' and out of order." But her mind was in too much of a whirl to maintain her side of the conversation sensibly, so she allowed him to lead her on to talk of what she meant to do.

She told him more about the research project that was absorbing data from the enquiry, about rumours that Marcus Walters had had his contract renewed for just two years, because he hadn't published since the doctorate, about a sabbatical at St Augustine that might produce a one-year opening, and about part-time hours at Mona that Marcus must now be even more paranoid about. Then, in a colourless voice, she added that she had sent in a letter of resignation that morning.

"I'll begin the onslaught again – applications to UWI, part-time, full-time, temporary, tenure track. The book I have in the pipeline should make some difference." But as a first step, the resignation was in.

Lex stared, as she described Francine's purring acceptance, the woman having cooled towards her again. "Well, perhaps it's wise," Francine had said. "You've really no hold on the institution as things stand, and that's so insecure for you. And, you know, it might be in your best interest to remember, should you ever land a little something elsewhere, that an ounce of collegial loyalty goes a long way."

"Whew!"

"Randall was completely in agreement about the resignation – Occam's Razor, he called it – although, I don't know that I'll ever get another permanent job anywhere," Candace confided to Lex, "let alone from a scrupulous institution. UWI? Let's face it. The barbarians are at the gate – only, we are the barbarians, and the gates of UWI are such that we may never penetrate the citadel. Anyway," she concluded with a stubborn set of her chin, "my letter's in. What's done is done, and it's too late to dissuade me." She shoved her copy towards him.

Dear Registrar,

This is to tender my resignation from the Institute of Tropical Studies on the grounds of differences between the ethical framework in which I choose to operate and what appears to be that of the institute.

I have tried over the past four years to resolve my differences with the academic and professional standards of the institute, but I have come to see that these are irreconcilable, and my reservations can no longer be set aside. I would be thankful if I could be released immediately once a suitable replacement can be found. Otherwise, I shall, of course, complete the sixth months stipulated for notice.

I record my gratitude for the kindness of many colleagues and my best wishes for their future advancement and success.

Yours sincerely,
Candace Clarke

Relief smoothed away a taut line on Lex's forehead. "What I'm going to tell you will confirm you did the only thing possible. But what prompted you to this sudden and, to all appearances, risky move?"

"I couldn't go on. It got to be a matter of intellectual life or death. I couldn't shut up about him; I couldn't turn him in. There was only the one way, and I'd drafted the letter before I went to that dinner. I think I realized where I stood before I even went to his house."

Candace told him about the day of the pit bull, and his lips tightened in revulsion. "Still," he said, "as a young girl left to take care of a helpless mother while fending for herself, you too seem to have been left to wither on the end of a chain. So the pit bull thing is . . . shocking but not much of a surprise." He regarded her carefully. "I understand Sonja has refused another extension."

"I think she's only been staying to see me through," Candace admitted. "I comfort myself that it can't have done her any real harm. God knows what association with ITS may have done to my prospects, for I'm not a Sonja Palmer."

"You're leaving barely in time." Lex's tone was uncharacteristically serious, his eyes brightly dark in the drawn face.

Through his mother's connections in the world of commerce, he had learned that the documents were indeed signed to render ITS an independent private university. Arrangements were in train with important financial houses that had seemed interested in a stake in the institution and willing to invest heavily – which would have sorted out much of the funding required. With his team of advisers, Earl Rider had sought guidance from Credit Suisse. But he had not taken it. He had completed the accreditation exercise to the initial satisfaction of the agencies involved; only, contrary to the advice of Credit Suisse, he had chosen for himself among a number of less expensive private equity firms, of which LMV Private Capital was the largest and Antillean Investment Group the smallest. He had not gone directly to Craig Harvey Renninger – the vast international firm that had been the primary recommendation of Credit Suisse. Instead he had selected these others and garnered supporters in the local business community – which was how Lex knew so much about the circumstances.

It was when Lex heard that negotiations were breaking down that he had given Sat a call. The conversation was stilted on Sat's side to begin with. (When a man with whom you have shared nothing but lack of mutual interest calls from hospital, you can only assume he wants you to do something for him.) Things got more strained when Lex asked him to drop in at the hospital to collect a package at the Provost's request. When Sat arrived, and Lex told him the Provost no longer had need of the material, Sat's face was murderous. But Lex had reached for his hand, and in the most heartfelt terms commended him on his truly statesmanlike behaviour. Not everyone would be large enough to restrain themselves from reacting to Courtney's betrayal. Sat had glowered at Lex as he continued. "I mean, how he appropriated the administrative leverage you two worked for, *together.*" He had watched it ignite in Sat's eyes, Lex told Candace, a flare of that fury that had been smouldering and was now eating its way out.

After that, it was a matter of time before Sat released to a number of ITS offices the first of the Courtney videos, the one his wife had hitched briefly to the intranet. Sat also leaked a remark that Elizabeth Woods instantly seized on and printed, about a staff member driven by rapacious sexual appetite to hound little girls in his class.

Yes, Candace confirmed, she had read that, and then she had noticed that not all colleagues actually cared, beyond the usual lip service to professional ethics and common decency. Secretly or blatantly, some of Courtney's male colleagues (and, alas, a couple female ones) viewed these exploits as redounding to Courtney's credit. So Courtney preened himself for a while, but Sat's obvious intention for the leak to be professionally damaging lodged deep. A much-quoted remark by Barham – that Sat would be a fine one to take the high moral ground on Courtney's indecencies – twisted the blade in the wound.

So Courtney began talking loudly about how Sat's swindling and blackmail had left a trail of traumatized students and undermined the credibility of ITS examination results. When Courtney referred to Sat's activities as a feeding frenzy, and this phrase too found its way into the press, Sat lost all control and began to proclaim Courtney's hypocrisy to all and sundry in the corridors, Courtney, he claimed, having been "involved in everything" from the start. And that was when Sat named Percy Stone as witness to a role Courtney had played in sourcing writers for some online organization.

"Percy?" Candace could hardly believe her ears.

"A satisfied client of Acadamentor in his day, I suspect," Lex said, "though I've no evidence apart from Percy's native incompetence. Could he really have produced a sound doctoral dissertation? I suppose one never knows."

"How can you know any this?" Candace demanded.

"Aah." Terrified of repercussions but helpless in the face of the very real likelihood that he could be dismissed and cut off from funding for his expensive lifestyle, Percy had cowered in the headlights for a time and then bolted to the elegant wing of the hospital in which Lex was recuperating, to ask his advice.

"He came to *you*?" Candace stared at Lex.

"He did. Why is that so incredible?" Lex turned a wounded eye on her. "Anyway, meanwhile, shred by shred, things at ITS had been unravelling." Everyone knew an outstanding report on examination security had been mentioned in the *Jamaica Observer*, resuscitating the unresolved rumour about exchanges of sex or money for grades. If Rider had dealt with a huge firm that had the resources to settle things swiftly, everything might have been signed by then. Things might have gone differently. But as it was, the idea that the credibility of qualifications from ITS might be called in question unnerved reputable but small firms, and they began to hold back, to postpone signing the remaining documents.

"Rider has been left holding it," Lex said. "At best, he'll have to put the whole thing in the hands of Craig Harvey Reninger, after all, and not as a functioning business with a profit – which was what it was when he had just negotiated the separation – but as a shaky enterprise, one on the way to becoming a non-accredited institution. Then the firm will call the shots as suit them best."

Candace stared at him, fascinated. "What the hell will he do?"

"We can only wait and see. Knowing him, he'll land on his feet. A guy in history at UWI told me Rider has almost certainly secured the post Down Under."

She stared at him blankly.

"Brisbane or Sydney or somewhere." He patted her hand. "But all this won't matter to you and your monk. And think of how it will contribute to your book."

"Forbidden Words? How?"

"I mean the one you're doing with your boyfriend, his unfolding saga of Earl Rider through the consciousness of his daughter." Lex paused, misunderstanding her silence. "Sorry. I guess I wasn't supposed to know."

"It seems" – her voice came thick, strange to her own ears, her head spinning – "*I* wasn't supposed to know." At his sudden sharp glance of alarm, she said, "Though, it stared me in the face. I've been blinder than ever."

In the first few seconds of realization, it was the irony that leapt at her. She felt nothing to begin with – so numb, she could glimpse what would have been the humour of it. Then, recognition, again so swiftly she felt nothing: the way people described a shark attack – the blow one registers after seeing one's blood spreading away.

She *saw.*

Even when Randall seemed slightly naive, at times even gullible, she had believed in him unquestioningly. Recollection oozed droplet by droplet, of how slowly, steadily in their talks, night after night, she had opened her mind to him, grateful for his patient ear, had surrendered herself to that selfless hold on her, as she clambered out the pit of her past. Only, his effort had been not a gift but an investment. She talked; he gathered data. He dissected her anguish for reassembly to a publishable story.

"I felt like I was surfacing from a nightmare, when . . . *that* was the dream. I was floating farther and farther from reality, while he . . . extracted the venom. For he did draw out the pain too. But to repackage it. Fictionalize it for sale. And then, the contrasts I clung to, between . . . were never there."

Lex's face was drained of colour. "My God," he whispered. "What have I said? It was just by the way – the man referred to plotting your father's effect on you, so I assumed this was something the two of you were co-authoring. I asked, and he clammed up, so then I thought he was protecting your interests. That you were doing this together."

"Oh yes. Apparently we were. Only, I never knew." She placed her hand on his absently. "You've done me a great service, Lex. Truly." She stood up and straightened her skirt fastidiously, as if it mattered.

But as she drove back to New Kingston, the road blurred with returning sensation, more and more of the past dislodging, falling in on her – the e-mail messages, Skype ponderings, occasional long-distance calls, the soothing timbre of Randall's voice offering to tide her over when she resigned, until she got something else – it would give them time to catch up – and his bright, encouraging, almost hypnotic eyes. The supports that had built up began to crumble – the calm, the healing and the hope; and the shards rained down on her, their edges razor sharp. Everywhere they sliced, the darkness poured in. The grinding screech forcing itself on her could only be that massive wheel smashing its way out from the inside of her head.

Chapter 16

Of High Degree

Lat no man truste on blynd prosperitee;
Be war by thise ensamples trewe and olde.

The turbulence afforded no right side up, as she hurtled on, or anything to clutch at besides the reaching hands she flinched from. Words lapped round her and receded. A crisp voice dismissed her as mildly concussed, then faded. Sonja's, more muted, said, "You're okay. Your car's badly off, but you haven't hurt anyone else."

Words mushed into each other. Sonja at the desk, reassuring Lex over the phone. About what? What was left? "Life," Sonja answered. Which cleared up one source of confusion for Candace – whether she was only thinking or actually speaking. "Life," Sonja repeated implacably. But what good was that, the darkness hissed, what more than an unending exchange of poisoned chalices. The ceiling and walls steadied and connected at their corners; then Sonja's face came in focus.

There seemed no escape from the TV news, from voice after voice demanding the Provost's statement. Sonja had heard that the Australian university that had honoured him had now announced their offer of a recently endowed Chair in Postcolonial Studies. Rider had gone to clear up a few matters in Texas and would return to Portmore to settle matters here, and then he'd be gone for good. Arrangements regarding the future of ITS would be in place in mere weeks, he had announced, and members would be unwise to trouble themselves about unsubstantiated rumour.

Candace persuaded Sonja to drive her to ITS for a brief meeting with the Master. She had never before been a passenger with Sonja driving, and Candace closed her eyes as the car swooped, bucked and swerved again, around pedestrians and between buses and trucks that blared their horns and acrobatic cyclists looping their way with one hand on the bar nonchalantly and the other uplifting a middle finger.

Once there, she got out shakily and made her way to the Master's office. She pointed out that the no-pay leave Dexter had promised to approve on the Provost's behalf would cover the period of notice that her contract required. Dexter had no difficulty arranging her immediate release. "As is you," he said. But Candace was obviously a complication he could do without. After all, when Rider moved on, Dexter must expect to move up – once the institute was retrievable – or he would jump clear. Either way, what good would an ex-Provost's daughter be to him?

Back in Sonja's car, Candace all but collapsed on the front seat, squeezing her eyes tight, as Sonja jolted and cursed her way back through the traffic to New Kingston. Candace was not aware of getting from the car into the house, only of Sonja's couch rising up to meet her and the fog closing on her mind and gathering in her body, seeping into her organs so her stomach felt tight, filling her lungs so it grew wearying even to breathe, let alone move her limbs. And this lethargy spread, suffusing even her face, so that when the phone rang, it took effort (useless effort, it seemed) to move her lips. She had no idea who was calling; she was aware only of her own voice, a flat, exhausted monotone, advising whoever it was to call back. It took strenuous concentration to raise her eyelids, and she gave up. Her eyes still closed, she let the phone drop from lax fingers onto the floor.

Again. For she had been brought low before. She had come through, but that only meant she knew and dreaded the unbearable depth of it and the gruelling climb needed to bring her out. In the distance, Sonja's voice again. First on the phone with someone, then beside her, trying to command Candace's interest. Lex had called to warn Sonja that Percy Stone seemed a sniff away from implosion, and, Lex not being up to it, he had directed Stone to her. And now Percy had rung Sonja and poured it all out on the phone – for it was not at his door, he sobbed. And the Provost was aware of everything, and Rider was, after all, the one ultimately responsible for the place, wasn't he?

If only they would not talk over her head, Candace begged. Or perhaps she said nothing, for on they went. However convoluted the path ahead might seem, Sonja advised, Percy would come out best if he were honest about all that had gone before. He must make a clear statement to distance himself from everything improper. A blessed pause fell, as Sonja listened. Then it began again. Well, distance himself as far as was possible, Sonja insisted. Then she sat by Candace and tried to divert her with Percy's dilemma. But Candace was out of it. She cared nothing for Percy's revelations (little undermining reptile). Whatever drama unfolded in the haze, her own disintegration felt closer and more brutally compelling.

"Of course, I'm keeping a full record, so you can catch up when you come around. But for now, you have to get up," Sonja insisted. "Cassidy, get off that couch and stop encouraging her to lie there; for once, you're not helping. Candace – do things. Write the book, visit Lex, curse your father. Rider needs to know, at the very least, how exposed he is on this side of the world."

What could it possibly matter?

By the time she was steady on her feet, it mattered. The forlorn hope of a personal life flourishing at last had turned out to be hollow. And no university post, however lowly, gleamed in the offing. Her mind fumbled for images of some other professional existence and came up empty. Her self-respect was about all she had left, and with it a need to somehow word her disassociation from her father, a final severing.

Outside, pulling open the car door, Candace thought of taking Cassidy for company, but the rented car was not, after all, hers to do with as she liked. In any case, the dog was probably safer at home than with a driver still unfocused and enervated. The cut and thrust of argument with her father had never held any thrill for her, but it was not fear that held her off, only exhaustion. Rider did not get high on contention for its own sake, like Francine, though engagement in public debate and controversy was as wine to him. The attention, the charmed audience, the intake of breath at the exchange of repartee – he swathed himself in the glamour of it. She was not ready even for a private exchange.

Now she wavered with her hand on the back door of the car. "Oh, get in," she told Cassidy, because she couldn't make it on her own and had too much pride to take along human support.

Mustering the energy to challenge Earl Rider felt so wasteful that Candace was washed out by the time she slowed in front the entrance. The ornate wrought-iron gates stood open, and the rented car bore her up to the house. She parked and sat there, spent, pretending to contemplate the structure before forcing her feet out. Hellshire Palms was in the hands of an agent, advertised for sale and ready for viewing – immaculate but for the persistent image of a gaunt canine body that haunted her, roiling her stomach. She sought around in her head for what she meant to say and found nothing, but she planted her feet on the ground and rolled a window down for Cassidy before locking up. The study was on the other side of the hall to the living room, the doors ajar. She walked in unceremoniously.

"I hear you totalled your car." He greeted her without a glance, flicking a speck of lint from the sleeve of his Ralph Lauren suit.

She had not come to exchange pleasantries. "You left the dog to die on its chain, you bastard." Weariness had thinned her voice to a husky rasp. "How low can you sink?"

"Sink? You obviously haven't heard. I'm out of this shithole."

"And you expect to live it all down?"

His familiar sneer. "My life on the other side of the world rests on my scholarship, which is formidable. What do you suppose I have to lose?" He looked up impatiently from the papers he was sorting on the desk.

"Everything." She practically spat it at him. "Your involvement with Vanessa Allison and the rest will transfix any institution contemplating your appointment to a Chair."

He paused, weighing her up. "You'll never publicize a thing. You haven't the nerve."

A threat? Virtually. Exposing him would implicate her, and he could extricate himself, using his own prominence to discredit her. Except that he knew nothing about her condition, of how shadows adhered to immediate thought and sensation, almost stifling her in despondency. Other urgent considerations flowed swift and lucid outside that, parallel to this curtain of gloom, and she was aware of them but too crushed by the present to engage in fear any more than in hope. His insinuation did not matter to her.

"The place in Brisbane will welcome you, with your trail of collusion? Closing your eyes and mouth, however obnoxiously Sat and Courtney behaved? Gallagher won't mind about you tolerating staff involved in academic fraud?"

"You're a greater fool than I supposed, if you don't know plagiarism from mentorship." But he sounded less assured, more irritable.

"Mentorship? A set-up like Acadamentor can only work through a network of unscrupulous scholars. It runs on intellectual prostitution. So you didn't dirty your own hands by profiting directly from the slime; but you certainly let your support base grow by looking away. Just what was I imported for? Part of a control group, publishing in solid, peer-reviewed journals and presses to keep the place credible?"

He smiled, unperturbed, reached for a document from his desk and held it out. It was an offer to her from Gallagher University at Brisbane. It was tenure track, tenure to be considered in two years and possible promotion to Senior Lecturer in four, at an institution high on QS World University Rankings. He had negotiated it as part of his package – a widower with a single daughter also in academia, the father and daughter team inclined to relocate together. All this was not tied to her living with him, he said, in case she leapt to that conclusion. Once she resigned from ITS and signed up for Gallagher, she need never speak to him again.

Nor about him, her mind processed rapidly, and then it swept on. For there it was – spread out before her. Never likely to come her way again.

"What choice do you have? You can't open your mouth anyway. A loving daughter who has worked for years with her father? You'd never hold a post again. Anywhere." She could see the taut flesh around his eyes relaxing in the knowledge that his usual cool-headed efficiency had brought him through again.

"Except I dumped you," she said, suddenly so drained she could only slide the copy of her letter of resignation onto his desk and on top of the Gallagher offer and turn away. She hadn't the energy to voice her most telling reflection.

Instead she made her way back to the front door, hugging to herself that two-edged sword: that she had turned over a trove of incriminating data to a third party who had no more compunction about hurting her than he did. Randall's book could carry Earl Rider down without effort on her part. And herself? Who knew how he might pitch it? The novel might implicate her irredeemably. What power could facts wield against invention?

As she approached the car, someone shouted. Perhaps he had called before, but this time he caught her attention and she glanced back. He had followed her out, demanding something she was too confused to make out; then she realized it was a file he was wanted, his résumé and instructions for revision. Why would she be carrying that about? Or talk to him at all?

She yanked open the car door, waving him away wearily and sank onto the driver's seat. He shouted again, but she ignored him. Grabbing the door, he held it open, seizing her shoulder hard. With a rumble of outrage, Cassidy lunged and clamped her teeth on his forearm, sinking them deep into his flesh. Even after she released him, she continued to growl, her jaws thrust forward, fangs bared.

He was screaming, his hand clenched on the bloody sleeve. "The brute bit me," he bawled at Candace, as she slammed the door.

"Fine," she snapped through the open window. "I figure she'll survive it."

Candace tore down the road from Hellshire Palms, the drive unreeling from her mind as fast as she sped along. Later she would remember nothing of how she got back to New Kingston, except for clinging to the thought that she must stay on the road for the sake of the dog.

"Good, good girl," Sonja crooned later, her arms locked around Cassidy and her fingers kneading the short tawny fur. "Always to be depended on to do exactly the right thing."

She had settled Candace on her couch yet again and handed her a cup with condensed milk on crushed ice. After a few minutes of silence but for the clink of ice and spoon, a faraway look came into Sonja's eyes.

"I had washed my hands of them, but I think I will arrange just one more conversation with Percy, in a week or two. Cassidy," she murmured, "you are an example to us all."

The next day, Candace cleaned her hard drive and walked away from her desk at ITS with nothing but her flash drives and the book manuscript for Forbidden Words. It was cutting-edge discourse analysis of equivocation on the misdemeanours of colleagues. Also, as a study of evasion, distortion and slipperiness, it constituted an account from which the top management of ITS could hardly recover, if she called names. But that was neither here nor there. Candace switched them off. She had already worked out more of the institute's way of operating than she could bear. As for its Provost – she no longer found relief in contrasting him with Randall.

Randall. She had basked in the thought that someone looking at her was actually *seeing* her; and what she had missed was that she was not seeing *him*.

The flight to Port of Spain would leave Jamaica before Randall's touched down. A staff member's medical emergency at St Augustine had opened up a temporary full-time position for the coming semester, and Sonja would oversee Cassidy until Candace could arrange the dog's transfer back to Trinidad. Or so their words went, skating around the knowledge that neither of them would subject a fourteen-year-old dog with an expected lifespan of ten to twelve years to the harassment of another relocation. Candace deleted e-mail from Randall unopened and then relegated his messages to spam, discontinued her Skype account and blocked his number on her mobile. She knew she was dismantling herself, the self she had come to think bearable.

She dipped in to see Lex, and neither of them mentioned Randall, but the room was heavy with the unsaid. Candace felt no inclination to cry, even when she left, because Lex would be well enough to go home in a week or so. Which was something.

Cassidy was a different matter. The dog's habitual air of solemnity darkened to deepest gloom, as Candace was taking leave of her at Sonja's house. Candace swiped her eyes in annoyance – because she was not the cry-cry sort, she insisted to Sonja.

She dried out in time for Sonja to drop her at the Norman Washington Manley Airport and boarded the Caribbean Airlines plane hugging her laptop with a view to forcing her mind back onto the project during the flight.

The plane took off at 2:40 with Candace jammed tight in the window seat against the cold curve under the window, the clouds prowling beyond the glass. The passenger beside her spilled over his armrest, and the seat in front tilted back towards her face. It was an age before the seatbelt sign went off and the narrow aisle became choked with bodies negotiating their way back and forth to the bathrooms. Cornered in her own company, Candace found herself revisiting Randall's part in the maze of betrayals that was her life. She resisted, forced her way from that cranny of her mind in search of some other space, any other. Only, it was bare. Walling off Randall left the landscape empty.

Which made no sense. Which was beneath her. With her ability. Her book, for God's sake. Her mind should be busy, bustling like the aisle of the plane, diverse interests forcing their way past each other. And they were there: except the fog obscured them, so that the grief alone loomed large and palpable and only what was lost seemed real.

Now she saw how far she had journeyed past that convenient picture of Randall as occupying some rarified intellectual plane of her life. The physical Randall, with whom she had chatted and laughed each night, had (even at that distance) grown on her, into her, transformed her into something other than what she had been, and fastened intimately into her body chemistry. She closed her eyes against the shock of craving for the flesh-and-blood man, a hunger so intense and visceral, she could imagine no way to safeguard herself against him but by purging him altogether from her system, and that would wipe out her last reserves of strength. It meant shutting herself down.

Her mother's addiction for Earl came back to her. But she blocked that; her connection with Randall had been different, *had* to have been. She inhaled painfully to press down the fancy of his being necessary for oxygen to enter her bloodstream or proteins to break down – all those silent secret transactions that went on inside and kept one going. Until – they stopped.

—)⟩(—

She climbed into the back of the airport taxi, so that the driver would be less likely to talk to her. A wave of empathy for her mother swelled and broke over her, but as the undercurrent of self-pity tugged at her, she pushed her way out. She grappled her thoughts, striving to reform them as prayer, but with every other support demolished, it was hard to hold on to, easier to let go of this last . . . prop. She had imbibed faith from Silver, and Silver was dear, good but ultimately ignorant, an unsophisticated woman of limited exposure – intelligent and well-read considering her situation, wise within her context. And dead.

She got inside the flat she had hurriedly located in Curepe and bolted the door, but the walls and roof were meaningless. This was what it was to be alone, with no shelter under an empty sky, no shrine for appeal or resource outside of herself. Then even that renunciation wavered, for she had grown up as a believer. But the darkness pressed in too dense, too heavy to permit a gleam. At least, from experience, she knew that this was as awful as it got.

But it wasn't. The days jumbled one into another, while she fluctuated between dismal and desperate and slid into self-loathing. She forgot to turn on lights and half awakened in the dark to the reverberation of Lex's disclosure. She lay spread-eagled on the bed, stunned, as if the blow had only just struck.

She tried gathering her mind around what was left – her entire life, obviously. But off-centre from the desolation, every rational argument for collecting herself and going forward played out like a film muted on TV in the corner of a room at dusk. She struggled to pay attention, but the smothering gloom swept in and blotted out logic.

Had it ever been like this? So eclipsing? In the twilight, a picture formed of swimming out at Maracas, treading water in a few panicky thrusts and then, with a sigh of relief, letting go, giving way so the rip tide could deal with the rest. But the thought of driving all that way, of keeping the car on the road for two hours, was insupportable.

It crystallized, stopping her – the idea that she would keep the car on the road to arrive at a rip tide. She recognized the ridiculous through a haze without feeling its humour and felt around for any restraint that might be asserting itself over her mind, but she was too tired, and her inability to pray paralysed her further. On some level of consciousness, she steadied herself and examined her rage, tugging it into a line of reason. After all, to reject the concept of suicide because of a belief in God made sense, but to believe in God so as to avoid contemplating suicide was weak-spirited and dim-witted. Her intolerance of mental collapse prolonged a fit of ill-temper that she supposed to be another dimension of her slide into abject misery.

And then there was her disgust – disgust at herself for letting yet another exploitative man drive her out of her own country and, curdling that further, a sour sense that she never had or would feel at home in Curepe.

Her hand slick with sweat, she reached out of the haze for her phone with the blurred idea of booking a flight back to Jamaica. The mobile skidded out of her fingers onto the damp tangle of bed linen. She let her fingers creep forward, feeling for the surface of the bed, the floor, a table. She slid her feet off the bed, stood up and walked inexpertly. The silence deafened her. The absence of scratchy pacing, of Cassidy's toenails (twisted over the years and perhaps sensitive, so she would not let Candace trim them) clicking on tiles – the emptiness of the house throbbed through her. Who would have thought she would find herself in her thirties with her life still unscripted.

When her phone chimed she ignored it as she had for the past six days. Sometimes she glimpsed the first few words of a message. *Call me,* Sonja said. *Where are you?* Lex texted. Perhaps she should try now, she thought once, but then the earth shifted, opened and crunched its jaws around her. But no, it was not the earth that had opened but a wound in herself as if Randall, *reading her,* had slit her open, spilling her insides out.

What had he once said? So many bloodless ways of taking a life.

The noise drilling her brain was the phone again, and she grabbed it automatically, struck at the green patch and bawled into it, "What?"

Sonja said, "What the hell is going on?"

She kept Candace on the phone for over an hour, refusing to release her, until Candace promised to answer every call from her or from Lex. "And you will resume you're habitually overstructured existence as of *now,*" Sonja shouted down the line.

That night the darkness was thick as ever but for pinpricks of light moving slowly, drunkenly, going out again only to come on elsewhere. Peenie wallies, the lightning bugs she had loved as a child. She registered a twitch that was almost a smile.

The next morning, Sonja relayed the substance of a message that had found its way from the department at St Augustine through ITS and into Sonja's box. A woman called Marcella Davies had been trying to reach Candace urgently for a couple of weeks.

Lord. *Marcella* – 2007 or 2008. Marcella Davies was a seriously troubled student with whom Candace had kept in regular contact for years. Six years ago (more? less?), Marcella had tried to slit her wrists, but either from indecision or incompetence, she had botched it, so her friends had had time to get her to the St Augustine Medical Clinic. They had called their lecturer, Dr Clarke, because they had no idea what else to do, and Candace had gone to the hospital and sat there saying everything that had ever been said to her about a positive attitude to existence, certain she was doing no good. Eventually she had convinced Marcella to see a counsellor. Then the girl steadied, and after a rocky start and two further minor crises, she completed her degree. By the time Candace left for Jamaica, Marcella had been talking about a master's.

Then, a short time ago, Marcella had begun to vacillate between the master's and suicide. She and Candace had talked by Skype and more expensively by phone. Marcella had registered for the programme, regretted it, called again. Then things seemed to settle down. But now, as Candace checked the missed calls and the girl's number came up again and again, and then no longer, not at all, she filled the gaps in the Marcella story – what must have been happening.

Now Candace phoned and phoned again, leaving more and more frantic messages, until eventually her mail showed up a brief message from Marcella. The young woman was sorry she had been unable to contact Candace . . . so as to invite her to her wedding.

Candace folded up, missing the chair and settling in a heap on the floor.

In half an hour, perhaps an hour, she forced herself to her feet. Groggy still but awake to the world outside her head, Candace felt for her shoes and keys, and compelled herself to leave the room. It was later that afternoon that she found herself in yet another rental car, driving through pounding rain.

When it rained, the average guard on the St Augustine campus waved entrants to the campus in through the gates from the snug safety of the security booths. Content in the knowledge that when it rained, car-theft, rape or other assorted mayhem was not in the cards, the guard turned no more than a cursory glance through the fat water droplets on the side window. She was not even aware of passing in through the gates or of parking and leaving the vehicle.

In keeping with the first week of September, students were everywhere

– the resigned, the eager, the clueless – peeping out from under inadequate eaves or sprinting from cover to cover. Candace came to herself as she plodded around campus in the rain, water trickling from her sodden hair and down the back of her shirt, her feet slippery with mud inside her shoes. She halted in front of the administration building, which had been duck-egg green, when she was a student, and was now terra cotta and some other colour between peach and coral. She remembered thinking it elegant, and then she looked down at her own bedraggled state and hastened in search of her car, glancing around furtively. Everyone must have noticed her.

Back in her apartment, she threw on all the lights she could and glanced about for the dog's bowl, and then she remembered.

She steeled herself to bathe, blow-dry her hair, file her nails, and she set out to show herself as a normal academic, however inconsistently employed, at some function taking place in the auditorium of the Learning Resource Centre. Any function. If she could pretend to be there, she might convince herself that she existed.

So she drove back to campus, where the programme unfolded jerkily, her attention wavering despite a rich procession of major artists. One dashed away a tear, gazed askance under his floppy brimmed hat, until he had collected himself and clinched his talk with a few obscure words that seemed to touch the audience but passed Candace by. Then another, a novelist, starting cool and self-possessed in spotless white, read from his book a passage the audience found so hilarious that the author too began to laugh, and the reading broke down (as inevitably happened amid mutual exuberance), and the people around her doubled over or threw back their heads, wiped their eyes when there was nothing left in the world to laugh over, overwhelming her with a flood of anguish, for in the midst of the tears and the laughter around her she was alone. She was stripped raw.

Nothing was left but work. Yet the thought sparked faint but real comfort. No foreseeable permanent job, but at least work.

Back in the apartment, the TV alerted her to UWI announcing the selection of a new Vice Chancellor, and congratulations poured forth in an exchange of mutual goodwill, official comments, and idle verbiage by those who delighted in the music of their own voices. One of the latter referred to the good wishes of Professor Earl Rider, "a respected colleague, the Provost of ITS and [could it be otherwise?] a treasured member of our own alma mater".

When she called Sonja, they agreed that no public reference could be expected to Rider's earlier interest in the UWI post, as that might imply his wavering interest in Gallagher, let alone ITS. According to the Jamaican news, Sonja said, sources close to the Provost acknowledged that a variety of reputable institutions were attempting to woo him but that he remained fiercely attached to ITS.

Candace forced herself to focus on Forbidden Words and, more particularly, on her analysis of modals from the BEAM data. The book was filling out and aglow in a deep place of her life. She had not only that but whatever had prompted her to research at all. It was at her core, irreducible. She felt a comforting, tickling nudge, like Cassidy's nose against her neck, an awareness that she could not abruptly and without cause transform into other than she had always been. And at that, something weightless, unformed, shifted in a recess of her mind, testifying to a significant thought lingering beyond reach. Then she must have fallen asleep.

She awoke to a sense of Randall, as she had known him for fifteen years. What felt like dawning realization might only be further self-deception, but she grabbed a pen and a sheet of paper and sat down at her desk to analyse things coldly. She blocked, as well as she could, that mischievous quiver that heightened the sensuous curl of his lips and lit his eyes with laughter, and she drew up his mind as best she could. Was this man she knew really a fabrication that had vanished, leaving behind some monster that had always lurked there? Had she accepted the worst interpretation of Randall based not on what she knew of him but on her experience of her father? (Perhaps in despairing of God, she had confused even Him with Earl Rider.) But then, there was that obsession at the core of comparison. For better or worse, Randall was more than not-Rider.

She collected a cup of tea with some crackers – all that was edible in the flat – and drew out another sheet of scrap. She was going to follow these thoughts as far as they could take her.

Though erasing her father from her thoughts was not yet possible, he was no longer the focus of her pain. He was now backdrop. Perhaps he suffered from never having been stopped; there was no question but that his ego had been overindulged. Yet he never had fulfilled his potential. She had been right about one thing – his innate brilliance – but he had stuck there, impaled on his own glamour.

And she had not driven herself this far, intellectually and morally, so as to remain fixed in a stale comparison with him (or what he could have been). She wrenched herself out from under that burden of longing, an almost muscular straining against the vast heaviness that pressed down on her, and it lightened infinitesimally. Relief came in minute releases.

She knew the chemical upheaval that propelled her mind towards despair did not switch off. That overwhelming sense of the world irretrievably spoiled lingered, so that no act of will on her part could banish the long shadow of dejection. From time to time, it might edge forward again, but for now, perhaps it was retreating and the world easing out of shadow. Drained, in its wake, she picked up soca pounding in a passing maxi and the smell of roti emanating from the neighbour's house. Taking shape around her was a world of no fixities, but at least the phantasm of an unattainable father had melted away.

More than that, much more, Randall's apparent lack of self-interest over the years rushed back to her, forcing her to question how he could now be trying to appropriate her most intimate thoughts for his own gain.

She examined the rush of warmth and light that spread through her at the thought of him running his hands through his dishevelled hair in dismay at one of her accounts of Francine's malice. She eyed the risk, took note of the desolation that might lie in waiting, acknowledged the potential embarrassment of miscalculation. She filed the likelihood of error and opened up the slim possibility that things might in fact be what they had seemed. She switched on her laptop.

The news was full of ITS and its mismanagement. Questions about the reasons for her resignation cluttered her e-mail. She deleted them, but the chair she sat on had steadied beneath her, the air smelled lighter, cleaner, and her mind ran clear, as if she could sit before the screen and write until morning without raising her head. But was this clarity, or was it self-deception, an almost drunken bout of wishful thinking?

By way of trust, or perhaps gullibility – she could not swear to which it might be – she found herself arriving at a decision to gamble everything.

She e-mailed Randall a brief message: "Path dark at present. Can see only one way forward, especially if you need help with the voices in your novel. Merge texts?"

She attached the files with unused data she had gathered on dialogue that suppressed information or unwillingly revealed it, on hedging or equivocating testimony. And half certain that she was finally, irrevocably, surrendering touch with reality, she attached a scanned copy of her father's instructions for fixing his résumé, as well as her notes on Sonja's files, leads to Sat's online business, and Sonja's notes on Percy's revelations.

Everything she had.

Chapter 17

Matter of Authority

For this ye knowen al so wel as I.
Whoso shal telle a tale after a [mayde],
He moot reherce as ny as evere [she sayde].

There was no response.

Randall had landed at the Norman Washington Manley Airport in Kingston and fidgeted in the pickup area outside, WhatsApping Candace, hammered by thick August heat. Solicitous taxi drivers swooped in, and he fanned them away as one would the long-legged mosquitoes that carried chik-V. Fewer drivers approached him as it got later with still no answer from Candace's mobile.

Randall had been to Jamaica only once since moving to the United Kingdom. Ten or eleven years before, he had come for a conference and rarely been off the Mona campus. Knowing little of the country apart from international news that fixated on crime, he was alarmed when Candace had not appeared by ten p.m. Visualizing the lonely Palisadoes strip he remembered between the airport and Kingston proper, he pictured her being forced to step out of her car at gunpoint or being thrown into what she had called macca bush. He told himself it was her country, and she would have taken needful precautions. He told himself that there was a rational explanation and that in the morning, he would laugh at his dark imaginings. He told himself that clichés would get him nowhere and he had to find a way to contact Candace before he lost it altogether. Fear pounded in his chest. He told himself to breathe.

By the time he decided to take an airport taxi, they were harder to find, but eventually he was speeding along between heaped sand and rock to one side of the road and the dark harbour with its far edge of lights to the other. He dug out her address and made the driver take him directly to New Kingston. But Candace's house was dark, except for a light or two outside, and the garage was empty. After knocking and calling to no avail, he thought of paying the driver to take him to the airport and back again, so that he could peer into the shadows along the way for some sign of her car. Then he searched his mind for the type of car she said she had bought, and he found nothing. Besides, he had seen none suspiciously abandoned along the way in.

And then he thought that perhaps she had mistaken the date and gone somewhere with her friend – what was the name? – Sonja. Yes. It must be something like that. But even his natural optimism could not disperse his apprehension. At the very least, he thought, she seemed surprisingly casual about his arrival, a lowering thought.

He could think of nothing but to check into a New Kingston hotel, so as to be near at hand when she called his cell, and the driver suggested Spanish Court. In his room, he had eventually drifted into a restless dose, when his phone alarm from a different time zone startled him. Candace calling at last, he assumed, pouncing on it. He answered groggily, demanding what had happened and whether she was all right. But he was only assaulted by a bewildering half-line of melody.

In the morning, he discovered at the desk that her address lay in easy walking distance of Spanish Court. He set out briskly and found himself – now it was bright enough to see into the dim house – staring through curtainless windows into vacant rooms. Next door a young woman was hanging clothes on a line, and he called out to ask whether she knew Dr Clarke and where she had gone, but all she could tell him was that the young lady did clear out everything and drive 'way, dawg and all.

So he made his way to the address where Candace would expect to find him, a town house near campus that she had located for him. Leaving a note on the door, he set out to rent a car, and by the time he drove that away, it was afternoon.

Remembering that Sonja lived a few minutes from Candace, he got into his account through the failing BlackBerry and retrieved an old e-mail with Candace's description of a brief drive to Sonja's for breakfast. Then he coasted up and down along the residential roads in the area, until he caught sight of a leggy brown dog pacing a fence. When he parked and came out, the old ridgeback sprang at the gate furiously; then she threw herself into a series of cavorting leaps that belied the white on her muzzle. She galloped around in circles, paused to pant, and then she hurled herself at the gate again.

"Cassidy," he hailed her in relief, shoving his hand through the gate to be slobbered over lovingly. "How can you remember?"

Relief melted his knees, and he grabbed hold of the iron bars. When he pulled himself together, he shouted for Candace and pressed the bell. Then he punched it with increasing fervor, but without response. Doors were open, a car stood in the garage, but no one answered.

He got back in the car and searched his phone.

The Net was no help. He had slipped off Candace's list of contacts for Skype and Facebook. The directory online listed no phone number for any Alexander Wright. (And what else could Lex stand for?) Before calling every Wright in the phone book, Randall decided to enquire at ITS.

The woman who answered his call said, "Dr Wright don't work here again. Dr Forbes-Garcia in a meeting, and Miss Gillian never come out today."

"I'm trying to make contact with Dr Candace Clarke."

"I know Dr Clarke."

He waited expectantly and finally prompted, "Could you help me contact her? Do you know where she is?"

After a pregnant pause, the voice replied doubtfully, "She . . . somewhere."

He ran through the numbers listed on the ITS intranet and decided on the one for central administration, but the phones rang unceasingly, so he tried the Cultural Studies extension once more.

"It's a holiday?" he asked the same woman who had answered before. "Because you say the secretary isn't there, and when I call Admin, the phones just ring and ring."

"No, is not no holiday." She was clearly amused. "In Admin, they don't answer the phones. They say they busy, and they not going get anything done if they stop to take every call."

He digested that, deciding that he had at least found a forthright informant.

"You'd advise me to go in, then?"

"I think that would be bes', my gentleman. Though, I sure they going say you shoulda call first."

He thanked her and drew up directions to Portmore. He made his way to the causeway and crossed the harbour, drove into the ITS compound and surveyed the parking lot. The hills behind the campus were dry and dull, lending no colour to the white uprights and corridors that stood out like a bleached skeleton, between which neglected cactus plants bared their spines.

A cleaner pointed the way to the staff offices of the Centre for Caribbean Cultural Studies. "That way, my gentleman," she said, and Randall felt a tug of recognition.

Randall found the Office of the Fellow easily. Dr Candace Clarke no longer worked there, Dr Forbes-Garcia assured him. He asked for Professor Sonja Palmer and drew a yet more reserved stare. Dr Forbes-Garcia offered to send on any message he cared to leave. With an affronted lift of her brows, she declined to share Dr Clarke's forwarding address.

He wandered back along the way and came to a sign that read *Office of the Provost*. Here he enquired, only to hear that Professor Rider was away. Randall enquired the way to the Provost's home, knowing that to be inappropriate, and he was not surprised to be reminded coldly that the Provost was *away*. On a whim, he turned back to the offices for Cultural Studies and followed the passage past the Office of the Fellow, until he came to a room with Candace's name still nailed to the door. He knocked furtively, pointlessly, and then he turned to see the draconian Forbes-Garcia regarding him with icy contempt.

"You thought it might slip my mind whether a member of my staff had resigned or still worked here?" she enquired.

"Excuse me," he mumbled, heading for the entrance.

On the way out, though, he dipped into the Master's office. It occurred to him that the assistant Candace had described might have forwarding information, and he tried to picture this . . . this Ms Mackhail from Candace's description.

When the Master's AA came through a door from one of the inner offices, Randall knew her at once. Pale eyes emphasized her faded, almost transparent quality, and the white dress clinched it. But she had no information except that Professor Palmer took care of Dr Clarke's mail. Meanwhile, Ms Mackail handed over a package to a younger man so unprepossessing that Randall felt little surprise about him turning out to be Sat, nor about Mackhail reaching for her hand sanitizer after their fingers made fleeting contact. An answering wave of revulsion passed over him at the thought of Sat's desecrating gaze and whisper, and perhaps Mackhail picked up his response, for she unbent enough to offer him a brief audience with the Master.

It was actually a bit of good luck to find Dexter Danraj in a frame of mind to say he remembered Randall Jefferies from some conference presentation a decade ago.

"So how you going, boy? How I can help?" asked Danraj.

Eventually Randall left with landline contacts for Sonja Palmer and Lex Wright. It was night by the time he returned to his house, and he called the first number repeatedly but without getting an answer. Remembering that Wright had been ill, Randall decided to wait until mid-morning the next day before telephoning his house.

It was another troubled night from which he rose early to complete some paperwork on campus. To have found Cassidy without Candace was itself unsettling, and as he moved from one office to the next, his mind was shot through with tales he had heard and read about people who disappeared in Jamaica and were later found executed, sometimes butchered. There was that Venezuelan student of Candace, he recalled. Never any explanation for her murder. Still, looking around at his safe and civilized surroundings, he reminded himself there were areas in London or New York that he would not dream of entering.

A mental survey of urban savagery across the globe brought no comfort, and he searched his mind for even the most unlikely lead. He was driving towards the main gate out of the campus at ten that morning, when it occurred to him to take a detour and look in on Marcus Walters. He was careful in his enquiry, introducing himself as an old classmate of Candace, making contact now he had arrived in Jamaica.

Marcus studied him. "The new appointee in literature? And you were a classmate of Candace at St Augustine? I was her classmate here, in the research methods course. Weren't you here too – for a short time? Like, one semester? Thought so. You guys were together a lot." He grinned knowingly. "Of course, she'll want to catch up with you, man. I'll let her know you're here, if she gets in touch."

Randall felt Marcus's eyes on his back all the way back across the grass. Just to make him squirm, Randall sat on a bench in clear view to check again for messages. Then he returned to the car and began his calls.

The helper at Lex Wright's house said, "Im don't come home yet, please, sir. Not till weekend. Im still in ospital." She was a chatty soul and shared directions and visiting hours without even being asked. Randall had a couple hours to pass before seeking Wright's help.

He jumped at a rap on the car window on which he was leaning his head and glanced out to see Walters signalling to open up.

"I was trying not to tell you this," Walters said, "because it probably means nothing, and I wouldn't want to be alarmist, but I've been wondering for a while whether Candace was okay. You know, there was a student she was very worried about and who eventually died. The last time I saw Candace, she spoke of going to meet this lady's partner, and I actually have a name Ariana gave us, with an address. Let me see."

Randall stared at the paper with Walters's scribble, almost overpowered by an urge to dump it. Out of the question, poking around in parts of a city he did not know. But then, to ignore a lead . . .?

The GPS drew him downtown and onto a grimy street he would not otherwise have chosen to enter. As the streets tightened, he slowed and began to rethink the afternoon. The next instruction took him to a yet narrower, more shattered road, and he paused, realizing that Walters's information had carried him into the other Jamaica he had read about and, up to now, had known better than to seek out. He craned his neck and drew down the glass a fraction to make out the name of the lane into which the GPS directed him. The bent lamppost stirred, as a one-legged man who had been indistinguishable from it separated, straightened and regarded him pityingly.

"Watch, Breds. You going wrang. Tu'n round, or man going bust two shat in you backside."

Randall switched off the A/C to hear better and slid out the paper with the address and name. He said, "It's just that someone told me to ask for this man."

The man stared at the paper without making a move to touch it. "Is dead you want to dead."

Randall made a five-point turn and reset the GPS for Mona Road. Not having had time to think of turning back on the A/C, he arrived home soaked in sweat. Inside again, he Googled the name Marcus had given him and found it in a *Gleaner* article on gangs and garrison in West Kingston. The man he had enquired for was also known as the Reaper. Candace would not have gone looking for him. And Walters, Randall thought with a shiver, as he got out of the shower and tried to dry off another burst of cold sweat, had to be a very sick man. Then it occurred to him that Walters might not have expected him to charge headlong into West Kingston. No one would be that fool. So the lead must have been just to mess with his mind.

The clean shirt Randall put on to visit Wright in hospital was soaked with perspiration before he got back into the car.

～)∣(～

Randall paused in front of the private room in the posh Phyllis Wright Wing. Then he knocked and was rewarded by a weary voice bidding him enter – a reluctant, hollow invitation. The tall thin man in the armchair at the window turned languidly and studied him, his gaunt face instantly transforming, when Randall identified himself, to radiate hostility.

"Get out!" Wright said.

"But is Candace all right? I've no clue . . ."

Wright reached for a buzzer and held it down, until a hefty orderly raced in. "Get him out of here," Wright yelled.

"I have to know!" Randall struggled helplessly against the iron fingers biting into his arm. "What happened?"

"You happened, you bastard. You didn't mention this book of yours was filched from her brain. So when she heard it from me, she drove into a truck and nearly killed herself. Now she's over that, God knows if she can ever . . ." Wright turned away with a spent gesture at the orderly, and before Randall could draw breath for another question, he was outside on the pavement.

Back in the car, Randall slumped, drained of the terror that had taken hold over the past forty-eight hours – of Candace lying dead, abducted, gagged, mutilated. A dumped garbage bag of body parts. The cold sweat and shuddering subsided, overtaken by a wave of heat: *She had dropped him.* Her friend Sonja had been right there in the house, listening to Cassidy's unmistakable reaction and refusing to look out. Treating him like a pariah. Candace had deleted him from her system. He dug his fingers into his hair and clamped his skull, which felt as if it would explode. Deleted him, after all that . . .

⟶〉〈⟵

Randall had not been looking for sex or companionship, when he encountered Candace at St Augustine; if he had been, he probably would have backed away. She aroused his curiosity. She had poise, was attractive in a tightly strung way, and her eyes were lively, searching, yet guarded. Most often fastened in a book. She was not given to greetings beyond the absolute demands of courtesy. No, not rude (usually), but not inviting. She was distant.

He had noticed that about her from the outset. Aloof – that was it. She seemed barely to register the occasional male student whose eyes followed her. Her remote smile politely marked the attention as gratifying, perhaps, but ridiculous and potentially intrusive, and soon the poor chap would drop without trace from her notice. It amused Randall, watching it play out. Most young men were too intimidated to persevere, and Randall pictured her history as littered with failed suitors.

But aloofness was the most he inferred at the time. "I can get along," she'd say, forestalling friendliness. But her mouth could break out of control into the most infectious grin, and, provided you didn't harass her with trivia, she could listen. She was an avid listener. They had become allies, then comrades. He could see that in aligning himself with Candace, he was signing up for propriety, an indefinite sentence, and he registered without a second thought for assessment procedures or course length. Because, once you gave her space, she was absorbing. Witty, mesmerizing. At the time, her unhurried pace and level tone projected not calm, certainly, but self-control, as if she were on top of everything. A short fuse, he suspected, but unflappable. No one, certainly not Randall, could have perceived her as having what the younger ones would call *issues* (pronounced, as Candace later grumbled, with an alveolar rather than a palatal fricative).

Issues? When she eventually managed to talk to him about her parents, moulding years of murky sensation into words, he saw she was much more messed up than he had realized. No. Wait. She was now a lot more . . . *whole* than she had been. She was still wounded but immeasurably better than when they met first – when she had looked as if she had it totally together. Now that she was revealing herself, he saw that *then* she had barely been holding her own: she had been a clutch of raw nerves cohering unexpectedly around a keen sense of the ridiculous.

There were times he had rested his hand palm up on the cushion beside her or stretched an arm behind her along the back of the couch. She would stand up to get him a glass of wine. Something. Even when he sensed her reaching for him, she refused to take hold. He came to think that if he scared her off, he would lose more than an unlikely girlfriend. He would lose part of himself.

And then, the whole Atlantic lay between them.

But these days, she said herself that she was the better for talking. If only what he knew of her now were not some invention, part of a story he was making up. At first his focus had been Earl Rider, the making of a brilliant, successful sonofabitch, but the fallout from such a character became impossible to avoid. So then – the daughter, under her layers of avoidance. Who was she? Because it was the "real" Candace he . . . . And that was where it all fell away into the unknowable. Wavering, slippery, flickering. And now vanished.

The thing was to get on with the rest of his life. Yes, Candace had occupied years of it, but now she had locked him out – not for the first time.

Time. It was time to wish her well mentally and move on.

Yet without Candace, there was nowhere he cared to move on *to*. Even as he rebuked himself for weakness, he confronted his own stubborn certainty that it was not weakness. Nothing so simple. He felt changed – radically, intrinsically changed in ways he did not think he could reverse, had no wish to reverse. He had become part of something he thought altogether worthwhile. He felt himself coded into her story and she into his, inscribed so profoundly that loss of her would reduce him to something like a subplot in his own life, fanciful as that might seem. No, not fanciful at all. For if he had never met her his life would have flowed smoothly; without the impediments, he would have found his way, though it would have been shallower. No tale is an island. If he had not made his way into Candace's story, he would not have known pain for another person, let alone the overwhelming urge to take that pain away. He was altered. Deepened.

But she had never sought admission to *his* mind. Grappling with how she must now perceive what he was about, he thought it must seem as if he had assumed the role of narrator, if not author, for her existence. And yes, he was writing the novel, the vicarious reliving of Candace's story.

It had begun as notes by a friend, towards understanding why Candace so cordoned off those corners of her past in which lurked the mutual disappointment of her father and herself. At first, Randall had thought that whatever inhabited those areas of silence must be horrible.

The suspicion must have played across his face, for she said, no, nothing like that. And she laughed away the thought of a psychologist. So then, she might speak to *him*, he suggested, a friend. And they did have that unshakeable trust often found between men or between women.

Yet there were gaps in her account she seemed unable to fill. Some of her knottier aspects might be simply cultural, like the Jamaicanness he thought as much an affliction as a blessing. A nationalistic arrogance intensified her mulish refusal to explain herself; but beneath that worked the introvert's evasiveness. So he had had to speculate in order to reconstruct parts of her past. In the manuscript, he at first distinguished those by font colour. Then, as Candace contradicted and second-guessed herself – because, she said, she had been a child and looking back now couldn't be sure – he marked those uncertainties by another colour. But it became impossible to distinguish levels of certainty in the account, and he gave up on colour coding, going where the story took him. He would offer her this tale, as based on someone *like* herself. . . . And then, well, they would talk.

Eighteen months it took to arrive at a design – first a framework for rebuilding her in text without violating her privacy, then a viable approach for producing a readable tale, because by then it was impossible to think of all this effort not going to press. After a while her liveliness and humour encouraged him to think she would easily come on board, when he could word exactly how he proposed to tell his story. Well, *her* story. It took another year for him to realize she might not want any story remotely connected with her out there, because she only pretended to be extrovert so people would leave her alone. So people would assume all was out in the open and there was nothing to pry into. It was her mechanism for hiding in plain sight.

As he refined the character, he saw how the extrovert pose made her come across, when she was withdrawn, as arrogant. Those who did not know her thought her snooty, disinclined to fraternize, they assumed, because she believed herself better than they were. He knew it was the reverse, and that she hid out of sheer disappointment in herself. Of course she realized she was intelligent, but in a vague way. Close as they were, it had taken Randall years to glimpse the scope of her mind, to gain an inkling of how ridiculously, frighteningly bright she actually was. But she didn't altogether get it. She was too traumatized by the idea of self-revelation to leave an opening for anyone to tell her about herself. But as she completed her degrees, published and delivered papers, that keen quick mind became her worst-kept secret.

Fast as she was on the uptake, though, he had felt sure she did not guess he was writing around her. She would not think herself interesting enough. And as time went on, he found he could not work out how to tell her.

Gradually his account of her had begun to take him over. Between lectures and marking, research and the writing up of scholarly papers, it began to annex his interim thoughts, and over a solitary meal or if he woke at night to change position or retrieve the quilt, his mind teemed with it. Eventually stopping to calculate, he realized it was occupying more time than any other single aspect of his life. He had taken up the habit of devoting every meal exclusively to the consideration of the book, and sometimes, afterwards, he did not know what he had eaten. Writing the novel had replaced the taste of food.

He convinced himself it was all for her.

Then there came a night of violent struggle. It was a novel he was writing – but what did that mean? The truth was, he had approached this mysterious woman like a novel he intended to create, and he was confused by the intersections between discovery and invention in what was unfolding from him. Bits that had been scrambled by Rider's carelessness had to be reassembled through painstaking narrative operations. Then Randall fell prey to all sorts of anxieties. What if in keeping with his own agenda he produced a simplistic rewrite of her life? Made her up, as it were.

The battles that waged inside his head had indeed been over the book: whether to involve Candace in the actual writing of it or even to put it to her at all – that it should be attempted. For what if she refused to countenance it? What if she were adamant it should not be written down? He told himself that he had been trying to work out whether the thing was a viable undertaking before sharing it with her, but now there was no escaping the fact that he had waited too long.

And suppose she had agreed. Wouldn't her expectations have differed from whatever he produced? Or what if she insisted on vetting page by page? Intolerable. He had to assemble events and reconstruct situations as best he could, adhering to what he got from her but recognizing that some of it was twisted by pain and some too private to reproduce unchanged. And then, the gaps: he had to invent or speculate, based on choices that presented themselves. There was one thing he had promised mentally – but faithfully, as if he had placed his hand on her grandmother's New Testament. He would not publish it against Candace's will. He would not put out anything she might find hurtful or intrusive, and, given the history, that might amount to much of the book.

That meant showing it to her when it was done and bearing with her objections. He would have to omit whatever she found offensive, and if that were fundamental to the whole, he could not publish. The acknowledgement of this mental pledge sliced deep. For how did one live with that? He must decide to live with it, or he could not write on. He must stop now, relinquish it altogether, or go on under the strict understanding that he might never put the book out. And that in itself would be a sort of self-betrayal, like submission to censorship. The thought was excruciating, but he bent his head before it as before an axe-stroke that honour bound him to endure.

He knew now that he had started on this project long before he became conscious of writing a novel. Month in, month out, over years since renewing contact with her, he had listened, noted, questioned. Gradually the possibility of dropping it after years of work had begun to needle him, and now, just short of completion, there was suddenly no way forward. With the connection broken, all hope of her authorizing the work had dried up, along with the work itself that had so possessed him. And his version of their future had withered. He woke up, sat over tasteless meals and went mechanically about his job.

The anger had dulled, leaving grief, before that too was overtaken by a resurgence of fear. For level-headed as Candace was, he had glimpsed, beneath, a delicately poised psyche. Her super-organized, meticulously ordered approach to life made her seem predictable, but that too was part of the pose. She had sat for most of her life on feelings that might be dangerously volatile. His anxiety about her, resentment over her distrust, frustration regarding the book intersected one another and undermined every other consideration except how she must view him now.

An obscure old poem came to mind, pre-Conquest, in archaic alliterative verse and strangely personal in an age of the heroic and tragic. It was a woman's lament over betrayal by a man she had called her closest friend. Readers understood them to be husband and wife or lovers, because that was what people assumed about relationships between the sexes. The lament conveyed rejection beyond the periphery of warmth and light and song – a curse binding him to solitude: *May he be cut off from all sources of joy beyond himself.* It reverberated in Randall as his own fate.

Only the job remained, and he clung to it. UWI had employed Randall as a generalist in British literature – in rather the same way, Candace had teased, that the odd British university had expected him to teach Naipaul by virtue of being born in Trinidad and having taken courses in West Indian literature. Similarly, now, he had found himself assigned courses in Shakespeare and in seventeenth- to nineteenth-century verse, all on the basis of his thesis on medieval English lyrics. It meant spreading himself over centuries, genres, literary movements, and demonstrating the relevance of these to Caribbean students. September was upon him, immersing him in massive class preparation. Somehow he found his way to lectures on time and whipped himself up to enough passion to teach on interventions between the mystical and erotic in Donne, on nationhood in Shakespeare, and on wayward breaks with tradition by the Brontës.

But it was impossible to escape Candace's silence. Garrulous media made it worse. Against a background of students pouring onto the ITS campus to register for the new academic year, TVJ commented gravely on the uncertain future of the institute, what with a growing number of resignations among academic staff that included the Provost's daughter. CVM *News Watch* demanded statements from the management about rumours that the Provost had accepted a high-profile post in another institution and asked whether it was true that a position had also been negotiated for Dr Candace Clarke, said to be a relative. A journalist called Elizabeth Woods reported that Ms Amelia La Mar, hitherto assistant to the Provost, had refused to comment on her duties and that the Provost's own daughter could not be located for a statement.

The fear edged up again, beating in his chest, until Randall felt his rib cage would explode.

Marcus Walters was kind enough to call and enquire whether Randall had managed to make contact with Candace. He had been a little concerned after their chat, Walters said. The truth was that he knew Candace was away, but he had felt it was not his business to say. He really had heard her mention that she wanted to get to the bottom of this Ariana Ramirez thing, but perhaps it was good they had not pursued that. It might have been risky. At the same time, Randall was so obviously concerned, and Candace would surely have contacted such a good friend by now – unless something really was wrong. He let a long pause elapse. Of course, she was a little like that, wasn't she? Played things close to the chest. Perhaps she had applied for the post Randall landed (she had been forever applying for everything, Walters knew) and was just a little put out that Randall got in instead of her?

Randall thanked him for his concern and said he felt sure all was well. He had been so tied up settling in that he had probably missed her call. He was on his way to a lecture at the moment.

Teaching had begun, but all the time, furious as he was at being hurled away, he checked messages obsessively between lectures and even, furtively, during a class, while his students contemplated some question he had thrown up on PowerPoint. His heart lurched at the alert for every message and plummeted when a glance confirmed it was not from her. At the same time, his BlackBerry was breaking down; sometimes it would not charge. So he would hang there wondering about mail that might have crawled through at last to his inbox. Then he would connect and, again, nothing. Quickly before the connection failed again, he would send, knowing her system would discard him as trash. Trash?

Eventually he tried sifting through his trash. And there it was, categorized as spam by the forces that resided in cyberspace. He waited and waited for it to open, hung because of a huge attachment.

Path dark at present. Can see only one way forward especially if you need help with voices in the novel. Merge texts?

He stood there at the podium in the lecture room, in week two of the semester, where he had been searching his system for her name while waiting on the second-years to settle down for the only lecture on sonnets that he could fit into a one-semester course. How long had the message been there? He studied the date. Eight days. His hands shook as he fired off the response that came instantly to him: *Let [us] not to the marriage of true minds / Admit impediments.* Candace's immediate reply was that she was dispatching an application for part-time hours at Mona, cancelling her acceptance of the St Augustine temporary post and booking a seat back to Kingston on the Caribbean Airlines flight first thing next morning.

He came back to himself to find the students watching him and whispering to each other. He had warned them from the first class about the discourtesy of using mobiles in class. However, a quick question established that they had not read the sonnets he had assigned, and he seized the excuse to storm out of class and return to his office. Later he would figure out how to make up the class.

He slammed and locked his door. Then he reread Candace's message and clicked on the attachments. That evening, when she telephoned from her new number, he stumbled headlong into a maze of words – feelings detoured, sidetracked; meanings skirted; explanations bypassed from sheer awkwardness. The quiet at the other end of the line, the waiting unnerved him, sent him fumbling hastily for topics, meandering on about dialogue in biographical writing.

"Especially the place of speculation – remembered dialogue being especially fraught," he heard himself saying. Blasted phone. His meaningless babble trailed off, as he gathered his wits to try again.

How would she react to a direct question on how she felt about him? There was no returning to their hitherto bloodless version of intimacy. "That question of merger you raised" – he tried to speak lightly between ragged breaths and the pressure of the phone on his lips – "was it to be . . . purely textual?"

"Actually," he heard her say, in the tone of one coolly deliberating a nice academic point, "I had nothing the least bit pure in mind."

❊

So, as it turned out, it was Randall who met Candace at the airport in Kingston. The sight of her struck him with almost painful force, yet the reunion turned out to be stilted. Having talked freely for so many years over the intervening miles, they found themselves – in each other's presence – tongue-tied. After an initial exchange of measuring glances, conversation came haltingly, amid a wary circling of each other.

"But what a marvellous coincidence." They turned to take in an ebullient Marcus Walters. "How wonderful to catch you both – only, I'm on my way out to Cave Hill." He emitted a sigh of resignation. "Meetings, meetings. But I can't stop, and I'm sure you two don't need me! Glad you caught up with each other." He squeezed an arm each and was gone.

"What a character." Randall grimaced.

"You . . . spoke to *Marcus*?"

"I was searching for you. I made discreet enquiries. I went to ITS and then in search of Lex Wright."

She wasn't following. "But Marcus?" Perhaps it was because in this start of the new semester she was, for the first time, not teaching – largely because of Marcus. But that was hardly what Randall expected her to get hung up on at their first meeting in a decade. She still hovered beyond reach.

It was evening before she asked, "So, is it finished?"

He noticed she didn't say *the novel*, or *your novel*. (*Our novel* would have been nice.) But he went along with her.

"How can it be? So much left untold. Undeveloped." He could hear his own unease. "So many things I've felt unable to ask."

"Just ask what you want to know." Her face bland, her voice crisp.

"Perhaps I don't know what to ask," he parried. "I suppose I need answers to questions I don't know I should ask."

And no doubt because she wanted it to work out between them, she seemed to sift her mind for things she had withheld. From him and from herself. He laid down his pen deliberately.

"Oh, you can take your damn notes." She studied him, not hostile but wary. "I don't think I can talk, if you look at me instead of at the page."

They had not recovered enough for him to say that he might want to look at her for the rest of his life. She was not forthcoming enough for him to lay down such a declaration in the space between them. Nor was it enough for her to have come back. She needed to say she should never have doubted him. But he held that back, so she began to talk.

She knew what Randall suspected, and it was not true, she said. Her father had never touched her in any way harsh or improper. Never. He never touched her at all. She had seen the child who lived next door with *her* father, seen him pull her onto his lap, rub his cheek on hers, run his fingers through her hair, stroke her. One of the things she discovered about the neighbour's dog was how much it wanted to be touched, and that had been the beginning of her kinship with dogs. She thought she remembered her father lifting her out of a car, onto a chair, that sort of thing. But as if she were a package. It was not a touch.

She had no horrible assault suppressed in her past and needing to be articulated and . . . treated. Her father had done nothing to her that was criminal; she was not repressing anything that terrible. She couldn't even say how much, at the time, she had minded her father's lack of interest. Perhaps when she was little, she was mostly sorry for her mother. *No.* He never hit *her* either. He would never do that. He was one of those men who was never going to do you physical harm, she said. Not your body. There was so much deeper inside to be crushed. Mind, psyche, soul – whatever glowed deep beneath your skin, whatever made you distinct from him or apt to shine – he had the ability to seek that out and quench it. He said . . . things.

He told her mother, "You waste time hanging round my neck. You have the child you wanted, or thought you wanted. Latch onto that, and let me breathe." When his wife's eyes filled up, he jerked his head in Candace's direction. "Don't say I didn't tell you it would be pointless."

He said things that encouraged Candace to say . . . stuff she would never have uttered otherwise. Hurrying them along through an airport, he saw Candace hesitate at a line on the ground.

"What now?" he demanded.

"Step on a crack," she said.

"Break your mother's back," he finished. "How many can you step on?"

He seemed in such a good mood that she chimed in, "Let's get cracking." Not that she wanted her mother to cry, but because she wanted to make her father laugh. Wanted to say something smart. He did laugh. Her mother didn't cry – just looked at Candace as if she understood. And Candace had felt soiled, like something for the trash or the toilet.

When he saw her suddenly downcast, he said, "Exactly like your mother."

And that lifted her up. For a few foolish seconds. "Pretty?" she asked, bouncing with excitement.

"Brainless," he said.

That was all. Trivial as that. But every day, between the quarrels, this was their peacetime conversation – a succession of small splintering remarks. Out of the blue, too, unprovoked except by her mother's presence. It was as if her mother were dragging her down. Sometimes Candace couldn't even look at her mother, couldn't stand her around. Which made Candace disgusted with herself.

Then one damp windy day in January, something happened at school, and she couldn't tell a soul. She tried calling her mother. She told the teachers she felt sick and wanted her mother, so they allowed her to use the phone. But when she couldn't get through to her mother, the Principal phoned her father, and Candace heard Miss arguing over the phone – that he should come, that the child said she felt sick and wouldn't talk to anyone about it. Then the Principal muttered to a secretary, "Some parents," and Candace tied the arms of her navy sweater around her waist and went to stand outside.

Her father's car tires screeched when he rounded the gate, so that everyone in the school could hear, and girls and teachers looked out through the windows at her standing there with the sweater tied and hanging, and when she got into the car, he demanded to know what the emergency was. She whispered that she didn't know – only something really was wrong, and she wanted her mother. All the way home, she thought she must be going to die and wondered how bad that would feel.

When she got out of the car, he noticed the car seat and started shouting. He wasn't worried about her dying, just about the upholstery. Her stomach heaved, and she ran inside but didn't make it to the bowl: she threw up in the bathroom doorway. It was on her shoes, everywhere. He shouted for Patrice and for the maid, but Candace was dying anyway and wanted it to be over, so he would stop shouting. Then he told her to get cleaned up – didn't she know she was a revolting mess?

It didn't matter what the helper told her, how Eudine patted and said none of it was Candace's fault, or that Eudine asked how it was Candace never know anything when she read so much; and it didn't matter when Candace's mother came in and explained what she could, because it was all too late.

"But you said you wrapped the sweater at school, and no one knew," her mother protested.

It was no use telling her about the car seat and the shouting and the bathroom floor.

So it was that sort of thing. Not what Randall had been thinking. Not abuse. Just remarks like razor blades. Slicing her mind, so the darkness poured in. Sometimes, only sometimes when she sat as far from the house as she could, beside the fence, the neighbour's Labrador would push his face carefully between the barbwire and lick her tears.

And the things that came back now, from earlier still, were like that. Words. It shouldn't have mattered so much, but she was alone in it. It was worse when she discovered she wasn't meant to be alone, about how she was a twin. Randall didn't know? Well, she was. Which was why Lex felt like a brother. A twin that made it.

No, there was no yearning in her for some "missing part"; they weren't identical. Just this: she was born alive, and he was not. First, Candace had learned, there was the boy. Dead. Then, the girl. The disappointment. After all that screaming. Her mother, according to her father, bawled like a cow.

Candace knew the wrong one had survived. Every time her father looked at her, he must have been seeing a dead baby. The dead baby that wasn't her, the dead baby she should have been.

When she grew older, she assumed that when he looked at her mother, he saw the woman who didn't give him the living son, but that wasn't it either. Because now another, keener edge glimmered. There was that other thing.

He told her mother, "Shut up about all the daddy crap. I never wanted any of it. I made myself clear from the outset. We agreed: no children. That was the deal. Remember? Then you came crying that it was an accident. *You* were supposed to take the precautions, remember? Okay. So now you were to go to someone and get it sorted out. You would get rid of it. That's what we said. Remember? Only, you didn't. You came crying that you *couldn't*. You said you wanted this; I said I was having no part of it. You said very well. I guess you thought the idea would grow on me. It didn't. You did some test in Miami and swore it was a boy – as if that would convince me. Then I'm landed with a smaller version of yourself that should never have seen the light of day. And now you come whining to me about her needing her daddy?"

Candace remembered her mother throwing her arms around his knees but not how Patrice got on the floor. No. He hadn't hit or pushed her; he hadn't needed to. She crumpled all by herself. He unfastened his wife's fingers and then gripped her face in his hands and turned it up, so he looked into her eyes.

He said, "If you couldn't get rid of it from the outset, you could at least have had the grace to dead in childbirth."

Neither of them had glanced at Candace. She had always known. She should never have seen the light of day. She had longed for a dim unfathomable place, a burrow, a nook underground, where no one need ever set eyes on her again.

After a while, she discovered she could sink herself deep into a book, lose herself.

"Rider has done so much better than he deserves," Randall said, "but he has no idea what he's missed." He stared at Candace. She was amazing just to look at, slender, tense. Dragonfly light and poised. And then, her mind a-shimmer. But how to approach a body so locked down, how to convey without scaring her off that he wanted her excruciatingly. He asked at last the question he had turned over for years and never articulated, because it was so obvious that its answer might be unbearable.

"Why didn't you and your mother cling to each other?"

She was instantly on edge. "There was no *each other*. Unreciprocated clinging is not my line."

"But surely she loved you."

"I suppose." Her voice seemed at first stifled, and then it burst out against her will. "She never chose me, when it came down to it."

"But did you love her?"

"Yes," she snapped. He had never heard a *yes* so negative. Then she added more tentatively, "When I could."

"Wasn't she good to you?" Trite questions, but how else to proceed?

"Yes." Again. But now, as the pause lengthened, Candace had to fill it. "Yes, she took care of me. She was gentle, and she brought me beautiful things and made sure I had my shots." Candace stroked Cassidy's flanks absently. "She got someone to make a dolls' house I did not want, and, though she could not understand what she termed my *addiction*, she bought me books. She took me places."

"But?"

"She never took my part."

Cover it, cover it. He could almost see her tugging the lid back in place.

"When?" he intervened hastily, before she could blot it out.

"When it came down to it. When forced to speak to him about me."

"You make me wonder whether your father was so much the problem – because you never gave up on him, while your mother . . ."

"You know nothing about it."

"Obviously," he said, his tone matter-of-fact but a little weary. "You've never told me, so I hypothesize."

"For the book?"

"Not if you'd rather not."

"How's this for dialogue? 'You need to balance all this excessive reading with nurturing your femininity,' my mother told me. I suppose it goaded me into slashing back. 'It's all that femininity of yours that keeps Dad devoted, ent? Or perhaps it's just your bookish ways that bore him?' I remember how the colour drained from her face, leaving it the shade of dried bamboo."

"Why?" Randall asked. "What made you attack her? If they were not intellectually matched, was that her fault?"

"Oh, she was bright. Straight As at school. Good Upper 2 in history at Mona. She'd have gone on to her master's, if he hadn't needed *full-time support*."

"What, then? What was her crime?"

"She said, 'Oh, Earl, I know. But can't we start again? Can't you forget that, when I'm so sorry?'"

"I don't get it."

"She *apologized*. When he reminded her of their original deal – marriage without children. Of the mistake – or was I some contrivance for trapping him more tightly? I don't recall. When he reminded her she was supposed to have terminated the pregnancy but had been too weak, she clung to his hand and begged him to *forgive her* and begin again, for she was *sorry*." Candace's voice had risen an octave. "You don't see? My mother apologized for letting me out of her belly alive."

She sank down on the couch and remained motionless, wordless, with no sign of wanting him to sit by her, let alone touch her. At her feet, Cassidy stretched her long limbs taut and then curled up with a grunt of discomfort, showing elaborate unconcern but keeping her eyes fixed on Candace.

"I was the ruin of my mother's life," she said, "a curse she vowed to avoid and then relented towards unwisely, bringing down my father's unending blame for his not publishing more or rising more swiftly or amazing the world with his genius. I was her eternal regret."

He moved over to the couch beside her. "So the gone parent that has throbbed on like a phantom limb was really – your mother?"

"If only I had stayed decently buried."

He grabbed her arms then clenched his around her. "You should be proud – to have refused disintegration. You're amazing. With the slightest imaginable aid, you generated a coherent self."

"Your aid was not slight." She rested her forehead on his chest. "And you are still here. Why is that?" But she did not pause long enough for him to frame his answer. "One day perhaps I'll be able to feel sorry for him," she continued wryly, getting up to return to the table with their work. "But not yet."

Randall had no sympathy for Rider, whom he loathed without reservation, but he wondered whether some part of Candace did mourn the dissolution that the media were gradually revealing. Even the solid base of Rider's reputation was growing suspect, with the rottenness of ITS coming more and more into view. Candace knew enough to be sure it was a matter of time before the rest would implode, and already – not a month since the glittering banquet in his honour – the dazzle had gone. She cast a nervous glance at the TV.

"How does he bear it?"

Although Randall sensed he had not bridged the distance between them, he knew there was no sense putting anything off any more, and he said, "Something I have to show you. I can't sidestep this one."

He flicked his screen and turned it to her.

> *Applications are invited for the post of Lecturer in Sociolinguistics and Discourse Analysis at the University of Belmont in South Florida, to become available in Semester 2, January 2015. The successful candidate will also be expected to teach courses on Language, Culture and Society and in Field Methods for Sociolinguistics and Discourse Analysis, as well as to supervise research on closely related areas. Special consideration will be given to applicants with expertise in Creole Linguistics.*

Before she could avert them, her eyes betrayed anguish as well as excitement. This was the first time in her working life that no employment had materialized.

"You can't not apply," he said, knowing that if they offered it to her, she would have to accept. He tried to shift attention from the unspoken thought loud in both their minds by adding lamely, "You may need to ask Marcus for a reference."

By late September a barrage of rumours assailed them regarding ITS. The sale of the campus, or at least its land – however uncomfortable it made the academic staff in Sonja's estimation – seemed to account for Earl Rider's unavailability for comment. The Provost as higgler, Sonja had remarked. Now she had satisfied herself that Randall was a decent man, she regaled them with descriptions of the excitement on campus, even of how Dexter had demanded, hoisting his oversize coffee mug, "What happen to the old Earl, man? Like he vanish off the face of the earth." But then the details of the sale slowly emerged, and the fact that the physical plant was changing hands deflected attention from the whereabouts of the former Provost.

At the end of the month, a hush had descended on the campus. Even the chiming voices of construction workers and their pounding of concrete and steel had quieted. The site lay deserted, while the new and returning students wandered confusedly from class to class, and as October began, ITS staff pondered the identity and intentions of the new owners.

Those who could comforted themselves by reference to the few precedents of which they had heard. Universities had changed hands before. Once the institution was private property, it could be disposed of, and presumably life would go on as usual. Whatever had happened about St Georges in Grenada? people began to ask each other. No, it didn't really sell; there was just some arrangement to bring in a major shareholder. Just the land, someone else added. "Same ting," someone else cut in – in a tone that said, *So there! These things work themselves out.*

Candace took up the subject of St Georges idly over the papers spread out between them across Randall's dining table, for this was only ITS they were talking about here, whereas St Georges had solidity. She seemed borne up on the reflection that she had completed a full draft of Forbidden Words, and while she overhauled it, she snatched time to speculate.

"Who would want ITS?" she wondered aloud. "Or, are they just interested in the pickings, whoever they are – wheeling over the campus, like those Anglo-Saxon birds of battle you admire so fervently."

"Nah. Just lurking behind a tapestry with a scythe." Randall shuffled some pages he had printed out.

"Can ITS sell, you think?"

Randall's thoughts were elsewhere. "I hope you'll finish skimming my draft, while I'm young enough to proofread," he grumbled, getting up to turn down the gas flame under the pot.

"I told you to send it off when you were ready." She showed no awareness of how uneasy she made him with this reluctance to read the novel.

"And if there's something . . . wrong?" He could not bring himself to say *unprintable*.

"I can't always work out in my head what I remember from what I hoped or feared might be the case," she reminded him, then added, "The difference is academic in any case." She raised her head, from the stack of paper he had pushed in front of her, to the smell of red beans simmering with scotch bonnet pepper and pimento seeds in coconut milk. "Shouldn't I run out for the jerk chicken now?" But she seemed to pick up his rising distress. "You see, I'd rather read the published thing. I wish you'd send it off." She added lightly, "Imagine me sinking into a book and finding myself. Not the version I know, it's true, but so much the better." At his glance of surprise, she said, "Yours is bound to be a better version of me than mine. Don't you think?"

He closed his eyes a moment in irritation. Worse than that. Her refusal to look at the work left him unsettled and offended. That she wouldn't or couldn't grasp what it meant to him – Or was she still suspicious? He shot a glance at her, as the pain at her distrust flooded back.

Trying to block it made him jumpy.

When her cell phone rang again, he said, "Why don't you change the number? All these blasted calls in search of Rider – I suppose it's natural for people to assume his daughter knows how to contact him, but the phone never stops." He pulled himself together and tried to think how to mend the proliferating rents. "I wonder whether I should have a word with him. He might even be back here by now, passing through perhaps. Mind if I try to see him? You'd have to give me directions."

"Whatever."

"Could you be any more dismissive?" He was more abrupt than he had intended. But he didn't care. The recent savage break between them yawned again like a gash in his chest.

"What is it? This . . . this impenetrable thing in our way?" She turned to him. "What can't you ask?"

"You actually believed I would siphon off all you had been through so as to publish it without your permission or knowledge?" His voice was inflected for humour, of the rallying sort.

"Stop pretending to joke," she told him. But at last she came straight to it. "I don't know what else I should have concluded from your silence about the novel."

Her sudden intake of breath made him look up, and he saw realization in the widening of her eyes – a flicker, hardly detectable.

"You put it off." And she laughed – hardly more than a hiccup. "I told you procrastination would be the death of you." Then her voice changed, throbbed with distress. "Oh, Randall, what was I to think?"

What answer was there for that vacuum where trust was supposed to be? He could only shake his head. "So what was different?" he demanded. "What made you know you were wrong?"

She shot him a glance that unnerved him. Taking it in, he sank down on the desk chair. She hadn't known – not for sure. Perhaps not even now. It swept over him like a rush of flame. Her lips moved, but the fire crackling in his brain blocked her out, and all that came to his mouth was a taste of ashes.

Without another word, he sprang up, grabbed his papers and walked out to his car.

When he returned three hours later from his office on campus, she was gone.

An hour and a half after that, when he arrived at her house, he could see her through the window at her desk, scrolling through e-mail in a desultory way. When she heard the bell, she jumped up to run to the door.

He stayed outside and tossed the manuscript and a handful of flash drives through the doorway onto the ground at her feet. On impact the unbound stack slid apart, sheered and fanned out, hissing across the tiles, the flash drives clinking here and there before the papers covered them.

He said, "I wish you well. I really do."

Then he got back in his car and sped off.

Chapter 18

Fall

I wol no lenger pleye
With thee, no with noon oother angry man.

*D*ays afterwards, the news broke that the Institute of Tropical Studies at Portmore was reported to be on sale for a sum in excess of US$1 billion. Sources who asked not to be identified revealed that the institution had been running at a loss for some years but had been funded (through negotiations by the parent institutions) by a huge financial group. No, the sources had not authorized this reporter to name the group; but it was a firm of the calibre to churn out hundreds of millions in US dollars for support of maintenance and payment of salaries. A conflicting report said that the separation documents had not been signed and that the original parent institutions were bringing to an end an offshore arrangement that had never quite suited them. Yet another version was that there were no potential funding agencies but that a private equity firm had been prepared to source a massive investment, and that this offer had been withdrawn on the directors learning of ITS's accreditation problems, so the current owner or owners (undisclosed) were selling out as best they could.

By now UWI was awash with ITS students trying to find out how they could move across into UWI programmes in mid-semester and get credit for what they had already done. Most of those seeking sanctuary had no equivalent to the Foundation courses but were sure they did not need them, so they bore down on Marcus unrelentingly. There was no way they could enter in the current academic year, but they had at least to be advised. A few tried for specially admitted status with a view to seeking credit later. As UWI border enforcement went into high gear Randall, like many others, found himself besieged by profiles from Admissions for assessment and guidance on credit or exemption. Nor were students the only ones seeking entry. Uninvited applications for academic posts poured in, and telephones in Appointments and in Human Resources rang incessantly.

But from Candace there was no word. Randall told himself he was glad she was safely out of it. He shouldn't give a rat's arse, he knew, but if she was okay, it would be easier to get on with his life – as he should have done years ago. He wasn't worried about how she would live; she could take care of herself physically. She was certainly unfit to take care of anyone else. He cursed himself for wanting to know whether she would apply for a full-time Instructor post in the AFP, go after the South Florida position or fall for whatever arrangement Rider might have wangled in Brisbane.

There you were. He couldn't even feel sure she was cured of Earl Rider.

That night, when he attempted to find recent word of Rider through the Net, he stumbled upon an old announcement that the offer of a Chair at Gallagher University in Brisbane to Professor Earl Rider had been withdrawn. Nearly two months before. So then, where the hell was he? Not holing up at The Habitat, or some reporter would have sighted him on the road. Randall cursed himself again for wondering. Every interest he had had in ITS had evaporated: the book, the woman, everything.

In the course of a meeting in late October, when an item came up on graduate throughput, a chance remark fell from Professor Crichlow that he had sent off a reference for one of his past students (probably the best mind he had ever encountered in his thirty-plus years of teaching) and that now she had been invited for an interview at a pretty sound place in South Florida, for something in January 2015. Walters was in the room, specially invited, because graduate student writing affected throughput. He threw a glance in Randall's direction. Randall managed to meet his eye with a smile, but he heard precious little of anything else that went on in the meeting.

Easier if she left the country. Yet it was outside of anything he could ever have imagined, the hollowness. Candace had lodged deep in his life, from undergraduate days. She was there woven into every design for his existence that he had contrived – but it had all been on his side, all those assumptions. Years of trust he had laid down, steadfast in his belief in her. That she could be uncertain of his disinterested devotion ignited a fury of which he had never suspected himself capable. He was ablaze with the injustice of it.

He tried telling himself he had taken offence at a natural misunderstanding, but it was no good. *He* had never given up on *her*, all this time.

The thought of years, *years* spent working her out, not just for the book, for that came later, but to bring her to some recognition of the person he could see – the thought of those years seared through his chest. He saw no end to this anguish and bitterness. His mind was an inferno.

But fires burn out.

Gradually a chill settled in. He set about reinventing his life to exclude her, his fury not spent but transformed. It was an entirely different anger now, with no spark of feeling, no rush of warmth. He released himself into work: courses, articles, those students he could bear to contemplate. Dealing with students brought Candace forcefully to mind. A problem arose – summoning back enough humanity to face students without, automatically, reflecting on how she might have handled them. She was good at that, he acknowledged to himself with cold justice.

He put away the pretension of writing fiction; the Caribbean had enough novelists. He was fleshing out an article on fabliau and carnivalesque, when a soft rap on the door jarred his composure. But it was Walters, come for advice about ITS.

It seemed Shade had been wooing him. They had had productive talks before the troubles over there became public knowledge. Now Shade was saying it was all a temporary hiccup that would right itself and that all those idiots who had panicked and run off had left vacancies a man like Marcus could pick and choose between. When the GKIA came back in, Shade had said, he planned to have a team ready for them to run with. And even if the talk about a sale were valid, so what? People had bought and sold colleges before – at least, in a sense. He had veered off into something about land grant universities that Walters did not understand, before returning to the future of ITS. The accreditation trauma a year or two back arose precisely so as to secure the value of the place, he said.

"What?" Shade had demanded. "Like a set of professionals would just dash away thousands of students – mid-programme? And staff with legal contracts?" He guaranteed everything would be back to normal in a couple months and that by January everyone would be getting ready for Semester 2, as if none of this had happened.

So Walters wanted to know whether Randall – who (it stood to reason) knew more about the place – could tell whether it wasn't likely, after all, that ITS might have a future. Because Walters was wondering whether he shouldn't consider it. The current position he occupied didn't allow time for the research UWI insisted on, and now these draconian procedures for assessment and promotions had led to him being given a two-year contract and a warning. So he had to work out what to do. What did Randall think?

What Randall thought was – this is why people write novels: because the material is hurled at us every day. Then, he thought of Candace struggling to keep a toe back in UWI and Walters dodging about trying to cut it off.

"Yes," he said. "Why don't you think about that carefully, man. Don't burn your boats here," he added, as conscience feebly reasserted itself. "But certainly nurture that contact with Shade. ITS may be where you belong." Randall gazed at the hills through the door Walters had left ajar. Perhaps, Randall reflected, he was wrong to have dropped the fiction. But where was the sense thinking about that? Hadn't he thrown away the book? Yes, of course, there were copies he could retrieve from the cloud, if he wanted (not that Candace would refuse to return anything he asked for, though contacting her was out of the question). Even if he could bear to take up the novel again, he would have to do a lot more than fiddle with diction and trim adverbs. He would have to rewrite the end. Like the part in which she said, *in the most offhand voice imaginable, "You were probably right last night about us getting married. Which house do you think we should give up?"*

"Come with me now," he said, turning off the TV images of gesticulating ITS personnel. "After my class, we'll run down a special licence or whatever it takes."

"No rush. Go to class. I won't disappear; I'm going nowhere over the next four hours except into my own manuscript."

He snatched up her laptop and the four-inch thick bundle of papers that comprised Forbidden Words *and hustled her into his car.* "Then I'm not letting that out my sight."

That scene would have to go. (He hadn't been satisfied with it anyway.) And later, when she said, *"I can't think why you have never just gone your own way."* That too. Along with all the linguistics metaphors in his response about their way being mutually intelligible and about concord and all that crap.

Then there was the fall of ITS. He had to recast that. He had imagined it at first as a physical ruin along the lines of Sodom and Gomorrah, or perhaps a plunging into the sea like Port Royal. But alongside that, he had fabricated the growing intimacy between the main characters, which he had thought inevitable.

Like when they would go for a walk and stop to look at the mountains. He closed his eyes and re-felt the passage where *she leaned back against him, wrapping his arms around her waist.* "Like sinking between the covers of a book," *she murmured.* "Something bound well with a good grain and grand typeface." *He shouted with laughter.* "I'm serious" – *she grinned* – "sans serif, that's you."

"Simple?"

"Certainly not. Just devoid of idle flourish, so one can focus on depth and nuance. Eminently readable."

Cross out all that crap. *They were laughing so much, they could hardly stand. Passers-by stared and began laughing too, shaking their heads in bewilderment. A rastaman nodded affably and waved.* "Get home safe," *he said.*

"But how shall we live? Do I accept anything I get abroad and commute? Otherwise I shall have to succumb to Marcus and let him have his wicked way with me. Or follow my father into disgrace. Or what about if I withdraw my letter of resignation to ITS?" *They held onto each other and once again gave themselves up to helpless mirth.*

Cross it all out and start the last couple chapters again. He couldn't carry off a romance even if he wanted to, and only some truly hot sex scenes would have been convincing, let alone interesting, to most readers – which he could hardly have put in, under the circumstances. He would have to reconceive the personal interactions entirely.

On the other hand, the ITS collapse was turning out to be as dramatic as if it had been physical.

Walters told Randall he had been in Portmore on the campus when
Percy Stone arrived at ITS – some arrangement by Professor Sonja Palmer,
Walters had heard. An administrator named Gillian had been really nice to
him. (Walters's discreet smile conveyed he was, after all, an attractive chap
and one likely to be perceived as well-placed to arrange a job for someone
who felt insecure where she was.) She settled him near enough to Sonja's
incompletely closed door to follow events. Elizabeth Woods sat demurely in
Palmer's office, in one of two armchairs that faced each other under strong
lights. She patted the other chair, and Stone sat and babbled it all out.

It was all there on the evening news: that students were never the point,
and it was all above board, because the Provost was fully aware. No, not
everyone. People had resigned, including the Provost's own daughter, who
had nothing to do with . . . Anyone who . . . Sat's thing? Yes. No, not Danraj.
Courtney perhaps, but mostly Sat. The Provost would know exactly. He
knew what he was doing and he was . . . The Provost had supervised Percy's
graduate work, so he had infinite respect for him. Very caring. Courtney
could be kinda . . . exuberant, and Professor Rider had accommodated
. . . No, the Board of Governors for Acadamentor, at Sat's invitation.
Acadamentor . . . Did he say that? Well, a group to assist students. People did
not realize how many students leave a doctoral programme with nothing to
show after being in it for eight or ten years.

―⁄₁∖―

A university is an ecosystem in which it is possible to threaten one or two
elements without compromising the whole, by juggling compensatory
movements in growth or decay. But this collapse was surely the whole she-
bang. Even as speculation spiralled regarding separation packages and lay-
offs, the situation remained shrouded in mist. If the news reports were correct, most of the employees had been clueless about what was underway;
many had no clear sense of how the system worked, or even that there *was* a
system. They awoke only to a world that was falling apart.

Overnight, reports churned in the machinery of newspaper firms for
the morning headlines. As usual, some of it was old information. The
institute had been introduced by parent organizations in the United States
as an offshore campus but had, over the past few years, negotiated its

independence (at considerable cost) under Provost Professor Earl St Rose Rider. The report went on to claim that sources had described financial backing for this newly independent institution as having broken down. According to these and other informants, ITS representatives had been privately brokering a sale over the past months and agreement had been reached with a firm seeking a location for a shopping mall. Hitherto, attempts by the owners of the mall to purchase extensive land nearby had been blocked through the action of conservationists working in the interest of the Portland Bight Protected Area and of the general environmental well-being of Portmore and its surroundings. "Now that an already developed site has come up for sale," remarked the new owners, "there can be no further objection."

It was reported that neither students registered for the institute's programmes nor academic staff employed on the campus appeared to have been aware of the extent or nature of arrangements underway. Yet a few had apparently taken precautions when they observed the tension in the upper administration, according to Marcus Walters.

Walters had inveigled his way into the bosom of the Centre for Caribbean Cultural Studies – just in case ITS could be resuscitated – and treated Randall to a series of unwelcome visits, apparently encouraged by Randall's advice to consider ITS as a potential employer. He reported that as rage spiralled out of control, Professor Francine Forbes-Garcia had lost it and boxed Registrar Harindra Baldeosingh. However, it turned out that Forbes-Garcia had, much earlier, privately opened a consultancy in Business Communication, an area regarding which it would have been pointless to say that she knew nothing whatever.

Walters seemed quite pleased that he had been invited into the coffee room and he told Randall that he had it from Danraj that the Registrar, Baldeosingh, was himself too busy trying to retrieve his children from a wife rapidly relocating to Boston for him even to seek out a new job, let alone think how to retaliate against Forbes-Garcia. A man named Barham was stirring his cup at a table behind them, and he had dismissed both Baldeosingh and Forbes-Garcia as beneath his contempt. Walters actually knew Barham anyway, the latter having already negotiated a few part-time hours per week at UWI in the AFP for the next semester. Barham seemed amused that someone called Olatunde had disappeared, presumably back to the arms of the Global Knowledge Institute. Danraj murmured that a journalist from the *Jamaica Observer* was trying to contact this Olatunde for a statement.

In all this, there was no word on the ex-Provost himself. It struck Randall that except for a report in the papers regarding the sudden resignation of Professor Rider, who had left to take up a distinguished position abroad – at great loss to the academic community, and so on . . . he was already fading from public consciousness. It seemed that those who could not afford to conceive of the absolute collapse of ITS insisted it was all just temporary. Walters dropped in again to confirm that hope was not lost. He had it from Morgan Shade himself that in advance of any instructions to do so, but knowing how long these things took, Shade had even begun searching for a new Provost, although in his view (which he supposed would be generally shared), Dexter Danraj seemed to be quite clearly the coming man.

Professor Forbes-Garcia had actually been unexpectedly kind to Walters – he expressed himself as really quite gratified. She was supportive of his interest in ITS and encouraging about the possible future of the place, once the GKIA resumed ownership. There was no way a flourishing US institution would surrender a campus to some mall in a little third-world country, she said. But Walters was well-placed as he was, surely? She had heard of all he had accomplished in the AFP and was even inclined to take a couple hours herself, but only if he found he needed that extra help.

Professor Forbes-Garcia was forthright about all that certain staff members had brought down on themselves. Left with even less likelihood of a future than hitherto, for example, the ne'er-do-well they called Percy Stone had overdosed and was in Kingston Public Hospital in critical condition. And there was nothing to rescue some perfectly awful girl called Althea, or Anthea – however much she had, over the years, ingratiated herself by shouldering courses for staff members who had fallen ill or by attending their parents' funerals. Despite the young woman's heartfelt representations to UWI, shifting institutions and carrying credit for courses completed was not an option in relation to an ITS graduate programme that did not yet exist. Anthea was history.

It was encouraging how open everyone was, Walters said. Even the

Master had chatted with him frankly about developments, including the scandals exposed on the news regarding people like Straker and Nagasar. Especially Sat Nagasar. No amount of croc punch could boost Sat's future, Danraj had remarked jovially; but perhaps, he added, the reptilian population would balance up. Francine said Dexter himself was okay (of course), because he had a back-dated letter of resignation that showed he had in good time distanced himself from a failing institution and had only been there up to recently so as to do what he could for his more endangered colleagues. In any case, he was a tenured faculty member of the US university from which he had taken a long series of leaves of absence.

All too soon, Walters ushered himself into Randall's office again, big with news. Rumours were rife about a bailout that had been organized by the Provost in advance, though Danraj had emitted a prolonged suckteet. "Bull" was all he would say. Randall got much less out of the media. Asked for comments by an interested press, the UWI management maintained discreet silence about an institution with which it had had no official links.

Despite excited press coverage of ITS, and Walters's hysterical updates, little actual information seemed available regarding the ex-Provost. "Financial ruin of ITS now horse out of stable. Campus is Riderless," quipped a smug newspaper reporter. The actual sale of ITS had turned out to be a sale of the physical plant only. The widening catastrophe of student programmes and staff contracts would emerge in time. Only the cleaning, janitorial and grounds staff were to be kept on, together with one or two of the lower-grade technicians.

In the babble of voices and fragments harvested from local talk and international calls and passed on, a few phrases emerged distinctly enough for Walters to quote. *The entire patriarchal monstrosity rotten at the root the whole time . . . Do not compete with an elephant when it comes to passing stools . . . Well, you know I was just passing through so as to advise them fellows . . . He gave also their increase to the caterpillar and their labour to the locust . . .*

Chapter 19

Memento

Paraventure ther may fallen oon or two
Doun of his hors, and breke his nekke atwo.
Looke whiche a seuretee is it to yow alle
That I am in youre felaweship yfalle.

*R*andall stared at three items in the inbox, just arrived on November 26, 2014, trying to decide which to open first. He chose Sonja's message, which was copied to Candace. Sonja wrote that Candace had left a bulky package for return to him – a hard copy of a manuscript and a pile of flash drives – and asked that he pass by and collect them. Actually she could have returned them before, but, being a retiree with limited obligations, she had decided to read the manuscript.

With a stab of annoyance, Randall read on. After all, he had thrown it away, hadn't he?

She wanted to say she quite liked the novel and looked forward to discussing it, when he cooled down (or warmed up – whichever), but meanwhile (not knowing how long the temperature adjustment would take), she thought she should set him right on a factual error she had picked up. She knew he had every right to invent what he liked, but just in case he thought the twin business was a fact . . .

Patrice never had twins. Candace was probably confused by whatever it was she had overheard as a small child, from the two of them quarrelling over her head; but there had never been twins. Patrice had conceived *before* her pregnancy with Candace. She had waited as long as possible before aborting, to the point where some doctor judged it might be a boy. Or so she told Earl. But it didn't convince Earl to start a family, so she gave in. Her letters to Sonja had been full of guilt over the abortion and pain from her husband's callousness – on top of which, she was pretty sick. The following year, when she was pregnant with Candace, again she waited dangerously long, until the same doctor said he couldn't confirm it was a girl but so far saw no evidence that it was a boy. And she decided it *was* a girl. She *knew* it, and she was keeping the baby, even if Earl left her. She chose to have that one. She had named the child Sheena, hadn't she? Sheena Candace. (Randall Googled the name *Sheena* and found it meant "gift from God".)

Randall would obviously tell the story any way he liked, Sonja had written, but she wanted the facts available to him.

The next message was from a press and copied to him, though addressed to Candace. The press was pleased to report that Dr Candace Clarke's proposal for a scholarly work, entitled Forbidden Words, was of interest, and they looked forward to receiving two copies of the full manuscript to send their peer reviewers. They had noted her concern regarding information she needed to share with the University of Belmont in South Florida and were therefore copying this correspondence to the university, as well as to Dr Randall Jefferies, to whom all her correspondence with the press so far had been copied.

He paused to consider where these earlier copies of correspondence had gone and decided she must have typed his name at the bottom of the page but never sent him anything. Apparently she wanted him to know her book was under serious consideration. Well, good luck to her.

The third message was addressed to him by the same press and copied to Candace. It acknowledged receipt of his proposal and the accompanying manuscript. It invited him to submit two copies of his novel for dispatch to their reviewers. The press noted his acknowledgement that the end of the work was still under revision and asked for his proposed submission date. Although his letter had stipulated that he was operating with only a tentative title, they rather liked the one with which he was currently working.

He sat, frozen, while it seeped in. She had submitted his novel through correspondence in his name, with her name merely a c.c. on the covering letter. He stared at the date of her letter as cited by the press – mere days after he had thrown it at her.

How the hell had she done it?

But it played out smoothly in his thoughts – the persuasive introduction to the book, his signature forged with a flourish that was half angry, half triumphant. The soft copy attached from his most recently dated flash drive, and an author's profile she could have written in her sleep. But a synopsis? She must have mocked up something from the sharp points of her life in and out of her father's shadow. Then she had packed it all off for publication without a glance and left it up to him. He could collect the flash drives and hard copy from Sonja. Or not. He could finish it as he liked. Or not.

A shiver ran through him, and he turned his eyes again to the date the press had quoted. She couldn't possibly have read the novel. He huddled before the screen in shock, going over the letter. Then he grabbed the car keys.

Far from showing any inclination to avoid him, Sonja brought out cassava wafers and the fiery smoked herring paste that Jamaicans called Solomon Gundy.

"You knew what she was doing?" Randall was as tense as Sonja was calm.

"I quite liked the book," she said inconsequentially, "but that's neither here nor there. It went in before I saw it. What was important was that it should get a fair chance. Aren't they prompt, though, for such a reputable press? I've never seen the like." She reached out a jug of coconut water. "You would know she had sold the flat her mother left her in Canada and invested in something in Miami? No? South Dadeland, she said. So when the last tenant left, she did not rent again, just dug herself in to edit her manuscript."

Behind them, the news of ITS played out on the TV. Cassidy heaved a sigh and forced herself to her feet and away into a sunny patch beside the window; then she turned her back on the furore before slumping down again and closing her eyes. (Had she been allowed early enough to get her jaws into things, so to speak, she might have spared Candace much unpleasantness. But people thought they knew best.)

The hour or so at Sonja's house passed in civilized conversation about minor characters of the novel, publication woes and joys, and the comparative speeds of operation among presses that Sonja knew well. Sonja treated him quite gently, as if he were at the beginning of an arduous recovery from a near-fatal illness. Indeed the numbness was wearing off, and the tingle of returning feeling that had not died but only been disguised as fury was growing unbearable. He found it hard to think against it, to work out what it meant for Candace to have submitted his manuscript without scrutiny, perhaps without a glance.

Randall had been home for hours, sitting on his small porch in the dark, before it occurred to him that two months before, Candace had fired off her material to him from Trinidad in much the same spirit. She had sent him everything she had then – not because she knew he was genuine but in case he was. A hazard. If she had refused to read the draft, it might be because that too was part of a risk she judged worthwhile. A gamble so absolute that it stopped his breath.

Two days later, he sat contemplating the advertisement for a tenure-track post in sociolinguistics at UWI Mona for 2015/2016. He had attached it to an e-mail message that read merely *FYI*. But his hand hovered over the key. To send or not. Of course, Candace would eventually know about the ad anyway, and she would feel the irony of it: a UWI post materializing just late enough for her to have received the USF offer. A near miss. At least, he supposed it would come down to that. Perhaps it would be as well under the circumstances, sparing them both the discomfort of working together in the same faculty. Yet suppose she didn't see it? She deserved the choice.

But then, if *he* sent it, that would be a message by implication. Could he risk that?

Turning over and over in his other hand the instructions the press had attached for formatting his novel, he pressed send. And the moment that was done, there rose a sense of a gap in understanding, lingering in his manuscript, that there was a character he needed to sharpen. And it came to him that he would drive over to Portmore and find out how to contact and speak to Candace's father for the first and last time. At least to lay the ghost.

—⁊⁊⁙⁊—

ITS was deserted but for those who had stayed on to clean up, before the crew descended to make renovations and restructure for the mall. At first it seemed there was no one there who could tell him anything, but then he encountered Admin Assistant Mackhail, packing away some files that she would not want in the wrong hands. She gave him directions to The Habitat, although she saw no reason to suppose that the Provost was anywhere else but where he should be – "Down Under, as they call it". Two men ran up, one shouldering a hefty camera, and Randall backed away.

Ms Mackhail, having arrived at an age well past that at which another institution would have enforced retirement, had little or no financial security to look forward to but seemed singularly untroubled. Into a microphone pressed on her by an insistent member of the press who desired comments from all levels of the campus community on what was in store for those found responsible for the disaster, her statement was succinct: "Their iniquity shall be upon their bones."

Randall arrived at Hellshire Palms, parked outside, pressed the bell and eventually climbed over the gate – pausing before a scene of surprising deterioration. What little foliage there was near the house had overgrown in the November rains, but the potted plants under shelter were withered. Even the cactus seemed drawn, and the spacious entertainment area was, inexplicably, floored with shattered tiles. The windows looked strangely vacant, seeming almost to give on an empty sky. Randall cast his eyes around hopelessly. He had thought to find a caretaker with some contact information. Yet, he supposed, someone must have tried that already. On the other hand, with his house partly visible from the road, the grounds unkempt, Rider's farewell at the institute complete – if only through an electronic message that was clearly an afterthought before tucking himself in – and with the starting date of his new appointment reported in the *Gleaner* as some weeks away, his absence surprised few people. Most could have no idea that the Gallagher offer had collapsed. All that was said on the TV news was that efforts to contact Professor Rider had proved fruitless.

With good reason – but that would take Randall weeks to assemble from fragments that came slowly and untidily together.

What was later revealed was that Professor Rider's flight had been booked for October 4, 2014, from Kingston to Brisbane via Miami and Los Angeles by American and then Qantas Airways. He had paid no attention to correspondence about withdrawal of the offer, because, as far as he was concerned, his legal position was clear. The agent Rider had called about the sale of his house eventually said the Professor had mentioned having shipped his stuff ahead. He said he planned a good night's sleep, having packed a light bag (because some injury to his hand was healing more slowly than he would have liked) and placed it near the door beside his briefcase. He said his BMW was gassed up and ready to go. The agent was to use the spare key to collect the car at the airport and handle that sale as well.

Who knows what followed? Perhaps Rider had had confused dreams in which the director of the accreditation body, the journalist (Elizabeth Woods), and the chair of his interview panel in Brisbane were bending over his mobile phone and reciting in his daughter's voice, *How low can you sink?* Or perhaps he enjoyed untroubled repose.

At any rate, when Randall knocked on Rider's front door and received no response, a wave of irritation made him give the front door knob a violent twist and shove, and the heavy metal door clattered off its hinges to the ground. On looking through the entrance, he stayed very still and then backed softly away. It was on the basis of what he saw then and what was uncovered later that he reconstructed what appeared to have happened.

Earl Rider probably awoke even before an unfamiliar noise, like a low groan, got his attention. If he glanced through the window, he might have noticed the birds in the tree overhanging the house erupting in a startled flapping of wings, like light artillery, and a galliwasp breaking cover from a small pile of dry palm fronds and sprinting across the yard for a longer stretch than it had ever before taken in the open, remaining exposed long enough for a bird to snatch it up, though none were interested. The groan would have deepened, thundered, as the last drop of acid water that had been working over thousands of years cut its final nick in the limestone and brought down the cavern under his house, snapping stalactites and splintering the Taino petroglyphs that Lex Wright had admired, in the collapse of the subterranean chamber and much of the foundation of concrete and steel supports for which the rock had been further weakened by drilling, by hammering and, at last, by the sheer weight of the edifice.

The bed shuddered violently beneath him, and a glance confirmed there was nowhere to set his foot, only crumbling brick and tile and showering plaster. He dug his fingers into the sheets as the bed plunged, the walls rushing upwards, until all around him was the rock wall of a shaft, its opening above him receding, nothing to clutch at, no one to catch his howl of terror. And then the bulging wall burst in, a slab toppling, jammed askew and blocking out the light and his eyes squeezed tight against showering stone and sharp particles, and the dust filling his nostrils, fogging his brain, stopping up the last cry in his throat.

The outer walls of The Habitat had stood on intact as the bottom dropped out of Earl Rider's life, carrying him down amid the shattered tiles and polished wood, and the designer grout that was powder now and held nothing together anymore. Nor was there anyone to retrieve or any art to reassemble the crushed and punctured body of the owner of this fine residential property with its attractive prospect on the Caribbean Sea.

—✦—

Randall called the police and drove to Sonja's. There he telephoned Candace on his BlackBerry and broke the news gently. But she was calm. Randall and Sonja had the phone on speaker, and it felt as if she were in the room. Cassidy sat forward in the doorway, her body crouched, eyes yearning.

"But surely an earthquake. A couple weeks back?" Candace said she had felt as if the ground beneath her rocked and then lurched back in place. "I actually stumbled and held on, to steady myself."

"I never felt a thing. Nor heard anything on the news." Randall glanced at Sonja for confirmation.

"Don't you want to come home," Sonja put in, "even for a while? You'd stay with me."

She would have to think about it, Candace replied. But she realized how much they had to talk about.

Then, as the shock wore off, leaving her emptied, it must have occurred to Candace that her father had escaped witnessing the public collapse of his image. She whispered, "Dead the whole time. He was always luckier than he deserved."

Randall stayed at Sonja's, and the three talked on Skype on and off during the day. By evening the media had caught up and ran the story as a tragedy. *Cave-in claims life of prominent son of the soil* was blazoned across an evening paper.

But all last testimonies floated down unheard by the Provost. Randall reflected that well before the extent of the damage Rider had wrought was known above ground, the small things that had flitted from secret crevices in advance of the limestone cavern collapse, those that had had their ears to the ground, so to speak, and slipped aside – shadows like spectral Amerindians emerging from their caves – must gradually have returned to reclaim possession of their little corners of the earth.

To Candace, Randall said as little about Rider as possible. Before they shut down Skype that evening, though, he said, "Congrats on your book."

At which point Sonja strolled away, into the garden.

"May I congratulate you on *yours*?" Candace said. "Of the three titles you had scratched down, *Grounds for Tenure* seemed good to me, and I see the press liked it."

"You know it only comes out if we stay together," he said.

"Then we must wait and see if it comes out."

In the end, she decided not to attend the funeral, though a fortnight later she flew in (as she explained it) to discuss the upcoming vacancy with Professor Crichlow.

But she told Randall, "Why I really came was to find out what you feel," and she listened, spellbound, as he talked on into the cool December night.

She had still said very little by the next morning, when she let Randall drive her to the cathedral for the memorial service on which Shade, Francine and others had insisted. As Randall's car pulled into the parking lot, she murmured, "You know how some characters are too good to be true? For a short while, I supposed . . . that I must have made you up."

"Are you ever going to tell me how I turn out?"

The car had stopped, and she had slid out of the passenger seat and was negotiating the uneven flagstones with higher heels than she usually wore, so it was a hurried glance she threw back through the car window.

"Real," she said, reaching in to draw a promissory finger along his lips.

Then she braced herself and went inside to find a seat, noticing that a

Christmas tree had already gone up but was screened off out of respect for the deceased. An usher recognized her and insisted on placing her in the front row.

But when Francine's eulogy referred prayerfully to the life and witness of Earl Rider, Candace picked up her purse and umbrella, and got to her feet. And she walked away unhurriedly and without a glance at the interested faces turning to her on either side of the aisle, without any sign of awareness that Francine's voice had trailed off, so that Candace's departure reverberated in an aftershock of silence.

A reporter who scurried after her tripped over a carelessly extended foot in highly polished Bally shoes, but by then, Candace was, mercifully, out of earshot.

Acknowledgements

This is a work of fiction. All its characters and events are inventions, and there is no Accelerated Foundation Programme at the University of the West Indies. The Institute of Tropical Studies, too, is entirely imaginary.

This book would not have been possible without decades in tertiary education at a well respected institution. For this experience I thank the University of the West Indies which has been my intellectual home. Nor would I have completed both academic and creative writing alongside family life had my family been other than it was. I thank my husband and children for their devotion, unflagging interest and good humour. I thank my sister and brother-in-law for throwing themselves so generously into my exploration of Portmore. Finally, I have been blessed with remarkable editors, as sensitive as they are meticulous, and I thank them unreservedly for their insight, wit and patience all along the way.

www.ingramcontent.com/pod-product-compliance
Lightning Source LLC
Chambersburg PA
CBHW030918050726
47498CB00003BA/793